PRAISE FOR
Elizabeth Gunn's

PAR FOUR

"A SUPERBLY WRITTEN, ENTERTAINING
NOVEL in a series to watch . . . numerous clever
plot twists keep the story interesting."
—*Booklist*

"A model of the small-town procedural."
—*Kirkus Reviews*

"The plotting is complicated, the characterizations
deft, the sense of pace dead-on. ALL IN ALL, A
VERY FINE MYSTERY."
—*Fore Word*

"The nuts and bolts police work is well-defined
and the large cast of cops and crooks is
exceptionally well-drawn."
—*The Plain Dealer* (Cleveland)

"A largely satisfying procedural."
—*Library Journal*

ALSO BY ELIZABETH GUNN

Triple Play

PAR FOUR

◆ A JAKE HINES MYSTERY ◆

ELIZABETH GUNN

A DELL BOOK

Published by
Dell Publishing
a division of
Random House, Inc.
1540 Broadway
New York, New York 10036

ISBN: 0-440-22636-8

Reprinted by arrangement with Walker and Company

Printed in the United States of America

Published simultaneously in Canada

January 2000

10 9 8 7 6 5 4 3 2 1

OPM

◆ ACKNOWLEDGMENTS ◆

When I began this book, John Sibley, deputy chief of police in Rochester, Minnesota, since retired, was my key resource in law enforcement. Besides his patient guidance, I got generous help from Roger Peterson, who was lieutenant in charge of the detective division when *Par Four* began, advanced to deputy chief while I was writing it, and has just been named chief of police for Rochester. Others who have earned my sincere thanks are: Lt. Ron Wegman, a literate and kindly practitioner of critical incident debriefing; Officer Mike Beery, one of the first POP officers in Rochester and an eloquent champion of the program; Sgt. Louis Bode, the vice detective who illuminated the murky world of the drug trade in the heartland; Lt. John O'Neil, tactical commander of the Emergency Response Unit, and the several members of his team who treated me to an unforgettable overview of their gear and procedures; Gary Kaldun, head scientist at the Bureau of Criminal Apprehension in St. Paul, an affable guide to the wizardry of forensic sleuthing; and Officer Greg Meyer in whose company I experienced the breathtakingly unpredictable world of the street cop.

• O N E •

THERE WAS PLENTY TO LOVE ABOUT MY ROOMY NEW OFFICE AT the end of the hall, beginning with a gleaming brass nameplate on the door that read "Lt. Jake Hines, Investigations." I intended to take my time moving in Tuesday morning and get all my stuff put away before I worried about earning my pay raise. But Lulu Breske blindsided me before I even got my computer set up. I was crawling around behind the desk, trying to remember how the monitor plugs into the CPU, when she banged the door open and yelled, "Jake Hines! You in here?"

She startled me, and I jumped. My head hit the corner of the desktop, and for a few seconds I thought maybe I'd gone blind.

"Jesus, Lulu." I groped my way to my feet and rubbed my head, where a lump was rising. "What are you hollering about? I'm right here."

"How come you never answer my messages?" She aimed her clipboard at me like an Uzi. "Three times, I called you yesterday. What's the matter, you forget how to work your voice mail? Okay, your CID is set for seven-thirty tonight, sign here." She pointed to the line with my name on it.

"I don't know what you're talking about," I lied. "What CID?"

"The drug bust, the high-speed chase, whatever that screwup was Sunday night. That's your name right there, isn't it? Know any other Jake Hines in the department? So sign it, and I'll be outta here."

"Aw, Lulu, that wasn't my collar, I just happened to get in the way by accident."

"Argue with the chief about that. He says notify everybody on the list, I'm gonna notify everybody."

"Well, I don't have time for any meetings right now, Lulu. I'm buried in paperwork." I waved my arm at my clean, empty desk. All the junk I usually keep there was still sitting in boxes on the floor.

Lulu stared at the shiny wood veneer for a couple of seconds. "Uh-huh." She turned to the door. "So, you want me to put down here that you're refusing your CID?"

"Of course not," I said, indignantly. It hadn't even occurred to me to refuse it. I was just trying to weasel out of it.

CID is copspeak for Critical Incident Debriefing. Conventional wisdom in the law enforcement community now says cops who encounter high-stress situations should debrief as soon as possible. We're supposed to blow off any leftover emotions that might be hanging around, so we won't turn into a bunch of crazies and self-destruct. Somebody noticed the high rate of alcoholism and suicide cops have, I guess, and decided we need counseling.

And not just cops. Firefighters after big fires, medical

crews that work disasters, they're all being encouraged to sit around afterward and tell how it happened. They're supposed to say how they felt about it, too, like, "I keep hearing that woman scream," or, "I feel like I never want to eat again." Sometimes, I've heard, they even hug.

"It's an idea whose time has come," an intern named Josh Hyde told me, beaming as if he'd just found gold in his sock. He helped with a Jaws of Life extrication on the highway after an eight-car pileup. Describing the debriefing he attended afterward, he said a couple of paramedics got into a screaming match, and a driver named Manahan cried.

"That made them feel better?"

"I don't know about them," he said. "But I sure got rid of a lot of baggage." Josh picks up jargon fast.

CIDs are usually run by peers, volunteers who get extra training in counseling. You can tell when somebody's signed up to be a debriefer. He starts toting books around with titles like *A Team Approach to Stress Management*. A guy whose conversation has reliably been along the lines of "How about those Twins?" will start using words like *epiphany*, and sooner or later he'll probably say, "We feel it's helpful to get those feelings out in the open where we can deal with them."

Which was just what I didn't want to do. Dodging an occasional bullet is an inconvenience I can live with, but spilling my guts in public is not. I'm not a big hugger, and I got more than my share of counseling while I was growing up as a ward of the state of Minnesota. Now that I'm a grown-up, I try not to let strangers mess with my head.

By accident, though, I got in the middle of a high-speed chase and a questionable arrest last Sunday night that left all the participants unhappy. When the chief heard the details, he set up a CID. Lulu's task, as his secretary, was to make sure I got word of the time and place. Mine, as I saw it, was to stay out of her sight till it was over or she forgot about me, whichever came first.

My phone rang. I pounced on it like a dog on a bone.

"Rowdy's Bar's been robbed," Schultzy said from the dispatch desk. I could hear the backchatter from the other consoles nearby. "They say the owner's taped up in the basement, and the safe is wide open."

"Anybody responded?"

"I sent two cars, Stearns and Donovan, but Ed says send an investigator. I can't find anybody, where is everybody? Can you go?"

I opened my mouth to say, "I'm not even moved into my new office yet," but Lulu was standing there with her list, so I said, "Sure. Hold on a sec." I put the phone against my chest and said, "Got an emergency, Lulu. Robbery call, possible injury."

"Fine. But I notified you about your CID, so now you know," Lulu said. "Seven-thirty tonight in the small meeting room, go or don't go, no skin off my nose." She stomped out noisily on her tortured heels.

To the phone, I said, "You send an ambulance?"

"They don't think they need one. You decide. You want the address? Fourteen—"

"I know it." My second year in college, I dealt hamburgers off the arm at Rowdy's Bar. "This owner, you mean Babe Krueger, right?"

"Uh . . . don't have that information. It'll be whoever's in the basement wrapped up in duct tape, I guess."

"You sent a fingerprint team yet?"

"No. You think?"

"Uh-huh. Soon's you can get 'em up there." Rowdy's must have fingerprints going back to the Hoover administration. Getting a team there fast might make the exercise marginally less futile. Physical evidence in a bar is always a can of worms. Everything's sticky and smells like secondhand beer. Rowdy's has a restaurant and pool hall, too, so add fifty years of grease and chalk dust.

I checked an unmarked car out of the parking garage. Driving up the ramp, I opened the windows to dump the underground air. Yeasty August street smells flowed in, still with a high percentage of toasted petroleum and rubber, but suggesting mulch and lawn cuttings too. The maple trees by the Second Avenue bridge stood motionless in midmorning heat, reflected almost exactly in the slow-moving water. Rutherford was having a hot, dry summer; the river was low. Where the stream turned, east of the bridge, a sand spit was growing out from the bank.

I turned right, drove east four blocks, and turned left again on Sixth Avenue, rolling past tidy redbrick apartment houses with hedges around small front yards. North of Tenth Street the houses began to get shabbier, and some of the lawns grew weeds and trash. At the intersection on Twelfth, one of the corner buildings was boarded up, and the house next to it had a broken window. I was driving into the failing neighborhood old-timers call the North End. Rowdy's was just ahead.

I parked by the front door, where a thin man in a white apron was turning the Closed sign to Open. He unlocked the door and said, "Hi, c'mon in."

I held up my badge and opened my mouth to ask for the owner, and he said, "Oh. They're all still downstairs. Go to the back and turn left."

Rowdy's looked pretty much the way I remembered it, not improved any in fourteen years but not deteriorating like the rest of the neighborhood either. Maybe the grease and smoke protect it. A massive old mahogany bar faced a few tables in front, with a lunch counter and booths behind. A long room full of pool tables adjoined through an open arch. Stairs at the back went down a short flight to the rest rooms, then doubled back into the basement storage area. I remembered the dim, bare lightbulbs, the woven wire enclosures full of booze and canned goods. The cramped office behind the stairs smelled of smoke and roach spray, money and sweat.

Babe Krueger was in her office chair. Duct tape bound her arms to the chair arms. Her legs were wrapped in tape to the thighs and then taped as a unit to one leg of the desk. Her mouth was taped shut, too. Little strangled sounds came out of her.

Stearns and Donovan were standing beside her, making tentative, unhappy moves. Suddenly Stearns reached across her face and ripped the tape off her mouth with one quick, gutsy move.

"Ah," she said, sucking air. "Hoo." She breathed while we watched, opening her mouth as wide as it would go, inhaling, exhaling, "Ah, hoo." She rolled her tongue around behind her lips and said, hoarsely, "Could you get me some water, please? Right in there."

I brought a glass of water from the bathroom and bent over her, holding it to her lips. Her cheeks were streaked with dirt and tears. Some gray hairs showed along the part in her sweat-caked hair. She gulped the water noisily, dribbling a little out of one side of the glass.

"Sorry," I said, and Babe came up for air and said, "Shit, don't worry about a little spilled water, honey, I wet my pants twice since those freaks left me this way." There was, I saw, a puddle under her chair. She squinted up at me suddenly and said, "Jake? Is that you?"

I've probably filled out a little since I was nineteen. She was changed, too; it made me sad to see how much. Guys used to come to Rowdy's Bar just to look at her, a lively mover with a wonderful mane of red hair and a what-the-hell smile that lit up the whole North End.

Her name was Babe Thorson then. She could carry nine hamburgers on one arm, and in my wildest dreams I used to enjoy guessing at some of her other skills. A steady stream of ardent boyfriends waited to take her out after work, but Babe surprised us all by marrying Art Krueger, the dour proprietor of Rowdy's Bar. Five years later, after she dropped the charges from the last beating he gave her, Art signed a divorce settlement that gave her the bar. From what I've heard, that's the last good luck Babe Krueger had with men.

"Yup, it's me," I said. "Let's see about getting you loose." To Donovan I said, "Got some gloves with you? This duct tape will give us great fingerprints if we're careful getting it off."

"Forget that," Babe said. "The guys who taped me up wore surgical gloves the whole time they were here."

"Oh," I said, "well." Wincing, Mary Agnes Donovan reluctantly peeled a couple of inches of duct tape off Babe's bare arm. Babe yelled in pain.

"How about we just cut it in enough places to get her out of the chair," Stearns suggested, "and run her over to the emergency room? The nurses'll have stuff over there to make it easier." His old-cop's eyes said, Find a way to bag this. The stuffy crowded office already stank of rage and urine and was getting worse fast as our anxiety added more sweat.

"No, piss on it, go ahead," Babe said. "I need to get goin'! Just pull it fast so it won't hurt so much, willya?"

We found a big pair of scissors and went to work. She grunted a couple of times through her set jaw, but she never yelled again. In five minutes we had most of the tape off.

As soon as she was free, she bolted for the bathroom. There was the sound of a lot of flushing, and then she came out and said, "Can you hang tough a couple of minutes while I change clothes? I stink like a damn sewer." She took some garments out of a closet behind her desk and disappeared again.

"Well, no use all of us standing around here, I guess," Al Stearns said. "You need any more help with this, Jake?"

"Better stick around till we're sure she's okay," I said, "and then, yeah, you guys might as well roll. Can't do much police work in a crime scene while they're serving lunch in it." I looked around the dingy office. "Is everything down here the way you found it? Except for the tape?"

"You were right behind us, Jake," Donovan said. "We never had time to touch anything but her."

"Fine," I said. "I'm going upstairs and talk to the employee who found her. Come get me, will you, when she's ready to talk?"

The thin cook who had opened the door for me was shaking grease off a basket of french fries as I slid onto a stool nearest the bar. He dumped the fries alongside a burger and set the plate in front of a white-haired man with a red nose.

"There you are, Neely, my man," he said. "You want some more coffee with that?" He poured it, then came to my end of the counter and said, "Now, what can I do for you?"

I held up my badge again, said, "Jake Hines, Detective Division. Were you the one who placed the call?"

"Yup. She all right?"

"She seems to be doing okay. We got her out of the tape and she's changing clothes. Were you the first one who found her?"

"That's right. Came to work the way I always do, turned on the range, and started some coffee—"

"Wait. Can we back up a little? Could I have your name first?"

"Sure." He shrugged his thin shoulders. "Have anything I got, I guess. Ain't much, though. I'm just the cook. John Floogey, spelled P-f-l-u-e-g-e. Call me Jack." He rattled off his address, phone number, social security.

"Okay, Jack, how'd you get in this morning? You have your own key?"

"Sure. Have to. I open up."

"So—"

"So I walked in and went to work, same as usual."

"Anybody else here?"

"No. Well, Babe was downstairs, but I didn't know that. All the lights was out, the air-conditioning was off, I figured I was the first one in. Turned everything on, started the grill up, made the coffee.

"Then Dozey come in, he's the dishwasher. Peeled some potatoes while I cut up cabbage for slaw."

"He have a key too?"

"Nope. I left the back door unlocked for him, like always. You wanna talk to him? He's swampin' out the johns."

"I'll see him next, thanks. Then what?"

"Bartender come in. Then we all started sayin', 'Well, where's Babe?' Time she got the tills out, set up the registers. We're supposed to open by eleven. I needed some sugar and catsup out of the storeroom, I said I'll go get that, and then if Babe's not here I'm gonna call her."

He squeezed his eyes shut, put his hands over his mouth, and breathed through them like a man fighting frostbite.

"I still can't hardly believe this next part," he said softly. "I turned on the lights ahead of me as I went downstairs. Had a bus box in my hands, for carrying stuff back up. The office lights are on the same switch, but the door was closed, so I didn't pay no attention to the light under the door . . . but when I went by it I heard these funny noises comin' out of there. Like to made my heart stop. I told myself, Must be a rat, but it didn't sound like no rat. I tried the door, holding the box out in front of me, ready to hit whatever come at me, but it was locked. So I knelt down and looked through that screened vent in the middle of the door. Boy, my ol' heart was just goin' like this, y'know? And then, hell's fire, there was Babe's eyes starin' right at me. An' her fastened up every which way to the desk and the chair, and doin' her best to holler through that tape."

"Did you try to get her loose?"

"I couldn't! I don't have the keys to her office!" Jack raised his arms, palms up in an I-give-up gesture. "I'm just the cook." It seemed to be his mantra. "I hollered through the door, 'I'll call the cops, Babe, hang on!' and I run back upstairs to the phone. Dialed nine-one-one, answered all the questions they asked me, best I could, and hung up and run back down and told her help was on the way. She nodded her head a couple times and rolled her eyes toward upstairs. So I said, 'Don't you worry, we'll get 'er open,' and that's what we done, Dozey and me and Red, he's the bartender. Only we still ain't got no money to work with. Lucky we only had a couple of regulars so far, we're just gonna have them sign chits till Babe gets some new tills ready."

She came up the stairs at that moment, dressed in clean clothes, with her hair combed and her lipstick on straight. She carried two cash boxes with a couple of bills and a few pieces of change in each one. Over her shoulder she told an impressed-looking Mary Agnes Donovan, "I always keep a little extra change in the cracker box. Only place they didn't look. Bastards even cleaned out my purse."

Al Stearns followed them, looking the way Stearns always looks on duty, like just possibly a few sticks of dynamite up his nose might get him excited. He's seen everything twice, and the closer he gets to retirement, the less anxious he is for the third time.

"Here, Jack," Babe told the cook, "this is pretty sparse, but you can—" She gave him rapid-fire orders for dispensing change, moved to the bartender, and repeated them. "Listen," she said, turning to us, "I gotta run to the bank right now—"

"Babe, Red can go to the bank," Jack said. "I can cover the bar till he gets back. Why don't you sit down and eat this burger I've got on the grill? Mooney ain't in no hurry for it. Are you, Art?"

"Huh?" Mooney's bald head and bushy white eyebrows appeared over the top of his newspaper. "Who, me hurry? Hell, I don't do nothin' all day, and I don't start that till afternoon." He lowered the paper to the counter and smiled at Babe. "Better sit down, darlin'. You look a little pale."

"Well . . ." Babe looked uncertain for a couple of seconds, then smiled shakily and said, "Okay. Thanks, I appreciate it." She sat down on the stool next to mine, and Jack poured her a big glass of orange juice. She took a swig, sighed gratefully, wrote a check and a change list, and walked them over to the bar. After a short conference with Red she came back and sat down again, sampled the coffee Jack had poured for her, and said, "You're right, I just realized I'm starving. Make that a cheeseburger with everything, will you? And plenty of fries?"

"Can I ask you some questions while you eat?" I knew she needed to eat in peace, but I wanted to get as many answers as possible while the shock was still fresh. Victims often reject their memories as soon as they can.

"Sure. You want some coffee?" She looked at me with sudden interest and asked, "How come you're not in uniform, by the way?"

"I'm an investigator now," I said.

"Like, a detective?"

"Yeah. Like that."

"Jeez, kid." The old barn-burner smile made a momentary reappearance. "Lotta water over the dam since I showed you how to carry a bus box without gettin' a hernia, huh? Remember how we used to herd drunks out the door together on Saturday night? One on each side and both talkin' so sweet?" She chuckled, lit a cigarette, blew smoke in the air, and sighed. "Can you believe it? All these years later, I'm still doin' it." She stretched, stuck her fist against the side of her neck, and rotated her head against it. "God, I got cramped in that chair. All my muscles are tied up in knots."

"I wish I could tell you to go home and take a long hot bath," I said, "but the sooner you tell me this story, Babe, the better chance we've got of nailing those guys."

"Oh, right," she said, not sounding confident. Jack slid the cheeseburger in front of her, and she began wolfing it down. "Well. Where shall we start?"

"Start wherever it started. Were you the first one in the building yesterday?"

"I was the only one. We don't open on Monday anymore. It's the slowest day, and I needed one day off a week to get caught up at home."

"So why were you here?"

"I came in about two in the afternoon to make up the weekend's deposits and go to the bank."

"Is that what you usually do on Monday?"

"Yes. I was a little earlier than usual yesterday because I knew I had a lot of cash to count. We had the biggest weekend of the summer, the regional pool tournament, and we were swamped for three days."

"Okay. So you came in the front door, back door?"

"Back. Parked where I always do, in my space in the lot on Seventh Avenue, and walked down the alley."

"Let's start there," I said. "When you're done eating," I added, apologetically, but she waved one hand in a no-problems gesture as she stuffed the last bite in her face and got up to lead the way. We walked through the open arch into the long, dim room full of pool tables, silent at this hour. I followed her to the rear, where she pushed the panic bar on the heavy back door, and we stepped outside. The alley smelled like Dumpsters. The back door was grease-stained and flyspecked but surprisingly solid, a heavy steel door that made a snug fit in a steel frame. It had a heavy-duty closer with a spring-operated latch bolt and a dead bolt above.

"Door looks newer than the rest of the building," I said.

"OSHA made the landlord do some remodeling a couple of years ago," Babe said. "Remember how we used to have to lock the back door from the outside to keep it closed if the wind was blowing? Feds said it would be a death trap in a fire. Long as they had to fix it, I persuaded them to go first class."

"You got a good lock."

"The best. Spring lock in the closer, see, always locked unless you set it on open." She showed me. "Whoever gets to work first, usually Jack, unlocks the dead bolt and sets the closer in the unlocked position till the rest of the help gets to work and we open for business. Once we open the front door, I reset the spring lock on the back door. For the rest of the day, nobody can open this door from outside, but in an emergency anybody can get out by pushing on the panic bar. When I close up at night, I lock the dead bolt on the way out."

"Sounds like a good system. Deliveries come in the front?"

"Mostly. Anybody wants to deliver from the alley has to arrange it with me first. And the crews for the later shifts come in the front, too. Jack has one set of keys, and I have the other one. Nobody touches the locks but the two of us. We watch who comes in the front, and we don't have to worry about the back. Getting to be kind of a rough neighborhood around here, Jake."

"Uh-huh," I said. "Lotta smoking going on."

"Yeah, and these days some of the smoke is from crack. Can you believe it? Right here in little old Rutherford? You know, with pot smokers, you don't have to worry too much, those dodos just get dreamy and worthless if they use too much. But crack users are something else. Crackheads like to fight. Tell you the truth, if it wasn't for my old-timers, I might think about selling this place."

"Does Helmer Krogstad still play pool in here? And Willie Finch?"

"Helmer's in a rest home now. Willie still comes in. Pat Fogarty, Mitch Carlson, you remember both of them, don't you? Tony Pease, Pete Peterson, Larry Tuohy. They may not be rocket scientists, but at least they seem to be able to choke down a burger and a beer without breaking up the place."

"So," I said, playing with the spring lock a minute longer, "when you come in on Mondays to do the weekend deposits, you unlock the door and then—?"

"Lock it right up again, leave it locked till I'm ready to go to the bank. Drive to the bank, make the deposits, come straight back here with the change. Lock up again while I put the money in the safe, phone in some orders, pay a few bills, and then I'm outta here."

"And you feel pretty sure you locked the door like always yesterday?"

"Not pretty sure. Damn good and sure. I've had a couple of bad scares here in the last year, Jake. I'm careful. Nothing distracts me while I see to the locks."

"Any chance whoever robbed you was already in the place when you got here?"

"No. Randy locked up Sunday night." She smiled. "You seen Randy since he grew up? He's way taller than I am now, eighteen his last birthday."

"Hard to believe." I vaguely remembered a sulky little boy in the back booth, eating ice cream while his doting mother finished her shift. Babe never talked about his father.

"Randy's closed up before?"

"Yeah, he earns his spending money looking after the place for me on Sunday night. To give me a break. We close at nine Sundays. Other nights we're open till one, so I stay."

"Makes a long day."

She shrugged. "I don't trust anybody else to do it. I usually grab a nap in the afternoon."

"Does Randy have another set of keys?"

"No. I leave mine with him. He brings 'em home when he's done."

"He still lives with you?"

"Oh, sure, he's still in school."

"Can I talk to him? Will he be in soon?"

She shook her head. "He went fishing yesterday and stayed last night with the kid whose dad owns the boat. They were going out again this morning. I don't expect he'll be back till around five."

"Okay. Let's walk on through this. You locked the back door—"

"Right. I turned on the lights, went downstairs to my office—"

"Let's do it," I said. At the door of her office, she began going through the motions, naming them like a child reciting a lesson: "Went inside. Closed the door. Opened the safe—" Her voice took on a jumpy edge.

"Sit down," I said. "Don't hurry. Take all the time you need." She fished a cigarette out of a pack on her desk, and I lit it for her. "You never heard anything?"

"Not a sound." She blew smoke for a minute. "I was just finishing the third deposit when they came through the door."

"How many?"

"Two. One big guy. I'm five-six, and he towered over me. The other one was a little shorter and a lot slimmer. But I never saw their faces. They had on"—her voice wavered ominously, "ski hats, I guess . . . those knit things with holes for the mouth and eyes? Looked like . . . terrorists . . ." She shivered and began to whisper. "Black sweatpants. Dark T-shirts with 1-long sleeves." A couple of tears slid through her fresh makeup.

"Babe." I picked up a straight chair that was sitting against the wall, set it down facing away from her, and straddled it so that our knees almost touched. "Listen, I know this is tough. But I urge you now: Don't get scared, get even. Help me catch these guys."

She put her hands over her face and made three painful sounds that combined the worst aspects of grunting and moaning. I handed her the box of tissues on her desk; she grabbed a handful and disappeared into it, blowing her nose. Then she gulped air, blew it out, and said, "The worst thing was, they never made a sound."

"No kidding? They didn't talk at all?"

"Didn't talk, didn't grunt, didn't even point. I swear, Jake. Like a pair of goddamn spooks. Just grabbed me and slapped that piece of tape on my mouth. Then, while the biggest one held me like this"—she got behind me to demonstrate a bear hug, with one leg wrapped around my lower torso—"the other one started wrapping me up. When they had my legs taped clear up to the hips, they sat me down and taped my arms to the chair. That's the part that hurt the most. They taped me up tight while my legs were straight, and then they bent them anyway to get me in the chair." She rubbed her knees to comfort them.

"After that they taped my ankles to the desk. But they did all of that without making a sound, can you imagine? It was like the worst nightmare I ever had. I actually kind of wondered when I was gonna wake up." She gave a shaky laugh.

"Then they started scooping up money. Methodical! They used a picnic cooler they had brought along. Went in the safe and got out the rest of the change. Went through my purse and the drawers of the desk. Moving right along but not hurrying. When they were sure they had it all, they turned off the lights and left. Never even glanced in my direction while they went out and closed the door." She shivered.

"Babe, did you check the rest rooms when you came in? Could they have been in the men's room?"

"Damn, I hate to think so," she said, fretfully. "But no, I didn't. Randy must have checked them, though, I've taught him well enough how to close up! Last thing we do, always, is check the rest rooms and make sure they're empty."

"Hiding in one of the storerooms, maybe?"

"Shouldn't be. Storeroom doors are supposed to be kept padlocked every minute they're not bringing out supplies. I mean, I have systems for all this, Jake."

"We'll take another look at both doors," I said. "But I don't see any signs of forced entry."

Babe shook her head. "Pretty tough to force an entry though the doors I've got now," she said. "Almost need dynamite."

"Think about it," I said. "This basement has no windows. What about the roof?"

"Vent fans for the heat and cooling, and the grill.

Maybe eight inches of access if you could pry off the fan housings."

"No trapdoor?"

"No."

I waited a minute. "How long has Jack Pfluege worked for you?"

"Oh . . . nine years? Going on ten. Jack's okay, Jake, don't worry about him. He was washing dishes here when Art's old cook—remember Bodie?—Bodie said he'd be damned if he'd ever work for a woman. The day after I filed for divorce, when he saw Art wasn't coming to work, he took off his apron and walked out. Jack said, 'I know how to cook, gimme a chance.' He burned a few fries at first, but he learned fast, and he's been here ever since. Comes to work on time, does his job and nothing extra. Just right for here. I watch everything like a hawk, I've never seen him try any funny business at all."

There was a lot of loud talking on the stairs. Ollie Green and Nick Kranz, the fingerprint team from downtown, appeared in the doorway. Between them stood a plump, excited-looking adolescent who seemed vaguely familiar.

"Hey, Jake," Nick said, and at the same moment the kid yelled, "Ma!" and Babe said, "Randy!" Mother and son began hugging each other, both talking at once. "Jeez, you okay?" Randy asked, and Babe said, "What are you doing here so early?"

"You sure you're not hurt? How come you didn't call me?"

"I thought you said five o'clock!" said Babe.

I met Nick Kranz's eyes, nodded toward the hall, and we walked outside.

"We won't get any useful prints from the office, I guess," I said. "Babe says the thieves wore gloves in here. I'd like you to lift what you can from the desk and safe, though, for comparison with employee prints. The front door is hopeless, everybody in town has a print on there. But try to get everything off the back door. I've got a hunch they came in that way, and they might not have wanted to put the gloves on till they got inside. And we want a full set from each employee." We went back inside, and I introduced Ollie and Nick to Babe. "Give them the name and address of any employees you have who are not working now, they'll follow up. We'll need your prints too, Randy."

"Oh, sure," Randy said. He seemed to be enjoying the excitement.

Babe's phone rang. She answered and passed it to me. Sally said, "Milo Nilssen's waiting in your office. Says you have a date for a pretrial interview?"

Damn! His appointment was written on the desk calendar that I hadn't unpacked yet.

"Can he wait? I can come back right now."

"That's what he wants. He said, 'Tell him to get his ass back here. I'll wait in his office.' Evidently it has to be done today."

"Right. Ten minutes, tell him."

I handed the phone to Babe and told her, "Green and Kranz are going to be here awhile, working in this office and on the back door. Will you keep everybody out of here till they're done? Oh, and Babe? Let me borrow your deposit book, will you?"

"What for?" She looked alarmed.

"I want to make copies of the weekend's deposit slips. Will you make up a list of the money they took that wasn't in a deposit? It helps to get as close as we can to the exact amount of the theft."

"You mean, like, to make it a felony or something?"

"Robbery's always a felony. No, I just mean, if we find

some deadbeat making large purchases all of a sudden, the totals might fit."

"Can't you just make note of the totals? I don't like the idea of everybody snooping in my business." She was starting to feel the shock, I thought; her color was going bad.

"Nobody's going to snoop. I'll make the copies myself, and I'll get them back to you this afternoon."

She gave me a long, hard stare, wrapped a big rubber band tight around the long tablet, and handed it over reluctantly. I crammed it into my already tortured briefcase and drove back to the station, pondering the probable hard knocks that had made a suspicious workaholic out of the once lighthearted Babe.

Milo Nilssen, his frayed Hush Puppies propped on my nice clean desk, was taking a snooze.

"Don't be formal, Milo," I said. "Make yourself at home."

"Nice of you to drop by, Jake." He got up and stretched. He wasn't really annoyed; Milo always needed rest. He worked for Ed Pearce, the handsome, showboating county attorney of Hampstead County. Ed was legendary for running his staff ragged and taking all the credit.

Milo had been on a high lope all summer, wrapping up the details of a case his boss was determined to take to the grand jury on Thursday. "The Teen Drug Bust," as Ed Pearce always called it when he talked to reporters, took place last spring near Madison High School.

"Why is the CA so excited about a few nickel bags of dope?" I asked Milo, back in May when they started putting the case together. "Does he really think high school kids never smoked marijuana before?"

"It's Doris, I think," Milo muttered, looking over his

shoulder. He always got furtive when he mentioned his boss's wife; he was convinced she had extrasensory powers. Mrs. Pearce took a keen interest in her husband's career, and Milo dreaded her scrutiny. "Doris wants him to run for governor in two years."

"She said that?"

"Well, not to me." Milo peered around him, shooting his cuffs and ducking his head. "And don't you tell anybody I told you."

"How's this little two-bit marijuana case gonna help him run for governor? Why not a crack dealer, if he wants profile?"

"You got one in jail?"

"Well, no. But it's only a matter of time."

"Sure. Maybe quite a lot of time. Crack dealers are tough and smart. Ed and Doris think this case will play well with parents and school boards, and it's ready right now when they need it. Ed's gonna talk to the jury about evil outsiders preying on our kids."

"Outsiders? Pinky Predmore lives in Blooming Prairie, for chrissake."

"Still. He's not from Rutherford. Ed thinks he can make it work."

Now, in August, Doris apparently remained convinced that this case had the sweet smell of success clinging to it, and had urged her spouse to spare no effort. Doris's urging being no laughing matter, shit was rolling downhill onto Milo, who had the case just about ready to go. Four high school students had been subpoenaed to testify to a jury how an evil dealer named Pinky Predmore had seduced them into buying cannabis in the school parking lot. And today I had pulled myself away from Rowdy's Bar, where I really belonged, to take part in this interview.

"I certainly hope," Milo said, ostentatiously choosing a pen from the row of implements clipped to his pocket protector, "that I didn't take you away from anything really important." Lately Milo had been groping for an attitude. Today he seemed to be working on irony.

"Just routine," I said. "One more robbery in section three."

"Aw, hell, what now?"

"Rowdy's Bar. Looks like it started out as a straightforward burglary, but the thieves surprised the owner counting the money and taped her up."

"The owner? You mean Babe Krueger? Aw, no kidding? She okay?"

"Seems to be. You know her?"

"Back in her party days she dated my older brother. They used to give me a ride to Little League practice. I never wanted to get out of the car." He blushed, remembering. "She was always real nice to me," he added, wistfully. Seeing me smiling at him, he slipped into defensive mode, shooting his cuffs, smoothing his hair, and looking at his watch. "Well, let's get at it, shall we?" he said, pulling forms out of his briefcase.

We went over the facts of the case again. Pinky Predmore, a layabout and loser from a small town west of Rutherford, had been apprehended in the parking lot at Madison High School in mid-May, selling, or attempting to sell, marijuana to students. No leaf had actually been found on the person of any student. Pinky had, in various pockets on his person, about a dozen nickel bags, which in Rutherford go for ten to twenty dollars, import fees being what they are. Buzz Cooper was the arresting officer.

"And Buzz got the complaint how, remind me?" Milo said, leafing through his notes.

"Lessee. Sally Hall was the call taker that day, passed it to Schultzy on dispatch, Schultzy called for the nearest car, and Buzz answered."

"Yeah, here it is, a nine-one-one call, and Sally couldn't understand the name of the caller. But a good address and description of the car, so Schultzy asked Buzz to check it out, and he scored. Longworth was backup. You ever find the identity of the caller?"

"Nope."

"How come you interviewed the suspect, Jake? I thought Bo Dooley was your head narc now?"

"He is. Dooley and Anderson did all the interviews pertinent to your case. I talked to him because I was looking for a trade. Chief said I could offer him a little leverage on his drug charge for some skinny on three stolen cars. We thought the suspects might be customers of his."

"Did he give you anything?"

"Nah. Pinky doesn't know anything. That's his problem. He's way down at the bottom of the food chain, Milo; he probably got those few bags of dope from some dealer in a one-time purchase and was just trying to double his money. His usual shtick is swiping CD players out of unlocked cars. Boosting wallets, stuff like that. He even works sometimes."

"No kidding, a solid citizen. Well, his next job's gonna be making license plates, I guess." Milo and I agreed on the final wording of my statement, and I was typing it up when the phone rang.

"Had lunch?" the chief asked.

"No. Is it noon?"

"Twelve-thirty. My wife sent too much food, how about helping me eat it up? I need to talk to you."

"Well, fine. Thanks. Be there in a couple of minutes."

Milo looked up from packing his briefcase, saw my face, and said, "Somebody gotcha, huh?"

"Chief wants to chat."

Milo punched my shoulder. "It isn't always more work," he said helpfully. "Sometimes it's just a cut in benefits."

· T W O ·

MILO'S SARCASM WAS PROBABLY RIGHT ON TARGET IN HIS OWN workplace, I reflected as I walked down the hall, but it was way out of the kill zone in mine. My boss has no need for dirty tricks. Frank McCafferty is an honest, confident man who settles his differences with a candid exchange of ideas. Sometimes he's so candid I'm halfway out of the building before the echoes die down, but at least I don't have to worry about getting knifed in the back.

And a summons to talk to the chief isn't all that unusual; lately we've had plenty to talk about. Last year, when Frank saw we were going to get moved into the new government center building, he lobbied city hall to marry a federal grant to some state matching funds and upgraded the whole department. First he got our patrol cars equipped with computers slaved to downtown. Then he spread his newly wired, more efficient patrolmen out, one to a car, and used some of the payroll he saved to put on three more detectives.

The two cops that tested highest on the Civil Service exams, Darrell Betts and Rosie Doyle, were finishing their training and joining the investigative section this month. Darrell was a shy, quiet farm kid from north of Eyota whose high scores surprised us all. Rosie was almost his logical opposite, a high school star in basketball and a bouncy extrovert whose grandfather and two uncles were Rutherford cops. We intended to start them both on burglaries, where the logjam of unsolved cases was highest. Always the entry-level crime of choice, burglary in Rutherford had increased 15 percent in the last six months. In neighborhoods where nobody locked a door five years ago, householders had begun shopping for alarm systems.

Next the chief took Bo Dooley off patrol, sent him to school, and designated him the department specialist in narcotics and vice. Bo had been a patrolman in St. Louis for five years before transferring up to Rutherford, and McCafferty felt he had experience with big-time drug traffic that we could put to good use. Gimme a break, some of the foot soldiers were heard to mutter, a narc in Rutherford? They took to calling him the Drug Czar.

"We already got the game, like it or not," Frank said grimly, "why be shy about using the name?" He exerted himself to establish liaison between Bo and his opposite numbers in the Twin Cities, and he told me, "Don't worry about the bitching from the troops. A lot of 'em swore they couldn't live with a computer in the car, either. Now they're turning into hackers."

I let that obvious exaggeration pass because there was other urgent business to discuss. Frank was putting me in charge of his newly enlarged investigative division.

I applied for this new job, tested for it, and was glad to get picked. I got a raise in pay and a lieutenant's rating. More money never hurts, and besides, I'd been a detective almost six years; it was time to take on more responsibility. But I knew it was going to be a roller coaster. My newly rated investigators were going to need plenty of help, and thanks to all these reorganizations, even the old hands were floundering. I was hoping soon to be the hero who led them out of this swamp. On my first morning, I was mostly trying not to let them see me sweat.

So now, if Frank wanted to talk some more about organizational matters while we ate some of his wife's marvelous food, I could use the help and advice. If, on the other hand, Lulu had put a burr under his saddle about my efforts to avoid a CID, I was in for a big case of heartburn. McCafferty is impervious to argument once he climbs on board one of his hot new hobbyhorses. He's determined to show the guys in St. Paul we're quick to respond to new ideas, that we're not just a bunch of hicks down here in little Rutherford.

I marshaled my excuses: the burglary this morning at Rowdy's, just when I was trying to get moved into my new office and organize my staff. A stack of faxes waiting for answers, somewhere in those boxes still on my office floor. Not to mention an angry lady named Millicent Porter, who was evidently going to call me every week for the rest of my life till I found the family heirlooms that were taken from her home last spring. I kept getting busier as I went down the hall. By the time I reached the chief's doorway, I didn't have time to spit.

It was all for nothing. Frank was humming contentedly as he laid out his lunch. He didn't seem to have anything on his mind but calories.

"Look at this!" he said, pulling Baggies out of a brown paper bag. "Sheila makes me a salad so I won't gain weight. Then she sends along enough garnishes to fatten a hog. You think maybe my wife is secretly working for the opposition?" He chuckled. His desk looked like something out of *House Beautiful*. He even had carrot sticks and flowered napkins.

I felt saliva spring into delighted action under my tongue. Frank was unwrapping a plate of deviled eggs, and I smelled cucumbers in vinegar.

We filled our plates with pasta curls and greens. Frank found a bottle of vinaigrette dressing, which he sloshed on like water, crowing happily, "This stuff is low-fat, see?" He claims his size is due to old-jock metabolism that never adjusted to his desk job, but he's a powerful hand with a fork, too.

We crunched through a few thousand vitamins. Finally Frank sat back, sighed contentedly, and began poking idly at a radish with a broccoli spear.

"Well, so," he said, "how's it going with the move? Gonna be able to off-load some of your cases and get on with supervising?"

"Hope so. Had to take a new burglary call this morning at Rowdy's Bar, though. Just as well I did," I said as I saw him open his mouth to protest. "It's gonna turn into aggravated robbery. Lucky it wasn't murder."

"What, somebody got hurt?"

"Babe Krueger was taped in a chair for almost twenty-four hours. Alone all night in the basement of Rowdy's Bar? Good thing she's tough. Most women would be in the hospital."

He shook his head. "See, there we go again, section three."

"Yep. Maintaining its average." In the near north watch area, east of Broadway and north of Center, the call rate this year had been roughly two to one over any other patrol zone in Rutherford. Lately, patrolmen assigned to section three got the adrenaline pumping before they even left the station.

"They robbed the safe, huh? While the place was closed? Anything else taken?"

"Storerooms weren't touched. Haven't had time to talk to the bartender yet, but he had the bar open, and it looked okay."

"So how much money?"

"Still working on the total. Close to thirty thousand, give or take."

Frank stared. "From Rowdy's? Hard to believe."

"Biggest weekend of the summer, Babe says. Pool tournament. I've got the deposit slips. She's still working on the change list."

"Seems like a lot. Whaddya say"—he stood up, suddenly irritated by the groceries spread over his desk—"had enough? Okay if I deep-six all this?" He scooped a lot of garbage into his wastebasket, sat down, and tortured his swivel chair for a minute. "I've been thinking about pop."

"What do you want? I'll get it." I started toward the machine in the hall.

"No, no, no." He waved his arms. "Capital P-O-P. Remember? Problem Oriented Policing. We talked about it in May, after I came back from the chief's convention. Then all hell broke loose around here, and I kind of tabled it. But I'm thinking about a POP program for section three."

The acronym approach to law enforcement makes me deeply uneasy. Why should we make it sound as if we're playing some cute game? "I gotta tell you, Frank," I said, "I feel quite problem oriented already."

"What? You think it sounds kind of la-di-da?"

"Uh-huh."

"I don't know." Frank kicked his desk three or four times. He has very large feet that he's always trying to maneuver into a comfortable spot. "This time I think maybe we're onto something. They call it the proactive approach. Instead of *re*active, see? I mean, for instance, usually we wait till we get a call, then after we know somebody's got a problem, we respond to that, right?"

I let three seconds go by while I recrossed my legs and then said, "Right."

Frank picked up the big glass paperweight from his desk and played with it a minute. I watched while he decided not to throw it at my head. Finally he put it back on a stack of spreadsheets, sat back, and gave me one of his big, innocent stares. He has prominent baby blue eyes. It's distressingly easy to tell when you're enjoying his full attention.

"All this reorganization we've been doing in the investigative section, you remember what got us started on that?" he asked softly.

"Rapidly growing town, rising crime rate. So many new cases—"

"Uh-huh. Accompanied by an even larger dip in the clearance rates, right?"

"Down a little from last year, for sure." I'd been hoping we weren't going to go all over that ground again. Hadn't we decided on a strategy, weren't we taking steps?

"I just got the June figures." He pulled one of the spreadsheets toward him. "Eight percent down from last year, which was five percent below the year before."

"So many cases all at once—"

He picked up the paperweight again and put it down again, but harder. "What do you think I'm saying to you?" His voice was going up despite his best efforts. Down the hall, I could hear doors closing. "We're just answering one call after another as fast as we can, and it's making the whole department look like a bunch of turkeys! Morale is in the toilet, and everybody's jumpy and mean because we're up to our armpits in a goddamn swamp! And the more swamped we get, the lousier our score is going to look!"

He slammed the paperweight down again, and Lulu came and closed the door to the outer office. "Your ass is on the line as much as mine is. You think the City Council is going to send you little bouquets of flowers saying, 'Golly, Jake, we're sorry you're having it so tough just when you got your nice promotion'? Think again.

"I just got this note in the mail." He waved a piece of paper over his head and then brought it to eye level and gave it a glare that should have set it on fire.

"The mayor wants to know if we"—he held the paper in front of his nose and read, in a voice like battery acid—" 'perhaps need interim assistance.' Which in plain English means"—Frank was beginning to look apoplectic—" 'When are you going to get your asses in gear over there?' You know what the next goddamn helpful sonofabitching memo's going to say? Huh?"

He was getting so worked up I didn't dare answer. He wadded the memo into a hard ball and hurled it into his wastebasket with a metallic twang. Plastic Baggies and a couple of shreds of lettuce flew out. "It's going to say, 'Help is on the way, asshole, and send us your resignation and don't forget to include one for your smart-ass new head of detectives.' "

He sat back and kicked his desk a few more times. He picked up the heavy paperweight again and sat looking at it curiously while I held my breath.

I watched my watch scroll through ten seconds before I said softly, "I'm sorry, Frank. I didn't mean to be rude."

"Like shit you didn't." He had me there. I had meant to poke fun at what I saw as a silly initialized everybody-into-the-pool approach to crime control. Now I meant to talk him out of beaning me with a glass knickknack. If I could.

"What do you want me to do?"

He stared out his window a minute. "I want you to quit being a pissant," he said, "and give this idea a chance."

"Okay," I said. I still thought it was crap, but I was sorry to have offended him. "What's first?"

He stared at me a minute. I must have looked sufficiently sincere, because finally he nodded, satisfied, swiveled his chair noisily, and said, "Look at this."

He had two blowups of section three pinned to a corkboard behind his desk.

"I had Lulu flag the addresses for calls in section three for the first half of this year, and for the same period last year." He poked the left-hand chart with his pen. "Here's last year. Blue is for no-arrest calls and misdemeanors, theft, vandalism, DUI. Red is for the serious stuff—assault, armed robbery, rape, domestic violence. Look where the pins cluster."

Three-quarters of the calls were between Tenth and Eighteenth Streets, along Fifth and Sixth Avenues.

"Huh," I said. "We all keep blaming section three, but really most of the calls are in the center, aren't they? Basically in what they call the North End."

"Exactly," Frank said. "The rest of section three, the brick apartment houses from Center north to Eighth Street, and the commercial sections along Broadway and out by the highway, I had Lulu run the averages, and they're actually a little lower than the rest of town.

"But here's what concerns me the most." He swiveled right. "Look at this year's map."

The clustering was equally obvious, but denser; there were many more pins. And now the most active area extended north almost to Twentieth Street, and was creeping east; Seventh Avenue had many pins.

"It's growing," I said.

"Like a cancer," Frank said. "And do you see how the color's changing? Last year it was nearly all blue pins. Now it's much redder. The level of violence is going up fast."

He sat down at his desk and turned his pop-eyed blue stare on me. When McCafferty thinks hard, his eyes open wider, and he starts to look like a deer caught in the headlights.

"Some of the problems in that neighborhood are obvious. It's the oldest part of town, a lot of the buildings are seriously run-down. Some of the bigger houses that used to be occupied by families have been divided into apartments, getting shabbier and shabbier. And there's a growing tendency toward absentee landlords. They don't check references, they rent to anybody that puts down the deposit, and they're very reluctant to evict anybody when the neighbors complain about noise and disruption. The houses go downhill fast.

"And now there's the crack trade," he said.

"Uh-huh. What Bo Dooley calls the Yellow Brick Road."

"Dooley claims supply follows the river up from New Orleans, creates its own demand as it goes along. Says he saw how it worked in St. Louis."

"He seems to think the gangs have divided up Minnesota," I said, "pretty much like the magazine salesmen used to."

"Yeah. Personally I still think he's exaggerating the drug problem a little for small towns like Rutherford, but he's right about one thing, crack isn't like other drugs."

"The quick high, I guess."

"Uh-huh. Instant gratification, made to order for the young. And compared to coke or heroin, it's fairly cheap. You can make enough swiping CD players and lifting wallets to get a hit almost every day."

Frank stared at his jolly colored flags a minute and sighed. "Also, we're not quite as small as we used to be. Chamber of Commerce assures me we'll top a hundred thousand in the next census. Gobbling up cornfields in all directions. I never thought I'd hear myself say this about my own hometown, but there are strong indications of a couple of street gangs up there in the North End." He turned on me indignantly. "In Rutherford! Goddamn! What the hell does a street gang do in this town?"

"Rob 7-Elevens."

"We've only got two. After that, what? But I have to go with the evidence; we've been breaking up fights that look like turf wars. Madison High is right in the middle of it, getting so troubled they can't keep teachers. The principal says it's turning into an arms race; he's asking me to detail an officer up there this fall doing weapons searches in the morning. I hate it."

"Trust me," I said, "whoever you put there is going to hate it worse."

"I know. And here's another thing. Think about the little stores that stayed in that neighborhood so long. Pete Niarchos had a shoe repair place on Eleventh Street for twenty years. When he quit, a pawnshop went in there."

"Yup. And where the Payless Drug Store used to be, on Fifth? It's a topless bar now."

"New stores turn over fast, too," Frank said. "It's only a couple of years since the Shell station closed on Fourteenth Street, but look what's happened since it left. First there was a martial arts school in there. Then that massage business, and now it's an X-rated bookstore. Steady downhill slide. More and more fringe operators, more and more trouble.

"But there are still places up there . . . well, Rowdy's is one. Been there forever, still going strong, or anyway going. Maybe not elegant, but they usually keep order.

And people, too—some of the smaller one-family homes—there's a core group of older homeowners hanging on. It must be getting kind of scary, though. Even the ones with paid-up mortgages are going to have to move out if we don't get 'em some help. And where'll we be when they're gone? Now, right there is where the POP idea starts to look good."

"Is this one of those crash things where we go in and arrest a bunch of people all at once?"

"Some of the bigger cities do that in their worst neighborhoods. I don't think that's a good idea for us. Where would we get the resources, anyway?

"What I'd like to do is assign a couple of officers full-time to just the North End. Start with one man, in fact. Have him make that section his very own, let the people there know he's their officer. Get him out of his car, walking the streets, getting to know people. I'm hoping he can get acquainted with some law-abiding people who'd like to take that neighborhood back. If he could get locals working with him, even a little bit, helping him spot the worst troublemakers, in time I could justify getting him a partner and make it a full-time thing."

"Maybe while he's poking around," I said, "he could look for the fence that's handling all the stolen merchandise that's being generated up there. That first contact must be nearby, Frank. Some of these thieves are fleeing the scene on bikes."

"There you go. He might pick up some gossip about drug dealers. And one thing I know he can do right away is pinpoint the worst hours at the toughest corners. I can get more patrols in there at the times and places when they'll do the most good." He swung his chair around. "You see the possibilities? Work the problem, is what they say. Try to do less policing and more problem-solving."

"Yes," I said, "well." The sociobabble was starting to

leak through again. In a minute he was going to say something about "making a difference." I tried hard not to squirm.

Frank saw me getting antsy. He planted his elbows on his desk and stared straight at me as if he was hoping to penetrate my skull. Some people find being in line with Frank's pop-eyed stare disconcerting. "Like having your nose hairs examined by a frog," Mary Agnes Donovan said once. I don't mind it except when he grinds his teeth.

"Now, to get this going I need to find somebody who's a good communicator," he said, giving up on my forehead. "Somebody very approachable, but with enough experience on the street to stay out of trouble. You got any suggestions?"

"Clint Maddox."

He sat back, impressed. "Just like that, one guy? Nobody in second place?"

"Remember that young runner who found Frenchy LaPlante's body in the park last spring?"

"Creed," Frank said. "Jerry Creed. Had a history of emotional problems."

"Uh-huh. He did all right, in the first few minutes after finding the body. Called nine-one-one and waited by the phone. But after Maddox and Cooper got there, he started to come completely unglued. Maddox held Creed in his arms like a baby till help arrived. Ask Buzz Cooper. He told me that day that Clint Maddox has superior people skills."

"Huh. I'll be damned. Maddox? I've always seen him as kind of . . . ordinary."

"I know. Because of his looks."

"Oh, come on," Frank said, offended. "I don't judge people for their beauty, for chrissake. Cops, especially."

"You can't help it with him. He has a funny face—a lot of freckles, and green eyes. Also his ears stick out."

Frank started a grin, then guiltily put a hand over his mouth.

"You see what I mean?" I said. "Thinking about his face makes you smile. He looks a little bit like Alfred E. Neuman."

"Who's Alfred . . . Aw, you mean the guy on the cover of *Mad* magazine?"

"Uh-huh."

"Oh, c'mon, Jake, jeez, that's terrible." He chuckled, though.

I wasn't trying to put Maddox down. But I live behind an odd-looking face myself, so I've come to terms with the fact that appearances count. To prospective foster parents, during my childhood, I was described as possibly an Arab with dimples, or maybe a light-skinned African-American with straight hair and the wrong nose. "I think I'm going to list you as Asian/Hispanic," a placement officer told me in fourth grade. "It's as good a guess as anything."

I don't have a clue who made my face, but I've always known that the confusing ethnic signals it sends out make many people itch in some subliminal way they can't scratch. My ex-wife once suggested I wear a lapel pin reading "Human Race." I told her I didn't want to seem like a troublemaker.

Clint Maddox's face is different, though, kind of homey. His funny map might actually work to his advantage in the job Frank's talking about. People open up to him; he looks harmless.

"Okay, let's get serious," Frank said. "Say, for the sake of argument, that Maddox is right for the job, how do I get him to take it? It's not gonna be any cakewalk, I'll tell you that."

"He won't really be all alone in section three, will he? You'll still have a squad assigned up there?"

"Oh, sure, but that's a big area. The patrol car can't be nearby at all times. For a lotta hours, he's gotta walk the pavement in the North End alone. Some of those tough little gang-bangers are gonna be watching his every move. So he can't take any crap, but he's gotta be approachable, too.

"Now, what would make all that extra aggravation worthwhile? I need a ploy. I can give him a merit raise, but that's all I've got in the way of money. What else does he want, I wonder?"

"Weekends," I said. "I think Maddox would wrestle alligators for weekends off. His wife works Monday through Friday, and she's been giving him heat because they hardly ever get a whole weekend together with their kids."

"Well, now!" Frank beamed at me. "Once I finally get you cranked up, you can really churn out some ideas, can't you? How come you know so much about this guy? He a particular buddy of yours?"

"No. I just noticed he made all the right moves during that crazy week at the end of May. So I started talking to him sometimes."

"Well, I appreciate your help. I'm gonna go after him right away. If he takes it, maybe you can get him in on the Rowdy's investigation, huh?"

"And the booze heist at Tom's Liquors," I said, "and Lou's rape case, and the apartment that just got cleaned out at the Kiowa Towers. Oh, you betcha. No shortage of places for him to get started in the North End."

"Right. Okay, I'll call you if this works out." He turned away from me and immediately began dialing his phone. Out in normal society, Frank is a courteous man, but at work he often forgets little niceties like hello and good-bye.

I was almost out the door when he turned and said

over his shoulder, "Oh, say, don't forget your CID to-night. Seven-thirty."

"Aw, Frank, I don't need that."

"Just do it, Jake. Don't argue."

I went down the hall feeling grumpy. It was almost two o'clock, the afternoon was getting away from me, none of my mail was answered, and my office still looked like a war zone. I felt fagged out from working in so much confusion, and abused at the thought of giving up an evening to do something I hated. I looked around for something to punish. The only paper on my desk was the note I'd written to myself that morning: "Call A to Z Rentals."

A to Z Rentals runs my apartment complex. Actually, I live in the infamous section three, but out near the high-way where there's plenty of noise but not much worth stealing. My building was always a dog, but it used to be owned by a nice old guy named Ernie Trogstead, who lived next door and was decent about coming to fix things when they broke. Ernie had a heart attack and sold out to a real estate consortium a few months ago. This week my kitchen sink was leaking at the joint underneath, and the closet door in my bedroom wouldn't slide. I'd already left two messages on the answering device at A to Z Rentals, and so far I wasn't getting any answers.

A year ago I moved into this drab apartment in a rage, when my then wife demanded I get out of our house. It was never intended to be more than a temporary squat, but by the time our divorce was final, I was too broke to put a deposit on a better place. Now that I was solvent again, I kept putting off moving because I had begun to dream that Trudy Hanson, my occasional weekend squeeze, would agree to a more substantial arrangement. I was conveniently vague about what, exactly, we would promise each other, or how we would manage her commute to a full-time job in St. Paul. I just kept having pleasant daydreams in which we drifted amiably together through chic, immaculate rooms. Meanwhile I tolerated this scuzzbag apartment.

I called and got a machine. It told me, as it had before, that my call was important to A to Z Rentals. It urged me sweetly to leave a message, promising to get back to me promptly. When the tone sounded, I reminded A to Z Rentals that two previous messages had gone unanswered. I assured them my sink and closet door had not healed by themselves since my last call, and promised them they would never see another penny of my money until both my problems were fixed.

Talking mean to the answering machine gave me a momentary boost, so I began to unpack. My desk blotter, appointment calendar, and pencil mug looked incredibly neat on the immaculate desktop. Then I thought anxiously, who ever heard of police detectives sitting at clean desks clearing cases? I decided to copy Babe's deposit slips, go back to the North End, and finish up the Rowdy's interviews. I had a desperate longing to see one task finished.

I was standing at the copy machine in the hall when Vince Greeley stuck his head around the corner and said, "Hey, Jake. You wanna see my new cammy jammies?"

"Your what?"

"My sexy new camouflage suit that I got for the ERU. Come in here, you're just gonna die of envy." Vince was beaming.

"What's an ARU?"

"Jake, *Jake*. Wake up and smell the coffee, for God's sake. ERU, Emergency Response Unit. The ay-leet corps of Rutherford's finest," he crowed as I followed him down the hall to the men's toilet.

"Oh, good," I said. "Just what we need, more initials to

learn. Why can't we just have a SWAT team like everybody else?"

"Count your blessings," Vince said. "The chief was going to call it the Fast Action Response Team till we showed him how the acronym worked out."

In the cramped space in front of the urinal, nine guys in various stages of undress were trying on complex clothing, speckled all over in shades of brown and green. Chad Frye was testing the Velcro on his many pockets. Buzz Cooper stood holding an enormous helmet with a plastic faceplate.

"You think you got a big enough hat?" I asked him.

"Believe it or not, with all the padding, this fits fine. Just barely room enough in here for my earplug."

"You're protecting your hearing?"

"No, it's got a wire that runs down to this little radio in the shoulder pocket, see?"

"Oh, a receiver? Where do you keep the microphone?"

"You'll never believe," Buzz said. "This little earplug is the microphone and receiver, both."

"You mean you can talk to it through your ear?"

"Whisper, even. Right through my head bones. It's for a silent approach. Ain't it the burning end? Here, let's show him, Vince." With their helmets on and their faceplates lowered, they carried on a silent conversation that delighted them more and more until some private obscenity reduced them both to hysterics.

The whole team was on adrenaline overload, high-fiving each other while they played with their fancy toys. Frye and Cooper showed me a steel battering ram with handgrips on both sides and a steel plate fixed to one end. "It's for breaking down doors," Frink said.

"We're gonna call it 'The Key,'" Cooper said.

"I've even got a body bunker, lookit this, Jake," Vince said, hauling a huge, medieval-looking device out of a

box. "It's for the guy who goes through the door first."
He propped it up, grunting, and peeked through the tiny
viewing slit.

"A body bunker? Do you really call it that?"

"Of course, what else?"

"Well . . . it's a shield."

"God, Jake, you just gotta get with the program,"
Vince said. "Look, I got my terrifying light beam, here—"
He showed me the battery-powered light under the viewing slit. "And then there's my Darth Vader gun, hey, this
thing's really a doozy." He aimed his new Glock at the
wall and hit a button. A red dot appeared above the urinal. "It's a laser-powered sight. Because I can't see around
this body bunker to aim my gun, see? So wherever my
magic dot appears, bang-bang, he's dead." His high, cack-
ling laugh echoed across the urinals. "Ain't it all just . . .
dye-aye-bolical?"

"You kind of like this stuff, huh, Vince?" His smile was
so incandescent, I felt I must be casting a shadow.

"He ought to," Frank said, coming out of the locker
room next door with Kyle Staley. Staley's suit was like
Cooper's, but black, and he wore a flak jacket that came
almost to his knees. "This stuff cost an arm and a leg."

"How do you decide who's black and who's speckled?"

"They've all got a full suit of each," Frank said.
"Black's for night."

"Yeah, the chief had to go around town with a begging
bowl to get the money," Vince said.

"The Elks came up with some of this," McCafferty
said, "Kiwanis and Eagles each had a bake sale, and the
clinics chipped in. I told 'em all, 'I hate fundraising, so if
we're gonna do this let's do it right the first time.' And
boy, we got the best. This is a Spectra vest."

"That's good?"

"Very latest thing. Lighter and more flexible than

Kevlar, feel it. And certified to stop a .357 Magnum. Did
you show him the flash-bang?" he asked Vince.

"Um. No." Vince unearthed a box from under a pile of
equipment. "It's kind of like a super firecracker. We throw
it in ahead of us on a high-risk entry, it scares everybody
half to death."

"You sure scare *me*," I said. "I hope we can find some
criminals bad enough to deserve you."

I went back down the hall, stuck the copies of Babe's
bank records in the Rowdy's file and crammed the origi-
nals back in my briefcase, dug my tape recorder out of a
box, went down and found my car, and drove back to the
North End. Jack Pfluege was cleaning the grill.

"Babe went home for a rest," he said. "Me and Red
and Dozey are mindin' the store." It didn't look like too
big a task. Three guys dawdled over half-empty beers at
one end of the bar. In a booth beyond the empty lunch
counter, a couple of students were drinking coffee. I heard
the murmur and click of a pool game coming from the
back room.

I talked to Dozey first. The dishwasher was a retarded
man in his thirties, missing half his teeth. He told me
proudly about his simple chores, asking me politely, "You
want me to show you where I keep my mop bucket?" I
told him I didn't need to inspect that right now, and tried
to get his version of the morning's events. But life had
taught Dozey to avoid involvement in a confusing world,
and he made a reluctant witness. He kept circling back to
his work routine, which he seemed to follow by rote.

The bartender, Red Eickhoff, was sitting on a high
stool, leafing idly through a two-day-old copy of the *Minneapolis Tribune*. The thieves hadn't touched the bar, he
said.

"Far as I can see, the only damage in this part of the
establishment is just the usual mess I face every Tuesday

morning from that shit-for-brains Babe's got working Sunday nights." His account of the morning agreed substantially with Jack's, except that in Red's telling, he became the hero of the day.

"I told Jack right away, I said, 'Let the police handle it. You just do what you always do, get the lunch counter open.' I mean, running around like a chicken with his head cut off." He rolled his eyes to the ceiling. "As far as Babe getting taped up like that, all I can say, it was bound to happen. Bound to happen. Whaddya expect? A woman alone hasn't got any business trying to run a place like this."

He had his name in at a couple of places downtown, he said; he would be giving notice soon. He had worked at all the best places in town, he didn't have to put up with this foolishness here at all. Never did like working for a woman anyway, and now thieves breaking in, it was just ridiculous. Business was going to hell here anyway, anybody could see that.

"Look around," he insisted, indignantly. "You see a lot of customers in here?"

"Looks pretty quiet. You had a good weekend, though, right? The tournament?"

"Friday night sure wasn't nothin' to write home about. Saturday got fairly lively for a while. I didn't work Sunday, but Sundays never amount to much, tournament or no tournament. And that boy's gonna chase away what little business we got left."

"Which boy is that?"

"Sonny boy," he nodded disgustedly toward the back room, "Candy-ass Randy in there. She leaves him in charge, and all he thinks about is playing with his friends. Hear that?" he demanded, as a chorus of laughter and shouts erupted in the other room. "Him and his worthless pals. How'd you like to be working for that? Even

when he works, he just makes problems. Today he volunteers to go fetch the liquor order, and he comes back with
a bunch of stuff nobody ever heard of." He held up a
bottle of bourbon with a label I'd never seen before.
"Look at this crap. What am I supposed to do with this?"
He leaned toward me with malice pinching his features,
and hissed urgently, "Some of these friends of his are
worse than worthless, if y'ask me. A couple of the ones
he's hanging around with now are *niggers*, for chrissake!"
Suddenly he looked at my face and became unsure of
himself. I stared back impassively, watching his jowls get
pinker as he debated whether an apology would make
things worse.

One of the men sitting at the end of the bar turned
suddenly and said, "Say, ain't you the young fella that
used to work here a few years back?"

"Hey," I said, looking, "Tony Pease." I walked over.
"You still like vinegar with your fries?"

He was pleased I remembered; he crowed to his
friends, "You see, I told you. You were thinner then,
weren't you? I probably was too, far as that goes. You
remember Larry Tuohy, don'tcha? And Pete Peterson? I'm
try'na think, was your name Jack or Jim?"

"Jake," I said, and we shook hands all around. "I'm a
detective now, with RPD." I showed them my shield, and
they passed it from hand to hand, wonderingly.

"Lookit that," Tony said, proudly. "This hardworking
young man went out and made something of himself.
Ain't that great?" They had all been getting close to retirement when I worked at Rowdy's, and they were really old
guys now, white-haired, with arthritic fingers. "You here
to find out about Babe's robbery?" Larry asked.

"Right," I said.

"Terrible thing," Pete said, and they all looked grave.

"Makes me so mad, to think of some smart-aleck

punks doing that to Babe, hard as she works for her money," Tony said.

"And Babe's decent to everybody," Larry said. "Rotten kids."

"Did Babe tell you they were young?" I couldn't remember that she had mentioned age to me.

"Oh, well, no, but . . . who's doing all the terrible stuff around here lately?" Tony said, getting agitated. "Bunch of punk kids have taken over this neighborhood, Jake, it's enough to make you sick. I've lived here all my life, I own my own house, and I'm almost afraid to come out on the front step. I hardly ever *do* go out after dark anymore," he said, and his two friends said, almost in chorus, "Nobody does."

"Really?" I said. "It's that bad? Since when?"

"Oh . . . well, it's been gradually getting worse, of course, but . . . year before last, around the time the pawnshop opened up, that's when we really noticed it. Right, guys?" The other two nodded. "The pawnshop and the"—he waved his hands around, embarrassed—"you know, the place with the dirty books. X-rated, ain't that the way they say it? Jesus," he added, staring into his beer, "what kind of people would want to . . ." Words failed him.

Pete looked at me and shrugged helplessly. "This wasn't a fancy part of town when you worked here, Jake," he said, "but people were holding down jobs and mostly behaving themselves, right? Am I right?"

"Well," I said, "except for St. Patrick's Day," and we all laughed. The year I worked at Rowdy's, St. Patrick's Day came on a Saturday night. A good many North End citizens started their celebration at lunch, and by midnight Rowdy's was the center of a neighborhood drunk of epic proportions. Babe and I needed all our strength and ingenuity to get the place closed that night. Larry,

Pete, and Tony were some of the last customers out the door.

"Aw, jeez, you would bring that up," Pete said, chortling delightedly. "Whee, boy, been quite a while since any of us hung one on like that. Of course"—he nudged me and winked; I had forgotten what a great winker Pete was—"it was Mr. Tuohy here that was really a disgrace; we had to carry him home, if I remember rightly."

"Oh yeah, well, at least I'm Irish," Larry said, "the rest of you was just fakin' to get at the booze. All them old songs about Mother Machree and like that, for chrissake."

"Now listen here, my mother was Irish! I learnt them songs from her fair and square!" Tony Pease yelled. "I admit I'm not much with the jig until I've had a couple of boilermakers."

"No, and not too much after," Larry said. They were all laughing and punching each other by then. Larry ordered another round and insisted I join them.

"I really can't," I said, "I'd get fired. Gimme a rain check, and I'll come back when I'm not working."

I left them shaking dice for the price of three beers and strolled into the back room, where Randy was trading taunts with three other pool players. The sweet smell of cannabis perfumed the air.

Randy turned toward me, smiling, recognized me, and said, more seriously, "Oh, hi!" He turned back and said something softly to the other pool players. One of them, a tall, very handsome young black man with dreadlocks, leaned gracefully toward an ashtray and snuffed out a butt with elaborate casualness.

"Mom went home to get some rest," Randy said. He was more authoritative in his mother's absence. "She'll be back around six, I think. Can I do anything for you in the meantime?"

He liked being in charge. His face had echoes of Babe's features, but blunted and babyish; he had soft, plump hands and a roll of fat around his hips. In his management persona, he copied her mannerisms.

"Well, yes, you can, Randy. I need to talk to you about the last two days, get your whereabouts since yesterday morning on the record."

"Oh, well . . ." He wavered, rather pleased to be interviewed by the police but reluctant to leave his game. "Okay, hang on a minute . . ." He went back to his friends at the table. They talked softly for some time while I waited. Finally they slapped hands and said, "Yeah, later, man," all around. He swaggered back down the long room to where I stood and led the way to a booth on the restaurant side.

I put the tape recorder between us, said, "You mind if I use this?" and turned it on without waiting for an answer. I wanted to jolt him a little. I resented the self-important way he had kept me waiting while he talked to his friends, and I had begun to blame him, unreasonably, for some of the changes in his mother's face. When I looked up from setting the recorder, I saw that I now had his full attention.

"C'mon, you don't need to do *that*," he said. "I'm not really involved in this at all!"

"Did I say you were?" His smile was fading. "I've got everybody else's story about what happened yesterday. Now I need to get yours. That's all." He began rearranging himself in the booth, crossing and recrossing his legs. "Any reason why you don't want to tell me where you were Monday?"

"Of course not." He paid a lot of attention to himself while he lit a cigarette. "I was fishing all day with a friend."

"Name?"

"Scott Rouse. His dad took us, it's his dad's boat. Norbert Rouse." He gave me the address on Third Avenue and the phone number.

"You left from their house?"

"Right. I rode my bike home after I locked up here, gave the keys to Mom and put a few things in a bag, then rode my bike back to Scott's house so I'd be there, ready to go, at six in the morning. We went to Lake Pepin."

"You fished all day?"

"Till about three. Never caught one fish. Pitiful."

"You came home then?"

"Yeah. Well, back to Rouse's. I stayed there last night."

"Any reason?"

"We were going to try our luck at Wabasha today. But the outboard wasn't working right, and this morning Mr. Rouse had a flat on his car, so he decided to get his gear fixed, and I left to go home." He fussed with a book of matches. "But then I decided to come here." He took a long drag on his cigarette, elaborately casual. "Well, you know that, you were here when I came in."

I leaned across the table till he met my eyes, and asked him, "Who'd you see on the way?"

"Nobody!" He slid back in the seat as far as he could go, trying to get more distance between us. "Why?" His eyes darted back and forth from my face to the ashtray, where his hand kept tapping that cigarette. "What makes you think I saw anybody?"

I almost felt sorry for him. He couldn't seem to see that I was just following where he led me.

"You got here about eleven-thirty," I said. "Their house is what, ten blocks from here?"

"I guess. Maybe twelve."

"What time did you leave your friend's house?"

"Oh . . . we were out in the yard awhile, shooting hoops. . . . I'm not sure."

"Well, how long does it take you to ride a bike twelve blocks? Five minutes?"

"Well, c'mon, longer than that."

"Ten minutes? Fifteen? We get that bike any slower, Randy, it's gonna fall over." I gave him a slitty-eyed look, very Sam Spade. "So when I check with your friends the Rouses, are they going to confirm that you were at their house, in their yard, till at least eleven-fifteen?"

"Well . . . jeez. Listen, I could have stopped a couple times on the way over here. I probably did, come to think of it."

"Where'd you stop, Randy?"

Randy puffed up and got red in the face, simmered and steamed a couple of seconds, and then decided to try indignation.

"Oh, the hell with this crap! Who the fuck do you think you are, anyway? All these stupid pushy questions! Who elected you God? You got some goddamn nerve, coming in here treating me like a criminal in my own place!"

"That's funny," I said. "I thought it was your mother's place."

He slipped over the edge then into genuine rage.

"Smart-ass motherfucker!" he yelled. He picked up the ashtray from the table between us and hurled it across the room. "You get out of here!"

The ashtray struck the mirrored wall behind the lunch counter, narrowly missing Jack, who had luckily squatted just then to put something on a shelf. The mirror shattered noisily. Jack popped up like a mechanical toy and stared openmouthed at the splintered mirror and the thousand shards of glass lying all around him. His shocked gaze swung around to the two of us in the booth. Randy was breathing hard through his mouth, his cheeks bright red.

I shrugged apologetically toward Jack and punched the recorder off.

"Tell your mother I'll come back tomorrow," I told Randy. "You and I can talk some more then." His face was turned to the wall, and his shoulders shook. He didn't look around when I left.

I debated, driving back to the station. Maybe I should have taken Randy in and let him cool his heels in a cell overnight. His behavior could have been called obstructing justice. His answers might have been politer by morning. But he was Babe's baby, and it seemed to me that she had had enough grief for a while. I didn't see how Randy could have had any part in the robbery. He'd given me an alibi that was easy to check. Besides, Babe would have known if her own kid taped her up, mask or no mask. I had just started leaning on him because his arrogance ticked me off, and then his devious answers kept me going. Something did seem to be bothering him. I should find out where he was getting his dope. When I did, I would no doubt have to add it to the pile of woe that seemed destined to keep growing around Babe Krueger.

As soon as I was back in my office, I called the phone number Randy had given me. Norbert Rouse confirmed Randy's story about yesterday's fishing trip, but he had no idea what time Randy had left his yard that morning. He called his son, Scott, to the phone. Scott said it was shortly after breakfast, "whenever that was."

"Can you give me an estimate?"

"It's summer," he said, "who keeps track?"

I was typing up my notes when I realized I'd forgotten

to leave Babe's deposit book at the bar. I dug it out of my briefcase and put it in the middle of my desk blotter, where I'd see it for sure in the morning. On an impulse, I picked it up and leafed through the pages, starting with the last one and working back.

There was a huge difference between this last weekend's deposits and those for the preceding days. Rowdy's Bar was only ringing up a few hundred dollars, weekdays. Last Friday and Saturday had grossed barely fifteen hundred between them. But this weekend . . . I dug out my calculator and added it up. Friday, Saturday, and Sunday came to $28,464.93.

I leafed back through the book. It was filled with neat pages recording pitifully small numbers; the worst day, a Tuesday early in July, was just over two hundred dollars. How did Babe pay staff and keep the lights on with so little business? Then I leafed back to the last weekend in June and found another winner: In three days, Rowdy's Bar had deposited over thirty thousand dollars, virtually all of it in cash.

I stared at the wall a minute. Then I locked Babe's deposit book in the file cabinet, put a note in the exact middle of my clean desk blotter reminding me to return it in the morning, and wrote a second note that said, "Call Chamber of Commerce." Somebody there could probably tell me what special events took place during the last weekend in June. Then I'd get Babe's explanation for her big June weekend and see if it tallied. I had to figure out some devious way to ask her, since I'd promised not to snoop through her deposit book.

I went home and checked my answering machine. A to Z Rentals had not called. I emptied the pan of water under my leaking sink, nuked the half pizza that was aging in my refrigerator, and watched the world news while I gnawed my way through some very tough cheese. When I finished it, I swept the crumbs into my napkin, flattened the can from the one beer I had allowed myself, brushed my teeth carefully, and gargled with mouthwash. I wanted to smell kissing sweet for my first CID.

·THREE·

TODD LOVEJOY WAS IN THE SMALL MEETING ROOM, HUNCHED
in the farthest chair from the door. I took the chair on his
left.

"I never been to one of these things," he said, "they
gonna hypnotize us or what?"

"It's my first one, too. We're just gonna tell what happened, I guess."

"I'm still not sure I know," Todd said.

Mike Zimmerman came in looking at his watch and
took the seat next to me.

"Hey, Mike," Todd said.

"Hope this thing isn't going to run late," Mike said. It
was 7:28. Bright sunlight was still coming in through a
crack in the drapes.

"Why," Todd asked him, "you gotta be someplace
else?"

"No." Mike looked at his watch again. "I just don't
want this to take all night, is all." He was just fussing

about the time to cover his nervousness. CIDs are strictly voluntary; he could leave anytime he wanted to.

Two cops I didn't know came in then, wearing uniforms. Their arm patches read "Austin, Minnesota." They took seats across from each other at the oval table. One pulled brochures out of his briefcase and arranged them in two stacks in front of him, taking care to get them lined up straight. The second man unbuckled the leather strap of his wristwatch and laid it on the table in front of him, then took a list out of his pocket and unfolded it.

Bo Dooley stood still in the open doorway for a few seconds, then came in and took the first seat he came to, at the head of the table. He had been a patrolman for five years in St. Louis before he transferred to Minnesota, and he drove a squad car in Rutherford for a couple more years before he made detective. Department gossip said he was kind of a loner. In theory I was his boss now. In practice, he'd been running his own show ever since Frank assigned him to narcotics, and I really had no idea how to manage Bo Dooley.

Vince Greeley walked in last, smiling. He greeted everybody by name and introduced himself to the out-of-town officers, shaking hands. He took his seat and looked around affably, like a guy getting ready to play cards. He was the only person in the room who seemed entirely at ease.

The man with the list looked around the table, counting, then called each of our names, checked us off a list when we answered, and put the list aside.

"I'm Lt. Norman Sieverson," he said. "Call me Norm." He nodded toward the briefcase man. "This is Sgt. Martin Houck, call him Marty. We're here as volunteers, same as you. We've come to talk about the high-speed vehicular pursuit that ended in an arrest here in Rutherford Sunday night."

His glance slid around the table while he talked. He seemed to be learning our faces. "This is not a critique. Nobody's going to evaluate your job performance based on what you say. It's not a test, there's nothing to pass. We're not taping this meeting, and we take no notes. Our only purpose here tonight is to allow each of you to tell the story as clearly as you can. Just say what you saw and how you felt. There's no right and wrong; this is just a chance to vent your feelings."

He looked around the table. "Who wants to be first?"

Nobody spoke. Sieverson waited a couple of seconds and said, "Okay, who made the initial contact with the suspect?"

Todd Lovejoy cleared his throat. "I did."

"Okay, uh, Todd." He watched a few seconds while Todd Lovejoy sat frozen silent in his chair. "Can you remember how it started?"

Lovejoy stared at his hands. His lips moved a couple of times, and then he looked up and said, "I work mid-shift, three to three. I'd just come on, it was three-thirty, I was doing my first set of drive-throughs. I had section one, my usual, twelve blocks downtown and a strip both ways along Center Street. I started downtown, checking the parking lots and the alleys in back of the bars."

He licked his lips, remembering. "Sunday afternoon in the summer, y'know, there's hardly anybody around downtown. I was expecting a pretty quiet shift. But back of BJ's, in the alley between Third and Fourth Street, I noticed four kids standing by a car."

"You mean, children?"

"Uh, no. Late teens, early twenties. Two young black males, pretty good-looking guys, one tall and one short, that I've seen around town, I think they're brothers. Then a white kid who's a cashier at Wendy's sometimes; I don't know his name, but I know he goes to Madison High. The fourth one was black, tall and strong looking, a little older, I've never seen him before. They were clustered around a black Jeep Cherokee, driven by a black guy in shades, wearing a fade haircut and a leather bomber jacket. It was parked in against the wall, underneath where the arcade goes over.

"I slowed down to a crawl. The small kid saw me coming and said something, and they all sort of strolled off. It seemed to me they were trying too hard to look cool, so I stopped where I was and ran the license number for the Cherokee." He looked around the table, suddenly cheerful, and said, "Boy, y'know, I bitched as loud as anybody when we first got those data terminals in the cars. It felt like putting an *elephant* in the front seat. Right in the way! And I *hated* learning how to work it. Oof-da. But lately, man, I tell you the truth, I think of my laptop as a pal."

"Squads aren't wired in Austin yet," Sieverson said. "We're hoping the grant comes through pretty soon."

"Yeah. You're gonna love it." Todd became suddenly aware of the rest of us sitting there stone-faced and stopped, embarrassed. "Well," he said. His eyes went to the wall behind Sieverson's shoulder and studied it. "My query came back with a name, Eugene Soames, and an address in Minneapolis."

"The name mean anything to you?"

"No. I had just enough room for a standard pull-up." He meant two car lengths behind the Jeep and offset left by one width, so the squad car would protect him, as he got out of it, from the car in front. "I turned on my overhead flasher and started to get out of the car. That's when he took off."

"Drove away, you mean? Fast?"

"Smokin'. Left a trail of rubber. Couple of those kids just barely got out of the way in time."

"You never spoke to him?"

"Never had a chance. He went blazing down to the end of that alley, hit the brakes, and skidded into a tight right turn. I had my siren on by then. Soon as I straightened out on Fourth Street, heading west, I saw he was almost a block ahead, so I called dispatch for help. While I was talking, though, I glanced right and saw one of our new Crown Vics with a flasher going, keeping pace with me on Fifth Street."

Sieverson glanced around. "Now, who was that?"

"Me," Bo Dooley said.

"You were in the unmarked car?"

"Yes."

"So you're an investigator, right? Not a patrolman."

"Right."

"How'd you get there so fast?"

"I was there all along. Tailing Eugene Soames."

"You know him?"

"No. I was watching the Cherokee."

Sieverson's face had begun to look the way Frank's does, sometimes, when he talks to Dooley: deeply thoughtful, like a man trying to decide if yesterday's fish is still good enough to cook. Dooley doesn't go out of his way to please. For one thing, he talks as if he's been given just this small allotment of words for each day, and he has to be careful not to run out.

Sieverson folded his broad, capable hands carefully together on the tabletop and said, "Why don't you just tell us the story, Bo?"

"I was in the drive-in lane at the First National Bank, with a good view of the driver's-side door of the Cherokee, waiting for him to make a sale."

"So you knew you were watching a drug dealer?"

"Had a tip. From a snitch. He didn't have a name or an address. Just said he knew for sure a big sale was going to take place on Sunday afternoon in Rutherford. I started driving around, and when I spotted a big new sport utility vehicle with Minneapolis plates and a young guy in shades and gold jewelry behind the wheel, I tagged along. He parked in the alley by the wall, which seemed promising, and when Farah Tur showed up I got really interested."

"He's that older Somali kid, right?" Todd asked.

"Uh-huh. Been in town about a year, him and his little brother. Been making connections. Getting ready to try some bullshit, I think."

"And you were getting ready to arrest him?" Sieverson asked.

"Not yet. I wanted to see who made the buy. Then I'd get my snitch to see if he could make a buy from the buyer. Soon as he brought product back to me and we tested it, we'd set up another buy, with marked bills, and if all went well we'd have a case. It's a long process."

"Which never seems to work," Mike Zimmerman said. "All this cloak-and-dagger stuff belongs in the movies, if you ask me."

Dooley's pale eyes settled on Mike Zimmerman and turned to blue ice.

There was a little silence. Zimmerman looked at his watch. Norm Sieverson checked the time, too, and said, "All right. Let's move along here. Who's next? Who answered Todd's call for backup?"

"I did," Vince Greeley and Mike Zimmerman both said at once. Vince shrugged amiably, and Mike said, "Well, dispatch called me first because they knew I was nearby. I'd just called in that I was back in service from a domestic disturbance, nine-ten blocks southwest of where Todd was."

"But I was only five blocks north," Vince said, "but the desk didn't know it. I was cruising the south end of section five. I called in and said 'I'm right here, can I help?'

and dispatch said okay, both of you assist nineteen-forty-five, he's got a suspect fleeing the scene."

Glances went around the table. We all knew Vince would have volunteered if he'd been any place south of St. Paul. Speed is Vince's chocolate cake with double fudge frosting.

"Right," Todd said. "Well, that Cherokee was pulling away from me, for sure, but the Crown Vic seemed to be keeping up, so I told Mike to head north on Twelfth Avenue and block the intersection there. And I told Vince, 'Try to meet us at the golf course,' because, you know—well, you don't, I guess"—he looked at the two Austin men apologetically—"but I figured if Mike blocked the intersection at Fourth and Twelfth, the suspect would have to turn north there, and there was a fair chance the other three of us could herd him into the cul-de-sac where Fourteenth Avenue runs into the northeast corner of the golf course." Avoiding Mike Zimmerman's eyes, he said softly, "But see, I meant block the intersection kitty-cornered, cut off the east and south options, so the Cherokee'd have to turn right."

"Woulda worked, too," Bo said.

"Oh, put a sock in it," Mike said, glaring at Bo. "You guys went off half-cocked, and now you want to blame me for it!" He turned to Sieverson and said, "I hate a high-speed chase. I've always said that."

"I don't," Bo said. "Anytime I see some fool trying to outrun cops in their own hometown, I figure fortune has smiled on me."

"But not necessarily on the innocent bystanders. A high-speed chase is a disaster waiting to happen. I get nightmares for weeks afterwards, thinking about the women and children we could have killed. We've had one discussion after another about this, about how it's better to hand off a suspect—"

"Except if we handed 'em off to you," Bo said, "they'd all end up on the beach in Miami."

"Now what the hell's *that* supposed to mean?"

"It means you drive like my grandmother," Bo yelled, suddenly infuriated into squandering some extra syllables. "Jesus H. Christ! You parked that squad car as straight and neat across Fourth Street as if you were going to some goddamn wedding. What were you thinking? He could hear Buzz and me coming on his right! Why would he turn that way if he didn't have to?" Bo turned back to Todd. "Something I still don't understand. When Soames turned left on Twelfth Avenue, where did you go?"

"Left on Tenth. I saw him turn the wrong way, I knew you and Buzz would be farther behind him then, so I figured it was up to me. Only, see, I never supposed he would turn and go west again on Third. Why did he blow his lead like that? I thought he'd keep on going south, so I kicked it in the ass and roared on south fast as I could. When I didn't see him after two blocks, though, I listened to the radio traffic a minute and realized you'd all gone west again."

Bo shook his head again, made a *tsk-tsk* clucking noise, and lapsed into mournful silence.

Sieverson waited a minute, glanced at the watch on the table in front of him, and sighed. "Okay, we better keep moving. What next?"

"Um." Todd cleared his throat. "By this time our shift supervisor was on the radio to me, trying to find out how the chase was going, and I could tell he was thinking of calling it off. So soon as I got turned west again, I called Vince. He said, 'No sweat, we're right behind him, looks like he's gonna end up at the south end of the golf course.' How do you get that kind of speed out of a squad car?" Todd asked, and Vince grinned at him and winked.

"And I was behind Vince on Fourth," Zimmerman said.

"Yeah, way behind," Bo said.

"I believe he was trying for the on-ramp to the high-way," Vince said, "and if he'd gone one more block south he'd probably have made it. By the time he saw the golf course parking lot ahead, all those cars sitting there and nothing beyond them but fence and grass, Bo was right on his tail on Third Street, and I was screamin' around the corner from Fourth. And of course none of us knew it, but Jake was right there, too."

Sieverson looked at me and said, "You weren't in the chase before this point?"

"I was never in it. I was playing golf."

"He got in the way," Vince said delightedly, "so we had to run over him." Bo and Vince and Todd all chuckled softly.

"It's just a little nine-hole municipal course," I told Norm and Marty. "You don't have to join a club, that's why I like it. Pay greens fees when you feel like playing a round, and that's the end of it." It seemed important to me to make them understand the casual, relaxed nature of the afternoon. "The city crammed nine holes into a very small space by running the holes alongside each other in a W configuration, and the last hole, the ninth, comes right up along the fence line by the parking lot. I was enjoying that last hole a lot, because I could look right across the fence to the parking lot and see my brand-new cherry red pickup that I've wanted for years, sitting out there with dealer plates on it because I'd just picked it up the day before.

"Number nine is a par four hole, with a water hazard where the creek goes through, and a sand trap on either side of the green. I'm not a very good golfer—" Little snickers sounded around the table. "I spend a lot of time in those sand traps." I saw Sieverson glancing discreetly at his watch, and I thought, You said tell the story in my own way, Normie, and that's how I'm telling it.

"Sunday, though, I stayed out of both traps and got on the green in two. I was very happy, walking up to my ball. Even with *my* putting, I had a better than even chance for par on number nine. Then I started hearing all these sirens—"

"And tires squealing," Vince said, looking pleased.

"I stepped up onto the green and looked across the fence. Five cars were coming at me at top speed."

"You moved very fast," Vince said, beaming at me.

"What did you do?" Sieverson asked me.

"I jumped in the sand trap. The deepest one. I thought they were all going to come through the fence and kill me."

"Did they?" Everybody laughed. Norm Sieverson smiled and said, "I mean, did they come through the fence?"

"They didn't quite make it. They wrecked my pickup instead."

"*I* didn't," Bo said.

"You know, strictly speaking that's right. Bo did not run into my truck. He ran into Soames's Jeep Cherokee and knocked it into my truck."

"Wouldn't've been much more than a fender-bender," Bo said, "if Vince hadn't collided with the rear end."

"I barely dinged his car! Just dented the back bumper a little, till Zimmie came tearing in there and ran into *me*—"

"Which I wouldn't have done," Zimmerman said, "if you'd answered me on the radio when I asked you where you were."

"Well, shit, I didn't exactly have time to chat," Vince said.

"When the noise died down a little," I said, "I stood up to see what was going on, and Eugene Soames ran over me and knocked me down again."

"Ran over you with his car, you mean, or—"

"No, his car was embedded in my pickup, which was halfway through the fence. Soames got the passenger-side door of his car open somehow and jumped through the hole in the fence, and just then I stood up and he ran into me. He wasn't having *his* best day, either. A lot of stuff flew off him when he hit me, dark glasses and something else—"

"You saw that too?" Dooley asked sharply. "See?" He stared at Todd, suddenly excited. "I told you I saw him throw something away."

"I know what you told me," Todd said, "you said it enough times, Bo. So I stayed out on that golfcourse with you until almost dark, crawling over broken glass and lost balls, with my ass in the air and my knees all grass-stained, and we never found squat. Dark glasses. That's it. There's nothing else out there, dammit."

"He had crack," Bo said. "He threw it away. I know he did."

"Okay, let me finish," I said, determined to tell my side of the story now that I was started. "Bo and Vince and Mike were all prying themselves out of their cars, screaming, 'Stop him!' 'Get that guy!' and then they started swarming through the fence. I had no idea what was going on, but since they were all yelling at me, I got up again and ran after the guy who had knocked me down. I was hoping very sincerely that he didn't have a gun, and as it turned out I guess he didn't. He ran north along the number nine fairway and waded the creek when he came to it. He ran along the other side of the creek bed a little way, and then climbed up the bank and ran north again on the number six fairway. I followed him along the near side of the creek till it narrowed, and I was able to jump it easy and gain a little ground. He still had plenty of speed in him, though, so when I realized I was still carrying my putter I threw it at him."

"I can't believe you hit that guy," Vince said, "running like you were."

"Actually I didn't, quite," I said, "but what happened was luckier. The putter flew between his legs, and he tripped on it and went ass-over-teakettle. I think he rolled three times."

"He was lying nice and still," Vince said, "by the time I got to him. I cuffed him, and then Todd came up and said, 'Well, I guess he's my collar, huh?' and we took him to jail in Todd's car."

He smiled benignly, and Todd added, "Which was the only one left undamaged by then."

"It's easier to keep your car nice," Bo said, "if you get to the suspect last."

Todd turned on him, suddenly furious. "Why don't you stuff it, you mean sonofabitch?" he said. "Christ almighty, is there anybody here you haven't insulted yet? How about Marty, can't you find something wrong with the way he parts his hair?"

Marty Houck, who had been the silent member of the debriefing team till now, looked mildly over his reading glasses and said, "Well, now . . . ," and Norm Sieverson leaned toward the middle of the table, extended his hands in a hushing gesture, and said, "Now, look, guys, this kind of recrimination won't get us anyplace. If you have questions about procedure during this incident, take them up with your supervisors. We're just here to tell the story."

"The story is, we blew it," Bo Dooley said. "We had a crack dealer right in our hands, and we had to let him go because we messed up."

"Oh, he's back on the street?" Sieverson asked.

"Where he has every right to be," Mike Zimmerman said, "as far as we can tell."

"He lawyered up," Vince Greeley said uncomfortably, "and got released this morning."

"He didn't have any priors or—?"

"Or anything *on him*," Mike Zimmerman said. He glared at Bo Dooley. "No controlled substances whatever, on his person or in his car, not even a can of beer. And no weapon. No gun, no shiv, no Boy Scout knife. You can *say* he's a drug dealer till you're blue in the face, but if you don't have any *evidence*—"

"Why'd he run, then?" Sieverson asked.

"Oh, his lawyer says we just chased him because he's black and we're biased," Todd said. "Eugene says he's been abused before by the police, and he panicked."

"They're threatening to sue the city for harassment," Mike said. "They say we endangered his life and wrecked his car for no reason."

"There was a reason," Bo said. "He had crack. He threw it away."

"Okay, Bo," Todd said. "If you're so goddamn sure of that, you go out there and crawl around that golf course by yourself and find it. I'm sick of helping a guy who can't even be civil." To his own horror, then, his lips began to tremble. He picked up the only thing he could reach, a pile of Marty's brochures, and flung them into the corner of the room. "Son of a *bitch*," he muttered bitterly, and blew his nose.

There was a terrible silence. Mike and Vince examined their hands. Marty got up and walked to the corner quietly and began picking up brochures. Bo Dooley sat silently in his chair with his arms folded, expressionless. He has curly auburn hair that fits his head like a cap, and a neatly trimmed dark red beard. He was wearing very old blue jeans faded nearly white by many washings, and a gray sweatshirt so frayed it had threads dangling from the cuffs. The diamond earring in his left ear struck an odd, antic note above his threadbare clothing. His appearance always seems to walk some interesting line between scruffy and elegant.

Sieverson looked down at his watch and sighed. "It's almost nine. We're not rigid about the time we allot to debriefings, but we've noticed that after about an hour and a half we start repeating. So unless anybody has anything vital to add—" He looked around and waited a couple of seconds. "Since you all seem quite dissatisfied with the results of this incident, I would suggest you consult your superiors and try to decide if anything should have been done differently. Not with a view to getting anybody in trouble, but just to settle the matter in your own minds so it won't keep eating on you. But that's just my suggestion. You suit yourselves. As I told you, CIDs are not meant to evaluate performance.

"Marty's got some brochures for you. One of them details the reactions that often follow stress, so you'll understand that your own symptoms aren't anything out of the ordinary. If you have trouble sleeping or lose your appetite, or if you start to have a lot of trouble at home with your family, we do urge you to ask for more help. We'll be glad to stay, too, if any of you want to talk privately with one of us right now.

"The second brochure has lists of books you can read, to increase your understanding of what job stresses can do to you. Also lists of organizations that stand ready to help. There's a lot of information on the Internet, too, and we've listed some of those addresses." He looked around the table, nodded, and said, "Good luck, guys."

We all drifted out except Zimmerman, who stayed to tell Marty and Norm about his nightmares. Todd went down the stairs fast and was outside unlocking his car by the time Vince and I got to the tall glass doors on the ground floor. Dooley was already pulling out of the lot on his Harley.

"Need a lift, Jake?" Vince asked me.

"Nah. I got a department car till mine's fixed. Thanks."

"This your first CID?"

"Yeah."

"My third. I can't seem to stay out of trouble." He chuckled. "So—whadja think of it?"

"Oh—it was okay. At least you didn't hug me."

Vince's gleeful cackle echoed in the empty hall. "Well, hey," he said, "I was tempted, don't think I wasn't. Dooley, too, I really wanted to kiss *him* on the mouth." He started out, turned back, and squinted at me in the dim light. "You aren't really pissed about Sunday, are you?"

"Why? Just because you wrecked my new pickup and spoiled my golf game and almost killed me? Whaddya think I am, a sorehead?"

His laughter started the noisy echoes bouncing down the hall again. "Okay, then." He hit my shoulder. "Long's you're not holdin' any grudges." He charged out the door into a fading sunset, letting in a swirl of late-August air, heavy with the scent of barbecue grills and fresh-cut alfalfa.

·FOUR·

SOMETIME TUESDAY NIGHT, I BEGAN DREAMING I WAS THE ONLY waiter in Rowdy's Bar, and that the place was crammed full of noisy, hungry people who all wanted beers and hamburgers. Red and Jack yelled threats and insults because I wasn't getting their food and drinks out, but the harder I tried to satisfy people, the slower I seemed to move. Bo Dooley, seated at a table with several other customers, began to heap contempt on my head as I got hopelessly further behind with my orders. In the dream I got hotter and hotter, till finally I woke up flailing angrily in a sweaty sheet. For a few seconds I lay still, grateful to be out of the dream. Then I realized I really was hot, and jumped out of bed.

The air-conditioning in my apartment building had quit. No air at all was coming through the vents. I played with the thermostat, but nothing changed.

The window in my bedroom seemed to be stuck. It was always a little crooked and difficult. I hadn't opened it

since sometime in June, and it must have warped a little
since then. I dug out my tool kit, found a pry bar, and
forced my bedroom window twelve inches up from the sill
with a lot of grunting and swearing. I knelt by the opening, trying to cool off.

The air outside felt only a few degrees cooler than my
room. I leaned out as far as the screen would let me,
longing for a breeze. Sweat dripped down my sides onto
the floor.

I turned the covers back and lay down naked on the
sheet in the sticky air. I closed my eyes and thought about
ice. My back stuck to the sheet. I turned over and thought
about kayaking in Alaska. My chest stuck to the sheet. I
peeked under my arm and saw that the luminous face of
the clock by my bed said four-fifteen. What the hell, I
decided, my office is air-conditioned, and I'm always saying I need more time there. I took a long shower and
dressed.

Outside, the air near the ground was a little cooler. The
sky in the east was getting light, and a couple of birds
were trying out chirps. On the highway, I found a booth
in the arctic chill of Ray & Ellie's Truck Stop and ordered
the Long Haul Special: sausage and a three-egg cheese
omelet with hash browns. It's a wretched excess I sometimes award myself when life begins to owe me.

I read the entire *St. Paul Pioneer-Press*, drank second
and third coffees, and still got to work before six. In my
office, I unpacked all the remaining boxes and put everything but the files away. I flattened the boxes and took
them outside to the Dumpster. Back inside, I began sorting case files into stacks for my crew. The routine burglaries could be divided equally between my two new
investigators, Rosie Doyle and Darrell Betts. If they chose
to see that as an invitation to sexual rivalry, I would not
interfere while they busted their butts. I wanted Ray Bai-

ley to continue working with Lou French for the scant year left before Lou's retirement. Lou was a master of the messy cases: domestic abuse, assault, and rape. Ray seemed to have some of Lou's avuncular air; maybe he could master tough love and be Lou's replacement. Bo, of course, would stay with vice and narcotics.

That left Kevin Evjan, whom I'd picked to be my second in command because he was smart and energetic and seemed good at pacifying people.

"I'm gonna want you to help with scheduling, answer a bunch of e-mail and faxes," I told him. "Handle outraged citizens. Put a lid on department whiners."

"Somebody to sort the shit," he said.

"Exactly." He took it because he knew it put him in line for my job. With Kevin riding shotgun, I hoped, I'd have time to steer the toughest cases through the system, and we could all end up looking smart.

"It's a hell of a plan," Frank said when I described it to him. "As long as when the shit hits the fan you all work together."

On the console by my desk I stacked case files to hand over to Kevin. Millicent Porter's old, dog-eared file was on the bottom. I had exhausted the department's resources trying to find her grandmother's serving spoons; ever since the thief got away, she had been exhausting me with abusive phone calls.

I piled on several more recent files, the top one being another section three crime, the weekend burglary of Tom's Liquors. I was a little sorry to let go of it. Tom Priebe was that rarity, a victim so likable you wanted to help him yourself.

The amount of his loss had been easy to determine, because the store was hit shortly after his monthly inventory on Saturday night. "I always inventory on the third Saturday of the month, after closing," he said, "I do it at night so I can take Sunday off." Rutherford still has blue laws; liquor stores have to close on Sunday. It's one of those family-values gestures we hold so dear in the heartland.

So the time of the burglary was equally easy to fix: sometime between one A.M. and eight-thirty Sunday morning. "Which is when I stopped in to get my windbreaker, on my way to mass," Tom said. "We were gonna go on a picnic. We canceled that, of course, when I found my store cleaned out."

There was nothing to indicate forced entry. Somebody appeared to have unlocked the back door, loaded up all the booze, locked up again, and left.

"But that can't be," Tom told me firmly, "because I only have one set of keys. My wife and I run this place together, just the two of us. We split the shifts between us. Nobody ever has the keys but Cindy and me."

"You don't have a cleaning service, a janitor, somebody who does routine maintenance?"

He kept shaking his head. "It's a small store. We're barely making it. Like it or not, we do everything ourselves."

"You don't have children? Never need to go anyplace together?"

"We got two boys, and we need lots of things, including time off, but we have to get along without it till the loan's paid off. Fourteen more months. Usually Cindy covers the hours when the kids are in school, and I take the rest. Her mother helps out with the kids in the summer. I hate it, but it won't last forever."

"Okay," I said. "Then explain to me how thieves came in your store without disturbing the steel grating you lock across the front, and without putting a scratch of any kind on the back."

"Beats the shit out of me," he said. He looked about

ready to cry. "I know the insurance adjuster would love to prove I'm in on this myself, but so help me I'm not. All I want in the world is to have everything go along nice and smooth till I pay off that friggin' bank loan and get my wife some time off. We been really strugglin'. You realize what a crimp this puts in my cash flow? I have to front the money to replace the inventory till the policy pays off. I'll have to put it on a card and pay interest on it for a couple of months." He thumped his pencil disconsolately on his desk pad. "Probably sounds like small potatoes to you, but it's serious shit for me," he muttered. "I would certainly like to see somebody's ass in jail for this."

"It doesn't sound small," I said, "and we'll do the best we can." Privately I wasn't optimistic. We clear between 8 and 10 percent of burglary cases in an average year. We do a lot better with robberies, where the crime is person-to-person and there's some kind of a description, however inaccurate, of the thief. But the person who enters your premises unlawfully and leaves with the booty without being seen has an excellent chance of enjoying the prize undisturbed.

"Tom, you own this building?"

"No, hell no. If I had money enough to buy my own place, I wouldn't be in this part of town. I got it on a sublet from Tony Marco; this used to be Tony's Liquors, remember? He wanted to get out after his heart attack, so he was willing to leave his deposit on the lease and let me take over the monthly payments. That's how shoestring this is for me; I didn't even have enough for the rent deposit when I moved in. Tony let me have three months to pay off the basic stock, and Cindy's dad loaned us enough to live on while we got started. Been a squeaker all the way."

"But you're making it?"

"Have been. Till now."

"Who's your landlord?"

"Bestway Realty."

"They take care of the building okay?"

Tom shrugged. "They don't bother me, and I don't bother them. I send the check to the bank every month."

"What do you do if you need something fixed?"

"The one time I had a drain go bad, I got sick of waiting for them and called a plumber myself."

"And paid for it yourself?"

"Yup. And took the cost of the repair off the next month's check. They never said boo."

"Kind of a weird way to run a company," I said.

"Uh-huh. But as long as they don't raise the rent, I'm living with it."

I stared out my window now, thinking. The value of the missing merchandise at Tom's store was close to eighteen thousand dollars. The apartment in Kiowa Towers that was emptied last week, what kind of values were being claimed there? I looked it up: a surprisingly substantial haul for a sleazy apartment. It was occupied by three or four college dropouts in their twenties, who seemed content to work odd jobs and live in sleeping bags in order to pursue their expensive hobbies. They had a burglar alarm to guard their loot: two racing bikes, bags full of photo gear, a closet full of ski equipment, and a pricey entertainment center that filled one whole wall. They had all worked the mid-shift at a downtown hotel and partied the rest of the night, coming home early last Thursday to find their place cleaned out. The neighbors were unanimous: No alarm had sounded. There were plenty of marks and scars on their old front door, but the locks and the alarm were undamaged.

I put the Kiowa Towers file on top of the Tom's Liquors file. The day shift was coming to work. Down the hall, Kevin Evjan was trying to unlock his door while holding

on to a briefcase, a cell phone, and a full cup of coffee. I
went out and held his coffee cup while he unlocked his
door.

"Goddamn," he said. "It's not even eight o'clock yet,
and you're walking around the building carrying an armload of work. You going to start right out being a slave
driver?" He pushed his door open and groped for the
light.

"You got time to take some files from me?"

"Sure, hell, yes, why not? Might as well add 'em to the
mess. Look at this place." His floor was still covered with
cardboard boxes. He leaned his briefcase against his piled-
up desk.

"Only take a minute. Never mind, I don't need a
chair." Kevin is the lucky recipient of all the best genes
from his Irish mother and Norwegian father. He has
glowing blond hair, bright blue eyes, and the open face of
an Eagle Scout. His career as an investigator has been
greatly aided by his guileless appearance; people trust him
on sight, and all but the deeply depraved tell him everything he wants to know.

We stood side by side, leaning on his desk, passing files
back and forth.

"You've heard me mention Millicent Porter, I think," I
said, passing him the dirty manila folder, soft from hours
of handling and stapled all over with notes, cards, and
phone messages.

"The spoon lady?" He laughed. "I heard you worked so
hard to make lieutenant so you could off-load the spoon
lady."

"Damn right. I want you to call on her in person. Take
all the time you need, go over the case in detail. Use your
boyish charm. Do whatever you have to do to get her to
stop calling me."

"Shee. Boyish charm, what a crock. Okay, you got it."

"Okay. The next two are more serious. These are first reports of burglaries that need follow-up right away." I leafed through the Kiowa Towers and Tom's Liquors folders, explaining a little about each case. I showed him six more folders, saying, "These I'm giving to Darrell and Rosie. Nothing very complicated about any of them, but I want you to ride herd on them and help them when they need it." I pulled the last folder out from under my arm. "I'm not leaving the Rowdy's Bar file with you. It was probably intended to be a burglary, but the guys who did it surprised the owner on-premise and taped her up, so it's turned into robbery and assault. I want to show it to you, though, because of some of the similarities with Tom's Liquors and Kiowa Towers. Three lucrative heists within a week, all in properties with good security systems, owned by careful people who lock their doors. None with any sign of forced entry. I'm thinking maybe we've got some real pros in town with very good tools."

"Mmm. Or a fresh shipment of groceries just came up the Yellow Brick Road, and all the crackheads got busy at once."

"Ah, you've been talking to Bo. Well, whatever. After you've worked with these, check back with me, and we'll see how we're all doing."

"Sure. You think we ought to have a meeting a couple times a month? The whole crew?"

"Maybe. Let's get some work done first so we'll have something to talk about." I hate meetings. Wasting time should at least be fun. I left Kevin looking for his desk calendar.

My desk was clear now, except for a note I'd written to myself when I first got to work. "Keep calling A to Z Rentals," it said.

What more could I possibly say to that bloody tape? Maybe I should tell it that Jake Hines had died of heatstroke in apartment 3-C last night. Say I was a concerned friend, and that I hoped the tape machine would send somebody to pick up the body before it got any puffier. I dialed the number. After the first ring a female voice said quickly, "A to Z Rentals."

"You're there!" I said, "In person! My God. What's your name?"

"This is A to Z Rentals," she said, coldly. "What number were you calling?"

"You! I was calling A to Z Rentals, don't hang up! This is Jake Hines. Apartment 3-C at 2803—"

"Oh, Mr. Haynes." Her voice changed suddenly, taking on the sticky sweetness of the answering tape. "Honestly, you must think I'm a terrible person! I'm so sorry I didn't get back to you sooner. I hope you can understand that I've just been so busy here, and—"

She went on for some time, explaining that she had been out of the office showing property, this was just such a busy time, and there was only her and so many calls, and now when she finally had time to play the tape she found all these messages from Jake Hines, was it Hines or Haynes? And she was just so very sorry. I was almost ready to start comforting her when she said, "Now, just tell me exactly what's wrong with your bathtub—"

"Sink," I said. "It's the sink that's leaking. But what's more important is, the air-conditioning quit work last night."

"Oh, yes, well, I know about that! Another tenant in your building, well, actually several others"—she tried an ironic little laugh that failed—"called me earlier. The repairman's on his way for the air-conditioning, rest assured! But now, you say your sink is stopped up—"

"Leaking. My kitchen sink is leaking. And the closet door won't slide."

"Okay. I'm writing all this down *right now*," she said,

as if writing things down were some heroic effort reserved for the most elite customers. "Is this the closet in the living room, Mr. Haynes?"

"In the bedroom. What's your name?"

"Um. Tammy," she said, reluctantly.

"Okay, Tammy, my name is Jake Hines." I spelled it for her. "I'm a detective with the Rutherford Police Department." I had lowered my voice a couple of notches and added all the gravity it would hold. "Will you try to remember my problems, please, Tammy, and take care of them for me as fast as you can?"

"Well, you bet I will, Mr. Hines," Tammy said. She subtracted a little treacle from her voice, going more for sincere now. "I'll get right on this today, and you can expect action, um, no later than close of business tomorrow."

Wouldn't that be good? Against all the evidence, I decided to believe her. I didn't have time for a funk about household affairs. I have cases to clear, I thought urgently, many cases to clear!

I trotted up and down the hall, passing out case folders to Darrell and Rosie, Ray and Lou. Bo was out of his office, probably back out at the municipal golf course combing grass. I decided to leave him alone till he proved to himself there was no crack out there.

I looked at my watch. Ten-thirty. Why not run up to Rowdy's and see what Babe had to say about her big weekend in June? I stuffed her deposit book in my briefcase and started toward the parking garage. On the way out of the building, though, I decided I'd ask Schultzy to send teletypes to some other towns, detailing these three high-yield burglaries I was curious about and asking them to contact me if they'd seen burglaries with big losses behind good security systems. I wrote out the message, fished out my plastic key card, and let myself into the

glass-enclosed dispatch room that's the nerve center of
the department.

Inside this bright fishbowl is a kinetic-feeling space
where five or six people work intensely in near silence.
The four main workstations face each other in a circle,
with a desk off to the side for the fire dispatcher, who cuts
herself in and out of police traffic as the load requires.

McCafferty used to put the walking wounded on dispatch and let them answer phones and talk on the radio
while their bones knit. But when the department went to
computer-aided dispatch, the communications center became more sophisticated. Putting laptops in the squad
cars added still another layer of complexity. Besides dealing with unforeseen emergencies fast, dispatchers have to
be big-time geeks now. The messages that flash and scroll
across their screens, guiding cops through the grit and
commotion of their lively days and nights, are simultaneously copied to the records unit, becoming part of the
immutable evidence that we constantly refer to, and eventually take to court if need be. The unsworn support people who work the dispatch desk have to be fast, accurate,
highly literate, and very cool.

Meaning it's made to order for Marlys Schultz. She
thrives in this job, which requires her to talk, type, read,
and listen simultaneously. With the universe finally crank-
ing along at her pace, she gets comfortable and happy,
banging away on her keyboard at warp speed and barking
out information like a big blond Saint Bernard. Marlys
was always an information junkie, and she loves telling
cops what to do.

Cunningham was supervising the shift, his rimless
glasses glittering in the indirect light. Schultzy was in the
lead dispatch slot, enjoying a quiet gab with her deskmate,
Neva Dudek, while they waited for the shift to heat up.
No use just sitting quiet for three seconds.

"I mean, here I am with my arms full," she was muttering across the little half-wall between them. Her screen lit up with a full page of details, she read it between one blink and the next, called car 2533 and shipped the page to his screen, heard his response, typed a couple more lines onto the page in front of her, and resumed her conversation while her eyes still scanned the screen. "And here's Jessica screaming in my face, 'I don't wanna go to Granny Goose! You can't make me go there!' And I'm five minutes late, and Ernie starts picking her up and giving her this line about, 'Now, sweetheart, you know Mama's not gonna make you stay no place if you're not happy,' and I'm saying, 'PUT her in the CAR, Ernie,' because this is just standard Jessica horse manure, we've all spoiled her rotten and she thinks she should get her way every time!"

She paused to blow hair out of her eyes and I said quickly, "Schultzy, you got a minute?"

She swiveled her chair slightly, showed me most of her profile, and said, "Hey, Jake. You gonna hang around in here now and pull rank on everybody?"

Schultzy's a pal of mine. She was pleased when I got my promotion. She hates having her stories interrupted, though.

I leaned across her shoulder and laid my handwritten message in front of her. "Will you send this teletype for me? It should go to the investigative division in Austin and Red Wing and La Crosse, and, let's see, maybe Winona and Des Moines, for starts. Okay?" I started for the door.

"Well, now, hang on here, Loo-tenant! Not so fast, please! I can't read this gobbledygook! What kinda henscratching is this? You better stick around and read this to me."

Schultzy always pokes fun at my terrible handwriting, and today, delighted to have a brand-new lieutenant by the balls, she took time to give me grief about every word, entertaining the room at my expense. I was standing by her left shoulder, arguing about how to spell "Des Moines," when Sally said, from the call desk, "Personal call for you, Schultzy." Schultzy grabbed her outside phone absently, cupped it against her ear, said "Schultz," and went right on typing. A woman's voice said something in her ear. Suddenly, Schultzy's strong white hands lay still on the keys.

"Whaddya mean, gone?" she said quietly. She lifted her right hand off the keyboard and set the tips of her fingers very gently against her lips. Her back had gone stiff. The voice in the phone was talking fast.

"Look in the street," Schultzy said, "she'll probably try to go home. Oh. Uh-huh. No place around there, huh? Listen, could you hold on a second?" She turned to Cunningham and said, "Jessie's run away from day care. Okay if I send a squad over there to help look for her?"

"Hell, yes," Tom said.

"Melanie, there's gonna be a marked squad car there in a couple of minutes, you tell the officer everything you just told me, okay? He'll help you look. Okay. Okay. Yeah, well, I better get on it, okay?" She banged the phone down, looking cross, and said, "Wants me to tell her it's okay that she let my kid get away. Jeez Louise."

"I thought your mother took care of Jessica," I said. We had all heard plenty about Grandma Bjorncamp's spanking theories.

"They were ragging on each other too much," Schultzy said. "I decided to try a change." Matt Coe answered her page. She fed details of Jessica's hair and clothing, and the address of the school, onto the screen in front of her, shipping it to his screen while they talked. Coe said, "Copy," and we heard his motor accelerate before his mike clicked off.

"Why don't you go ahead and call Putratz?" Cunningham said. "To assist?"

"Really? That's okay?" Schultzy asked.

"Sure, go ahead," Tom Cunningham said. Ordinarily he'd wait, on a runaway. Dispatch has to be stingy with squad cars, because they're spread pretty thin. Schultzy got Putratz on the radio and gave him the address, then called Coe and told him about his backup.

"Okay, I see the school now, Schultzy, listen," Coe said, "I'm gonna make a quick sweep of the area before I go in, okay? Might get lucky here."

His transmitter went dead. We hung over the blinking console, listening to traffic from other parts of town. Sally and Neva were taking all the other calls, so Schultzy could stick with Coe and Putratz. The news had spread outside the fishbowl, I saw; people working on the floor kept turning to look in through the glass walls of the dispatch area. Then Coe said, "Two-three to base," and Schultzy said, "Base."

"We didn't find her when we circled the block," Coe said, "so we'll go on in now and see this Melanie, uh, Eisenman, that right?"

Schultzy said, "Eisenman, right." Her face was losing color.

There was silence for a few seconds, then Sally took a call and told Schultzy, "Nguyen and Miller say they've finished their first set of drive-bys, want them to join the search team?" They both looked at Cunningham, who nodded, and Schultzy pressed her mike button and said, "Yes. Take Twelfth to Center and—" She set up an east-west grid for them to drive, on the streets above and below the nursery, her instructions scrolling across their screens as fast as she typed it in. When Stearns and then Donovan called in a few minutes later, she gave them a north-south pattern in the same area.

Sally answered an outside call, put it on hold, and said, "Schultzy, there's a person on this line, I can't tell if it's a man or a woman, that says they've got a girl named Jessica."

Schultzy hit her phone button and croaked, "Schultz." Standing behind her, I heard a falsetto voice talking high and fast. I couldn't understand the words. Schultzy listened a minute, squinting in concentration. When the voice stopped she said, *"What do you want?"* A shrill giggle came over the line, and then a click and a dial tone.

Schultzy stared blankly into her screen.

"Some man with a weird voice said he's got Jessica," she said. "He didn't seem to know I was her mother. He just said tell all the cops he's got a little girl named Jessica Schultz downtown—that's what he said, downtown—and he'll decide pretty soon what he's gonna do with her. I asked him what he wants, but he wouldn't say. He just laughed and hung up. He's got . . . he's got the craziest voice . . ." She yanked the headset off her ears suddenly and flung it clattering across her keyboard. She raised her arms over her head in a groping gesture and then whirled and threw herself over the back of her chair, burying her head in her arms. A high-pitched wail began to come out of her, something like, "Ohmigodohmigodohmigod—" I tried to put my arms around her, but she pushed me away and went on keening.

Frank stuck his head in the door. Cunningham stepped over and spoke to him softly; Frank went away, but then came right back. Without a word, ignoring all of us, he walked directly to Marlys Schultz, pulled her upright by her shoulders, and slipped a brown paper bag over her head.

We were all shocked speechless. It seemed like such a brutal, insensitive thing to do. It worked, though. Schultzy quit yelling almost at once. Oddly, then, for a few seconds even the phones stopped ringing. In the sudden silence, a roomful of law enforcement professionals stared open-mouthed at the distressed mother quivering under a grocery sack.

Frank watched the clock on the wall a few seconds, then leaned over and said softly, "Schultzy, can you hear me?" The bag nodded. "Listen, I know it's hard. But I don't have to tell you that the quicker we find Jessica, the better her chances are. So I want you to calm down now and help us. Can you do that?"

There was a little sound, like a tiny grunt, and then the brown bag bobbed again, and Schultzy's voice, muffled, said, "Mm-hmm," and then, clearer, "Okay."

Frank lifted the bag off her tousled head. Schultzy rubbed her face, blinked her eyes a couple of times, and whispered, "Thanks."

"Let's get to work," Frank said.

The next hour was a blurry sweat. Frank told Cunningham to put everybody that wasn't currently arresting somebody on the search. Cunningham got all but two squads from the day shift headed downtown, and Lulu started calling in off-duty people to help.

I called Sheriff Grant Hisey and requested a K-9 team. In Rutherford, the county keeps the dogs. Grant said he had two dogs trained, and asked if we could use both.

"Sure appreciate it," I said.

"Hey, their handlers need the practice," Grant said. "Tell Schultzy not to worry. These puppies are pretty good. Be sure you have something for them to smell."

I told Schultzy, "They need a piece of Jessica's clothing. For the dogs."

"Should be something at the school," Schultzy said. "I'll check right now." Her color was improving. She was talking to squad cars, rattling off exact details of Jessica's size, weight, hair color, and dress, typing perfect messages at breakneck speed. The faster she worked, the stronger she got. Between radio transmissions she made tensely controlled phone calls that collected her husband, Ernie, their other four children, and both sets of grandparents at her house. Once she got them there she bombarded them all with precise directions for the care and feeding of one another. I began to wonder if they might not all want to run away.

I went out to my section and found Kevin Evjan. Together, we mobilized the entire investigative force to walk the downtown skyways and subways that keep Rutherford citizens from freezing in the winter. I described the voice I had heard on the phone, and told them if they saw a man walking with a blond female child they should do something, anything, to get him to talk.

Bo Dooley walked in just then and said, "This could be somebody needing money for a fix, couldn't it? Shall I talk to my snitches? They usually know who's getting desperate."

"I want you to do it," I said, "but help with the downtown search first. I want to get over to that day-care center."

Before I left, I asked Schultzy, "Did you find out about Jessica's clothing?"

"Melanie found her extra sneakers in her locker. You going up there now, Jake?" Her face wanted to ask to come with me, but knew better.

"Yeah." I touched her shoulder. "I'll be in touch."

Granny Goose was swarming with cars. As fast as cops stopped circling the area and headed downtown, parents who'd heard the news began arriving, anxious and resentful, to take their children away. Melanie Eisenman looked frayed.

"I want you to know that nothing like this has *ever* happened at Granny Goose," she said, "and I'm *sick* about it. But I want to go on record as stating that I did what I had to do under the circumstances. Jessica is a *very* difficult child—" She flared her slender nostrils.

"How did she get outside?"

"I put her in the laundry room for time-out. It's warm and clean in there, and there's plenty of light, so it's safe but it's *boring*. That's why I use it. The children have to understand they're being deprived of the company of their playmates for inappropriate behavior."

"What did she do?"

"Smeared finger paint all over Timmy Grover," Melanie said grimly. "It wasn't an accident. She wanted his picture. When he wouldn't hand it over, she attacked him."

"How'd she get out of the laundry room?"

"There's one set of shelves—here, I'll show you—" She led me to the laundry room, which was, indeed, a boring place. "In the closet, here, you see? Always full of clean towels. The shelves go clear through—" We walked out one door, in another, and she showed me how the shelves went through into the bathroom, so that clean towels could be pushed in one side and removed from the other. "Jessica climbed through, apparently. We found a stack of towels pushed onto the floor, where she came out. Then I guess she went out the bathroom door and down the hall and found the back door, here. She's tall and strong for her age. I suppose she managed to push on the bar, see, and get out." She showed me the panic hardware.

"Let's go out."

We were in a play yard filled with swings, a jungle gym, a big sandbox in one corner. A steel mesh fence, four feet high, ran around it, with a gate at the back.

"The gate was closed?"

"And padlocked. Always, when the children are here." She showed me.

We were looking at the locked gate when the dog teams arrived, in a van. Two smiling deputies hopped out of the front seat, obviously eager to show their stuff. They gave their quivering dogs a good whiff of the sneakers. Melanie unlocked the gate, and the deputies brought the dogs into the yard, where they went gleefully nuts. After running excitedly in circles for a while, they bayed over to a spot in the rear corner and began lunging at the fence. Their handlers took them to the same spot on the outside, where they howled and jumped some more and then took off southbound along the sidewalk. Melanie and I trotted along, too intrigued to stay behind. Our chase lasted only half a block. In front of a redbrick duplex with stone gateposts, the dogs plunged abruptly into the street and began baying in circles around an oil spot.

"Looks like she must've got into a car here," the thin deputy said.

"You mind running them through it again?" I asked. I did not want Jessica in a car with the man with the high voice.

"Sure," the K-9 guys said, their faces carefully neutral. "Good idea." The dogs followed the scent again, willingly, ran to the same oil spot, and howled in frustration. For the first time in my life I thought I understood how dogs felt.

"Are you looking for the little girl?" a voice said suddenly at my elbow. I turned and found a short, round-cheeked woman pushing a twin stroller containing two round-cheeked, fussing babies.

"You saw a little girl?"

"A blond girl? About four or five?"

"Exactly! When did you see her?"

"A couple of hours ago—give or take. I was on my way to the Valu Mart on the highway. I came past this yard, and she was standing inside the fence all alone. When she saw me she said, 'Will you lift me out?' and I said, 'Well, honey, I don't know whether you're supposed to be out of there or not.' She said, 'Well, I just wanna go home,' and I said, 'You better go inside the school there and ask some- body if you should be out.' She looked real disappointed. After I went on I thought, Heck, I bet I should have gone in there to the school and told them one of their kids was in the yard trying to get out. But I had shopping to do, and with these twins I have to hustle to stay on schedule. In fact, as you can see, I'm a little behind right now, I better get 'em home." She gave me her name and address while she rocked the unhappy babies with her foot.

"You didn't see a man hanging around here, did you?" I asked her.

"No. A man? What kind of a man?"

"Don't know. Probably in a car."

"No, I'd never of left her if I thought . . . She's miss- ing, huh? Son of a gun. Now I feel real bad. Jeez, listen, I'm sorry, but I've really gotta get these kids home." Her babies were beginning to sound like the dogs.

"Sure," I said. "Thanks a lot."

I called the station and brought Frank up to date. "Anything new there?"

"Everybody's searching downtown, no leads yet," he said. "But listen, Maddox is walking the North End today, and I've started him talking to people. He just got a tip about a place to look, why don't you run up there and see what you think? Hold on, I'll find him—" I heard many voices, the rattle of the radio, and then Frank said, "He'll meet you in front of the pawnshop there on Eleventh."

I went north on Center Street, hit the lights just right, and in eight minutes pulled up in front of Clint Maddox, who was standing at parade rest in front of the Kwik Kash Pawn Shop. A dozen young males crowded around him.

I leaned across to open the passenger-side door, and he slid in beside me. "Boy, you make friends fast," I said.

"I'm the new girl in town," Maddox said. "Some of these kids have never seen a lone cop on foot before. They're all dyin' to know what in hell I'm doin' up here." He smiled. "What am I doing, Jake? You got any idea?"

"Taking the neighborhood back," I said.

"All by myself?"

"Frank said he'd try to get you a partner soon. Listen, you heard about Schultzy's little girl?"

"Yeah. Poor Schultzy, I bet she's goin' nuts, huh? I'll tell you one thing, though, whoever took that Jessica, I bet he's having a long day."

"You know her?"

"She used to play with my girls sometimes on Saturday. We had to cut it out, my kids always ended up crying. Jeez, I feel sorry for Schultzy, though. You got anything on the snatcher?"

"Just that he talks like Mickey Mouse and won't say what he wants. And he said he was holding her downtown. But Frank said you had another idea?"

"It may be nothing, but—a couple of people have said to me in the last few minutes that a man went into the house with the broken porch railing on Fifth Avenue, and he had a little girl with him."

"You found it yet?"

"No. Wanna go look?"

"Sure." We drove east. "You don't have an address?"

"Between Fifteenth and Sixteenth Streets, they said."

Half the houses in the block had serious maintenance problems, and straggly ill-kept lawns. There were three porches in various stages of decay. We drove the area twice, then parked the car and started walking. As we passed a house set close to the sidewalk, a voice asked softly from inside a window, "You lookin' for the dope house, Jake?"

I peered through the screen. "Tony?" He was sitting just inside the open window, in a sleeveless undershirt. He had a cup of coffee on the windowsill, and a lighted cigarette on the stand ashtray beside him. "This is Clint Maddox, Tony, he's working in this part of town now. You think there's something funny about one of these houses?"

"Fifteen-ten," he said. "Other side of the street, two doors down. See it? The one with the spokes broke out of the porch railing."

"Uh-huh, I see it. What do you know about it? Loud noise, big parties at night?"

"Not noise. People. All kinds of people in cars. Some nice cars, some rattletraps. And all ages, not like you'd see in a club or anything. Starts about four in the afternoon, pretty much every day, goes on till midnight, later on weekends. They drive up, they go inside, they stay a few minutes, and they leave."

"So, buying something, you figure."

"And plus, Jake, nobody really lives there. No car there in the morning, no lights on till evening."

"Grass looks recently cut," I said.

"Some lawn service comes a couple times a month. Talk to Pete. His house is on Sixth, his backyard's right across the alley from the backyard of that Fifteen-ten there. He says the same thing, people in and out all night long."

"You seen anybody go in there today?"

"Uh-uh. Still too early. You gonna go in and take a look, Jake?"

"Having a lot of company's not illegal," I said. "We need a little more than that to go on. But somebody said a man and a little girl went in there. You didn't see that, huh?"

"No. But I'm pretty sure Pete's home. You wanna walk around in the alley there, he'll show you which yard it is."

"Uh-huh. Maybe we'll do that."

"Nice to meet you, young fella."

"Clint," Maddox said. "Glad to know you." As we walked away, Clint said, "Whaddya think, shall we take a look in back?"

"Why not? Let's get the car." We idled north on the alley between Fifth and Sixth Avenues, counting backyards.

"Fifteen-oh-six, oh-eight . . . there it is," Clint said. "The one with the tan hatchback parked by the path." The house was in serious disrepair, with cracked siding and peeling paint. A screened porch ran across the back of the house, its rusty screen sagging above dilapidated steps. A path ran through the weedy yard from the alley to the porch. No lights showed in the house.

"Look under the car," I said. "That look like an oil spot to you?"

"Might be leaking a little, yeah. Why?"

"Can you back up a little? Maybe park by those bushes back there?" Clint put the car in reverse while I grabbed the radio to page the K-9 van. When Wayne answered, I said, "Remember the oil spot on the street where the dogs dead-ended? I might be looking at the car that made it."

"Where are you?" Wayne said. I gave him the address and described the alley.

"We'll come in right behind you," he said.

"We need a nice quiet approach, if that's possible."

"We'll put the muzzles on."

As soon as I put the mike down, every car on the search started calling me, stepping on each other so I couldn't understand any of them, and making a lot of noise. I turned the sound off and called Cunningham on the phone.

"Tom," I said, "call all the squads and tell them we need a silent approach here. Let's not stir this up till we see what the dogs think of this car."

"Copy that. Uh, Jake, you think you can hold the dogs off a few minutes? The chief's called in his new ERU team, and they're gearing up right now."

"Tell 'em to hustle. I'm not sure how these dogs do their work."

"Copy," Cunningham said. "Hold on a sec, Jake, the chief wants to tell you—" Frank came on and said, "Just want you to know I got a no-knock search warrant signed by Judge Levy ten minutes ago. Vince is bringing it."

"Good. Dogs are coming, I gotta go."

I walked back to the K-9 van as it nosed into the alley. Fritz rolled his window down. "That the car?" he asked.

"Uh-huh. The neighbors say they've been watching this house. Lotta late traffic, they say, no regular tenants." I looked back to where the dogs lay, quietly alert, their eyes gleaming above their screened masks. One of them raised his dark head and growled, low in his throat. Wayne turned and spoke to him, low and sharp, and the dog put his head back on his paws, but kept his unblinking stare on me.

"The chief's sending up his new emergency response team," I said. "He thinks we might want to use them on the entry. Will the dogs be okay if we wait a few minutes?"

"Long as we stay in the van, they're under full control, they won't make a move or a sound till we tell them," Fritz said. "Once we get out, we'll give them the shoes to smell again, tell them to follow that scent, and lead them to the car. After that it's up to them. If they smell the little girl around the car, they're going to make plenty of noise, and they'll go where the smell leads them. Can't ask them to be quiet while they do that."

"Understood," I said. We stood silent a few minutes, smelling the garden smells of Rutherford in August, corn in the husk, zucchini, and ripening apples. Then Vince Greeley walked up to my elbow and said softly, "The Joy Boys are here. Whaddya want busted?"

He looked awesome. His king-size bulletproof vest bulked up his torso to improbable size, and his head had all but disappeared into his masked helmet. Staley and Frink crouched behind a maple tree, holding their six-foot "key," its metal battering ram glinting in the sunlight. Cooper and Frye, in their cammy jammies, made odd speckled patches pressed against the hedge. Someone had left a garden rake on the ground where they were kneeling, and I wanted to warn them not to get snagged in it.

"Guess it's time to go, then," Wayne said. He got out and opened the back doors of the van. Fritz brought the two dogs out on their leashes. They stood trembling silently while the muzzles came off, and then Wayne, wearing gloves, took Jessica's sneakers out of a paper bag and put them on the ground. The dogs sniffed the shoes a couple of times, whimpering a little while he talked to them softly. Wayne and Fritz each took a leash and walked their dogs to the tan Escort by the gate. The hounds circled it excitedly, nosing it, and when they reached the passenger side they set up that god-awful yapping noise I'd heard at the nursery. They dragged their trainers up the path toward the porch. Then my heart banged against my ribs as a child's scream, high-pitched and horrifying, came from inside the house.

The alley exploded, as five cops in speckled suits ran flat out for the house. Cooper ran toward the corner of the house, carrying the garden rake before him like some improbable lance. Without breaking stride, he drove it with all his might through the rear side window. Then he leaned back, pulling on the handle with his whole weight. The screen and a great spill of shattered glass came out of the window and slammed onto the grass. Frye came behind him, hurling his outsize firecracker through the hole in the window as he ran past it. It went off with a blinding light and a noise like the end of the world.

Staley and Frink took the porch steps two at a time and hit the door with their battering ram, smashing the lock and the top hinge in one mighty lunge. Smoke poured out of the house. Vince ran through the ruined back door behind his body bunker, the red dot of his magic Glock dancing on the billowing smoke. His four teammates, clutching their 40-caliber semiautomatics, followed close behind him. The child's desperate screaming went on and on.

Most of the Rutherford police force had emerged from the yards around the block by then, and were running toward the house with their weapons in their hands. Before they reached it, Vince reappeared in the doorway. Keeping his shield between him and the house, he backed across the porch and down the steps. The screaming came with him, I realized suddenly. He was holding Jessica Schultz behind the bunker.

I ran up to him in the yard and grabbed her out of his arms. She felt like hostile rocks. Her torso was hard and rigid, but she seemed to have eight arms and legs, all scratching and kicking. Vince turned as soon as I took her and ran back into the smoke and noise.

Jessica abused me mercilessly while I carried her down the alley to Fifteenth Street. At the curb by the corner I found Mary Agnes Donovan, sheltering behind her squad car with her Glock pointed at the alley. All around the

block, cops were similarly deployed. We could spare one
of them, I figured.

"Donovan," I yelled across the squalling kid, "will you
take Jessica back to the station?"

"Sure," Donovan said, "put her down." Jessica staggered when I set her down on the sidewalk, then planted
both feet firmly, took a deep breath, and went back to
screaming with fresh energy. Tears and snot poured down
her cheeks. Her face was very red. She was making enough
noise for a train wreck. Mary Agnes holstered her weapon
and peered critically at the child for a moment, then
leaned over and said quietly into her ear, "Jessica, do you
want to go see your mom?"

Jessica stopped screaming, took two or three snuffling,
raspy breaths, looked into Donovan's face, and said, "Ye-
heh-heh-ess."

"Good," Donovan said. "Hop in the car, then, and
we'll go." Jessica climbed across the front seat like a
mountain goat. Donovan slid in beside her and picked the
radio mike off its mount. "Tell Schultzy I'm bringing Jessica in right now," she told Sally, "and she's okay." She
handed Jessica a handful of Kleenex while she backed out
of her spot. Donovan has four boys. Noise does not im-
press her.

I ran back down the alley and into the house, where
five cops in multicolored uniforms were running around,
slamming doors open and shouting to whoever was in
there to come out. They pointed their weapons at the bare
walls and blank windows on the ground floor, then sidled
up the narrow stairs and threatened the second floor. Finally Vince came back downstairs, sweating profusely. He
threw open the front and back doors and waved, and
most of the Rutherford police force crunched into the
dirty old house and stood gaping.

The air was full of dust and flying slivers of old wood.

The shattered remains of the side window glinted on the kitchen floor. The dogs were still howling, too, and all the squads began yelling questions at each other. There was so much noise in the small crowded space I thought my head would burst. I groped over to Wayne and Fritz and yelled into Wayne's ear, "Ask them to stop barking."

"It doesn't quite work like that," Wayne shouted back, grinning. But he nodded to his partner, and they took the noisy, excited dogs back to the truck.

Maddox walked in and asked me, "Who's got the kidnapper?"

I looked at Vince. "Nobody, so far," Vince said. "Jessica is all we found."

"Did he run away?"

"From this house? There were cops in all the bushes for two blocks around."

They searched, though. Blue uniforms spread up and down the sidewalks and out into the street. They talked to the neighbors they found peeking anxiously out of windows. They looked into cellars and backyard sheds. After a fruitless hour, they trailed back to the station.

I was standing in the chief's office by then, reporting on the debut performance of the ERU team. Schultzy was in his spare chair, looking like Viking Mom, holding her daughter.

"The rake worked okay, huh? And that flash-bang thing?" He was crazy about the lo-tech hi-tech symmetry of the rake and the firecracker.

"Yup. If the bad guy had been there, we'd've had him sure."

"But he wasn't? You're sure? How could that be?"

"Hold on a sec, I just saw Cooper and Frink come in." I ran downstairs to the supply room, where the last of the ERU team was checking in their extra gear.

"All this razzmatazz and nothing to show for it," Buzz

Cooper said, looking tired and hot. "There was nobody in that house but the kid, Jake."

"Nobody." I went back up and told Frank. "The house was empty except for Jessica."

"So is this a kidnapping or what?" Frank demanded, staring at me indignantly.

"Beats me," I said. "He called us. What has he got if he lets her go?"

"Tell me again," Frank asked Schultzy. "What did he say he wanted?"

"He never said. I couldn't get him to answer me. Jessica—" Schultzy rolled her daughter off her lap and set her on her feet. Jessica swayed groggily; the scare had exhausted her, and now she was falling asleep. "Jessica, how did you get out there to that house? Huh? Somebody took you there, right? Who was it? Tell Mama!"

Jessica squeezed her eyes shut and began to cry again. She really did have an extraordinary voice. "Bad boy, Mama!" she howled between sobs. "Bad boy!" She hurled herself back onto Schultzy's chest and clung there.

"What did he do that was bad?" Schultzy demanded. She tried to pry her daughter loose so she could look at her, but Jessie clung to her fiercely.

"Chief," Schultzy said, looking up across the noise, "I'm sorry, but I think I oughta get this kid home and calm her down."

"You're right. Hey, I'm gonna have Donovan drive you." Frank held up a hand as she started to protest. "Because I want you to stop off at the clinic and get a check with a sexual assault kit. Only takes a few minutes," he assured her hastily, "and it would be foolish to skip it. I'll call ahead and tell 'em to expect you."

He followed her out the door, fussing, admonishing. "And then, as soon as you get her home? Let Donovan take off all her clothes and put 'em in an evidence bag, will you? Has to be paper, not plastic, and it's safer if it's done by somebody with experience. We'll want to check them for hair and fibers and—" He stopped himself before he'd said "semen." I heard him, farther down the hall, saying, "You call me after she's had some lunch and a nap, and we'll see if she feels like talking by then, huh? Maybe she can tell us more about this bad boy."

He came back in his office, and we stared at each other in the glorious silence.

"Rape kit?" I said. "We're looking for a molester with a show-off streak?"

"Makes just as much sense as a kidnapper that calls the station and then turns the kid loose."

"Maybe she told him her mama works for the police," I suggested, "and he chickened out."

"Uh-huh. Or maybe he used to rape little girls, but he reformed," Frank said, "after he heard how this kid can yell."

·FIVE·

MOST OF THE RUTHERFORD POLICE FORCE WAS STOMPING around the station, angry and frustrated. It was wonderful, of course, that Jessica was back unharmed. But knots of uniformed figures kept forming, in the break room, on the stairs, demanding of each other, "How did that shitheel baby-snatcher get away from us? We were all around that house watching every minute, how could we lose that filthy dickhead?"

"You looked in all the closets, under the beds?" Frank was almost beside himself with frustration, asking the same questions over and over as the groups came in, driving everybody to distraction until just staying away from Frank became a goal in itself. "How about the basement? You sure you didn't miss anything down there?"

"There isn't any basement," Cooper said.

"Oh, there has to be."

"Well, there isn't," Cooper said, wiping sweat and dirt off his face. "There's no down stairway on the first floor, so we went out in the yard, and we searched every inch of the outside of that house. We looked for a root cellar, a coal chute, anything. Trust me, Chief, that old shanty's got nothing underneath it."

"Buzz, this is Minnesota," Frank said. "It's got running water, hasn't it? A kitchen, a bathroom?"

"Yes, it has."

"Well, then it has to have a basement. Pipes'd freeze solid if it didn't."

"Yeah, well, good luck finding it," Cooper said, his face stiff with anger. He had decided that the whole ERU business was a case of ridiculous overkill, and he was sorry he had ever volunteered for it. He felt foolish about taking part in an operation in which five grown men did nothing but terrify a little girl. Hot and disgusted, he stomped off muttering that he was goddamned if he was going to say there was a frigging basement under the frigging house when there frigging wasn't.

Frank let him go. But as soon as Cooper was out of hearing, he turned to me and said, "Jake, there has to be a basement in that house. Go on back up there and find it."

"You want me to go along?" Vince asked. "I've got a couple hours left."

"Yeah. Sure. I guess so. Hell, I don't know where anybody belongs now, anyway," Frank said.

"What about impounding the car?" I asked him.

"I'll see to it," Frank said. "You take a good look at that house, Jake. Find me something."

We met Bo Dooley coming out of his cubicle as we went down the hall. "We're going back up to the kidnap house," I said. "Why don't you come with us? You might as well have a look, everybody else has."

"You want me to bring my Valtox kit?" He's got a little suitcase about the size of a kid's lunch box, for field-testing common drugs.

"Bo thinks everything's going to turn into a drug case sooner or later," Vince said.

"Bring your gun, too," I said, "and plenty of ammunition. It's an unpredictable day."

I drove while Vince bitched. He's hardly ever in a bad mood, but right now he was seriously pissed. Frank, he said, ought to be happy to have Jessica Schultz alive in her mother's arms, and quit harassing us about details.

"What the hell, Jake?" he said. "Couple of hours ago he'd of given anything to be where we are now. But then he turns right around and has a worm about whether this stupid old shack has a hole under it? I mean, who *gives* a shit?"

"He feels like everything's out of control," I said. "We chase a guy, and he turns out not to be carrying anything. We find the kid but not the kidnapper. Seems like nothing goes right lately."

"Yeah, well, that's life," Vince said. He was hunched in the passenger seat, scowling all over his handsome face. "I mean, but let's remember to blame the bad guys, huh? It's not the cops' fault, for Christ's sake."

I parked by the tan hatchback, which was still waiting for somebody in back of 1510 Fifth Avenue. Maddox was standing there, talking to Pete Peterson, whose neat backyard contrasted sharply with the mess across the alley. The kidnap site had evolved, in the last couple of hours, from slum housing into a trash heap.

"Used to be a family named Schwartzkopf lived here, for many years," Pete was saying. Maddox looked as if the story had been going on for a while. "He worked for the Great Northern. Always raised a big garden, took real good care of the place. But you know how it is, their kids grew up and he had a stroke, and the missus sold the house to a real estate company and moved to her daughter's place in Sioux Falls." Pete looked older than he had yesterday. "Seems like there's not much market for these older houses anymore," he said. "Kind of a problem for the rest of us."

"It's going to be quiet enough for a while, anyway," Maddox told him. "We'll put a lock on it, treat it as a crime scene, and it'll be under close scrutiny till we get some answers."

"You want to come in with us," Vince asked Maddox, "and help us find a basement under this house? Whether it's here or not?"

"Hey, anything works for me," Maddox said, "I'm making up my job as I go along."

The four of us crossed the weedy yard and climbed onto the porch. "How did it feel," I asked Vince, "going through the door first behind that bunker?"

"Over*loaded*," he said. "That big vest is so hot, I was just cookin' in there! And all the gear is heavy, especially the bunker, that damn thing weighs a *ton*. I'm gonna have to pump some iron to play on this team, I see that." Behind the idle bitching, he was pleased with himself, though; he had boldly gone where the rest of us hadn't been. He stood with his hands on his hips, shaking his head at the door that hung crookedly from its bottom hinge. "What a mess, huh? We gonna get somebody up here to board this thing up?"

"Chief said he's sending a crew," I said. We stepped inside. The stove and refrigerator were gone from the kitchen; a hot plate stood on a counter by the sink. Cockroaches skittered away as I pushed open the door to the bathroom. The tub stood on ancient claw feet, its finish etched gray and brown, with rust streaks running from the faucets to the drain.

In the living room, a dirty plush sofa sagged against the side wall. A matching chair trailed stuffing near the front window. Above it, like a family portrait, Vince's copy of the search warrant was neatly taped to the wall.

"You just gonna leave that here?" Maddox asked him.

"That's what the directions say, if you can't find an owner or renter to deliver it to, leave it posted in a prominent place."

"Kind of hard to pick a prominent place in this dump, isn't it?" Maddox said.

"Damn straight," Vince said. "And if you think this is a little tacky, take a look upstairs." Bo and I followed him up the narrow stairway that ran along the side wall of the living room. There were two bedrooms, their doors standing ajar. One very dirty mattress lay in each of them, with a moth-eaten olive green blanket crumpled on top.

"This is it," Vince said, "what you see is what you get. One little closet in each room, nothing in either one. Plenty of trash, though—" He bent toward one of the many pop cans lying on the floor.

"Don't touch it!" Bo said sharply. "Let me—" He fished a pair of plastic gloves out of his pocket and pulled them on. Carefully, he picked up the pop can by the ridges on both ends and looked at it contentedly. "Oh, *yes*," he said.

"What?" Vince said. "You got a thing for bent pop cans?"

"See these holes?" The can had been mashed down in the middle, on the same side as the pop-top hole, and the saddle that the bend created was riddled with small punctures.

"Ever see one of these? The stains are from the heat," Dooley said. "It was used to smoke crack."

"What, instead of a pipe?" Vince asked.

"Right. You score some crack and don't have your gear with you, you can bend a pop can, punch some little holes with a nail or a needle, lay your rock right there in the saddle, and light 'er up. Suck the smoke out the drinking hole."

"Shee. The price is right, too, huh?"

Clint Maddox pussyfooted up behind us and said softly, "Hey, guys. I just found something." He turned and went back down the stairs, walking on the balls of his feet, and we all followed him, attempting weightlessness.

At the bottom step Maddox turned with his fingers on his lips and pointed along the wall under the stairs. In the slanting light of afternoon, we could see a little shadow, deeper than the others in the board-and-batten siding. Maddox had found what all of us had missed before, a cubby with a flush door under the stairs. The door was a fraction of an inch ajar because a cigarette butt had wedged in the opening, causing the magnetic latch to fail.

I drew my weapon and slid along the wall. Greeley stepped silently across the door and backed against the wall with his Glock in the air. Dooley and Maddox braced behind me as I stepped away from the wall and kicked the door open.

It swung into an empty space about three feet wide, just missing the far wall. Nothing moved or made a sound.

Greeley turned quickly away from the wall and peered into the dark space. He stepped in with his gun cocked and swung the door back so he could look behind it. "Nothing back here. This end slopes down behind the stairs." He swung the door back and looked again at the tall end of the closet. "Hey, there's a hatch cover leaning against the wall here, though." He directed his light at the floor. "Hole in the floor, too. Look here."

We all crowded in to see where his Streamlight was pointing. "Ladder goes down," Maddox said.

We all looked at each other, and then Maddox stepped across the hole, shone his light around the bottom of the ladder for a few seconds, said, "Oh *well*," and stepped on the top rung of the ladder, shining his light anxiously downward. When Maddox's head dropped out of sight, Greeley followed him, saying as his torso disappeared into the hole, "Shit, I'm sick of this day."

As soon as Greeley's hands were out of the way, I stepped onto the top rung of the ladder and followed him down, staring bug-eyed into the bright beam of his flashlight where it pierced the dark. I got occasional glimpses of cobwebs and a stone wall. Greeley's breathing sounded loud below me, and Dooley's feet were groping downward from above.

The ladder had twelve rungs. The bottom felt like dirt. I turned around and said, "Smells like a sewer."

Maddox said, somewhere in the dark, "We both already said that." He was shining his light around. "Hole in the wall over here."

We followed his light, groping with our feet, brushing off cobwebs.

"Feels like I got creepy-crawlies all over me," Greeley muttered, and Dooley said, "Shut *up*."

"I can hear water running," Maddox said. He stuck his big light through the hole in the wall, leaned in, coughed, and pulled his head back out.

"It's the sewer," he told me, passing the light. "You wanna look?"

"Not really," I said, but I did. The space was probably three feet high, lined with ancient hand-cut stones, glossy with slime and grouted with moss. A small river of dirty water and human waste ran along the bottom. The smell made my toes curl. I shone the light around. Nobody crouched in the shadows. I came out and asked Maddox, "You ever been in the Rutherford sewer?"

"Can't say I've had the pleasure. You gonna make me go now?"

"No. This is the oldest part of town. All the new parts of the city have cast-cement storm sewers, with access points clearly marked on cast-iron covers above, and signs down below to tell you where you are. And the sanitary sewers are heavy-duty plastic, and much smaller than this. But apparently in this part of town we've still got a few blocks of storm drain and sewer lines combined. Illegal as hell, now, I should think, but they must be grandfathered, waiting for the budget to replace 'em. We'll have to ask one of the city engineers if there's a map of the sewer lines in the North End."

"What are you thinking? That our guy went out through the sewer?"

"Looks like it, doesn't it? The closet door was open, and the cover was off the trapdoor."

"Tight fit in that sewer." Maddox shuddered. "No way to stay out of the shit. Jeez, bad trip, talk about."

We heard heavy footsteps over our heads, so we started back up the ladder. Putratz and Coe were coming in with the repair crew, saying, "See, we gotta put plywood over this window and—"

I stuck my head up out of the hole, and Putratz yelled, "Freeze!" and reached for his gun. I said, "Chill. It's me," and he stopped in the middle of drawing his weapon, stared, and became unreasonably furious, yelling, "Well, Jee-sus, Joseph, and Emily, fuck a goddamn duck, Jake, it's a wonder I didn't blow your stupid head off!"

"Hey, I'm sorry," I said. "We didn't know you were coming." Which was untrue, of course; we came up because we heard them coming. But at least he quit yelling. The four of us crawled out of the hole and began beating spiders off each other. Putratz said lamely, "Oh, you found the basement, I guess."

"Boy, that's gonna make the chief happy," Coe said.

"Well, now," Greeley said. "That'll be a nice change, won't it?"

My pager sounded three notes. I went out to the car, plucked my phone off the dash, and called the station.

"Jake," Frank said, "anything yet?"

"We found the basement. Nobody there, but we think we know how he got away."

"Good for you! I knew there had to be one. Listen, I just wanted you to know the rape test came up negative."

"Jesus, that's good news."

"Yeah. And we can use some, huh? I sent Donovan along to Schultzy's house, she brought back Jessica's clothes for testing. Lou's on his way out now to see if Jessica can talk yet, haven't heard from him. But why I called, I've got a Toastmasters breakfast tomorrow and Rotary at lunchtime. So can we get together around ten o'clock, to review all this horseshit from today? I've got about a million questions."

"Join the club," I said. "Ten o'clock's fine." I wrote it on a Post-it and stuck it to the dashboard. Now, if I can get this car back to the station without being struck by a meteor, I thought, maybe I'll remember to put this note on my calendar.

I leaned against the car a minute in the quiet alley, smelling the hydrangea hedge we had all hidden behind earlier. It was just starting to bud, I noticed; it would bloom gloriously in September, oblivious to the detritus piling up around it. Hollyhocks were blooming right now around Pete Peterson's back steps, leaning top-heavy against the mellow old brick of his house, in a flower bed that was outlined by river stones. The blooms looked peaceful and optimistic, as if they were just waiting for all of us to shape up and behave ourselves. For one wildly rebellious moment, I considered the feasibility of faking amnesia for the rest of the afternoon. "I just forgot what I was doing entirely, I guess," I imagined myself saying, "and I took this wrong turn and ended up in Chatfield." I got a distinct inner vision of myself, sitting in the creaky silence of the library across from the park, reading old copies of *National Geographic*, and then walking down the sleepy street to the Liquor Store Bar for a draft beer.

The memory of my new pay grade surfaced just in time. I went back inside the sordid house and asked, "Okay, who's ready to ride back with me?"

"I am," Dooley said, cradling his bent pop can like a treasure. "Me too," Greeley said, but Maddox said, "I've got my own car. Hold on a sec, Vince, lemme get that spider out of your ear." When Vince began slapping frantically at the side of his head, Clint laughed happily and said, "Oh, I guess that's just dirt after all."

"How'd you like a fat lip?" Vince said. They batted each other like third-graders, high on the relief of climbing out of that stinking cellar.

Back in my office, I watched the shadows lengthen over downtown while I wrote three pages of notes, with question marks sprinkled everywhere like confetti. Why did the squeaky-voiced man call us? Why did he tell us they were downtown, but then take Jessica to the crack house? And why did he abandon her there? I printed my notes and read them over, trying to remember what they reminded me of. Finally I got it: that old Cosby record in which his girlfriend keeps asking, "Why is there air?"

I made two stops on the way home, for a six-pack and a large assortment of Chinese takeout. I'd forgotten about my apartment problems, but when I got home I found to my delight that the building was air-conditioned again, and the sink drain worked. I set up a tray in front of the TV set. All through local and national news and a couple of inane sitcoms, I washed down salty vegetables and tiny slivers of pork with plenty of icy beer. Then I hung up my clothes behind a smoothly sliding closet door, lay down, groaned once, and slept ten hours without turning over.

I woke at six, so thirsty my lips felt crisp. I drank a big glass of ice water and stood under the shower for some time with my mouth open. Feeling vague and bloated, I dressed slowly and was walking toward my door, dreaming of orange juice and coffee, when my phone rang.

"Oh, good, I caught you," Neva said. Dispatch was already buzzing around her. "Listen, on your way in to the station, could you stop by the Second Avenue bridge? You'll see Eldon Huckstadt there somewhere, look for his squad car. He'll probably be down by the river by the time you get there. Somebody phoned in that there's something big floating in the river. After Eldon got there, he said he was going to need help getting it out, so I called Halvorson and had him come to the station and get that piece of line with the grappling hook that we use to fish stolen bikes out of the river. After Halvorson got there, he called in and said I better get somebody over there to take a look, because he's never seen anything like this before."

"Why am I not surprised?" I said. "The way this week is going, it's probably a dead elephant."

The morning sun looked hot and brassy above the maples by the time I reached the river. Two blue-and-whites were parked by the curb north of the Second Avenue bridge. I parked by the opposite curb, walked across the street, and looked down the embankment. Halvorson and Huckstadt were standing on the sandbar, which had grown a little farther into the stream since I noticed it Tuesday morning.

Eldon Huckstadt held a coiled length of nylon line with a grappling hook on the end. As I climbed down the bank, he dropped the rope onto the sand beside him and uncoiled several loops of it. Balancing himself with spread legs and his left arm extended forward, he leaned back and threw the hook as hard as he could. The sun glinted off it as it turned, flying far out across the water. When it splashed in midstream, Huckstadt tugged a couple of times on the line. When it went taut, he yelled, "There! I think I got it!" Halvorson helped him haul in the line. I saw something red in the water; then a shadow of blue as it turned. By the time I reached the edge of the stream, the two men were hauling a multicolored bundle onto the sandbar.

"Oh, hell, that's what I was afraid of," Halvorson said as I walked up to him, "it's a person."

"Holy shit," Huckstadt said, "it's got feet on both ends." They both straightened up at once, spooked, and looked at me as if I owed them an answer.

"Lemme see," I said. Pulling on gloves, I stooped and pulled some of the soaked clothing out of the way.

"Dammit, I know this kid," I said. "It's Randy Thorson." Thin nylon cord was wrapped and knotted many times around the whole length of his body. A pair of naked feet stuck up on either side of his drowned face.

"Will you help me roll him?" I asked Halvorson. "I don't want to mess up anything, just . . . If we can get a look at the other . . ."

We rolled him on his side. I knelt and looked a minute at the body Randy was tied to, then got up and walked away, to the wet gravel at the edge of the stream. I stood squinting into the brightness reflected off the moving water, listening while a bird sang the same three notes, over and over, from the bushes on the opposite bank.

"Jake?" Huckstadt said softly behind my elbow. "You sick?"

"No." I swallowed. "I know that woman, is all."

"Come to think of it, so do I," Huckstadt said. "That's Babe Krueger, isn't it?"

·SIX·

POKEY GUNNED HIS OLD RAGTOP JEEP ACROSS THE BRIDGE AS IF
the tires were on fire. He made a highly illegal but elegant
U-turn to park nose-to-nose with Halvorson's squad car
and opened the driver's-side door before the wheels had
quite stopped moving. Carrying his little black coroner's
bag, he appeared at the top of the slope, saw me, and
began skidding down the bank on his heels.

I went to meet him. "Pretty good time," I said. "You
leave a skin cancer in mid-burn?" Rutherford can't afford
a full-time medical examiner, so Pokey combines part-
time coroner's chores with his dermatology practice. The
arrangement doesn't usually stretch his work days much;
mostly he certifies death by natural causes for old people
in rest homes.

"Eight o'clock patient no-showed," he said. "Was
headin' out for second coffee when you called. Perfect
timing, already peed even." Pokey learned English while

he was on the run from a work camp in the Soviet Union. You have to fill in the blanks. "You found drowned guys?"

"A woman and a boy. Mother and son, actually. And they're tied together."

"You ID'd them yet?"

"I know them. Talked to both of them this week, believe it or not. Their bar was robbed day before yesterday."

"You mean Rowdy's Bar? This the lady got all taped up? Saw story on TV. Shee. Some lousy week she's havin', hah?" We crossed the sandbar to the soaking muddy bundle by the water. "Hoo, boy, these two really *tied*, hah?" Pokey made a couple of clucking noises while he looked them over, set down his bag, and pulled on latex gloves. He knelt on the hot sand, peering into eyes, ears, mouths, taking temperatures. He pushed gently at Randy's jaw and neck, then got interested in his hands, looking carefully at his fingernails and comparing them to Babe's.

"How long ago you pull 'em out?" he asked me.

"Huckstadt was just getting a line on them when I got here. Quarter to eight."

"So. Half an hour. Sun's warmin' up fast, huh? Any cover around?"

"I got it. Here." Huckstadt came puffing back down from his car, carrying a black plastic sheet and a roll of crime scene tape. "Halvorson's gonna stay up topside," he said. "People are startin' to ask questions up there. We'll have a crowd down here in a minute if we don't move 'em along." He set to work marking off the area with tape.

"You got gloves on?" Pokey asked me. "Ah, good—I'd like to"—he rolled his hands like a flight instructor demonstrating yaw—"wanna get better look at her." I helped him roll the bodies a quarter turn. The corpses picked up sand with every move, and they were beginning to draw flies. I knew Babe didn't care anymore, but she had been a much-admired woman, and I felt bad about leaving her lying there, getting uglier every minute.

"Her face more messed up than his, huh?" Randy's cheeks and forehead were scraped from tumbling across gravel, but Babe's face had two deep horizontal cuts, running from cheekbone to jaw on the right side, and a slash across her nose. Pokey gently brushed some sand off her face, and pulled the tangled collar of her red robe away from her throat. When he did, we saw another long slice on her neck.

"Don't look like rock cuts," he said, pulling at the tattered front of her robe. "More like knife wounds, huh?" He found the zipper on her robe, slid it open to the waist, and groped aside the wispy nightgown underneath. The flesh of her bosom was covered with cuts; she had been stabbed repeatedly all over her chest and upper arms. One nipple was sliced open.

I must have made a sound. Pokey sat back on his heels and squinted up at me. "This woman mean something to you, Jake?"

"Not like that," I said. "We worked together once. She was nice."

"Ah." Pokey has a quiet generic sigh that wonderfully shortens sad stories. His adolescence was supervised by murderers, so he's hard to surprise. He bent over Babe again, briefly, then asked me, "How long since you seen her?"

"Um, Tuesday morning. Just about—not quite forty-eight hours ago."

"Looks like she died soon after."

"Well—I don't think so, Pokey. I had accounts of her whereabouts all Tuesday afternoon. And yesterday, far as I know, she was back at Rowdy's. Must have been. She had employees, customers, she couldn't be missing all day without somebody saying something."

"Mmm." He looked at his watch. "Hearse comin'?"

"Not yet. I called BCA. They say they've got a new rule, they're gonna transport the bodies to St. Paul and do the autopsy there."

"Hell you say," Pokey snorted. He pushed up his glasses with the back of his gloved hand. "Whose bright idea is that? Huh? I'm supposed to sign death certificate without seein' autopsy? Don't think so."

I knew how he felt. The state Bureau of Criminal Apprehension has more scientific gizmos than we can possibly afford in Rutherford, and it's great to have their help on major crimes, especially homicides. But we do lose some control.

"They said it's their price," I told him. "They take the case, they take the body. We have to pay for the transportation and lab work, too. I checked with the chief, he okayed it."

Pokey flounced around some more, muttering "numskull diffugilty," and then something in Ukrainian, followed by "buncha jerkoff bozos." He learns his American slang from three generations of patients and uses it with freewheeling disregard for what's in and what's out. Under stress, he flings in snippets from two or three of his native tongues. Some basic laws of language must govern the mix, because I usually get most of it. Finally he asked me, "How long we gotta wait for big-time St. Paul weenies?"

"I called them just before I called you. They said they had their vehicles clean and loaded, they'd get on the road right away. So, eighty miles, and they never heard of a speed limit . . . they'll be here all too soon. Let's do as much as we can by ourselves before they get here. What made you think Babe died Tuesday? Show me."

"Rigor mortis nearly gone, see? Boy's different, see how stiff his whole body is? Here . . . and here . . . feel.

Like marble. But woman's tissues already breaking down. See how loose fingernails are?"

"So you're saying they didn't die at the same time?"

"Or even in same way," Pokey said. "Look at his hands."

"What—so dirty, you mean?"

"Uh-huh. Fingernails full of dirt and gravel. Hands scratched up bad. Like he struggled, tried to push off bottom or grab stuff. Now look at her hands. Just lying at her sides, almost clean. Should have some defense wounds, though—" He pulled at the loop of rope over her left arm till he could turn her hand over. It was unmarked. "Help me," he said, and we rolled her body again, and slid the loop of line around till it was loose enough to let him look at the inside of her right hand and arm. "Oh, yah," he said, "see here?" There was a long slash down the inside of her right arm, and a deep cut in the palm at the base of the thumb.

"Almost anybody, getting attacked by knife, will put hand up—" He illustrated, conveying a dreadful picture of Babe fending off a knife with her soft white arm. Pokey went on staring down at the bodies and presently added, "Clothes funny too."

"What? She's in a long red . . . bathrobe, I'd call it. And Randy's wearing what most of the kids in town have on today, cutoffs, some old T-shirt, ratty sneakers. What's funny about any of that?"

"She got nightgown on under robe. No panties. Dressed for bed. He's in daytime clothes."

"Seventeen-year-old boys usually stay up later than their moms. He probably—" I looked up from note-taking suddenly, distracted by a big new sedan honking on the bridge. It parked in front of Pokey's Jeep, legally, headed the other way, and two people got out. One was a small young man in nondescript clothing. I gave him scant attention because the other person on the sidewalk was Trudy Hanson, BCA's expert photographer and fingerprint technician. Seeing her no-nonsense yellow braid dangling down her back, I felt my heart pump faster, sending blood to all the parts of my body that had just demanded resupply.

I met her last May during a difficult and scary murder case. She was so good at her job and so totally professional in her demeanor that it took me a while to diagnose my onset of rapid breathing. She was not a woman to be understood in one afternoon; her CD collection included Ornette Coleman, Flatt & Scruggs, and Yo-Yo Ma. She was fun to be around, because she never struck a pose; she climbed rocks or made fudge brownies with the same intense absorption she brought to her work. I had seen her tuck a bag of crocheting into the duffel she was taking on a white-water rafting trip.

I began longing to touch her almost as soon as I saw her, but was at pains to figure out an approach that wouldn't seem presumptuous. She responded generously to my plea for help with some camera work, and then one lucky night a mutual passion for dancing carried us along to lovemaking. We had shared a few blissful weekends since then, but I was still making very careful moves. She seemed to like her space. I was hoping to show her I could add pleasure to her life without foreclosing any options.

Mindful of working decorum, I gave her a sedate wave and climbed the riverbank at a sensible pace. By the time I reached the sidewalk, she was halfway into the interior of the car, sorting through the equipment heaped in the spacious backseat. It occurred to me to tell her that her jeans gave new meaning to the phrase "properly fitted," but there were people all around, so I just said, "Hey, great car. Where's the van?"

"Right behind us," she said, backing out. "Ted Zumwalt, this is Jake Hines." He was little and wiry, with round wire-rimmed glasses on a baby face and blunt-fingered hands a little outsize for the rest of him. "Ted's our new sketch artist."

"No kidding," I said, "you're going to draw pictures of this mess?"

"Yes, I am." He had a nasal twang and a wry way of speaking, like a country judge twice his age. "I will make quite a number of drawings, with precise measurements and many notes." He used his odd vocal mannerisms to create an impermeable shield of humorous irony, behind which he sheltered.

"And the next time you come up, Jake," Trudy said, raising my respiration rate another notch, "I'll show you the new computer software that translates Ted's pictures into three-dimensional drawings."

"Wow," I said, "too cool." I didn't care if he turned his pictures into balloons and flew away in them. In fact I wanted him to do just that, right now.

"So—you brought two vehicles so Ted could have a seat?" I asked her.

"Oh, Ted's the least of our problems," Trudy said. When Ted winced, she laughed and said, "Well, sorry, Ted, I didn't mean it that way—" She waved at the back-seat. "Look at the gear in this car! We're carrying a video camera now, as well as all the thirty-five millimeter stuff I had before. Plus all the exterior fingerprint equipment"— she squinted down toward the riverbank—"guess we don't have any use for that today, huh? And Ted's got all his sketching tools, and an easel—"

"This is your bigger, better BCA crew," Ted intoned, "and we've got the hernias to prove it."

I stuck my head inside the car door beside Trudy, brushing against her discreetly, and said, "Help you with any of that?"

She smiled her big toothpaste-ad smile and said, "Oh, thanks. Just grab these bags right here, will you?"

"What is this vile crime, anyway?" Ted asked, opening the trunk and pulling out his own stuff. "Couple of drowning victims? Why are you calling it homicide? Drowning's almost always accidental," he told me, doing the kindly sage to perfection.

"They're tied together."

"Don't see what that proves," he said, wrestling with his easel.

"You ID'd the victims yet?" Trudy asked.

"I know them."

Trudy looked up in consternation and said, "Oh, hey—"

I shook my head. "We weren't really friends. I worked with the mother for a while, years ago. But earlier this week her bar got robbed, so I've talked to both of them in the last couple of days. Maybe it's just a coincidence, but it feels kind of weird."

"I should think so," she said. We started down, skirting past Halvorson and his crowd of curiosity seekers. The extra weight made it hard to stay upright on the steep slope, and the sun beat down on us out of a cloudless sky. We concentrated on maintaining a controlled slide while staying erect and hanging on to our burdens, which quickly grew slippery with sweat. All three of us were red-faced and panting by the time we reached the sandbar.

"Hey, Trudy," Pokey said, getting up, grinning all over his foxy face. He shook her hand about twice as long as necessary. Trudy turns his crank big-time.

"Ted Zumwalt, Dr. Adrian Pokornoskovic," she said, getting the whole mouthful right. "Everybody calls him Pokey, but trust me, he is not slow." Pokey looked as if he might be going to roll over and wag his tail. His long-standing turf issues with the Bureau of Criminal Apprehension are set aside when he's dealing with Trudy Hanson, whom he once described to me as "Cat's pajamas, that girl, totally rad."

Ted walked over now to the bodies on the sand. "Wow," he said, "I see what you mean. These two are really all tied up together. Wow. Tied up good."

"We've tentatively ruled out suicide," I said, waggling my eyebrows at Trudy. She ducked her head to hide a grin and began pulling cameras out of bags. She made a sand-free beachhead out of containers and pulled film and filters out of the labeled compartments that keep everything straight for her. One of the many pleasures of watching Trudy Hanson work is the serene mastery she maintains over the tools of her trade.

Alternating 35 mm color slides with video, she did distance shots first. When she was ready to shorten the focus, Pokey began to follow her around the disordered bundle, asking for close-ups of Babe's head and chest and helping her get good pictures of the hands. Ted, meantime, had set up his easel and was making quick outline sketches, placing the bodies in their surroundings and noting distances and elevations. Then he, too, moved closer, making detail drawings of hands and feet and several pictures of the knots in the rope that held the bodies together. He worked his tape measure as hard as his pencil, and his pictures had the quality of architectural drawings, very precise, with all the dimensions noted.

Another horn sounded in the street above, and I climbed back up to meet the BCA van. It paused by the squad cars, while the front-seat passenger rolled down his window and leaned out to speak to Halvorson. He was evidently negotiating for a parking spot, because Halvorson left his crowd of sightseers long enough to move his squad car down the street. The BCA van took two tries to jockey into the tight space, and Jimmy Chang got out on the passenger's side, looking at his watch.

Time is never long enough for Jimmy Chang. He's a tense Chinese-Hawaiian workaholic locked into a horrendous schedule that combines state lab work with study and teaching at the university. I'm waiting to see if he finishes his Ph.D. in forensic pathology before he flames out.

"You made good time," I said.

"Yes, well, this woman," Jimmy said, nodding at his driver, "should be wearing a cape and a big red S. She leaps whole suburbs at a single bound. Jake Hines, Megan Duffy." Megan was an athletic-looking brown-haired girl, wearing a Toronto Blue Jays T-shirt and a reversed baseball cap. She laughed, showing a full set of braces on her teeth, and shook my hand, saying, "This guy's a regular fussbudget on the highway." Underneath the needling they seemed to be hitting it off; Jimmy looked marginally less tense than usual.

Megan opened the big rear door of the van, revealing a densely packed interior that was saved from chaos by scrupulous organization. Jimmy climbed in and began pulling gear out of drawers and cupboards, once consulting an alphabetical list of contents that was stapled inside a door. Megan followed him in and began to disappear under the heap of parcels he hung over her shoulders and heaped in her arms.

"Let me help," I said again, more reluctantly this time. They loaded me up, and we repeated the sweaty, slidy trip downhill. At the bottom, Jimmy set his bags carefully in a patch of grass, pulled a plastic sheet out of a bag, and spread it carefully on the sand under the aspens. "Put it all down here," he told Megan and me. "Be careful not to get any sand on the sheet."

We leaned painfully far out over the black plastic sheet

to avoid stepping on it while we dropped our burdens in the middle. Jimmy went and got his own bags off the grass and added them to the pile. He fussed over the possibility of a breeze, decided in spite of a dead calm to add a cover sheet, and tucked the edges in all around. When he was finally satisfied, he pulled on a lab coat and gloves and said, "Okay, Jake, show us what you've got."

We walked over to where Pokey, Trudy, and Ted were bent over the intertwined bodies. Pokey gave Jimmy a perfunctory greeting and asked, "What's all this about taking bodies to Cities for autopsy? Who says?"

"It was a board decision," Jimmy said. "They feel if we're going to take the responsibility for the information that ultimately goes to court, we have to control the entire process."

"Oh yeah?" Pokey said. "What about our control? Who covers my backside when I sign death certificate fulla information I can't verify?"

"We do," Jimmy said. "Don't worry about it."

"Like hell!" Pokey said. "Is my job to worry about it!"

Jimmy said, exasperated, "Well, it's my job to do only preliminary tests here and then take these two bodies to St. Paul. You're welcome to ride along if you want to take part in the autopsy. But I'm on a very tight schedule"—the watch came out again—"so please, Pokey, I'd appreciate if you'd just let me get on with it."

He turned to Megan and began a rapid-fire dialogue full of Latin words and blizzards of initials. In response, she trotted over to their cache of supplies and brought him several pieces of equipment, then picked out a kit for herself and began taking samples of sand, river water, and slime she scraped carefully off underwater stones. Jimmy, meanwhile, began to repeat all the temperature, muscle tone, and lividity examinations that Pokey had just finished.

"You got your phone?" Pokey asked me. I dug it out of my briefcase, and he punched out a number impatiently, walking away from us to stand in the shadow of the bridge. I heard his conversation start on a reasonable note and spiral quickly into a higher register. After a few minutes he punched the end button and slapped the cap shut as viciously as he could.

He came walking stiffly back to the group just as Jimmy looked up from the bodies and asked, "How many weeks did you say these two have been missing?"

"They were never reported missing," I said, "and I saw them both myself two days ago."

"Oh. Thought you said they were floating."

"They were."

"Couldn't have been," Jimmy said. "No way, Jake. Drowned people sink right to the bottom. They don't float for days, sometimes weeks."

"Jimmy, I stood right here and saw Eldon Huckstadt pull them out of the river."

"Well, they may have been in the river, but they couldn't have been floating. Until a lot of decomposition takes place and gas forms, drowning victims stay submerged."

"Speeds up in hot weather," Pokey said.

"Not that much," Jimmy said. "They'd never float in just a day or two."

"Hold on," I said, and went up the bank one more hot and sweaty time. I found Huckstadt on the sidewalk talking to a sixtyish woman in laced oxfords and a hair net. "We're all gonna wind up murdered in our beds here, I think," she said, "if the law don't clear these foreigners out of our town."

I stayed three steps away and said, "Can I see you, Officer Huckstadt?" He said, "Excuse me, ma'am," tipped his hat to the woman, and came over. "Thanks," he muttered.

"Need your help down here," I said. We moved together down the slope, which I was beginning to regard as my punishment for any bad behavior I ever got away with.

At the sandbar I said, "Jimmy, this is Eldon Huckstadt. He and Ray Halvorson pulled the victims out of the river." I asked Huckstadt, "How deep is the water here? When you snagged those bodies to pull them out, were they floating?"

"Sure. Well . . . not exactly. We had to drag them across the stones and gravel. The river's way low right now."

"Any idea how deep?"

"Maybe a couple feet in the deepest pools. Less than that in most places."

"So the bodies weren't moving at all, huh? Just stuck out there on the stones?"

"Not exactly. This is the fastest part of the river, remember, right here where it comes down off the hill. When I first saw it . . . them, I mean—" He shrugged apologetically and told Jimmy, "See, I thought it was just one big bundle of . . . something . . ." His eyes flicked over the bodies on the sand, and he shook his head. "It was moving, just a little, from time to time, getting bumped along through the rapids out there in the middle."

"Can you say for certain if you ever saw it float?" Jimmy asked him.

"Well. I don't know if I'd say float, exactly. More like rolling around, tumbling a little. It sure as hell moved. For sure. Because the person that phoned the station reported it right under the bridge. I found it downstream a couple of yards when I got here ten minutes later, and by the time Halvorson brought the towline, it had moved down here almost to the sandbar. It would stay in one place awhile, and then the water would tug it loose from whatever it was snagged on and move it a few inches farther."

"What color was it, mostly?" Pokey asked.

"Red. Isn't it still red? Oh. I see what you mean, his clothes are mostly blue, aren't they? Hmm. Well, in the water it looked like it was all red."

"Ah-hah," Pokey said. "Because she was on top. Floating. The woman was ready to float. Dead about eighteen to twenty-four hours, on land, before she went in the water. Betcha anything. And she's not gonna have any water in her lungs."

"That doesn't prove much," Jimmy said. "Lots of drowning victims have very little water in their lungs. What are you suggesting?"

"She didn't drown. He's gonna have weeds, dirt, all kinds of junk in his lungs, and hers are gonna be clean."

"Yes, well, maybe so and maybe not," Jimmy said primly. "Let's just wait till the tests are done before we go leaping to any conclusions, okay?"

"Wanna bet me?"

Jimmy gave an impatient little shrug, and I saw him open his mouth, getting ready to blow off Pokey's improbable sporting proposition. Then a curious thing happened. His glance traveled across Pokey's right shoulder to where Megan Duffy stood watching him, wearing an expression of amused curiosity. A feisty little spark appeared in Jimmy's dark eyes. He squared his shoulders, turned back to Pokey, and smiled. "Ten bucks okay?"

Ted had just agreed to hold the money when the county attorney's slate-blue Mercedes crossed the bridge, paused by the long line of vehicles, and went on down the street to park. I climbed back up the incline and walked along to his car to greet him. My motive was not unselfish, nor was I sucking up, exactly. Pearce, I knew, needed enough information to face the press, a part of his duties at which he excels. But from past experience I also knew he has a tendency to melt down at horrid scenes. I once saw the chief insert his big body between a gagging county attorney and a camera, and answer searching questions in a loud, confident voice until Pearce got his cool back. I thought maybe this morning I could do us both a favor by feeding Pearce the salient facts at street level and sending him on his way.

Doris was with him. They were plainly on their way to work, a power couple in perfectly fitted suits. A stranger might have wondered how Ed Pearce, on a Hampstead County salary, afforded Italian suits, Hermes ties, and a cream-puff car. In the department, we all knew Ed's wife operated the biggest travel agency in Rutherford, and Milo wasn't the only one who'd noticed that she liked to keep her mate in the limelight, looking his best.

"Morning," I said, leaning in the driver's-side window. "The chief call you?"

"Just now," Ed said, putting his hand on the door handle but not getting out. "Drowning victims, Frank said, but he seemed to think you were going to treat it as a homicide. How come?"

"They're tied together. Bound with several knots."

"Huh," he said. He tapped his fingers on the steering wheel thoughtfully. "Son of a gun. Hard to prove, homicide drowning. Don't think I've ever seen one prosecuted in Minnesota." He swung his perfectly creased legs out onto the sidewalk and got out, taking his time about straightening his jacket and smoothing his hair.

"Pokey's here," I said, "and a whole crew from BCA in St. Paul. And everybody who's looked at them so far agrees that they couldn't have tied themselves up that way."

He was ready to take the names of the victims and go on. I saw him reach for his notebook and gold pen, but then Doris leaned across the seat and said, "Well, hon, go ahead and have a look if you want to, I can wait." She gave him a loving, open-eyed look, sitting there handsome and perfectly groomed in her soft gray suit, and somehow the look moved him away from the car and along the sidewalk toward the river. Talking with Pearce, you felt you had to check every few seconds to see that you still had his attention; he was always darting little quick glances at the people around him, and would break off conversations in midsentence to greet a constituent. "Who are these victims, Jake?" he asked me. "They local folks?"

"Babe Krueger. Owner of Rowdy's Bar?"

"Hell you say." He stopped and blinked at me a couple of times. "No kidding. Really, Babe? Helluva note. I used to know Babe fairly well at one time." His handsome features took on the fatuous expression of the sexual scorekeeper. "Didn't that bar just get robbed?"

"Two days ago."

"Any connection, you think?"

"Don't see how." We reached the bank and began to climb down.

"Wow, some workout here, huh?" Ed said, slipping a little.

"Kinda steep," I said. The backs of my legs were begging for mercy. "Watch your shoes there, it's a little muddy." He picked his way across the damp gravel to the group already gathered by the water. His immaculate person looked ridiculously out of place above the muddy bundle of bodies and the sweat-streaked crew working over them. I introduced him around. He said, "Sure glad to have your help," to Jimmy, and "Nice to see you again, Doctor," to Pokey, and he took his time with the ladies, repeating their full names and making eye contact. By staying very involved with the crew, he managed to give only darting glances to the bodies. "See what you mean about the way they're tied," he said. "Who's the second person?"

"Her son. Randy Thorson."

"Be darned. Didn't even know she—" He decided to let that go. He asked Jimmy Chang, "Well, now how does this work when we call you people for help? Does this mean it's the state's case from now on?"

"We'll do all the forensic workup," Jimmy said. "But of course it's still yours to try in court."

We all looked up then because Doris was coming down the hill, slipping sideways anxiously on her high heels. "Ed?" she called out as she came down, her eyes searching for him in the group. "Listen, darling, I think you'd better get up here, the TV news truck just arrived, and they're getting out the cameras and mikes and everything. I asked them, and they said they're going to do a remote from right up there. They want—" She arrived, breathless and a little hot, at the sandbar where we clustered. The sheet had been pulled off the bodies while the crews did their work, and before any of us thought to block her line of sight, she got a good look. Babe was lying on top, with her poor ruined face turned up to the blazing sun, her hair spiking out from her head in stiffening strands, and flies gathering ravenously at her gaping wounds. I moved as quickly as I could toward the sheet, but I was too late. Doris Pearce made a horrified choking sound and fainted.

You don't often see a person collapse from a standing position. It happens in Victorian novels and I suppose in hospitals, but rarely in ordinary street life. One moment she was coming toward us, talking fast, a tall, chic woman any man would notice and admire and then probably decide was out of his price range. Then she made that strangled noise, there was a soft thump, and she was lying crumpled and helpless on the sand.

She surprised us all so totally that for a heartbeat we froze. If Trudy had been ready, she could have photographed a remarkable tableau of eight figures standing openmouthed around three prone bodies, two very messy and one well dressed.

Pokey came to life first. He grabbed a little bottle from his bag, opened it while he ran to Doris's side, stooped, and held it under her nose. Megan found a jacket, rolled it up, and stuffed it under her head. Ed came over and knelt by her, rubbing her hands and murmuring little soft baby-talk words that I had never imagined he would know.

She opened her eyes after a few seconds, blinked a couple of times, and immediately tried to sit up. Pokey said, "Lie still a minute," and Ed said, "Yes, be quiet, Dodie. Poor baby. You just stay right where you are for a minute, my poor sweetheart."

She turned her head toward her husband's voice. He stroked her hair, talking to her softly like a mother tucking a child in bed. He rubbed her hands and babbled soothing nonsense about how sorry he was, he'd never have let this happen in a million years if he'd only thought, and he wanted her to take her time now, just take all the time she needed to feel better before she tried to get up. What he said was unimportant; the point was that the hunky, egotistical career politician crouched in the wet sand without a thought for his beautifully clad knees and talked his wife out of a panic. It was a bravura performance. I saw a side of him I would never have guessed existed.

It worked for Doris; she lay trusting and quiet under his hands, and in a couple of minutes I saw her eyes grow thoughtful and clear. When her color came back and she said she was ready, Ed helped her to her feet and began brushing her off. We had the victims covered by then, and we all stood between her and the heap of bodies. So her gaze traveled calmly across all of us and up the hill. And what she saw there was a TV crew getting ready to haul a big camera down. The sight restored her to her old self at once.

"Never mind now, I'll fix myself," she told her husband, pulling on her skirt. "You better go talk to that TV reporter." He fussed over her a moment longer, but she gave him a little push and said, "Go *on*. I'm fine. The officer will help me, won't you?" She turned her compelling smile on Huckstadt, who moved to her side at once. Her husband sprinted obediently a couple of jumps uphill, turned, found me with his eyes, and said, "Come up here and help me, will you, Jake? I'm pretty fuzzy on the details."

He picked my brains expertly while we climbed toward the TV truck, and went on asking questions while Greg Prentiss posed him in front of the Second Avenue bridge, with the government center for a backdrop. At the last minute he got concerned about the sand on his knees, but Greg assured him they'd stick to a head-and-chest shot. So I checked his hair and tie while Greg consulted light meters, and then I stood out of camera range but near enough to feed him some facts if he needed them. He never did. He gave a lucid, beautifully modulated performance, expressing concern for the victims and assuring his listeners of the law enforcement community's mighty reach. Ed Pearce confronted a TV camera as a sunflower faces the sun, knowing instinctively where to turn.

The hearse arrived as we were winding up, and the cameraman turned his equipment to get ready for a long shot of the body bag coming uphill on a stretcher. It was a hard climb for four men. Huckstadt had put Doris Pearce into her car just in time to get dragooned onto the low end of the stretcher, and I could see he was getting just as sick of this hill as I was.

I saw Trudy packing up below, so I hustled down again, hoping to grab a minute alone with her. Before I reached her, my pager sounded again.

Damn! I couldn't remember if Pokey had given me back my phone. I found my briefcase buried in the junk heap of paraphernalia we had created by the river, with the phone on the strip of Velcro where it belonged. I pulled it out and punched the #1 button for the station.

"Hold on for the chief," Sally said. There was a little clatter and then soupy Muzak as she put me on hold. I saw Trudy start up toward her car and made a time-out signal with my hands, but she just waved cheerily and went on. Then the music broke off in mid-whine, and Frank's voice said, "McCafferty."

"Chief," I said, "I just remembered we had an appointment this morning, but I'm still here at the river where we found—"

"I know all about that," he said. "I wasn't expecting you. I just wanted to tell you something."

"Please," I said, "make it good news."

"Well, in a way it is," he said, "but it's damned odd. Two young fellas came in here a few minutes ago and confessed to robbing Rowdy's Bar."

·SEVEN·

THEY WERE SITTING SIDE BY SIDE AGAINST THE WALL IN THE
holding cell, a scared-looking blond kid, staring at his
feet, and the handsome dreadlocked dope smoker I had
seen playing pool with Randy Thorson. There were two
other prisoners in the receiving tank with them. One was
an elderly drunk talking to himself. The other was a fat
man with many tattoos and a full gray beard, stretched
full-length on the floor, passed out or sleeping.

"I've seen the black one before," I told Bo Dooley, "in
Rowdy's Bar."

"I've seen him too," he said. "That's Farah Tur."

"Oh, yeah? One of the guys you saw by the Cherokee?
On the day of the high-speed chase?"

"Bingo." Dooley was staring happily at the self-possessed young man.

"You know the other one?"

"Seems vaguely familiar."

"His name is Scott Rouse," I said. "I talked to him on

the phone once. He's the friend Randy Thorson was supposed to be fishing with, the day the bar got robbed."

"Now he says he's the robber? What a pal."

"Did anybody talk to them about the drownings yet, do you know?"

"No. The chief said we didn't know all the details ourselves yet, so shut up about it and just book 'em for the crime they were copping to. I was just getting ready to interview them when you got here."

"Good. One thing I want to be sure of: They're both over eighteen? You know for sure?"

"Yeah. The blond one's got a driver's license, and the other guy carries a green card."

"Okay. Let's see about getting them separated, then. I want these two as far apart as possible," I told the sergeant at the desk. "What have we got available?" Hampstead County runs the adult detention center in Rutherford. The sheriff's deputies give us great cooperation, but we have to ask for what we want. Politely.

"No sweat," the sergeant said. "Slow day, I've got openings." He punched up a rooming chart.

"Put Farah Tur in the most isolated one."

"This end one here okay?"

"Super. We're gonna take Scott Rouse to an interview room right now, but when we bring him back, will you put him as far away from Farah as you can? I don't want them to be able to talk to each other."

"You got it, Jake."

"I'd like to be in on Farah Tur's interview, okay?" Dooley said.

"Absolutely. You and I will do both interviews. I'll question Scott while you run the recorder and take notes, and then we'll switch for Farah." I handed him the tape recorder and an extra roll of tape. "But hang on a minute," I said, "I gotta make a couple of calls."

I called the dispatch desk and asked Sally to find Maddox and ask him to call me. Then I got Kevin Evjan on the phone and told him to look up Babe Krueger's home address and send a marked squad to secure the place. "Then get a search warrant," I said, "and go there. Call me when you're inside."

"Inside how? You got a key?"

"No. Try a credit card. Take along a pry bar and a glass cutter in case it doesn't work." We went back to the holding cell, where a deputy unlocked the door and stood by.

"Scott Rouse?"

"Yeah?" he said. He got up and came to the gate.

"You come along with us," I said.

"Am I gettin' out?" he asked. "Did my dad bring my bail?"

"It's a little soon for that," I said. "We're going to ask you some questions in another room."

Farah Tur said, without getting up, "I am not comfortable here. Please call Mrs. Glover at the United Methodist Church and tell her that I am here and that this place is not acceptable." He had a very precise accent, Brit schoolboy overlaid with African lilt. He was admirably composed, sitting erect against the wall with his long, graceful hands holding each other lightly in his lap.

"Stay cool, Farah. We'll get to you soon," Bo said, smiling at him the way a hungry man smiles at a steak.

We walked Scott Rouse around the corner, found an empty cubicle, and told him to sit. Bo and I brought two chairs to the other side of the table and got the recorder ready. Scott watched us nervously. Bo punched a button to start the tape rolling and said into the hand mike, "Interview with Scott Rouse, ten-thirty hours, Thursday, August 23—" When he was ready, he adjusted the little legs so the mike would stand between us, and wrote the date and time on the top of a lined tablet. He hit the mike button again and said, "Present at the interview are Lieu-tenant Jake Hines and Sergeant Bo Dooley." He looked at me.

"So, Scott, how much did you get?" I asked.

"What?"

"Money. How much money did you get when you robbed the bar?"

"Um . . . close to twelve thousand." He blinked a couple of times, staring at the wall behind Bo's head. He was very pale, with a light glisten of sweat on his upper lip. "I don't remember the exact figure."

"Lotta money. You bring it in with you?"

"Uh, no. I don't . . . I didn't get my share yet."

"Who's got it?"

"Farah had it. But then . . ." His attention wandered away for a few seconds and came slowly back. "He gave it to somebody else to look after, and now I don't . . ." He concentrated on the table awhile. "I don't exactly know where it is."

"Jeez, Scott. You want money bad enough to steal it, seems like you'd hang on to it."

"It's safe." He was traumatized, I thought. He had trouble following my questions, and his answers sounded detached and hollow. "Farah has it."

My phone rang. I said, "Hang on a second." Bo punched the recorder off. I stepped out of the cubicle and answered. Maddox said, "I'm at Rowdy's Bar."

"Is it open?"

"The door's open, but the cook says they haven't seen Babe since the day before yesterday. Right after she talked to you here? She went home to rest, he says, and she hasn't been back. Randy closed the bar Tuesday night and came in yesterday morning to open. But then he said he had to see some people, and he's never come back. The bartender didn't show up today either, and Jack says he hasn't got any money to work with, so he's thinking maybe he should close."

"Better tell him what's happened, Clint."

"Which is what?"

"Oh, sorry. You've been out on foot patrol, haven't you? We fished Babe and Randy out of the river this morning."

"Aw, shit. You mean they're dead?"

"Yes. Better tell Jack to lock up. And then bring him in to the station. Deposit the bar keys in the evidence room. Then call me, or one of the other detectives, Lou French or Darrell Betts. Somebody should take his statement."

"I'm kind of concerned about the dishwasher," Maddox said. "That Dozey? Guy's not really dealing from a full deck, and he's confused."

"Bring him along too, if he'll come. Maybe we can get him together with Victim's Services. He's probably going to need some help."

"Right," he said. "You be there awhile?"

"Probably, but if you can't find me, get one of the other detectives to take their statements, will you?"

"Sure. Soon as you have some time, I'd sure like to talk to you about the pawnshop."

"What pawnshop?"

"The one up here on Eleventh, Kwik Kash."

"Oh, yeah. I'll get to it as soon as I can, Clint."

I went back inside the cubicle, said, "Sorry," and nodded to Bo, who started the tape rolling. "What made you decide to come forward?" I asked Scott.

"Oh . . . Farah's mom. She found out, and she got really mad. She said we had to come in and tell. She's real religious," he said, looking at us earnestly.

"Mmm. How'd she find out?"

"Oh, Farah's stupid little brother tells everything."

"And Farah tells everything to his little brother?"

"No. But this time . . . he was waiting outside, so he knew."

"You mean you left him in the street for a lookout?"

He twisted in his seat. "Somethin' like that, I guess."

"How did you get in?"

"In . . . oh, you mean the bar?"

"Pay attention, Scott. Of course the bar. How did you gain access to the bar?"

"Randy gave us the keys."

"Oh, he did? So Randy was in on this too?"

"Well . . . sure. I mean, this one was *all* his idea."

"This one?" When he realized what he had said, he flushed pink, and his eyes watered.

"I didn't mean that like it sounded."

"Some of the other jobs, you and Farah planned those, huh? Tom's Liquor Store, for instance, was that one your idea, Scott?"

"I don't know what you're talking about," he said, bunching up smaller in his chair. "All's I know anything about is Rowdy's Bar."

"When did Randy give you the keys?"

"Well . . . um. Sunday night. Yeah, right, Sunday night, the night we got the money."

"You got the money Sunday night?"

"Sure. Had to. Randy said his mom would take it to the bank on Monday. So we got keys from him and waited till after he closed—"

"Wait, now. I want to be sure I understand. Randy gave you *his* keys, the key ring that he got from his mother to run the bar with. That right?"

"No, no. He had to take those keys home to his mom. The keys he gave us were copies."

"Randy had copies made Sunday night?"

"I guess. Or he mighta had 'em made earlier. Anyway he had 'em for us Sunday by seven o'clock."

"Where'd he have 'em made?"

He shrugged. "Here in town, I guess."

"I mean, which shop?"

"Oh . . . I dunno."

"So you got the keys and waited around till, what? Two, three o'clock?"

"We went home first. And went to bed. So our families would know we were in bed. Then when everybody else was asleep we, uh, we snuck out and came back downtown."

"What time was that?"

"Musta been close to three."

"Where'd you meet?"

"Oh, uh, in the alley behind the pawnshop."

"You were walking, driving?"

"Riding our bikes."

"Okay. Then you went to Rowdy's, used the keys Randy gave you—"

"Yeah."

"Entered by the front door, back door—"

"Front."

"And went to the cash registers—"

"No, no. Downstairs. The office is in the basement."

"Were the lights on or off?"

"Upstairs they were off. But they were on downstairs. When we got to the office, Randy's mom was there, working with the money. So we had to tape her up. We never meant to do that," he added apologetically.

"Why didn't she recognize you? She's seen you, hasn't she?"

"Sure. Plenty of times. But we had masks on."

"How come?"

He shrugged. "Farah thinks it's a good idea," he said.

"That right? What kind of masks does Farah think it's a good idea to wear?"

"Oh . . . you know. Um, nylons—"

"Stockings? Women's stockings?"

"Yeah. You pull a pair of panty hose over your head. It flattens your face so nobody can tell what you look like."

"You had all that along with you? And the tape?"

"Yeah."

"How come you had the tape?"

"Huh?"

"How did it happen that you were carrying that big roll of duct tape?"

"Farah always carries one." I sat and stared at him a minute, and he added nervously, "He says it comes in handy."

"For all his burglary jobs, you mean? Like when the two of you go in and clean out an apartment at Kiowa Towers, for example?"

"No! I never said that!" He looked appealingly at Bo, who gave him a nasty smile. "Listen, I came in here *voluntarily*," he said, trying for indignation. "It seems to me I should get some consideration for that—"

"Uh-huh." I got up. "You just sit tight a minute there, Scott. We have to see about something, and we'll be right back." Bo put the tape on hold. I stopped at the desk and asked the dispatcher to keep his eye on the prisoner in the cubicle. "Let's get a cup of coffee," I said, and Bo and I walked down the hall to the break room.

"Not the sharpest knife in the drawer, huh?" Bo said.

"Couple of things he said are very puzzling."

"For instance?"

"Well, he's way short on the money. The deposit tickets for that weekend come to over twenty-eight thousand dollars, and they got all the change from three cash drawers besides."

"Farah's probably holding out on him."

"Possibly. But then his description of the masks is all

wrong. Babe said they were wearing ski masks, balaclavas."

"She was getting taped up, she might have made a mistake."

"Babe Krueger would know panty hose if she saw them. But the oddest thing is that he says they robbed the bar Sunday night, and I know that isn't right. Babe told me how she always went in on Monday to write up the deposits, and that's when they found her and taped her up, early afternoon Monday."

"Why would he lie about the time?"

"No idea. But why would she? More to the point, why would Babe get up in the middle of the night, on her one night off, and go down to her place to write up bank deposits? After she already paid Randy to close up the bar for her?"

"No reason. I just don't see any reason why he'd change the time. Anyway"—Bo finished his coffee and scraped his chair back—"you ready to go back and tackle him on the murders?"

"No. Let's see what we think of Farah Tur first."

Bo snorted. "I already know what I think of him."

"Put that aside, will you? Drug charges can come later. Right now I think you and I should review the tape of Scott's interview together. Then we'll get Farah at the table, you ask the same questions we asked Scott, and we'll see if their stories match."

My pager sounded. I called the department and got a patch-through from Kevin Evjan. "I'm in Babe Krueger's house," he said. "The door was unlocked, the keys were in the middle of the kitchen table. In the middle of the worst—this is a helluva mess, Jake, totally trashed, and there's blood all over the place."

"Shit," I said. "I should have thought to check it before the BCA crew left."

"Well," he said. He was working for me now. He didn't want to hear about my mistakes.

"Tell you what," I said. "Lock it up. Who've you got there for security?"

"Stearns."

"Fine. Post him on the front door and start talking to the neighbors. I'll be there as soon as I can." I hung up and told Bo, "Will you go ahead and start the prisoner exchange? Put Scott back in his cell and bring Farah Tur to the interview room. I have to make a couple of phone calls, and then I'll be there." I watched the energized way he moved toward the door and said, "Don't start with him, huh? Till I get there."

"Oh, right," he said.

Lulu answered in the chief's office and said, "He's just walking out."

"Catch him! Can you?" For once, she didn't argue. I heard her in the hall, and then heavy footsteps came back and the chief said, "McCafferty."

"Chief, I sent Kevin to check Babe's house. He just called me, and he says it's a mess and there's a lot of blood. Sounds like I might need to call BCA back. You got any objection to that?"

"No," he said. "Get 'em if you need 'em. Uh . . . you been to the house yet?"

"No. Gonna go as soon as I can get clear here."

"Of what?"

"I'm halfway through these interviews with the boys who claim they robbed the bar. But Bo can finish that for me. Seeing the house is more important."

"Uh . . . Maybe I'll go with you," Frank said.

"Don't you have a lunch?"

"It's no big deal," he said. "How soon you gonna be ready to go?" Frank loves being chief of police in the town he grew up in, but sometimes administration and booster luncheons get to seem a little tame to him. I could tell he was hearing the call of the wild.

"Ten minutes?"

"We'll take my car," he said. "I'll be outside the garage."

Pokey's secretary said he was with a patient. I gave her Babe's address and told her, "Tell him Jake Hines wants his opinion of a crime scene." When I hung up, I realized I could have just said I wanted his opinion; he'd come across town any day for that.

I called Rosie Doyle's number. "Can you break away from what you're doing to come over to the jail and help with an interview?"

"Absolutely," she said. She'd been sniffing down cold trails on old burglary cases all morning, so she was ready for a change of pace. I told her where we'd be, and walked down the hall to the interview room. Bo was seating Farah at the table.

"Have you called Mrs. Glover yet?" Farah demanded. "When is she coming?" It was only in jail that his take-charge manner seemed outrageous, I suddenly realized. Put this guy in a boardroom in a good suit, and we'd all be calling him a winner.

"Sure, Farah," Bo said. "We called the bishop too while we were at it." Farah turned his upper body slowly toward Bo and fixed him with a stony stare that said, Don't let me catch you alone on a sand dune, white boy.

"Farah, did they tell you when you were booked that you could have a phone call?" I asked him.

"Yes."

"Who'd you call?"

"My mother."

"Why'd you call her?"

His regal features projected exaggerated patience. "So she would know where I was."

"Have a seat," I said, and asked Bo, "Can I see you?" In the corridor I told him, "Remember he said that. He called his mother so she'd know where he was. Scott said they came in here to confess because Farah's mother insisted. Now, listen: I have to go with the chief to look at Babe's house. Will you go ahead and talk to him?"

"Sure." He tried to conceal his delight.

"Good. Ah, here's Rosie. I asked her to sit in on the interview." Bo barely nodded when Rosie gave him a cool hello. Bo wanted Farah to himself, and Rosie had apparently heard some department buzz about the Drug Czar. They're grown-ups, I decided, let them work it out.

"Rosie, I want you to run the tape recorder and take notes. Bo will ask the questions. Let's agree on a couple of things," I said. "Your primary task is to find out whether Farah tells substantially the same story as Scott about robbing Rowdy's Bar. I still don't want you to question him about the killings. First we need to decide if these two really did the robbery together, or why they'd confess to it if they didn't. So take as much time as you need, stop and consult notes whenever you have to, make sure you cover all the same points. How'd they get in, what time was it, what were they wearing, where'd they put the money."

"Right."

"As much as possible about the money, huh? What denominations, how many checks. I've got copies of the deposit slips, and we can compare. Ask him was it on the desk or in the safe, anything like that we can go back and ask Scott. Babe said they cleaned out her purse—see if you can get him to tell you that. Rosie, pay close attention to his voice, eyes, manner, try to decide if you think he's telling the truth."

"I understand."

"And listen, Bo, I know you want this guy for dealing crack, but unless he opens the door to that, just concen-

trate on the crime at hand, will you? Get this guy's statement, put him away, and have lunch, and when I get back,
we'll talk to both of them again and see how they look for
the murders."

"Gotcha."

Sometimes Bo's laconic answers make me want to stick
a firecracker up his ass, but I was grateful for them today
because I was out of time. I ran down the back stairs and
found the chief idling his motor at the top of the ramp. I
jumped into the front seat beside him, then grabbed the
door handle and said, "Oh, shit, I forgot to get the address."

"Sit still, I got it." He wheeled expertly into traffic.
Frank was my trainer when I came on the force, and he
nearly drove me bananas trying to make me as good a
driver as he was. I think I got close, because it was that or
throttle him with my bare hands, but there's a level of
quiet elegance to his car handling I never quite attained.

"I guess this is not gonna be a pretty crime scene,
Chief."

"Why, what did Kevin say?"

"Everything broken up, and a lot of blood."

"Well, you saw them at the river. What about it? Did
they look like they'd been in a big fight?"

"Babe had a lot of cuts on her arms and chest, and
Pokey kept saying he thought Babe was dead longer,
probably before she went in the water."

"But he thought the boy drowned?"

"That's what he thought. Jimmy didn't want to specu-
late. But that's Jimmy."

"What did you get from the two boys who robbed the
bar?"

"Just finished the first one. The white kid, Scott Rouse.
Bo's interviewing the Somali guy now. We want to see if
they tell the same story, first."

"You don't believe they'd work together?"

"Mostly I just don't figure either one of them for an attack of conscience. So I'd like to find out why they're in the police station copping to a felony."

"So would I." Frank hit the left-turn arrow just right, turned off South Broadway, and drove through a couple of blocks of bars and small businesses and into a modest residential district. "Damn surprising about the Rouse kid. I used to play ball with his old man. Always seemed like an okay guy. Whaddya think about Scott?"

"He's got the time wrong, for starters. He claims they robbed the bar Sunday night. Babe told me herself she was robbed while she was writing up deposits Monday afternoon. And he's way too low on the money."

"Like they stashed some, you think?"

"Maybe. But why confess at all?"

"Maybe they did something worse than robbery Sunday night, and they want an alibi for the same hours."

"Like killing Babe Krueger, you mean? Only we know they didn't, because I talked to her Tuesday."

"True. Well, so what'll we charge 'em with, overzealous confessing?"

I laughed. It felt wonderful. "Tough one to figure penalties for."

"Right," he said, "and we wouldn't use 'em often."

We stopped in front of a tan stucco bungalow with a honeysuckle hedge, where Stearns stood in front of the front door. He looked bored out of his skull, but to be fair he would have looked exactly the same way if six nubile maidens had been dancing naked on the lawn in front of his eyes. I asked Frank once, "When was the last time you remember Stearns showing any emotion?" I thought I was making a little joke, but Frank replied, promptly and soberly, "Late fall of 'seventy-eight," and then refused to discuss it any further.

Kevin Evjan was standing in the open doorway of the two-story house next door, talking to a woman wearing an extra-large T-shirt and polyester pants so tight they were turning her ankles blue. She looked animated, and seemed to be getting more so as she looked up into Kevin's bright blue eyes.

Waiting for him in front of Babe's house, I looked over the few scrawny begonias clinging to life in a dried-up flower bed by the step. Behind them, I could see through a half-window into a basement laundry, where a naked bulb hung over a mismatched washer and dryer. A steam iron stood upright on an ironing board with a badly scorched cover. Babe's rewards for a life of hard work did not appear to have been large.

Kevin came over with the key, saying as he led us through the door, "The neighbor says there was a big fight here the day before last."

"What time?"

"Late afternoon. She and her husband were watching the news on TV, she says, and even though he likes the sound turned high, they heard the fight."

"Yelling, you mean?" Frank asked.

"And swearing, and a lot of crashing around. Look here—" The little house had no foyer; the door opened directly into a chaotic living room. "Watch the lamp," Kevin said, moving in ahead of us. Just inside the door, fragments of a porcelain base lay on the shag carpet around a torn lampshade. We stepped over it to confront smashed pictures, two overturned chairs, and a TV set lying on its face.

"This is nothing," Kevin said. "Come in the kitchen. Everybody got gloves?" We pulled them on. "Favor the middle of the doorway," Kevin said, "there's bloodstains on the woodwork. Watch where you walk out here, blood on the floor too."

We stepped carefully through the doorway and hopped over bloodstains and broken crockery to stand in the few clean spots we could find. Blood speckled the porcelain-topped table, the broken plates and cups, and the overturned chairs. A great smear of blood crossed the porcelain stovetop and continued onto the tile counter, slid down the cupboard door under the counter, and ended in a sticky pool on the floor. One fine, graceful spray of blood arced across the ceiling, and a huge spatter pattern decorated the middle of the wall by the pantry. There was an almost perfect bloody handprint at the top edge of the spatters, and a smudge of blood just below it.

"Kevin," Frank said, "I think you better get back outside and talk to as many neighbors as you can find. We need to find out who heard this fight, whether they heard what it was about. See if anybody can say whether it was Babe and her son fighting. If there were other voices yelling that day, try to get them to describe them. I know it's tough," he answered Kevin's dubious look, "but people surprise you sometimes, what they can remember. And Jake . . . Jake?"

"Yes," I said.

"What's the matter, you sick?"

"No. I used to know this woman."

"Oh . . . well. You want off the case?"

"No. What were you going to say?"

"That you're right about BCA, we gotta get 'em back here. My phone's in the car, use that. Then let's see if we can find the knife."

I hopped carefully over islets of gore in the horrifying slaughterhouse that someone had made of Babe's modest kitchen, crossed the living room, which now appeared almost neat to me, and stood blinking on the front step. Marigolds and zinnias bloomed in neat rows along the front walk of the house across the street, and a speckled cat sat grooming itself on the railing of the white-painted porch behind the flowers. It was hard to fit the sun-drenched cat and flowers into the same universe with the horror behind the door. Three doors east, I saw Kevin holding his badge in his left hand while he knocked at a door with his right.

Pokey rattled into the space behind the chief's car, grabbed his bag, and came toward me, saying, "You gonna find a stiff every place you go today?"

"Haven't got a body for you here. This house belonged to the dead woman you examined at the river. I want you to see the kitchen." He opened his mouth, and I said softly, "I know it's not really your job, Pokey. But you saw how she was cut. I want you to look at this house and tell me if you think it happened here. Okay?"

He screwed up his foxy face and said, "Old Ukrainian asshole s'posed to do all the dirty work, huh?" I could see he was pleased.

I guided him through the rubble to a clean spot by the kitchen table. As soon as he was settled, I went back outside, called BCA, and persuaded the operator to put me through to Jimmy Chang in the morgue. Jimmy protested when I asked him to come back. He had hours of work right where he was, he said, and then a class. "Get your own guys to do the fingerprints, and get a techie from the clinic to take blood samples. Somebody from the department can run them up to me." But when I told him about the spatter pattern on the end wall he said, "Don't let anybody touch it, Jake. Don't even breathe on it! I'll be there as soon as I finish these autopsies."

"Bring Trudy," I said, "this kitchen could be her masterpiece."

In the house, Pokey stood silent on his bare spot, looking as busy and contented as a woman making jam. Every few minutes he turned a few degrees left.

Frank was prowling softly through cupboards and drawers. "Thought I might get lucky and find the knife," he said.

"I'll look around outside," I said. I walked out the kitchen door onto a small entrance patio, a few stones set in the dirt with a little overhang protecting it. A rake and a spade leaned against a trellis alongside a couple of garbage cans. I lifted the lids. One held two bags of foul-smelling days-old garbage. I replaced the top quickly, hoping I wouldn't have to go through that. The second can held only one trash bag, but it was filled with garbage so rancid and moldy it made me feel friendly toward the first two bags.

I put the second lid back and stared at the weedy grass of Babe's small, empty backyard. I decided to divide it into imaginary cornrows and walk them slowly, scanning to either side as I moved. I began at the cedar slats of the left-hand fence, paced across the patchy turf to the metal posts and woven wire on the right-hand side, made a quarter turn, took two steps, and made another quarter turn. I was three steps back on the second row when something flashed in the sun, off to my right.

I went and looked at it, then stuck my head into the kitchen and said, "Chief? Think I found it." Frank came out in the yard and walked across the grass where I led him.

"Chrissake," he said. "Right here in the middle of the yard? What was he thinking?"

"Nothing much, I guess."

"Not much of a knife," he said.

"Good enough for impulse killing, I guess." It was an old cheap butcher knife, the blade worn down from use, the wooden handle cracked along the rivets and chipped on the edge. A few hairs stuck to the smeared blade, and the handle was bloodstained.

I stared around the quiet neighborhood. "Kinda hard to believe, isn't it? This terrible fight went on with people all around, and we never got a call."

"People don't like to interfere. Well—" He started toward the kitchen door. "Depends on the lab now. Hope the blood's still good enough to test. No rain the last couple of days, that's lucky. Been some dew, though."

"It's probably okay," I said. "I'm going to get a marker tag out of Kevin's car. I'll just mark it and cover it with an evidence bag till the BCA crew gets here."

"Good. And say, that reminds me, we need to send Jessica's clothes back with them, too. You think you can get them to stop at the station?"

"I doubt it. Jimmy Chang will be ready to fly to St. Paul on a broom by the time he's done with this job. I'll send Kevin down to the station for them, and give them to him here."

"Okay. Listen, I better get back too. Wanna have lunch?"

"Sure." I marked the location of the knife and went looking for Kevin, who was still knocking on doors. I got the house key from him, picked his brains about his survey so far, and sent him downtown, saying, "Get some lunch. Then check Jessica's clothes out of the evidence room and bring them back here to Babe's house, and I'll meet you here in an hour." I went back inside, walked into the kitchen, and stood in front of Pokey. When I interrupted his line of sight, he said, "What?"

"We're gonna have lunch," I said. "Care to join us?" I watched him morph from an inscrutable Asiatic sphinx into a jolly East European skin doctor.

"Hey, yah," he said, "lookin' at all this gore makes big appetite, hah?" We picked our way carefully through the wreckage. I locked the house and told Stearns, "We should be back in an hour," and he nodded a quarter of an inch without taking his eyes off the lawn. Pokey followed Frank's car to one of the slick-menu places that line the highway east of town.

"Did Kevin get anything more from the neighbors?" Frank asked me after we'd ordered. Lunch should have been time out, but there was no chance we'd sit there not talking about the mess in Babe's house.

"Musta been quite a fight," I said. "They heard it four doors down on the left, and across the alley in back."

"Anybody recognize voices?"

"Oh, they're all firm about it; it was Babe and Randy."

"And nobody else?"

"Nope. They all heard Babe and Randy. Yelling and throwing things, they say. Helluva fight that went on and on. Nobody remembers hearing any other voice."

"Figures," Pokey said.

"Why?" Frank said.

"Everything so broken up. Blood all over the place. Whole house says big anger, terrible rage." Pokey smiled benignly. "Families do rage best of anybody."

"Also soccer lessons," I reminded him.

"And orthodontia," Frank said. He has five children. He munched thoughtfully on a bread stick. "Whaddya say?" he asked Pokey. "That kitchen match up with the bodies you saw at the river?"

"Perfect match for the woman. Broken dishes, chairs tipped over, lotsa blood. Just what you'd expect, cut up like she was."

"So deep, you mean, or what?"

"No." Pokey shook his head. "Big cuts is when somebody just wants to kill and get it over. One or two deep stab wounds and then throat cut. But this woman had random slashes all over, like from fight. . . . Probably got more cuts on her back, too, Jake, whaddya bet? I never could see that, they were tied together back to back and I had to leave 'em that way for big cheese from St. Paul."

Frank fixed his goggle-eyed blue stare on Pokey and left it there for ten seconds. He knew about the coroner's resentment of outside help from BCA, but he didn't want to hear about it. He appreciated Pokey's coming out cheerfully at all hours, and he had heard me praise the quirky doctor's intuitive leaps, but at the bottom of his commonsense soul he knew he could replace this man in a heartbeat. In a showdown, Frank would side with the pros from St. Paul and consider Pokey foolish for picking a fight he couldn't win. I sat and watched while Pokey absorbed that information, took a big drink of cold water, and went on with his remarkable life.

"She had defense wounds, too," he said, illustrating with a hand over his head, "just what you'd expect to see when somebody been attacked with knife. But her son—" He shook his head. "Kinda hard to say. Wounds mostly looked like they came from river. Big question is, why was he tied up to mama like that?"

"He didn't have defense wounds?"

"Maybe some scratches. Hard to tell because of scrapes from river. Sure wasn't cut up like mama, nothing to die from. Looked to me like he drowned."

"After he got tied to his mother or before?"

Pokey gave Frank a Mona Lisa smile. "Wouldn't I be rich doctor if I could tell you that?" he said.

· E I G H T ·

KEVIN WAS SITTING ON THE FRONT STEPS OF BABE'S HOUSE when I got back, holding a one-sided conversation with Al Stearns, who occasionally indicated consciousness by blinking into the sunlight like an old lizard. I sent Stearns to lunch and asked Kevin, "Wanna see the knife?"

"What, the knife that caused all this mess? Where'd you find it?"

"Right in the middle of the backyard."

"No shit?"

"Yup. Like the killer just stood in the back door and tossed it."

"Jeez. You gonna be able to tell that one in court with a straight face?"

"You're gonna help me. Come and look." We went out back to my marker and stared down at the unimpressive old kitchen implement.

"Shee. Doesn't even look very sharp," he said. "And the handle's cracked."

My beeper sounded. "Damn," I said. "I don't want to use the phone in the house before it's been dusted. I should have brought my car over here!"

"Use mine. Lessee, where is it?" We hopped together through the bloody kitchen and he found his briefcase in the front room. He fished out his phone, and I called the station.

"Hold on," Sally said, "I've got Clint Maddox on another line." For one terrible moment, I couldn't remember who Clint Maddox was. Then I remembered, and it seemed incredible that only two days had passed since I recommended him to Frank as a POP officer in section three.

"Jake," Maddox said, "how soon you think you'll be able to get up here to the North End so I can show you some stuff?"

I bit my lip. When I agreed, mostly to get Frank off my back, that assigning one man to a troubled neighborhood was a good idea, I never intended to volunteer my services as mentor to the operation. Now Maddox seemed to think I was his adviser, and I had not had time to demand that Frank get him reattached to a squad leader. The POP mission had seemed only marginally useful to me on Tuesday morning, and now, compared to the horrifying crime smeared all over Babe's house, it seemed even less urgent. I had touted Clint for this strange job, though, and it didn't seem fair to dump him till I arranged for other support. So I said, "What's happening?"

"Mostly, it's what's not," he said. "At the pawnshop, and that adult bookstore? They hardly do any business at all! And don't seem to care!"

"Um. Why is that our problem?"

"It's just so weird! Y'know, my brother owns Al's Smokes. That newsstand and tobacco store on South Broadway? He busts his hump every day, stays open all kinds of crazy hours in order to make it. These two stores up here, they open up any old time, close up again anytime they feel like it. Just put a note on the door and take off."

"Clint, it may not be your work ethic, but it's not illegal," I said.

"No, but it's a sign of something," Maddox said, "and at the pawnshop I think I know what it is."

"What?"

"I'm almost sure he's got another place. When he closes his store during business hours, he does the same thing every time."

"What's that?"

"Gets in his car, drives north to Fourteenth Avenue, and turns right."

"Well, hey," I said, "that sure does sound suspicious."

There was a little silence, and Maddox said, "Okay, forget it," and hung up. I stood holding the dead phone for a few seconds, first disbelieving and then so angry my chest hurt. He hung up on me! I didn't have time for horseshit like that! Now he'd be crying to Frank that he wasn't getting any cooperation in the department. My brain ran amok through idiot swearwords, damn shit fuck sonofabitch bastard. When the roaring in my head eased enough so I could think, I called the station. Sally answered, and I said, very calmly, "Page Maddox, will you?" It took several minutes to get him back on the line. I counted backward by ones from one hundred to keep from sliding back into outrage. When he answered, I said, too fast for him to interrupt, "I was sarcastic because I'm in the middle of a pile of shit here that has nothing to do with you. I want you to accept my apology and then tell me quickly what you want, and I'll try to do it."

"Okay." He took a deep breath and said, "What I need is somebody to help me for a couple of days. If I just had

one guy, staked out in the neighborhood in some nondescript car with a radio. Then when I called him he could
follow these guys when they close their shops, and maybe
we could figure out what they're up to."

"I've got just the man. If I send him to the front of the
pawnshop in about an hour, will you meet him there and
brief him? I haven't got time."

"I'll do it. Thanks, Jake." He added sheepishly, "I'm
sorry I got pissed."

" 'S'awright." I punched off and called Frank. "Is the
old Dodge van in good enough shape to run?"

"Just about. What's up?"

"Maddox wants help. Okay if I take the van and tell
you about it later?"

"Sure. You need manpower?"

"I gotta guy. Will you switch me to my section?" Lou
answered and found Darrell Betts for me. Darrell was
thrilled to be picked for a stakeout, and he promised to
remember my admonition not to let the gas gauge on the
old van get below a quarter full, lest he stall out in traffic
and kill a taxpayer. "Take a sandwich," I said, "and pee
before you go."

"BCA's here," Kevin said as I hung up. Megan was
coasting toward us, peering at house numbers, when we
stepped outside and waved. As soon as she backed into a
spot, Jimmy jumped out and began throwing open doors.
When I walked up to him he said crossly, "We don't have
time for this crap, Jake, you should have told me this
morning there was a house to check!"

"Didn't know it then," I said, and walked away from
him. I'd just recovered from one fit of rage; it was too
soon to start another. I climbed up into the van, where
Trudy was hanging camera bags on herself as usual, and
said, "Your pack mule is here." She grinned, said, "Oh,
Jake, really, you mean it?" but then pulled me close and

murmured into my ear, "Why don't you see what you can do for Jimmy before he has a *worm*?" I touched her cheek and moved reluctantly away from her sweet-smelling softness. Sidling warily through taped and bungeed equipment thickly hung from pegboard side panels, I found Jimmy rooting in a rear cupboard.

"Why don't you let me show you the house first," I said, "and then Kevin and I will carry stuff in for you." He turned angrily with his prim little mouth open to tell me he didn't need any help, but just then Megan Duffy vaulted up the back step in her ratty baseball cap, grabbed his list out of his hand, and gave him a bump with one hip. "Go on, I'll get the stuff out," she said. "You want the spatter kit? Luminol? Coomassie Blue? You gonna need a vacuum filter?"

Megan's air of affectionate disrespect seemed to loosen up something in Jimmy that was usually wrapped very tight. He gave a funny little shrug, flung half a dozen incomprehensible terms at her, and followed me into the house. I guided him around the bloodstained hazards I was coming to know so well and found him a safe viewing spot in the kitchen. As soon as he got a good look at the carnage, I could see I wasn't going to have any more trouble with Jimmy Chang.

"Jesus," he said. "It's like a demo kit. Some of everything."

"First thing we need to find out," I told him, "is how many people were in this fight."

"Yes, well," he said, "plenty of blood to test."

"The neighbors say they only heard Babe and Randy. The two people you saw at the river. But if you find more than two blood types, or an extra set of fingerprints, we have to rethink this family fight."

"For sure," he said dryly. He looked around some more. "One thing I may be able to do, after I've analyzed

the spatters and those two big smears, is reconstruct the
fight from the point of view of the woman."

"You serious? God, that would be great."

"Well, you see, I've just finished her autopsy. I've got
her wounds firmly in mind. I should be able to match up
that information with what we see here. Did I hear Kevin
say you found the weapon?"

"Uh-huh. One, anyway. It's in the yard." We went out
to my marker. He walked slowly around the knife, knelt to
get a better look.

"Okay," he said finally. "This could be it. The blade is
long enough for the deepest wounds and slender enough
to have made the smaller cuts, I think. I'll be able to make
a careful match back at the morgue. I don't want to pick it
up till Trudy takes pictures of the location." We went back
in the house just as Kevin and Megan, chatting amiably,
squeezed through the front door, loaded with gear. "Oh,"
Jimmy breathed, "be careful—" Trudy was right behind
them with her own bags. The little house began to fill
with physical mass.

We addressed the crowding first. Trudy took pictures of
the broken lamp and TV set, and we bagged them and
took them away. The overturned chairs in the living room
could be fumed in our box at the station, we decided, so
we tagged them and put them in Kevin's car. Soon we had
a path through the front of the house. Competition for
work space in the kitchen continued fierce, however, so I
told Kevin, "Let's you and I look upstairs," and he followed me up the narrow painted steps.

Three doors led off the small linoleum-covered landing. Babe's bedroom had sprigged wallpaper and a pink
spread turned back on pink-checked sheets. Babe got up
for the last time in her life from the right-hand side of the
bed, stepping onto a pink throw rug that was shaggy from

many washes. Her purse was on the dresser, but the wallet was missing.

Randy's chaotic bedroom had olive green walls and dark-gold-painted furniture. Posters on the wall featured football stars and race car drivers in heroic poses, the Stones and Kiss looking gleefully crazed. A red print quilt and matching pillows were heaped on his unmade bed, dirty clothes festooned the two chairs, and the red shag throw rug by the bed was a jumble of socks and shoes, sweatshirts, and a backpack.

"Bathroom looks pretty clean," Kevin said from the hall, "wonder why it smells so bad?"

I went in and looked in the toilet and closet, lifted the lid of the clothes hamper, and said, "Here." A bloody white T-shirt lay on top of blood-soaked cutoffs.

"Wait, Trudy'll have to get pictures before we look at them," I said.

"I'll get bags and stuff," Kevin said, and went out to his car. I stuck my head in the kitchen, found Trudy flashing away at the counter and stove, and asked her, "Would it foul you up if you took a couple pictures upstairs right now?"

Without looking up she said, "Whatcha got?"

"Bloody clothes in the hamper. We'd like to look, and we can't till you get pictures."

"Uh—okay. I can make a note and come back to this. Hang on." She noted the shot number and the subject in a small spiral notebook, wrote the next shot number on the line below, and followed me up the stairs. The first thing I liked about Trudy was the seamless way she fit into her team's work, so well organized inside her head that she could deal with the commotion around a crime scene good-naturedly, without getting confused. In the bathroom she took one look at the mess in the hamper, said, "Uh-*huh*," and started flashing away at high speed.

Kevin came back with paper bags, labels, and a flare pen and laid them out in the hall. Trudy finished her shots, noted the numbers in her journal, and said, "Okay, it's yours."

"Thanks. You're a pal," I said, and she flashed one of her 200-watt smiles as she went back down the stairs.

Kevin watched her all the way down and said, "She's a real doll, isn't she?"

"Uh-huh. Don't even think about it."

"Oh-ho," he said, "like that, huh?"

"Hope so. Lay out three or four of those bags in a row, will you?" I pulled on fresh gloves and began dropping bloody clothes onto the paper bags. We laid the shirt and cutoffs out flat and added the socks and shorts I found underneath.

"God, blood on the undershorts, even," Kevin said.

"Uh-*huh*. Matches that mess in the kitchen, doesn't it? Still damp in places, too. When you check these in, downtown, be sure you tell the guy on the evidence door to hang them till they dry out, so they won't mildew. Isn't it funny? To judge by his room, they're the first clothes he ever put in a hamper," I said. "I wonder why he did that?"

"Musta been in shock," Kevin said.

He wrote up the labels but left the clothes laid out so Jimmy could see them. The rest of the bathroom looked clean, except for a small brown streak on the outside of the sink that might have been blood, and one brown smudge by the shower at elbow height. We went back in Randy's bedroom, raised the blinds, and went over all the walls and woodwork without finding any bloodstains. His desk drawers and pockets and the backpack yielded a couple of dollars in change, the only money we found in the house.

We went back down to the kitchen. Jimmy and Megan

were working together on the spatter pattern by the pantry. Megan, using a magnifying glass and a tiny metal tape, was measuring the length and width of half a dozen widely separated spots on the wall. As she called numbers to Jimmy, he fed them into the sine function on his handheld computer, wrote the answer on a sheet of paper, and measured and cut a length of waxed string off a spool. Megan took each string from him as he handed it to her, speared it with a pushpin, and fastened it to the spot she had just measured. When six lengths of string hung down from the wall, Jimmy gathered them gently together, sliding the ends he held till he found a point in front of him where the ends of six taut strings met.

"Here's where the victim was standing when she was struck," he said. Trudy took several pictures over his shoulder. "Once you find the location," Jimmy said, "you can see very plainly how the blood flew. Want to look, Jake?" I stood behind him and traced with my eye the separate paths a thousand drops of Babe's blood had traveled from her body to the wall.

"Trudy and I want to lift that handprint intact, if we can," Jimmy said, "and Megan's going to finish getting slides from each blood smear on the floor. Then we can put down paper and quit this hopping over everything."

"Jimmy," I said, "you've got something, haven't you, that tells you if there was blood on something and then it was washed off?"

"Sure. Luminol. You mean this maniac actually washed something?"

"Himself, I think. Upstairs."

"Okay, soon as we're done here we'll test it."

Trudy took several close-ups of the tragic handprint above the spatters.

"Seems to fade out a little from the flash," she said.

"Hang on a minute," Jimmy said, dug through his

stash of treasures, and came back with a bottle that looked like glass cleaner but was marked "Coomassie Blue."

"Wait," she said, "I haven't lifted a print yet. Where's my duster kit?" She disappeared into the living room and came back with a small jar of powder and a long-handled brush.

"Looks like a makeup brush," I said.

"It is," she said. "My contribution to the state of Minnesota. It's softer than the one they furnish, I like it better." She twirled it between her palms to fluff the bristles, dipped the brush lightly in the black powder, and began delicately brushing black powder onto the tops of the ridges in the handprint. When she had applied enough to suit herself, she blew on the wall, gently, in a couple of places, took the brush and powder back to the living room, and came back with a sheet of lifter paper and a hard rubber roller. She handed the roller to Jimmy, held the sheet of paper two inches from the wall, and made tiny adjustments till she was satisfied that it covered the handprint.

"Okay," she said, "now," and pressed the sheet of paper to the wall. Jimmy, standing a little ahead of her, raised the roller between her two raised arms, pressed it hard against the wall, and rolled it down the paper. When he stepped away, I realized they had both been holding their breath.

"Wow," I said. "All in one swoop."

"One is all you get," Trudy said grimly. "You fuss with it, you ruin it."

Trudy turned the paper, and they stood looking down at it, intently, the way fingerprint experts do, never quite satisfied. "Mmmm," Jimmy said, pointing his little finger at something, and Trudy sniffed and said, "Nnch." To me it looked flawless.

"Megan, you got your blood sample from this hand-print yet?" Trudy asked.

"Uh-huh," Megan said from under the table.

"Good. Give it a shot of that Coomassie Blue, then," Trudy said, and Jimmy sprayed the handprint. It turned dark purple, and Trudy took more pictures, with Jimmy fussing around her, muttering requests.

Finally Jimmy quit mooning over the handprint and said, "Okay, now! Megan, you've got a few more blood samples to get here, right?"

"Ah-hah," Megan groaned, from a tight space between cupboards.

"Good. Trudy and I will have a look upstairs."

Jimmy and Trudy were able to get into the bathroom together, if Kevin and I stayed in the hall. Jimmy sprayed the sink and the shower from a bottle marked "Luminol."

"Turn out the hall light," he said, and closed the window blind. We stood in the dark together like kids at a teenage party, and after a couple of minutes the sink and shower began to fluoresce. They turned blue-white, glowing brighter as we watched.

"Be damned," I said, "still works after two days, huh?"

"Oh, much longer than that," Jimmy said. "Months. Years, sometimes. In fact, the older the blood gets, the longer it will glow."

"So he washed blood off his hands in the sink and then took a shower," I said.

"Somebody did," Jimmy said.

"There's a little smear on the outside of the sink, might be blood," I said, "and one mark on the wall there. Is that enough to test?"

"Yes, I should think so. I'll get Megan up here, she's the best with these tiny samples."

"You got yourself a good new assistant, huh?"

"Indeed. The best. If I can put up with her mouth," he

said, with an uncharacteristic, rueful laugh, and then clamped his Awesome Asian look back on. "Trudy, now you need to get out in the backyard and get some pictures of the knife that Jake found out there. When you're done, go ahead and bag it and tag it."

"You need any help?" I asked her.

"Let Kevin help her if she does," Jimmy said. "If you want to talk to me about this fight, it's got to be now." He stuck his arm out and glared at his wristwatch.

We went down and stood by the chalk mark in the living room where the broken lamp had been. I turned on my tape recorder and spoke the date and time into it. "The argument appears to have started here," Jimmy said. "We didn't find any blood in here, did you? No. But somebody got excited enough to knock over the lamp and a couple of chairs. Then for some reason they moved to the kitchen.

"As we've all observed, a great many dishes were thrown. No way to know who threw them till the fingerprint work is completed. Maybe not then. The first knife cuts were probably the small, shallow ones you saw on her face and neck. They look somewhat tentative. Then maybe she threw that roaster and hit somebody. It's dented. The battle escalated, for whatever reasons, and I believe the first deep wound was administered here," he said, moving to the table.

"He, or they, must have held her, bent backward over the table, and brought the knife straight down. That's the deepest cut I found on her. It punctured her lung, and caused this." He pointed up at the fine brown spray arcing across the ceiling. "Blood tests have to confirm this, of course, but that's the way blood would spray out of a lung that was still working. If that's not the woman's blood on the ceiling, then you're looking for another seriously injured party, because there's no wound on Randy's body that would have produced that spray. You can tell Pokey he was right; Babe almost certainly died before she went in the river."

"About when, do you think?"

"We'll be arguing about that for a while. Being in the water confuses everything. If your officer is right that she was somewhat buoyant, then I want to say the longest time you can possibly afford me."

"I talked to her myself Tuesday morning. Could have been anytime Tuesday after that, I guess. But Kevin's witnesses all say the fight took place late afternoon Tuesday."

"Right. Well. After that big knife thrust, I think she somehow got away, and from then on it was a free-for-all. Looks like she threw everything she could get her hands on, and her attacker, or attackers, pursued her and cut her whenever possible. She slid across the stove, there, and on across the counter, and collapsed onto the floor. You can see that plainly, from the smears and the puddle of blood on the floor. It was probably then, while she was on the floor, that she got all those slashes on her back. A couple of dozen of them," Jimmy said, grimly, "some so close together I can't tell if it's one wound or two. They would have been very painful, but none were lethal. Those wounds all argue for a family fight, you know," he said, "because there's a tentative quality to the depth of the cuts, and the placement of the wounds shows no planning. A person intending to kill from the beginning would have got it done faster."

"That's what Pokey said."

"Yeah. Well. Pokey really nailed it, there at the river, tell him I said so. Sometimes I find him just about unbearable, but he has a very good eye. Now—" He pointed out a trail of blood drops crossing the kitchen from the stove to the pantry wall. They crossed so many other smears of blood that I hadn't noticed them before. "See this? The wound in her chest would have been disabling ordinarily, but it looks as if desperation kept her going. Somehow she got up again and tried one last time to get away. That's when somebody threw this chair at her—" He picked it up and showed me the blood and hairs clinging to the bent leg. "We'll take this one along with us, to confirm it, but I'm pretty sure the chair hit her right there, where I showed you the strings coming together. Besides causing blood to spurt out of all her wounds and spatter on the wall, the impact caused a subdural hematoma."

"Translation?"

"Knocked her out, caused massive bleeding inside her brain. The momentum of the blow propelled her toward the wall, so she put her hand up—her last conscious act, I should think—and made that perfect print. We have to get it back to the lab to match it, but Trudy's got a good short-term memory for prints she's working on, and she's almost certain it's Mrs. Krueger's. The smear on the lower part of the wall indicates she slid to the floor. Probably died there. See how thick the blood is?"

"That's blood?"

"Yes. It'll turn black and flake like that when there's a pool of it. She must have lain there some time. Hunched on her side, I think; there's some lividity on her right side. She may have lain right there till she was picked up and carried to the river."

"Have you finished the autopsies on both bodies?"

"Yes."

"Well, what about Randy? Did he drown?"

Jimmy made a wry face. "Yes, but don't quote me. Drowning is famously hard to prove. But for your purposes, right now, Jake, while you're trying to sort out this crime, go ahead and figure he drowned. His lungs were full of weeds and dirt from the river. That's one thing we'll do for you right away: We'll match the junk in his lungs to the scrapings and samples we took from the river. Then at least you'll know he drowned in that part of the river."

"Good. Then all I have to do is find out who tied him to his mother."

"Somebody who's spent some time on boats, I bet," Trudy said, coming in the back door. "We had quite a time with some of those bowlines, didn't we, Jimmy?"

"They were good knots," he said. "How close are we to hitting the road?" He began checking his list, firing rapid questions to the two women. I helped them load the big mound of evidence they were taking back. Kevin picked up a double armload of zippered bags and staggered to the van like a burro.

"You be home tonight?" I asked Trudy as I helped her out the door.

"I guess," she said. "What day is this?"

"Thursday. I think." We both laughed. "I'll try to call you, okay? Maybe we can think up a plan for the weekend."

She opened her mouth to answer, but just then a silly argument erupted by the back of the van, where Kevin, standing to be off-loaded, noticed Megan's Chicago Cubs T-shirt and asked her if she enjoyed backing losers. Megan yelled, "Hey, be nice! This year's gonna be different!" and in no time they were hurling stats at each other, arguing about Molitor's batting average and the strikeout records of Steve Trachsel and Rick Aguilera. They quickly escalated to the loud, uncouth insults so favored by sports fans everywhere, which brought Jimmy hurrying out of the house saying irritably, "Okay, now, what's all this nonsense?"

"Aw, we're just—" Kevin began, but Jimmy brushed past him, snapping at Megan, "Could you at least try to behave like a professional?" He stomped to the front of the van and got in on the passenger side, slamming the door.

"Hey, I'm sorry," Kevin muttered, but Megan made a shushing gesture and said softly, "Don't worry. I think he's getting his period," and they giggled hilariously. Trudy waved good-bye to me, and climbed quickly into the backseat. Megan hopped up in the driver's seat, started the motor, checked the traffic, and began to back out. Suddenly Kevin said, "Oh, jeez, that kid's clothes are still in my car," and I ran wildly after the van, yelling, "Wait! Wait!" Megan rolled down her window and said, "What?"

"Remember, I told you we'd be sending the clothes from the little girl who was kidnapped?" I said. "Remember, Jimmy? For hair and fiber sampling?" Kevin trotted up with the bag of Jessica's clothes, handed them to Megan, and said, "Forgot your lunch, darlin'," and they started another giggling fit. Jimmy, glowering blackly, reached across Megan and grabbed the sack of clothes out of Kevin's hand, hissing, "Can we for chrissake get going?" Megan backed fast into the middle of the street, reversed gears with a head-snapping screech, and left a trail of hot rubber on the turn at the end of the block.

"God, it's after four o'clock," I said. "How much have we got to take back with us?"

"Just the two chairs in my car," Kevin said. He was grinning at the corner where the BCA van had just disappeared. "Isn't that Megan a kick in the pants?"

"Yup. Let's lock up and see if we can get back to the station before all our guys go home."

Lou and Ray were standing by the elevator when we walked out of it. "Good, you're right here," I said. "Come to a meeting at eight in the morning, will you? In the small meeting room. We're gonna divide up the tasks on the double drowning and the kidnapping, all work together for a while."

Hustling on down the hall, I asked Kevin, "Go see if Darrell's back, will you? I'm gonna try to find Bo and Rosie."

They were in Bo's office, transcribing notes off my tape recorder.

"You get anything worthwhile from Farah?"

"He did it for the money," Rosie said.

"No kidding. Where is it?"

"In a coffee can, he says, buried in the woods."

"He draw you a map?"

"Not yet. He's trying to find a way to trade it for something. We explained to him that until he leads us to the money, we've got nothing to trade. He's thinking about it."

"How's his story compare to Scott's?" I asked Bo.

"Well, the masks, he says they were long knit things with holes. Sounds like balaclavas. He gave us some details on the money. A close estimate on the cash, and a couple of checks he remembered. He described Babe's office. We'll have this run off for you in a few minutes, both the interviews."

"Bring it in as soon as you're finished, will you? The tape too. And while I'm thinking of it, come to the small meeting room at eight in the morning. Work is piling up, we're gonna each take a chunk and run with it."

Darrell Betts was waiting in my office, trying not to smirk. "Hey," I said, "how'd you like spying?"

"We did some good, I think," he said, bouncing a couple of times in his chair.

"Those evildoers lead you to the loot?"

"Led me around, anyway. I waited about an hour in the van, and then Clint called me to follow the pawnshop man, that Sewell guy. Did you know the kids in the neighborhood call him 'Mr. Sewage'? Good name for him, what a dork."

"So, did he do this terrible thing Clint is talking about? Go to Fourteenth Avenue and turn right?"

"Yeah, Clint said you made fun of that, but listen! Clint's right, there's something very odd about that operation. Clint called and said Sewell was closing his shop, so I pulled around to his street and waited a couple doors down, and when he pulled out of the alley just like Clint said he would, I followed him, and sure enough, he turned right on Fourteenth Avenue. He followed Fourteenth to the highway, went south on Fifty-two, and turned in at that storage place out there on the Stevensville road, Southeast Self-Storage."

"Well, so then?"

"Well, I couldn't follow him inside, it's just a couple of rows of storage spaces. I didn't want to blow my cover, y'know," Darrell said, grinning all over his face. "Might have to dive off a cliff then, and kill a buncha guys."

"For sure. So what did you do, quick-thinking action hero that you are?"

"Waited in the parking lot of the little strip mall just past there, the one with the paint store and the feed-and-seed place. He stayed almost half an hour, then he pulled out and went right back to his shop."

"Well, there you have it," I said, "we've got to put a stop to this right away. Can't have guys going to their storage bins and then back to their stores in the middle of the day."

"Jake, I know it's funny on the face of it, but do you understand that Clint really thinks he's onto something?"

"Or he'd like to be. The old-timers in that area, Tony and Larry and their pals, they hate those new people that they believe are ruining the neighborhood. Clint has adopted their attitude toward the X-rated bookstore and the pawnshop: They're sleazy, they don't work hard enough, they must be doing something illegal. He's just about ready to start a witch hunt. We can't do that."

"You don't think it's odd when a small storekeeper has something more important to do than tend the store?"

"A pawnshop takes in stuff. It's what pawnshops do. Stuff has to be stored."

"And adult bookstores? What stuff do they take in?"

"You followed him too?"

"He goes a different way," Darrell said, "but he ends up at the same storage place."

"Huh." I kicked my desk a couple of times.

"Besides," he said, "both these outfits are run so funny."

"Funny how?"

"They don't care whether they take care of customers or not. Small stores, Jake, they really have to hustle to make it."

"So maybe they're not making it."

"The pawnshop's been in that location for a year and a half. The dirty bookstore moved once, but it's been in the North End almost two years."

"All this you learned in one day?"

"Clint's been asking questions. And we talked to Tony Pease awhile."

"Well, I'm impressed you learned so much so fast, and I'm glad you got along with Clint Maddox, he's a damn good cop. Tell you what. Write a report on what you saw today, leave it on my desk. Later, if we can clear up the kidnapping and double homicide we're currently working on, I'll assign you to some more undercover work with Clint, and we'll see what the two of you can dig up."

Darrell looked sad. "I told him you wouldn't go for it."

"For what?"

"Clint was hoping I could hang around his section

tomorrow, watch these two stores for him while he's off. He works four twelves, y'know, like all the uniforms. So he can only cover Monday through Thursday."

"Right. And he's got his assignment, which is policing the North End, and we've got ours, which right now is finding out who killed Babe Krueger and her son, and also who kidnapped Schultzy's child. Big jobs, lotta people counting on us to do 'em right, you hear what I'm saying?"

"Sure. Hey, I didn't mean to rag on you, Jake."

"No problem. Small meeting room, Darrell, eight in the morning. We've got a shitload of work to do, we're gonna divvy up the tasks and run like hell."

As soon as he was out the door, I called Frank and said, "Got a minute?"

"Just about. If you come right now."

"I'll do it by phone. Has anybody talked to Jessica Schultz?"

"No. Lou went over there, but Marlys said the kid was still too upset to talk. You get the clothes to BCA okay?"

"Yes. You know anybody in Planning and Zoning?"

"Uh, yeah, a couple guys, why?"

"I'd like to find some old city hand who'd come up with a map of the sewer lines in the North End, in a hurry, without making me get down on my knees."

"Well, lessee," I heard his big chair groaning as he leaned back, shifting his weight, "y'know who you really probably oughta try is Building and Safety. Ask for Angus Ferguson."

"He's an engineer?"

"Self-taught, mostly. Planning and Zoning's got all those bureaucratic engineers now with master's degrees, you can start a turf war over there just asking for a paper clip. But Angus is an old-fart tinkerer who goes back to the days when the whole town was managed by five or six guys with a few tools in a pickup. Betcha he knows where a set of those old plans are buried, and he'd probably enjoy walking you through 'em."

"Thanks."

"Wait. How'd it go at the house with BCA?"

"Fine. They went away with about a ton of blood samples and broken dishes, and they'll call when they're ready to talk about it. Bloody clothes in the hamper upstairs. It's looking more and more like a family fight that got out of control."

"That so? You're thinking the son killed the mother?"

"Looks that way. When the blood tests and autopsy results come back, we should know for sure, about Babe."

"But the boy—?"

"Tougher," I said. Rosie was standing in my doorway, and I motioned her in. "But listen, Frank, about Jessica? I'd like to go see her myself in the morning. Any reason you know why that wouldn't be okay? Did Schultzy say she was a real basket case, or—"

"Oh, no, no. Just that she was taking some kids' tranquilizers their doctor prescribed and sleeping a lot. They thought it was important to give her a couple of days to calm down. Just ask Schultzy if she's ready yet, she'll tell you, you know Schultzy."

"Sure do," I said. "Talk to you later, Frank."

I hung up, took the report Rosie held out to me, and asked her, "Bo gone home?"

"Yes. He said tell you his sitter's sick and he needed to pick up his kid."

"Didn't know he had one," I said. "You got a minute to go over this?"

"Sure."

"What do you think of Farah Tur?"

"Hard to know." She grinned suddenly. "Bo said, 'Ain't no chatterbox, is he?' "

"Meaning he's quieter than Bo? Wow."

"I'd call it a toss-up myself. One thing Bo wanted me to point out, Farah gives the same time for the robbery as Scott does. Sunday night." She flipped through pages and pointed. "Here . . . 'We waited in the park till all the bars closed and the street was quiet. Then we hid behind the Dumpsters in the alley behind the bar, till we were sure there was nobody around. We went downstairs sometime after three, maybe three-thirty.' "

"Huh." We stared at each other. "Isn't it odd? Why are they lying about the time?"

"Bo figures they did something else that was worse, and they're using the robbery to give themselves an alibi."

"That's what the chief said. So we're waiting for still another vile crime to surface? Shit. He says the same as Scott about the keys? They got them from Randy?"

"Yes."

Farah had given a fair description of Babe's office—"dark and stale, with one good light on the desk." They found Babe there, he said, counting the money and putting it into bank deposit sacks, "bags like leather with zippers at the top."

"Why didn't you leave, when you saw she was there?" Rosie asked him.

"The money was right there too. Easy to get."

"But attacking the owner like that made it a big-time felony, didn't you know that?"

"We did not hurt her really." I could imagine his leisurely shrug. "And we were wearing the knitted caps. She could not see our faces. And since we did not speak, she could not describe our voices."

"Babe said that, too," I told Rosie. "She said that was the scariest part, that they never spoke."

"I asked him, 'You did all that, taped her up and everything, without talking?' and he said, 'That's right, we never talk.' So Bo asked him, 'Never, on any of your jobs?' and Farah said, 'I mean we agreed before we started that we would never talk.' "

They put the money "in the picnic box," he said. I sat and stared at that line, remembering how Babe had said, "They had one of those Styrofoam coolers—" All along, the idea of Farah Tur confessing to anything had seemed ludicrous to me, and I had focused on his motivation: Why is he confessing? If he got away clean with a lot of money, why come in here and screw it up? But suddenly, with the inclusion of that unlikely detail, the Styrofoam cooler to carry the money in, and the spontaneous awkwardness of the phrase he used to describe it, "the picnic box," Farah Tur had made himself a credible suspect in my mind for the robbery of Rowdy's Bar, even though I had no clue why he was confessing to it.

They went home without counting the money. "I had to hurry," he said, "my father goes to work early." Incredibly, this handsome, self-possessed warrior, who wore his air of menace like a row of medals, was also a dependent teenager who, at home, would be expected to explain an all-night absence. Only after both his parents had gone to work in the morning did he and Ali, his little brother, count the money. They had expected about twenty-five hundred dollars, he said, "perhaps three thousand if we were lucky," when they went into the bar. He had known it was more than that as they loaded it in the cooler, but, "We were extremely pleased," he said, "when we found that we had almost twelve thousand dollars."

So Scott and Farah were telling the same lie about the money. They both said they robbed the bar on Sunday night, which I knew to be wrong. Both claimed they got the keys from Randy, which might or might not be true. They agreed they wore masks, but described them differently. What about . . . I paged back through Scott's interview till I found what I was looking for:

JH: Okay. Then you went to Rowdy's, used the keys Randy gave you . . .

SR: Yeah.

JH: Entered by the front door, back door . . .

SR: Front.

"Scott said they went in the front door," I said. "Farah says they waited by the Dumpsters in the back. He didn't specify going in the back door, but—did you ask him which door he went in?"

"Um. No. I'm sorry, I'm afraid I took that for granted. Wrong, huh? See, I figured, they were there in the alley by the Dumpsters, why would they go around to the front?"

"No reason. But Scott said they did," I said. "I'll make a note to ask Farah."

"Bo said you'd want to see this about the money, too," Rosie said, and showed me the page:

BD: Was the money mostly cash?

FT: Yes. Only three or four checks.

BD: Can you describe any of those checks?

FT: There was one on the First National Bank for fifty dollars, I think . . .

BD: You remember the name?

FT: No.

BD: Anything else?

FT: I remember one curious check, for one hundred dollars. It was blue all over, and was signed in two places.

I pulled Babe's deposit slips out of the file. On Saturday's deposit, she listed an American Express traveler's check for a hundred dollars, and a fifty-dollar check on a local bank.

"You know," I said, "Farah's starting to look good for this crime. I think I'm going to stroll over to the jail and ask him which door he went in, and maybe get him to describe to me how you overpower a victim and tape her up without saying a word. And why. Lessee, what time is it?"

"Six-thirty," Rosie said.

"Aw, no kidding? Jeez, listen, you better run along. I'm sorry, I just forgot the time. I don't want to burn you out your first week on the job."

"I'm not tired," Rosie said. "You mind if I come along? I'm new to interviewing, I'd like to observe how you do it, see how he responds to you."

"Well . . . you sure? Okay. You carry the tape recorder, I'll bring the files and a fresh tape." We walked down the broad front steps of the building and out the tall front doors, crossing the courtyard in sunshine so hot and bright it felt like noon. I slid my ID card through the heavy brass lock, and we entered the cool gloom of the jail, where time took a sudden lurch into evening. The empty supper trays were being collected. All the TV sets were turned on high, prisoners and guards moving as little as possible, trying to keep their eyes on the nearest set.

I asked the sergeant on duty to have Farah Tur brought out to the visitors' room used for nonaggressive prisoners.

"He's already in there with a visitor," the sergeant said. "You can interrupt if you want."

"I'll see," I said, and walked into the gray-carpeted L-shaped room, where tables and seating arrangements were pushed around at random intervals. On the couch nearest the door, a set of tired-looking parents groped for words to say to their stonefaced son. A young woman, standing a few feet beyond them, wept quietly into a tissue while the prisoner who faced her pleaded for understanding. We stood quietly, trying not to intrude, and scanned the room for Farah. Suddenly I became aware of a conversation going on somewhere behind me, in the short end of the L, around the corner from where we stood.

"—Don't give shit wha'chew want, dickhead," a falsetto voice said. I knew the voice; it froze me.

"I will not allow my brother to do it," Farah said.

"Not *allow*? Wha'chew mean, allow? Where the fuck you think you are?" Incredibly, but unmistakably, it was the voice I had heard on Schultzy's phone, saying he had a girl named Jessica. Why would Jessica's kidnapper be visiting Farah Tur?

Holding one finger against my lips, I leaned across Rosie and pushed the start button on the tape recorder she was holding. I bent to her ear and whispered, "Don't move," pushed the door open just enough to slide out, and hurried to the sergeant's desk.

"Floyd, you've got a Polaroid camera here, haven't you?"

"Sure. You need it?"

"Could you bring it and help us a minute? Rosie and I are going to stand behind two guys at a table, and I want you to take our picture and get theirs too. Will you? Right now?"

"Sure," he said, his heavy body suddenly quick and adept, reaching in a drawer, coming out with a camera, and checking the film as he fast-walked behind me. We sidled in through the half-open door, and I grabbed Rosie's elbow and whispered in her ear, "Laugh!" We chortled around the corner together as I cried merrily over my shoulder, "Aw, come on, Floyd, how often does a guy get engaged? You can spare a coupla pictures!" Tugging Rosie's elbow, I guided her on a semicircular path till we were behind the table where Farah leaned toward the squeaky-voiced man. Then I threw my arms around her and yelled, "Cheese!" and Floyd shot three pictures without pausing, the first two tumbling out of the slot onto the floor while Farah and the other man stared.

The man with the strange, high voice began to get up. I said, "Oh, excuse us, folks, guess we got carried away," and pulled Rosie away from him. Floyd scooped his first two pictures off the floor and moved ahead of us out of the room, asking Rosie over his shoulder, "What do you see in this bozo?"

"Good *man*," I said softly in the hall, grabbing the pictures from Floyd. "I'll call you."

We trotted down the long, dusky corridor to the heavy front door. In the courtyard, where sunshine still blazed, I told Rosie, "That was very well done, Sergeant Doyle."

"Thanks," she said. "What did we do?"

"Got a picture of Jessica Schultz's kidnapper, I hope. Why the hell is he visiting Farah Tur, though? Anyway, let's go see if we got his voice on tape."

We went up to my office and spread our treasures on my desk. Color was coming up nicely on the pictures. In the first two, Farah's visitor was turned away from the camera, watching Rosie and me, but in the last one he had turned toward the camera, and Floyd got a full-face shot. He was part African-American, copper-colored, tall and big, with mostly European features, thin lips and nose, but kinky African hair.

We rewound the tape and played it. The high, breathless voice said, "You in the slammer, numb nuts. Where you think you comin' from with this *allow* shit?"

"He is my brother, and he will do what I say," Farah said.

"That so? You think he gonna keep doin' wha'chew say when I got his nuts in a vise, asshole? Huh?"

"If you touch my brother, my father will kill you," Farah said, and then my voice drowned his out with the nonsense about the picture.

"We got enough, I think," I told Rosie Doyle. "Go home, Rosie. You did a helluva job. See you in the morning."

I called Floyd, explained what the craziness with the camera was all about, and asked him, "The man visiting Farah Tur, you got him on the sign-in sheet, right? What's his name?"

"Uh . . . lessee." There was a long pause while he breathed and moved his chair around. Finally he said, embarrassed, "He signed in, Jake, but I can't read his damn writing. We gotta be more careful about this! About twice a year we have a meeting about watching what people put on the sign-in sheet, then we're careful for a while, and pretty soon we start to let it slide again. Damn! I got his phone number, though." He read it out to me: "555-574-2250." He breathed again for a minute and said, "Damn. That's not a Minnesota prefix, is it?"

"No. Where is it?"

He looked on his chart and said, "Tucson, Arizona."

"I'll try it anyway," I said. "Thanks, Floyd."

I called the number. It rang ten times before an operator came on the line, checked the number, and reported it out of service. I stared out the window a couple of minutes. It can't be the same man, I thought, I must be mistaken. Why would Jessica's kidnapper go into the jail, of all places, to visit Farah Tur?

Still pondering, I called Schultzy's house. She answered, speaking loudly from what sounded like a dance class in a machine shop.

"What's going on?" I said.

"Just the usual," Schultzy said. "I need to come back to work, Jake, this family is too hard to take full-time." She tried to make it sound like a joke.

"How soon do you think you'll be back?"

"Should be Monday. Jessie's fine. She's going back to my mom for day care. They been having a love affair ever since Jessie's big adventure. That's what she calls it, 'My big a'venture.' "

"Will you be home tomorrow morning? You and Jessica?"

"Um, yeah, I guess so. Why?"

"I want to show Jessica some pictures."

"You want to show . . . you mean it's possible you've got a suspect?"

"Possible. Don't go counting on it now."

"I won't." But then she said at once, "Oh, Jake!" and I could tell she already had her heart set on it. "Honest to God? Where? How . . . ?"

"Just got lucky. I can't tell you any more, or I'll taint the identification. Don't tell Jessica anything except I'm coming to ask her a couple of questions, okay? We don't want to put any pressure on her to say she recognizes somebody if she doesn't. You think she can take it?"

"Sure. She's okay. She's already bragging to the neighbor kids."

"Good. I'll see you in the morning, then."

"Oh, God, Jake, you just don't know . . . Oh, wait'll I tell Ernie! We've been afraid to let her outta our sight!"

"I know. It's not for sure, now. But I hope I'm right. So, what time—?"

"Oh, whenever it's good for you, Jake, we'll be right here waiting for you."

"Shortly after nine, then, probably. I'll call if there's a hitch."

To make Jennifer's ID legal, I needed five other pictures

of youngish men, similar in appearance to the squeaky-
voiced man. So, to begin with, they all had to be black.
Booking photos would do, though. I called Floyd and
asked him, "How many black guys' pictures have you got
in the current booking file?"

"Uh . . . lessee." He slid a file drawer open and made
rustling noises. "Two, looks like. This Farah Tur that's in
here now, and that Eugene Soames you brought in from
the car chase last week."

"That's all? Damn! Okay, thanks." I checked the film in
my Polaroid camera, and walked around the building in
search of Art McGee, the night janitor. I found him cleaning the urinal on the third floor, delighted, as always, to
be offered any distraction from his lonely job. He's a great
kidder, too, so it took five minutes to get a serious shot.
Then I remembered an Ethiopian exchange student I
know, who sometimes works evenings at the library. I ran
across the overpass, found him shelving books, got
shushed a couple of times, but got a second picture of a
young black man.

I called the dispatch desk then and asked them, "Does
Greg LaMotte work tomorrow morning?"

"Lessee. No. He's marked up for a personal day. He's
here till nine o'clock tonight, though, if you want to talk
to him."

"Fantastic," I said. "Thanks." I walked out to the big
room where the support staff works. It was nearly all dark
at that hour but showed one patch of glow where Greg
LaMotte sat hunched over his 4.2-gigabyte computer, motionless except for his flying fingers.

Greg was a wizard at several record-keeping functions,
but his new specialty was image enhancement. He's got
software that allows him to pull a face out of a blurry old
crowd photo, tweak it and tease it a bit, and produce a

clear, recognizable portrait of a face you thought was lost in the sludge.

"Hey," I said, "you're working tonight? Outta sight. I need your help. Desperately."

"Is there any other way? Whatcha got?"

"I got this Polaroid kinda by accident, see. But this guy here, the one getting up, I suspect is the kidnapper who snatched Jessica Schultz."

"No shit? How'd you find the guy?"

"Like I said, by accident. But now if I could get his face lifted out of this picture, and put on a photo strip with five other black faces, I could try for an identification from the child. If she picks him out of the lineup, I can get a warrant to pick him up."

"Well, I can lift him out of that picture all right. No problem. What else you got to go with it? They have to be reasonably similar so you're not leading the witness."

"Well, I've got these two Polaroids—"

"They'll work fine."

"Okay, and Floyd says he's got two booking photos of young black men, can you use those?"

"Yeah. They're not enough alike to start with, but I can make 'em close enough. Long as I'm not changing the image of the one you're after, we should be okay."

"That still leaves me short one shot. You know any other black guys working around the building tonight, besides Art McGee?"

"How about you?" he said.

"I'm not dark enough, am I?" I'm actually about the color of a spice muffin, but in Minnesota, a little skin color goes a long way. "And she's going to be looking at me when I hand her the picture."

"I'll darken you up and lower your forehead and broaden your nose," he said. "She won't recognize you."

"Okay, here." I handed him the Polaroid, and he took my picture.

"I'll have this ready in a few minutes," he said.

"Any chance you'd put it on my desk before you go home?"

"Sure," he said, absentmindedly, without looking up. I left him there, motionless in the dim light except for his hands, with the screen light dancing on his face.

Back in my office, I decided to plan tomorrow morning's meeting. I turned a legal pad sideways, wrote the names of my six investigators along the double margin line of the page, and made columns under their names. I stared at the page for a couple of minutes, then changed my pen for one with a finer tip. I stared a couple of minutes more, got up and found a tissue, blew my nose, sat down again, and lined up my desk blotter with the edge of my desk. Assigning work, I decided, was not as easy as it looked. There was a lot to consider, and I was too tired to remember what most of it was. Outside my window, the last of the light was fading. Watching a Chevy Camaro pull out of the parking lot, I fell asleep, waking with a yelp when I started to fall out of my chair.

Feeling stupid, I did knee bends till I figured I could safely drive, then walked downstairs stiffly and got my car out of the parking garage. At the deli counter of the grocery on Broadway, I got chicken and potato salad and a bottle of Chablis. In front of the TV set in my living room, I ate hungrily while I watched an ancient *I Love Lucy* rerun. I made a game of leaving the sound off, deducing the dialogue from the body language. Lucy was funnier silent; I could even tell where she waited for the laugh tracks.

Holding my third glass of wine, I dialed Trudy's number in St. Paul.

"Oh, Jake, hi," she said.

"Did you have a pleasant ride back to the Cities?"

"Nice and quiet. I don't know what it is with Jimmy lately, he's really having mood swings."

"Megan seems to cope with him pretty well."

"Off and on. Sometimes I think she's part of the problem. Jimmy's so sedate, you know, and she's kind of a loose cannon. Good at her job, but you never know what she'll say next. Maybe I'm wrong, but it seems to me he gets testy as soon as she comes around."

"Must not be much fun for you."

"Oh, I'm just giving them plenty of space to work it out."

"Good. Listen, I had an idea for this weekend," I said. "Why don't we drive up to the North Shore? Walk on the beach, maybe get lucky and pick up some agates. Watch the big ore boats come in. We'll eat a nice big Kamloops dinner and then sit on a rotten log in the moonlight, and do a lot of kissing and giggling."

She gave me a wonderful sample giggle and said, "Oh, that sounds like fun!" But then, suddenly serious, she said, "But I can't. I've got a bunch of jobs piled up for this weekend."

"Jobs? What kind of jobs? Can I help?"

"Um, no. Not Saturday. But I'll tell you what, if you mean it about helping, I've got some stuff to haul Sunday. Would you really be willing to get involved in that?"

"Of course. I'm a proven hauler, as you know. You want me Sunday morning? Or maybe I should come up Saturday night, take you out for a meal, keep your strength up for all this extra drudgery." Lechery, I feared, must be dripping off my chin.

"Well . . . I really can't tell when I'll be done with my chores on Saturday, so probably I'd better not. But if you can come Sunday, say ten o'clock or so? I'll make pancakes."

"Glorioski, pancakes," I said, and she laughed.

"Bacon and eggs, then, how's that? And around noon we can load all these things in the car and deliver them around where they belong. That sound okay to you?"

Actually it didn't. Okay, for me, would have involved a Friday night drive to St. Paul, ending when Trudy Hanson opened her door, I wrapped her in my arms, and we spent the next forty-eight hours exploring the outer edges of our pleasure envelopes.

But I was still haunted by the nightmare of my disastrous marriage, which dissolved when my wife and I somehow turned life into a zero-sum game in which each mate's gratification seemed to cost the other an equal amount of dissatisfaction. Determined to stay out of that box with Trudy Hanson, I had schooled myself to take only what was freely given. Never implore, I resolved when we began dating. Hold her so lightly she will have no bonds to chafe at. So I agreed, without further comment, to be at her house by ten, and she purred her appreciation and promised me a good breakfast.

Just before I hung up, though, my disappointment burst out, cravenly disguised as a silly joke. "If I finish my chores extra fast," I asked her, "will you turn on the hose and let me run through the sprinkler?" There was a funny, puzzled silence, and then she chuckled amiably and said, "Sure," and I hung up quickly.

·NINE·

I WOKE UP AT FIVE O'CLOCK FRIDAY MORNING WITH THAT FEEL-
ing I get sometimes, that a large gray wolf is standing just
outside my bedroom door, salivating. Pale-eyed and ravenous, this slavering carnivore has stalked my life at intervals since I was about nine years old. I don't know where
he stays when things are going well, but I know where
he comes when he's hungry, and his message is always the
same: Your ass is in a sling again, Jake Hines.

I jumped out of bed and showered in three minutes,
microwaved a bowl of oatmeal, and ate it standing up.
Dressing quickly in my neatest clothes, I drove to the
government building by the shortest route. The wolf had
sharpened my focus, as he always does. I was fiercely concentrated on the dung heap of disaster confronting me: A
kidnapping and a double homicide had been added to the
major problems confronting my department, just since
Frank's Tuesday morning tantrum about unsolved cases.
Pernicious behavior was spreading unchecked. My sector's

efforts to fix blame and arrange for punishment were pitifully ineffective. Rutherford's investigative team was looking like a bunch of schmucks.

Ed Gray looked up from his night supervisor's charts, glanced at his watch, and said, "Jeez, kid, you don't have to earn the whole promotion in the first week."

I said, without smiling, "May I have the key to the small meeting room?" Ed handed it over, looking at me sideways while I signed the sheet.

"Must be a full moon, is it?" he said. "Seems like everybody's antsy tonight."

"How long can I keep it?" I said.

"What?"

"The small meeting room."

"Oh—" He waved his arms around, annoyed by confronting a question he ordinarily didn't have to answer. "How long do you need it?"

"Today. Over the weekend. Monday?"

"Today, the weekend, sure. Monday—" He shrugged angrily. He is a tall, strong man with a commanding voice, who did not become the tyrant of the night shift by saying, "I don't know."

"I don't know," he said. "Check with the day shift. Or the chief," he yelled after me as I walked away. I could feel him staring after me resentfully, thinking what a pain in the ass these jumped-up minority types are when they first get a taste of authority.

Two walls of the windowless meeting room had large white boards, with a supply of colored marking pens. I fiddled with the switches by the door till I got all the lights on and adjusted the rheostat to take the glare off the boards. I chose a red marker pen and wrote KIDNAPPING in huge capital letters on the left-hand board, and then MURDER x 2, even bigger, across the right-hand one. I wanted everybody wide awake during this meeting.

I pushed the chairs and tables into an open vee facing the boards, and turned off the Muzak. Back in my office, I printed the notes I had typed Wednesday night, put them on top of Rosie's notes from Scott's and Farah's interviews, and took them all into the meeting room, along with the tapes. Using the legal pad I had set up the night before, I assigned jobs to each investigator, working from the notes and tapes. When I had the day's work assigned, I started out the door to make copies. Then I thought, No, let them make their own lists. I went out to the supply cupboard, found six spiral steno tablets, and wrote crew names on the front covers.

Kevin poked his head in the door at seven-forty-five, and I sent him out to round up the rest of the crew.

"Keep 'em out of the break room, get 'em in here," I said. "We gotta move our butts today." He was back with the whole crew in ten minutes. We demolished all existing departmental promptness records by starting an eight o'clock meeting at seven-fifty-seven.

"We got these two big, bad cases, one on top of the other, this week," I said, pointing at the lurid red titles on the white boards. "They've got to take precedence over all old business. There's a lot of concern out there. The kidnapping scares parents of small children to death, and I don't have to tell you how your neighbors feel about the double murder. Everybody's asking you questions, right?" Six heads nodded ruefully. "So the chief's taking heat from the media and the City Council, he's passing it along to me, and you're all gonna get a share. Get used to it, I'm going to be on your ass for a while.

"We're gonna headquarter in this room till further notice. We'll all be working together, sharing information as fast as we get it. Set the answering tape on your phones; don't return calls till five in the afternoon. I'm going to hand out jobs; you're going to get as many answers as you can by noon, have lunch, and meet back here at one o'clock. We'll share what we got, divide up what's left, and keep going." I slid three notebooks down each table, and they all grabbed.

"Write down your own assignments as we go over this together," I said, picking up my list. "Make notes on the others' assignments too, so you know where to go when you're looking for help.

"Rosie first. Get all the financial records you can find for Rowdy's Bar and for Babe Krueger personally. Talk to her bankers, see if they'll cooperate without a subpoena, if not get on the horn with the legal staff and get whatever you need. Emphasize the need for speed with everybody. Tell them the public's demanding to know. Also, search the bar itself, get the keys from the evidence room. Bring in everything that deals with money: correspondence, register tapes, paid-out slips, ledgers. The bar office is in the basement, but you might find cash tapes under the counters upstairs, too.

"Babe must have an accountant; find him and talk to him. Also her attorney. You're looking for signs of financial distress, fresh debt, refinanced equipment, dunning letters. I put Jack Pfluege's phone number in your book, talk to him. He keeps saying he's just the cook, but I have a hunch he knew most of what went on there. The bartender seemed to think the business was failing. See if Jack agrees. Ask Jack if Babe seemed to be discouraged. You're going after both hard and soft information about Babe Krueger's financial affairs now, so don't be too proud to listen to gossip."

"And you want us back here at one," she said, "whether we've got anything or not?"

"Yes. But have something." She gave me a hot look, and I gave her a cold one back.

"Now. Kevin. You talked to several of the neighbors

around Babe's house yesterday, so you're a little bit acquainted in that part of town. I want you to go back out there today and talk to all the same people again, and as many more neighbors as you can find. Find out all you can about the personal side of the Kruegers' lives. Nothing's too personal or too trivial in a murder case. Did Babe have a lover? Did Randy? Are there relatives? Did they go to church? How about clubs? We don't know anything about these people but where they worked; there has to be more than that.

"Ask Scott Rouse, who's right here in jail, how long he's known Randy, where they hung out, and who Randy's other friends were. If your job overlaps with Rosie's, feel free to consult each other."

"I'm gonna start with the woman next door with the tight pants," Kevin said, eliciting moans and a low wolf whistle from his peers, "she seemed like she wanted to talk some more."

"Fine. Have fun, but don't forget how mad I'm gonna be if you don't come back with useful information." I made a check mark under his name and moved on. "Bo, look in your notebook."

He flipped the cover. "Angus Ferguson?"

"Right. He's an old-time engineer at Building and Safety. The chief recommended him, says he'll know how to read the old maps for the sewer system in the North End. Call him, tell him about the hole in the cellar at the crack house where we found Jessica. Get him to help you figure out where her kidnapper might have gone from there."

"You want me to go out through the sewer like the snatcher did?" His teammates chuckled, and he gave them his icy-eyed look.

"Only if you have to. Ferguson can probably show you

on the map where the nearest manholes are. Find them and look for signs of recent use."

"What, like shit smeared around or that?"

"Yup. Or scrapes, tracks, anything recent."

"Gotcha." Days like this, I loved Bo's short answers.

"Darrell."

"Yo."

"Take the yellow pages, find all the places in town that make copies of keys. Talk to them till you find one who remembers making copies of the keys to Rowdy's Bar for Randy Thorson last week."

"Wow," he said, "must be a ton of them guys."

"Yup. And they're usually not freestanding. They're in hardware stores, Home Depots, Mail Boxes, Office Depots, Insty Prints. Mostly cash-and-carry businesses that don't do a lot of record keeping."

"So I can't ask by name, right? I gotta describe the guy?"

"Start in the North End, where they might know his name, and keep widening the circle from there. Use your instincts. Get lucky." They all laughed, and I said, "Why don't you go up to Rowdy's Bar with Rosie first, help her bring back the tapes and ledgers that we're all sure she's going to find there, and get the picture of Randy that's on Babe's desk? Take it along, somebody might remember his face."

"Right," he said, brightening at the prospect of face time with Rosie. Far from developing a rivalry, the two were becoming my crew's best buddies.

"Ray, the first thing I want you to do is sort of weird, but it's important. Find the place upstream from the Second Avenue bridge where the river gets shallow."

"Say what?"

"The river's narrower and deeper north of town, right? Okay, and we know the two bodies we fished out of the river yesterday had to be put in shallow water, somewhere upstream from where we found them."

"How do we know that?"

"Babe may have been dead before she went in the water, but Randy almost certainly drowned. Drowned bodies don't float for weeks, sometimes months. If the water was deep enough where they went in, those bodies would have gone to the bottom and stayed there. They didn't, though; they rolled and bumped along till they got to the Second Avenue bridge, where we found them. So what I want to know is, how much of a stretch of river does that give us to search?"

"You want all the shallow spots, or—?"

"Ray, listen to me. I want you to find out how far north from the Second Avenue bridge you can go on that stream before you start to find deeper holes, places where those two bodies could have gone down and stayed down. Then we'll search the shallow segment till we find the spot where Babe and Randy were thrown in."

"What's that gonna do for us?"

"I don't know. Find it first, and I'll tell you."

"I'll call my dad," Ray said. "He and his uncles used to fish that river when the town was smaller. He'll know."

"Okay. Now, Lou. I want you to go to Planning and Zoning, the tax assessor's office, and wherever else you have to go for the answers to the following questions: One, who owns the building that Rowdy's Bar is in? Two, did Babe own her own house, or was she renting it—if so, who owned it? Three, who owns the crack house? Four, who owns the tan hatchback we impounded at the crack house? By the way, has that been fingerprinted yet?"

"Don't know," Lou said. "Is it in the impound garage?"

"Yes. Find out and get it done if it hasn't been. Now. Everybody listen up. If you can get what you need today by being polite, fine. If not, lean, push, get rude if you have to, but get what you're after. Any complaints, send 'em to me. See you all back here at one o'clock."

They charged out of the room like a herd of hungry buffalo. My watch said twelve minutes to nine. I hustled back to my office, grabbed the picture strip off my desk, slid it carefully into my briefcase with the recorder and the tape Rosie and I had made in the jail, and ran down the stairs to the parking garage. I was on the street by six minutes to nine. Damn! Where did time go?

Schultzy's house was in a sprawling suburb northeast of town, a big split-level with a yard that looked like a school playground. Jessica's swings were in one corner, surrounded by a volleyball court, horseshoe stakes, hoops, and a trampoline. The garage held enough sports equipment to open a small fitness center.

Jessica was looking out the big front window when I drove into the driveway. Her blond ponytails whipped around her shoulders as she scooted off the couch, yelling back toward the kitchen. Schultzy opened the front door as I walked up to it, with Jessica standing beside her.

"Guess you two didn't really meet formally, did you?" Schultzy said. "Jessica, this is Jake Hines." We shook hands gravely.

"I'm the man who carried you down the alley," I said.

"I'm sorry I kicked you," she said, smiling winsomely. For the first time, I began to understand why Jessica Schultz was her family's darling. A glowing apple-cheeked beauty, she was bright and charming this morning.

"Ernie and the boys are at work," Schultzy said, "and I sent the big girls to the pool. We've got all the time we need, and no distractions. Coffee?"

"Good. Black. Over here?" We moved to the round table in the family room, and they sat on either side of me.

"What I'm going to ask you to do isn't easy," I told Jessica. "But you're the only one who can do it. That man who took you the other day, you saw his face, right?" She bobbed her head, blinking nervously. "And you heard him speak?"

"Yes." Her throat sounded dry.

"Okay. Then you can help me find him. You ready?" She looked up quickly at her mother, who nodded. She turned back to me and repeated her mother's nod to perfection.

I laid my photo strip in front of Jessica.

"Look at the pictures on this strip, and tell me if any of them looks like that man."

Her large pale eyes passed calmly over the first two pictures and stopped on the third. She pointed to it, then put her small, blunt-fingered hands up to her face in a gesture of distress rarely seen in children, and whispered, "That's him." Tears formed on her eyelashes.

"The man who took you to the house where we found you?" She looked up at me and nodded, and one tear ran down each cheek and trickled across her hands, which were still clutching her face.

"Good," I said. "Hang on, Jessica. You're doing a great job."

"Can I see him?" Schultzy asked. I slid the picture strip in front of her, pointing to the third man. She sat staring down at him, looking shaken. "He looks so big and strong," she said, incredulously, "but his voice—"

"Wait," I said, "wait. Okay, Jessica, ready to go on?" She bobbed her head.

"I'm going to play a short section of this tape," I said, looking from one to the other, "and I want you to tell me if there's a voice on it that you recognize." I punched the on button. The squeaky voice said, "You in the slammer, numb nuts. Where you think you comin' from with this *allow* shit?"

Schultzy gasped. Jessica whimpered. I turned the recorder off and asked, "Was that a yes?"

Schultzy said, hoarsely, "Yes."

Jessica leaned toward her mother and said, "Can I sit on your lap?"

"Sure," Schultzy said. Jessica ran around the table and leaped into her mother's arms.

They held each other. "Just give us a minute, huh?" Schultzy said. I nodded. We sat. "Have some coffee," Schultzy said. I sipped.

Schultzy bent toward the yellow ponytails on her shoulder and murmured, "You're doing really fine, honey, I'm proud of you. Do you think you can talk some more?"

Jessica sat up and shouted indignantly, "I was scared, Mama! That bad boy scared me!" The cups rattled in their saucers.

"Jessica," I said, hoping to harness her anger before it burned out of control, "you're right to be mad. And if you can tell me a few more things, I'll put that bad boy in jail where he can't ever scare you again."

"I was all alone with him," she roared, turning red. "There wasn't anybody there to help me, and I was scared!"

"We came as fast as we could," I said, and for some reason that information seemed to catch her attention. She stopped yelling and stared directly into my eyes while the tears dried on her cheeks. "You did?"

I nodded. "We all tried really hard to save you. Honest. We even called out the dogs, weren't they noisy?" She remembered the dogs; she asked, "Were they fighting?"

"No. They're trained to bark like that whenever they find little girls that want to go home." She smiled at that, so I ventured, "Now, can you tell me a couple more things so I can catch this bad boy with the squeaky voice?"

She gave a long, shuddering sigh. Her mother wiped her nose. "Okay," she said.

"First thing I want to know is, how did he find you? Was he looking for you, or—"

"I was in the yard, see, because"—she darted a little sideways glance at her mother—"I didn't like that school where they took me."

"I understand. Did the bad boy come in a car?"

"Uh-huh. He was driving along, and he saw me and stopped."

"He stopped the car and came over to where you were?"

"Uh-huh. And I said, 'I wanna get out,' and he said, 'I'll lift you out, okay?' and I said 'Yes!' and he did it. And then he said we could go in the car, um, wherever I wanted to go? So I said, well, then, he could take me home, and he said he would." Her face clouded ominously, and she shouted, "But then he wouldn't!" Jessica, the never-opposed darling of the Schultz clan, shook with outrage. "He took me to that other place!" Her world had been turned upside down by the discovery that there were people out there who didn't care at all what she wanted.

"I know it's hard," I said. "Just a couple more questions—"

"She'll do it," Schultzy said. "We want this bad boy locked up, don't we, baby? Huh?" Jessica burrowed into her mother's shoulder. She snuffled while Schultzy nuzzled her ear and patted her back. Finally Schultzy murmured something, and she sat up, blew her nose, and explained to me earnestly, "See, I got scared that day."

"Of course you did." That brought me to the question that had nagged at me ever since I carried her down the alley. "Why didn't you yell when he scared you? You did a great job of screaming later on—"

"He put cloth in my mouth!" she said. "Like this," she mimicked stuffing something into her mouth, "and then he put another rag around and tied it in back." Her small capable hands described a knot behind her head. "I was afraid I couldn't breathe!" She rolled her eyes to her mother to illustrate the panic, adding curiously, "But I could. Did you know that, Mama? That you can breathe with just your nose?" Schultzy nodded, too near tears to speak.

"Were you too scared to try kicking and scratching?" I asked her, remembering the punishment she had given me on the way to Donovan's car.

She held out her small, sturdy arms side by side. "He put my arms together like that and tied a rag around them too. In the car."

"Your feet too?"

She shook her head. "He made me walk in the house. You know what he did, Mama? He held me by my hair like this," she grabbed one of her ponytails, close to the scalp, and pulled to illustrate, gritting her teeth against the pain. "Boy, it hurt! I wanted to cry, but I couldn't! You can't really cry with your mouth full of rags," she confided in me, " 'cause the sound comes out all mooshy, like uhh, uhh, uhh." She delivered a show-stopping imitation of gagged distress, and asked her mother, "Don't you think that was mean, what he did?"

"Yes, it was," Schultzy said. "We're gonna have to have some nice treats, I guess, to help you get over that."

"Like what?" Jessica asked quickly.

"Uh, frozen yogurt, maybe. And a movie, as soon as we can, would you like that?"

"*Star Wars?*" Jessica pressed.

"Again? So soon? Tell you what, let's finish Jake's questions first and bargain after he's gone, okay?"

"Okay. But I want *Star Wars*. All three of 'em." She flashed me a triumphant grin, and I smiled back, pleased to see her normal spoiled-brat persona return.

"Okay. One more question, you ready? I understand now why you didn't fight or yell while he took you in the house. But then, why did you start yelling just when we got there?" She looked at me, puzzled and shrugging, and I realized she had no idea when we got to the house. I tried again. "Did the bad boy stay with you after he took you inside?"

"Yes."

"What did you do while you were there?"

"Just sat there. I hated it!"

"What did he do?"

"Nothing. Looked at his watch once in a while."

"Well, then, what happened? Why did you start yelling when you did?"

"He pulled the rags off my head! Some of my hair was caught in the knot, and he pulled it right out! And then he pushed his hand into my mouth to get that cloth out"—she imitated a ruthless rip—"and when somebody has junk stuck in your mouth and just grabs it out like that, and it sticks to your mouth and he pulls it out anyway, it hurts, oh, you would not *believe*—" Her vocal tones and hand gestures were so perfectly copied from her mother that I felt myself sliding helplessly into a laugh and coughed instead.

"You got a bad cough, huh?" she asked me.

"I think I'm getting over it, thank you," I said. "Where did the bad boy go then? When you started screaming, and all the cops and dogs came in?"

She turned her large pale blue eyes on me and said, calmly, "He went in the wall." I knew about the flush door to the cubby, luckily, so I didn't waste time, as I surely would have earlier, trying to get her to explain how a person could vanish into a wall. To Jessica, it was no big deal. She was five; her abductor was a big person. Who knew what big people might do?

"Jessica, you've done a great job of explaining," I said. "Thanks to you, I believe I can catch this bad boy now. I'll let you know when we've got him locked up. He didn't happen to tell you his name and address, did he?" I asked her, winking at Schultzy. Jessica stared rather forlornly out the window, shrugged, and said, "Bad boy is all I know."

"Good name for him too." I gathered up my stuff.

"God, Jake," Schultzy said, following me to the door, "you really think we might get to the end of this nightmare pretty soon?"

"We're all working on it," I said. "And Jessica came through like a champ today. You really raised a winner there, didn't you?" She nodded, beaming. "We're on his trail, Schultzy. We'll get him soon."

Pondering Jessica's answers, I drove back to the station as fast as I could. She had identified her abductor with no hesitation. Schultzy was sure about the voice, too. Their certainty gave a big boost to the kidnapping investigation, but left me with a new problem: Why was Jessica Schultz's kidnapper visiting Farah Tur?

Ray Bailey pulled into the parking garage just ahead of me and hurried over to my car. "All my jobs should be so easy," he said. "My dad knows exactly where the river gets shallow. He rode out with me, took me right to the place. It's just above the Adelaide bridge on Nineteenth Avenue."

"Terrific," I said. "If you've got your answer, come up and help me with an interview. You can run the tape machine while I ask the questions." We went up to my office. I called the Adult Detention Center and asked them to bring Farah Tur to my office.

"They say it'll be a few minutes," I said. I put my tape recorder on the desk, rewound it, and said, "Listen to this."

The falsetto voice said, "You in the slammer, numb nuts. Where you think you comin' from with this *allow* shit?"

Ray turned toward me, startled by the strange voice. I held up my hand, and we listened together as Farah said, "He is my brother, and he will do what I say."

"That so?" the Mickey Mouse voice said. "You think he gonna keep doin' wha'chew say when I got his nuts in a vise, asshole? Huh?"

"If you touch my brother, my father will kill you," Farah said.

I turned the tape off and told Ray, "The last voice on the tape was Farah Tur, the man we're about to interview. He walked in here yesterday and confessed to robbing Rowdy's Bar. The other voice, the high one, was just identified by Jessica Schultz and her mother as the man who kidnapped Jessica on Wednesday."

"Hey, no shit?"

"Right. So now we're gonna talk to Farah Tur and get him to tell us how to find the man with the baby voice." I rewound the tape, put the machine on the end of my desk, and said, "Pull your chair up to this. When I nod to you, play it. As soon as you reach the end, rewind and be ready to play it again."

They brought Farah Tur up in chains.

"Why must I be bound like a slave?" he demanded, his face a mask of contempt. "You people have all the guns." I looked a question at the deputy, who said, "He got a little feisty coming out of the cell, so we put him in restraints."

"You can take them off now," I said.

When he was free, I pointed to the chair in front of my desk and said, "Sit there." Ray and I sat down across from him. "I want you to hear something." I nodded, and Ray pushed play.

The high-pitched voice said, "You in the slammer, numb nuts. Where you think you comin' from with this *allow* shit?"

Farah's face became an iron mask, his mouth clamped in a straight line below half-closed eyes. Motionless as marble, he listened to his own voice on tape saying, "He is my brother, and he will do what I say."

His composure never wavered as the shrill voice came on again, saying, "That so? You think he gonna keep doin' wha'chew say when I got his nuts in a vise, asshole? Huh?" and on the tape Farah's velvety voice responded coolly, "If you touch my brother, my father will kill you."

I nodded to Ray, who turned off the tape. I slid my Polaroid snapshot in front of Farah. "Who is he?"

He took his time over the picture. To be fair, it was a peculiar shot, of himself seated on one side of a table while his powerfully built friend, caught in the act of rising, peered into the camera's lens, and Rosie and I clowned around behind them. I watched as he recalled the disruptive intrusion in the visitors' room. The ruse seemed to please him. He sat back in his chair and regarded me with a spark of new interest. Finally he said, "He calls himself Bad Boy."

Jessica had said it over and over. I had never guessed that she was reporting a street name, not an opinion.

I asked Farah Tur, "What's his real name?"

"I do not know."

"Where does he live?"

"Why would I know that?"

I took a deep breath to hide my anger and said, "Well, see, I think you better know it, Farah, or the shit is gonna hit the fan and fly all over you. This man is a kidnapper. The victim just identified him, positively. You know the penalty for kidnapping? Hard time and plenty of it. And here I have this picture, and this tape, of him visiting you in jail last night. He didn't come in here just to be sociable, right? He was here to talk business. You're partners with this guy, right? Which makes that felony charge you copped to for the robbery at Rowdy's bar the very least of your problems. Now you're looking at conspiracy to kidnap."

"That is entirely wrong!" he said, indignantly. "I had nothing to do with seizing the child."

There was a wonderful, echoey silence. Ray and I looked at each other and then back at Farah. "Did I say there was a child? What child, Farah?"

"You said—"

"I said I was beginning to think you had something to do with a kidnapping that Bad Boy pulled off a couple of days ago. I never said he took a child. The only way you could know that is if you were in on it." His eyes were going dead again, so I rapped on the desk. "Pay attention! You're in slime clear up to your eyeballs, Farah, and your life's not gonna get any better unless I help you. And the only way I'm gonna help you is if you tell me where to find Bad Boy."

He roused himself just enough to smile ironically with one side of his face and ask me, "Oh, and then what wonderful things will you do for me?"

His incredible arrogance made me want to jump on him and pound his handsome face to mush. People think cops beat the hell out of prisoners all the time, but we don't, at least not in Rutherford. We have a whole manual detailing the evils of police brutality, in addition to Frank McCafferty's succinct rule, "First guy abuses a prisoner in my department is out on his ass."

I got up and went to the window, where I watched a long line of cars frying on hot asphalt in front of the First Avenue stoplight, while I counted backward from a thousand by tens. By the time I reached seven hundred and thirty, I was able to remember the rest of Frank's dictum on physical abuse: "Anybody who has to beat on a guy to get answers is too dense to be in law enforcement anyway."

When the light changed, I went back and sat down. "Farah," I said, "what does Bad Boy want your brother to do?"

"Oh—" He looked into the corner. "An errand—"

"And why don't you want him to do it?"

"He is a schoolboy. I don't want him to have anything to do with Bad Boy."

"Good thinking. What's your brother's name?"

"Ali."

"How old is Ali?"

"Fourteen. He looks younger. He was a child in the famine, and he did not grow."

"That why you don't care about him?"

His eyes blazed. "You don't know *anything*," he said furiously.

So there it was. I leaned toward him and said softly, "Well, if you do care about him, you better think about saving his life. Bad Boy doesn't kid around, Farah, he's a mean bastard. He tied up that little girl, hurt her, and scared her half to death, probably would have abused her worse if we hadn't found him when we did. You want a guy like that grabbing your brother?" Farah looked at the ceiling. His lips moved, but no sound came out. "Tell me where to find him, Farah. I'll put him away, and Ali will be safe." He turned his head away then and closed his eyes. "What's the matter, you didn't believe what he said about squeezing your brother's balls? You want us to play it again?"

I nodded to Ray, who hit play. The ridiculous yet somehow terrible voice came on again, saying, "You in the slammer, numb nuts. Where you think you—" Farah held up one long slender hand in protest and said softly, "Please," and I nodded to Ray, who turned off the tape.

"He meets people at Rowdy's Bar," he said, "or at a store called Kwik Kash."

"The pawnshop?" He nodded.

"Not good enough, Farah. Rowdy's Bar is closed now, and the pawnshop's only open a few hours a day. You want me to get this Bad Boy before he gets your little brother, you tell me where he lives."

We gave him time to think. There was evidently a lot to go over. He twisted in his chair a couple of times, scratched his head, opened his mouth once, and closed it. When he was ready he said quietly, "He has a room above the bookstore."

"You mean he lives right here in town?"

"Sometimes."

"Sometimes? What about the rest of the time?"

"Some days he stays in Minneapolis."

"Where in Minneapolis?"

"I have no idea." He said it so simply I believed him.

"Okay. Here in town, which bookstore?"

"The one with the . . . it is called 'Play Time.' "

"The adult bookstore?"

"Yes."

"Is the entrance through the store?"

"No." He hated to volunteer anything, but at last he did. "There is a stairway outside. In the back."

"Stay with him," I told Ray. I went down the hall to the chief's office. He was on the phone, but I made a time-out signal, and he asked the person to hold.

"I've got an identification on the kidnapper," I said.

Frank held up his hand, got back on his phone, and said, "Otis, I'm gonna have to call you back, okay?" He hung up and said, "Tell me."

I told him about the tape and showed him the picture. "Schultzy and Jessica both recognized the voice right away, no hesitation. And Jessica positively identified the picture."

"You did a regulation lineup?"

"Yes, yes, six photos, six black faces, all fairly young. It'll hold up. We don't have his name yet, but his street name is Bad Boy. What I want to ask you, can I have some extra help to go after him?"

"Anything you need. You want the ERU team?"

"Maybe, if we can make sure he's home. If they miss him on the first grab, he's gone, though. Farah Tur says he commutes to the Cities. If he's gang connected, he could go anywhere from there."

"So, whaddya have in mind?"

"I'd like to put two or three guys in the North End, around his room and the places he hangs. Bo and Darrell know some of his friends. If we could catch him in the open . . . Can I call in Clint Maddox, if he's able? He'll be on overtime—"

"Do it," Frank said. "Let's get this asshole. You starting this up right now? Excellent. Keep me in the loop, Jake, okay?"

I went out and asked Tom Cunningham, who was running the day shift, to page Bo and Darrell and call Clint at home.

"But listen," Tom said, "is it true, you got an ID on that guy that got away from the ERU and the dogs? No kiddin'? That his picture? Lemme see."

I showed him my original Polaroid. "I don't have his real name yet, but his street name is Bad Boy. I've got his voice on tape, too." I played the little segment of taped conversation. "How would you describe that voice?"

"Sounds like Mickey Mouse," he said.

"That's what I said. Not very scientific, I guess, but—"

"Close enough, though. Got that funny little squeak in there." Tom studied the picture curiously. "What kinda moves you layin' on Rosie Doyle, here?"

"That was just an excuse to take the picture."

"Sure." He clucked a couple of times, shook his head, and said, "You still don't get it about sexual harassment, huh?"

He was breaking himself up, and I had no time for jokes. "Will you get the description out to all the cars?" I said. "But tell them, 'No known address.' " I didn't want every cop in Rutherford climbing the stairs at the back of the bookstore. "Can you get it ready for BOLOs, too?"

"Oh, for sure. Starting this afternoon." BOLO stands for "Be On the Lookout." Patrolmen get a list of them at the briefing that starts every shift. "Lemme see if I can make a decent copy of this picture. Any ideas what weapons he might be carrying?"

"I don't know about that, but I think we better say he's dangerous."

"A kid snatcher? I'd say."

I called for an escort deputy and went back to my office, where Farah sat with Ray in profound silence. While we waited for his escort, I tried asking Farah some more about the conversation on the tape. "What did you say this errand was that Bad Boy wants your brother to do?"

But he had built a new wall around himself while I was gone. "I should have an attorney, I think," he said. "I need to talk to Mrs. Glover at the United Methodist Church. Will you call her for me, please?"

"You can call her," I said. "Use my phone." I handed it

to him and was pleased to see that for once I had startled Farah Tur. He looked up a number that he kept in an inside pocket and dialed it with a shaking hand.

Bo Dooley walked in, saying, "Your shit sniffer is back. Whaddya want?"

I took him out in the hall and said, "You don't smell bad."

"Angus fixed it so I didn't have to crawl through. He's kinda fun, isn't he?"

"I don't know him. The chief gave me his name."

"Well, he remembers everything back to Prohibition. He says Rutherford was better when it only had twenty-five thousand people, and he calls IBM 'them Eye Bee and Emmers.' He says the IBM factory ruined the town, that and the big clinic. Ain't that a hoot?"

Coming from Bo Dooley, this was an outburst of chatter, and I longed to let it run on. But not today. I asked him, "What about the sewer, did he help you with that?"

"Oh yeah. Soon's I showed him the house and described the hole in the cellar, he said, 'Betcha they found the old dump culvert,' and took me to the place where the city used to let raw sewage run into the river. Lotta towns did that, back in the good old days. It's been sealed shut since the fifties, he says. A piece of the culvert collapsed, and the riverbank is falling in through the hole, but nobody's noticed it because the spot is covered with sumac bushes. Somebody from the crack house must have found it and realized its potential for an escape route. Wait'll you see."

"I want to see it," I said, "but right now I've got an ID on the kidnapper, and I want you to go and help bring him in."

"No *shit*?" He lit up like fireworks.

I walked him out to Tom's desk to see the picture and

hear the tape. While we were standing there, Darrell called in.

"How you coming with the key makers?" I asked him.

"I took your advice and got lucky," he said. I laughed. "No kidding! Just now! I was leaving Hardware Hank's on North Broadway when I happened to see a new Package Depot store in the old A&P space on Twelfth Avenue. They just moved this year, so they weren't in the yellow pages, I'd never have found it except by accident. I went in and showed the picture, and bingo! They said sure, we know him! He gets keys made here often!"

"Great work," I said. "Hold on to everything you've got and don't come back to the office. I want you to meet Bo at—" I looked at Bo.

"The Dairy Queen by the Shell station on Twenty-first," he said. "We'll have lunch."

I explained his new assignment, and Darrell said, "Why not check out that old van and have him meet me in that? It's pretty good for hanging out."

Clint Maddox was waiting on another phone. "I don't mind coming in," he said, "but I've been helping my brother pour a driveway, and I'm covered with cement."

"That'll be absolutely perfect," I said, "come just as you are."

We checked out a side arm for Maddox and put a couple of short-barreled Remingtons in the back of the van. "You're in charge of this team," I told Bo, "but don't overlook what Clint's learned from walking that area all week. Darrell spent yesterday up there in this van, watching the adult bookstore and the pawnshop, so use any insight he's got. We want to catch this bozo in the open if we can, or inside his apartment alone. I'd like to make it a clean grab, no escape and nobody hurt."

"Right," Bo said, monosyllabic once more.

I poked my head in the chief's office, found him talking on the phone, and started to back out. He waved me in while he said, "Sounds perfect, George. Good. Good. Talk to you later," banged it down, and said, "What?"

"Just want you to know the team's dispatched," I said.

"Good. But you'll call the ERU unit if you need 'em, right?"

"Absolutely."

"I'm confused about something. You taped this guy's voice in the visitors' room—"

"Uh-huh. Took the picture there too."

"Okay, but he was visiting the African kid that claims he robbed the bar?"

"Yup."

"Well, what's the connection?"

"Sure wish I knew."

"Huh. Could it be they just happen to know each other?"

"The man who took Jessica doesn't seem like the type to make social visits."

"S'pose not. Well, so, whaddya think he wants?"

"Maybe the money from the bar. He wants Farah's little brother to go get something. Farah's saying no."

"Interesting. You talked to the brother yet?"

"This afternoon. Soon as I have a meeting with my crew—" I looked at my watch. "Damn! In twenty minutes!"

"Better get a cup of coffee. And here," he pulled open a drawer, "have a granola bar."

I munched on it while I made several phone calls. At one o'clock I carried a cup of coffee into the small meeting room, where Rosie and Kevin were waiting.

"Jake, do you still have deposit slips for Rowdy's Bar?" Rosie asked me.

"Hell, yes, I do. One book." I went to my office and got them. By the time I came back, Ray was at the table, too.

"Lou called me," he said, "and said I should tell you he's got a lunch date you're gonna love, and he'll see us later." He shrugged and rolled his big eyes at me apologetically.

"Okay." I didn't figure Lou French, in his late fifties and so asthmatic he couldn't use the stairs anymore, for a behavior problem. "Should be a good story when we hear it. Bo and Darrell won't be here either." I told Ray and Kevin about the tape Rosie and I had obtained at the jail last night, and showed them the picture. "I didn't want to waste your time with this till I was sure, but this morning I got a positive ID from both Jessica and Schultzy. Bo and Darrell are up in the North End looking for our suspect now. So the kidnapping case is looking close to wrapped up."

"Hot damn," Kevin said. "Can we all go up and help?"

"No. They've got Clint Maddox with them, and they can have an ERU team whenever they call for it. If he's there, they'll get him. We're gonna stay on the evidence track. Rosie, let's hear what you got this morning."

"The bank can't move without a subpoena. Legal's putting it out this afternoon, so we'll have the bank stuff Monday. I brought back what there was from the bar. Pretty sparse. I've got appointments with the lawyer and accountant this afternoon, and with Jack Pfluege. I'm looking for the bartender, too—you said he was good for gossip, right? You need a report on this today?"

"Nah. Write everything down and hang on to it. Kevin?"

"I've pretty well dished all the dirt in the neighborhood. Babe's last romance seems to have been five or six years ago. Since that ended, everybody thinks she just worked and slept and took care of the kid. None of the neighbors like Randy, but when I ask for specifics I get items like he never mowed the lawn, he was always hitting on his mother for money, and his friends were a sleazy bunch. Kid stuff. Nothing to get drowned for."

"Girlfriends?"

"One of the neighbors thought she saw a girl in the yard a couple times. I'm gonna try Scott Rouse and his father this afternoon."

"Good thinking. Okay, Ray, since you've finished your task, why don't you come with me? We're gonna talk to Farah's family. Everybody? Meet back here at quarter to five."

In the car, Ray asked me, "What kind of a name is Tur?"

"They're from Somalia. Came here after the famine."

"Minnesota seems like a funny choice."

"Doesn't it? From one of the hottest nations on earth to one of the coldest states in the Union."

"Any idea how they found us?"

"Some church group, I think."

We stopped in front of unit five of Perry Homes, a four-story block of rent-subsidized apartments below the south overpass to Highway 52. One of twelve identical buildings in the complex, it was painted that awful vomity green so favored by government designers, and it bore the scars of a decade of hard use.

"They gonna be home? Did you call?" Ray asked.

"No phone," I said, "but I had a squad stop by at noon. They were here then, and I asked them to wait for me." We stood on the wooden stoop, squinting at the names under the doorbells. As I bent toward the smudged labels, the door in front of us opened silently inward, and a pair of dark eyes stared out from tie-pin level.

"Hello," I said. I held up my badge. "We're looking for Mr. and Mrs. Muhammed Tur." The door opened a little farther, and another dark pair of eyes looked straight into mine. A woman wearing a light-colored head scarf and a long flowered gown stepped forward and pulled the door back decisively. "Come in," she said. "I am Farida Tur."

In the hall, she pointed toward the stairs and followed me up. Ray came behind us, followed by the small boy who had opened the door. A dingy hall led to several doorways. Behind one of them, a baby cried insistently. The building smelled like a men's room with a dash of garlic. Mrs. Tur opened the last door on the right.

Her apartment was less depressing than most low-cost housing because it was nearly empty and the floor was clean. A kitchen table with chrome legs and four mismatched wooden chairs stood in the middle of the room, which had a stove, sink, and refrigerator along the end wall. There was one closed door, which must have led to a bedroom.

"My husband—" She waved her hand and looked at the child.

Ali said, "He's asleep. He works in a bakery, so he goes to work early." His mother nodded vigorously and added, pointing to the child, "My son. Ali." After some hesitation she explained, "He speaks." We looked at him.

"She means I speak English," Ali said. He had high cheekbones and a handsome domed forehead like Farah's. It was hard to believe he was fourteen; I'd have guessed eight or nine. His narrow shoulders were sharp under his T-shirt. There was nothing childlike about his eyes, which were bright and careful as a hawk's.

We sat down around the table. I told them, speaking slowly, "Farah is in jail. He says he robbed a bar." The four of us looked at each other. Farida's poor English simplified the interview, in a way; I didn't try for tact or persuasiveness, only for the simplest words. "Do you have the money?"

The mother was puzzled till she conferred with Ali,

and then alarmed. She shook her head violently and said, over and over, "No. No, no, no, no."

"Do you know where it is?" Again the anxious conversation in Somali. Ali turned to us and said, "She doesn't know where it is."

"Do you?" He shook his head, wrinkled his nose, and smiled, as if acknowledging that I had asked a silly question and did not expect an answer.

"Ali is a child," his mother said sharply. She had practiced that one, I thought.

"Fourteen, Farah told me. Is that right? Fourteen years old?"

"Yes. But small—" She made a tiny gesture toward him, and he slid an inch farther away from her on his chair.

"Because of the famine, right?" She nodded. Ali sat with just the right touch of solemnity around his sweetly curving mouth. He could convey "famine victim" in a few economical gestures. He had learned to use what he had.

"Farah got enough to eat, then, huh?"

"He rode—" She flapped her hand at her son, and Ali said, "He became a technical. For Ali Mahdi." I remembered the TV news shots, of crazed-looking boys careening through the hellish streets of Mogadishu, in trucks with automatic weapons mounted on the back, carrying rifles that they constantly fired into the air.

Farida said something more, and her son shrugged impatiently. She tugged at his sleeve and repeated it. "What does she want to say?" I asked him, and he looked at his feet sullenly and mumbled, "She says tell you Farah can't seem to stop." Farida got up from the table then, held one finger up to keep my attention, and hurried to a drawer by the stove. She pulled an envelope out of the drawer, came back to the table, and laid a picture in front of me.

It was of a much smaller Farah Tur, smiling in front of a school. She tapped the picture and said, "Good boy." She looked to see if I understood her and repeated several times, "Good boy, good boy." Ali looked at the stove.

"I understand," I told her.

"The warlords," she said. She shrugged hugely and raised her hands to elbow height, palms up, in a gesture of bewildered despair. "Then, the warlords. Now, the break." Ali said something soft and dismissive, and she shook her head in exasperation.

I looked at Ali. "The break?"

He twisted toward the one window and sat staring out. His mother said something as hard as iron to him, and he turned back to me reluctantly and said, "She means crack."

"Crack? She thinks crack has something to do with Farah robbing the bar?" He nodded and went back to scrutinizing the stove.

"He's hooked, you mean?" Ali shook his head emphatically without taking his eyes off the stove. "So—he was raising money to start dealing?" His head never moved. He wouldn't give his brother up, but on some level he wanted to share some of his terrible secrets.

"Ali, what is it Bad Boy wants you to do?"

He peeled his eyes off the stove a little at a time. Finally he looked straight at me and asked, "Who's Bad Boy?" putting so much innocence into it that I knew he was faking.

"I think you've met him," I said. "We'll play a tape to remind you." I nodded to Ray, who was holding the recorder on his lap. He pushed the button, and once again the childish singsong taunted, "You in the slammer, numb nuts. Where you think you comin' from with this *allow* shit?"

The mother's reaction to the tape was pure curiosity, I

thought. She was more interested in watching the tape player work than in listening to the voice, and she couldn't follow the words at all.

Ali was mesmerized with fright. His big eyes rolled up till they were almost all white. He drew his bony little knees up and clamped his arms around them, holding on to himself as if he expected to fly apart.

The spool whirled on, and Farah's voice said, "He is my brother, and he will do what I say." Farida gasped when she heard her son's voice coming from the tape, and cried out something in Somali. Ali shook his head in a quick, fierce gesture that silenced her, and just then a tall black man, an older, more dignified Farah without dreadlocks, jerked open the bedroom door and stared into the room. He gaped all around the table, looking for the Farah he was sure he had just heard, as the tape spun on and Bad Boy's falsetto piped once more, "That so? You think he gonna keep doin' wha'chew say when I got his nuts in a vise, asshole? Huh?"

Ali sat forlornly hugging his own skinny elbows, his jaw clenched against his chattering teeth as Farah's composed voice said, "If you touch my brother, my father will kill you." The man in the doorway made a strangled sound and came toward the table with his arm outstretched. Ray turned off the machine. Ali jumped up at once, and his father took his chair as a matter of course. Ali's mother reached out to draw her son to her side, but he moved to the other side of his father and stood looking down.

"My husband," Farida said. "He, um, no—"

"My father doesn't speak much English yet," Ali said automatically. He pointed to the tape and asked, "Where did you make that?"

"In jail. He was visiting your brother. What does he want you to do?"

He shrugged. His father spoke then, demanding something in Somali. Ali bent toward him obediently, then turned to me and asked, "Is Farah okay?"

"He's fine. Tell your father his older son is fine, but his younger son is in danger."

Ali looked at me, obdurate as stone. I leaned toward the mother and said, slowly and distinctly, "Ali should tell me what he knows. You understand? He is in danger, DAN-GER, does she know the word *danger*, Ali? Ali is in danger till he tells me what he knows." I put two of my fresh "Lt. Jake Hines" cards on the table, one in front of each parent, and said, pointing, "Call me at this number when Ali is ready to tell me what he knows."

My pager sounded. I pulled my cell phone out of my briefcase and called the department while Ali sulked and his parents watched me with expressions they might have turned on the starship *Enterprise*.

"Thought you'd want to know," Tom Cunningham said, "Bo's got the kidnapper, he's bringing him in now."

"Be right there." I stood up. The parents stood up. I shook their hands in turn, saying, as distinctly as I could, "Thank you. I will help you if I can. Call me anytime." I tried to shake Ali's hand, but he skittered behind his father, pretending shyness. Going down the stairs, I could hear the excited questions beginning behind me.

·TEN·

What's his real name?" I asked Maddox.

"Alvin Jackson. That's what he's got on his driver's license, anyway. Which is expired, by the way. Three years out of date."

"That right? We'll have to come down hard on him about that. Where'd you find him?"

"Grocery shopping. Can you beat that? This dangerous felon was toting a six-pack and a frozen pizza out of the Piggly Wiggly."

"How'd you think to look there?"

"It was Clint's idea," Bo said. "He said we just impounded Bad Boy's car, so he'd probably be borrowing wheels. Clint and Darrell know all the cars in the North End by now"—they all looked at each other and laughed—"so we drove around the pawnshop and the bookstore, and sure enough there was a black Grand Am missing from behind the bookstore, and the proprietor was inside. After that we just cruised the area till we spotted the Grand Am parked in front of the grocery store."

"Any trouble making the arrest?"

"Nah," Clint said. "We waited till he came out with his arms full. We decided since I was in these fancy duds"— he held up his arms to show his filthy, cement-covered Levi's and T-shirt—"I could probably walk right up to him before he'd even look at me, and that's just how it worked out. When I showed him my badge, he started to run, but Bo and Darrell were all over him from behind by then."

"Just as well there were three of us, though," Darrell said. "This guy's been eating his Wheaties."

"Also he was carrying," Bo said. "A nifty little Glock 27 in an underarm holster."

Bad Boy was standing under blazing fluorescent lights in the booking stall at the jail, facing the wall, while the booking officer, Jason Hailey, strip-searched him. He measured a bit over six-three, and weighed 230 with very little fat. His chest and shoulders were massive, defined hillocks of muscle, and his buttocks stood up like boulders. He augmented his size with an angry scowl and very deliberate movements, to create an air of sustained menace. He wore a vast assortment of body-piercing ornaments in his ears, eyebrows, nostril, and navel, and many gold chains. At Jason's request, he began removing his jewelry. The chains thunked heavily on the counter when he set them down. "Careful with mah shit now," he squeaked. "Mah shit worth a lot of money."

"I'm careful, don't worry," Jason said "Unbutton your shirt. Unbutton your shirt! What's this you got here? Oh, a beeper." It was clipped at the back of his low-slung jeans, just below the three inches of Jockey shorts that showed above the waistband.

"We might be able to trace that," Bo said, watching Jason list it and put it in an evidence bag.

"That and the gun," Clint said.

"Except the gun's probably stolen," Bo said.

"Take off your pants now," Jason said, and when the prisoner was slow to move, "You want me to take 'em off for you? Take 'em off, then." Alvin was actually sort of enjoying his strip search, I thought. Taking off his shirt, he had done discreet little mini-crunches to show off his washboard abs, and now with his pants off he was making sure we all got a good view of his massive thighs.

"I'm gonna need to make a phone call right away," he told Jason.

"You'll get your phone call soon as we get you booked," Jason said. "Well, lookee here what we got." He unbuckled an ankle sheath from Alvin's right leg. "Goodness gracious, is that a real knife?" Jason found the button, and the switchblade popped up gleaming under the overhead lights. "Gentlemen," he addressed the gallery, "somebody better serve up a fresh ration of shit to the arresting officers about this. They shoulda found this hogsticker in the pat-down. Damn good thing he was cuffed behind his back on the drive in. But if he'd've injured my precious body with this thing, I might be feelin' real testy about now." Beside me, Bo, Clint, and Darrell began muttering profanities. Alvin stood preening ominously in his shorts and socks. He was looking forward to showing us what he had under the shorts, I thought.

"Call me when he's ready, will you, Jason?" I asked the sergeant. I wanted to get my three men out of there before they got any gloomier.

"Let's go up to the break room," I said, "see if we can find Maddox a ride home."

"How'd we miss that fucking knife?" Bo said. He

looked as if somebody had stuck it right through his heart.

"He fought so hard," Darrell said. "All I could think about was getting him subdued without killing him."

"I don't think we ever did do a pat-down, did we?" Clint said. "We were all hanging on to him so tight, and afraid to let go."

"Tell you what," I said. "Why don't you all just shut up about this right now? You made a helluva good search and got a very bad actor off the street. I'd be pleased to hear no more about that damn knife. And listen, Clint, thanks for coming in."

"My pleasure," he said. "This is the first time I started to think maybe this crazy POP job is gonna work out."

"Hell, yes, it is," Bo said, "wish we had somebody memorizing cars all over town." The three of them chuckled in a subdued way. They had been riding high after their success with Clint's bright idea, and I was sorry to see the hidden knife spoil it.

"You did good," I said. "See you Monday." As I crossed the blinding glare of the courtyard with Darrell and Bo, I said, "Bo, before we interrogate your prisoner, will you get somebody in the records room to run his name and stats through NCIC and MINCIS?" NCIC is the national crime information database, and MINCIS is the Minnesota version.

"Right away," he said, and went off toward the support staff.

"And Darrell? Better make notes on your morning's work. Every little detail."

"Including the knife?"

"Don't get hung up on the frigging knife, dammit! Just tell how you found him and how hard he resisted arrest, and list the knife along with the rest of the evidence. Because you know, Darrell, when indictment time comes, no matter how much evidence we give 'em, the county attorney's office always wants more. So put in every scrap you've got."

"I'll do it," he said, "but then can I get in on the interrogation with you?"

"Absolutely. I'll come and get you when he's ready."

Ray was typing up the notes from the Tur family interview when I found him. He looked up and said, "I was thinking."

"Yeah?"

"Well, there's a little patch of woods on the slope behind the Osco store, comes almost down to the water by the Adelaide bridge. Something about it, ever since I got back from there, I been wishing I took a better look at it."

"We'll do it Monday," I said. "Just finish what you're doing and come to the meeting at quarter to five." I was having trouble enough keeping pieces of this puzzle hung together. If each investigator started following his hunches, I was lost. In the hall, someone called, "Anybody home?" I stepped out and found Lou French, carrying his suit jacket and breathing hard.

"How was lunch?" I asked him.

"Outstanding. You got a minute?"

"Sure. Come in my office." Lou is the oldest investigator in the department, in both age and seniority. He would have got my job if his health permitted. But stress makes his asthma worse, so usually he stays in the station doing follow-up on recidivists and addicts and processing handgun applications. More and more, lately, he saves his breath to run his lungs and waits carefully for retirement. Something about this morning's work had lit his fire, though.

"Let me show you a fascinating fact about Rutherford real estate," he wheezed.

"You're racing your motor over real estate? The way you look, I was counting on sex and violence."

"That comes later. First call this number." He read off seven digits while I dialed. A sugary voice said, "Hello, this is Bestway Realty. Your phone call is im-PORT-ant to us—" and went on to entreat me to leave a message. I stared at Lou with my mouth open. It was Tammy's voice.

"Got that?" Lou said. "Remember that voice, now, because I want you to call—" He gave me seven more digits, I dialed, and the same sweet voice answered for a company named Pioneer Property Management, imploring me to brighten her day by leaving my im-PORT-ant message.

"This is totally weird," I said. "Lemme show *you* something." I dialed my nemesis, A to Z Rental, and handed the phone to Lou.

"Oh, yes," he said, listening, "A to Z, I know about them." He hung up the phone. "Your apartment?" I nodded. He sat back contentedly and began to tell me about his day.

"I went to the county assessor's office. Babe's house belongs to Bestway Realty, but she leased the bar from Pioneer Properties. The same voice on an answering machine kept answering the phone at both numbers. Finally I looked up the crack house. A to Z Rentals was listed as the owner, so I called that and got a live human being with the same voice as the answering machine, and I persuaded her to give me an address. She didn't want to, but I said—"

"Lou," I said, "I've got about five minutes. Can we cut to the chase?"

"Oh, sure. Sorry." He riffled through his papers and said, "Anyway this Tammi Fae Boe, that's her name, works in an office about the size of a broom closet, in the basement of the Kiowa Towers."

"Kiowa Towers," I said, "really?"

He nodded. "Thought you'd like that. Funny little girl, green fingernails, sort of a ditz. When I said I needed to ask her some questions, she said no, she couldn't talk, she was too busy to even eat lunch. So I went out and got us some food, and while we ate she explained how one small, not very bright female can manage almost all the low-rent housing in Rutherford."

"How?"

"Very swiftly. In a slipshod manner. With four phones."

"And?"

"I asked her who her boss was, and she said, 'It's a consortium of attorneys and physicians,' very lofty, like I was supposed to fall over and faint from being so impressed. I couldn't persuade her to be any more specific, so after lunch I went back to the tax assessor to find out who writes the checks. It's a person named F. Alexander Gainesborough. Sounds phony as a three-dollar bill, doesn't it? But his signature's on every check from Cigna Corp. Which also just happens to own the car we've got in the impound garage."

"No *shit*?" I had been trying to figure out how to get away from Lou without seeming rude. The car changed everything. "What about Kiowa Towers? Who owns that?"

"Um," he consulted his notes, "Bestway. Which I guess in the end really means Signa Corp."

My pager sounded. I called dispatch, and Neva said, "Your prisoner's ready."

"Ask them to bring him to my office, will you?" Damn! Too much going on!

"Lou," I said, "I wish we could go over this some more right now, but we can't, I've got a prisoner coming up. Organize your notes and bring it all to the meeting, okay?" He headed off to his own space, and I called Bo and Darrell, started out to get extra chairs, and was suddenly hit hard by a craving for coffee. I hustled toward the break room with my cup in my hand and ran into the chief in the hall.

"You know we brought in the kidnapper?" I asked him.

"What? I been in a budget meeting. Oh, jeez, you got him? Damn, I'm glad to hear that! What's he look like?"

"Come in my office in a minute, and you'll see. We're gonna . . . Oh, *piss!*" The coffeepot was sitting on the burner almost empty, smelling evil.

"Here, come in *my* office," Frank said. "Lulu always keeps a fresh pot ready. Why are you so upset just when you finally got a break?"

"Because there's so much happening at once!" I said. "And it all keeps running together. And this kidnapping makes no sense at all as a moneymaking venture, Frank. Jessica just happened to be standing in that yard because she sneaked out of the school. There's no way he snatched her except on an impulse."

"So you mean we got a real child abuser on our hands? Shit. Hard to prosecute, hard to prove. And it's gonna give Schultzy the creeps for a year."

"And when did you ever know a child abuser to call the cops just before he took his pleasure? That's just crazy, Frank."

"I know. You're right. But he took her, and he called us, and we've gotta go ahead with what we've got. Goddamn, however this turns out, I'm glad you got that bastard off the street, though. You just made my day there, Jake."

"I'm glad, too," I said. "You coming in?"

"In a minute."

Bo and Darrell had brought in chairs for themselves and were sitting against the wall, one on each side of my desk. Darrell looked as pleased as a kid at a picnic. Bo sat straight on his chair with his knees and feet close together and his hands clasped tightly on his knees; a muscle twitched in his jaw, and his eyes were hard as blue marbles. Something about grabbing Bad Boy had wrapped him even tighter than usual.

Bad Boy looked more impressive than ever in prison fatigues; they showed off his bulging biceps and powerful throat. Stripped of jewelry, his scowling face conveyed more menace. He lowered his massive forearms onto the armrests of his chair with a meaty little slap.

I started my tape recorder and asked him, on a sudden hunch, "Are your folks from down around the Cayman Islands?" It was the only place I'd been in the Caribbean, and his face looked like some I had seen there, with the European features of visiting sailors and the black skin of the girls they left behind.

"Antigua." His voice surprised me all over again, piping frail and infantile out of his massive chest.

"You a citizen of the United States?"

"Yup. Born in Minneapolis." I glanced at Bo, and he nodded.

"Why'd you kidnap Jessica Schultz?"

"Kidnap!" He shook his head. "You got the wrong man."

"See, now that's not gonna work, Alvin, because the victim has identified you."

"How could I have a victim when I ain't done nothin'?"

"The child you took out of the play yard at Granny Goose day-care center says you did."

"Man, why would I be hanging around a day-care center? Thass just crazy! You juss got the wrong man, is all." He crossed his arms and glowered. "She's white, right? This girl you're sayin' identified me? People in Minnesota think all black men look alike."

"She picked you out of six pictures of black men, Alvin. Without any hesitation."

"Don't mean nothin'. You told her to pick one, she picked one. Mah lawyer will be here soon and straighten all this out."

"He's not gonna straighten anything out, Alvin. You're in the can for kidnapping, which is a very serious crime. Do you understand that?"

He glowered. "Nnnhhh." He had this thin, high nasal squeak, an all-purpose noise he evidently used when he didn't want to answer directly.

"Actually it's a federal crime. If we hadn't found Jessica right away, we'd have had to turn the search over to the FBI. And if the case isn't closed right away, we might still have to pass you along to them. You think you're gonna enjoy having the Feds on your case?"

"Nnnnhhh." He sat there, big as a boulder, giving me nothing, a wiseass waiting for his attorney.

I looked at Bo and Darrell and shrugged. Bo pulled a sheaf of computer printouts from under his arm, put them on the desk, and said, "Kidnapping's not your usual gig, is it, Alvin?"

"Dunno wha'chew mean."

"I mean I been going over your record, and it looks like what you usually do is deal drugs." Bo laid his pages out on the desk and began to read. "Lessee, we got two short stretches at a juvenile boot camp, '89 and '91, you were pretty young then, weren't you? Both of those for shoplifting. Then three arrests in '92, one breaking and entering, two burglaries, no convictions in any of those. Working your way up, though. In '93, you were arrested for armed robbery of a gas station, and they made that one stick. You got five to ten and served two years in St. Cloud. Since your parole from there, it's all been drug busts, though, hasn't it? Five arrests, all for dealing. And no convictions. Alvin has good connections," Bo told me, sitting back and folding his arms. "Alvin's connections get him good lawyers, and the good lawyers keep him out of jail."

Alvin sat watching Bo closely. I could almost hear him thinking, What the fuck is this we got here? Bo's anger was so palpable I could feel it pumping where I sat. I was beginning to wonder about Bo myself.

"Them arrests was all a mistake," he said, placidly. "I didn't do nothin'."

"Right," Bo said, "we understand how innocent you are. What we can't understand is why you suddenly took it in your head to grab that kid the other day. That was a bad mistake, Alvin, and it doesn't seem like your usual MO at all. Why did you do that?"

"I didn't."

Frank walked in then, carrying a folding chair. He held a hand toward me, palm out, to indicate he didn't need anything, set up his chair against the side wall where he could watch all of us, and sat down. Bad Boy looked at him a few seconds, decided he was harmless, and turned back to Bo and me.

"What did you have in mind to do," I asked, "if we hadn't showed up when we did?"

"Do?"

"What was next? You had Jessica there in the crack house with you. How were you going to get the money?"

He shrugged. "You keep havin' fun with that idea if you want to, but I wasn't there, and I didn't grab nobody."

"Oh, bullshit. You're smarter than that. Your lawyer isn't going to be able to talk you out of this one, Alvin, because your pal Farah Tur gave you up too. Did I forget to tell you that? He told us how you grabbed that little girl and put a gag in her mouth—" A little flash of concern showed through a tiny crack in his composure and disappeared quickly. "He decided he didn't want to risk a death sentence over some stupid plot to grab a little girl and try to get money out of her hardworking parents—"

"I don't think you understand this man, Jake," the chief said, suddenly. We all jumped at the sound of his voice and turned to look at him. His big body was hunched awkwardly in the little armless meeting-room chair, his hands hanging idly between his knees. Staring morosely at the prisoner with his big pop eyes, he looked like a rather obtuse man contemplating a corpse at a wake. "He's ashamed of what he intended to do with Jessica, you can see that all over him. He's hoping that since we interrupted him, maybe we'll never figure out what his intentions were, that we'll think he did it for money. Which I for one don't believe for a minute, because just look at him," waving his arm toward the prisoner, "he's got pedophile written all over him."

"Peda-wa'?" Bad Boy quavered.

"Pedophile, Alvin. Jesus, you do it, and you don't even know what to call it? You get your rocks off with little kids, right? You meant to abuse Jessica sexually, didn't you?"

"Whaaat?" Alvin had been feigning menace before. Now he got angry, and seemed to grow a couple of inches in all directions. His face darkened, and the big vein at the side of his neck began to pulse and swell. "You think I wanted to do some little child?" Under stress, his voice got higher. "Man, thass disgusting!" he squeaked, glaring at Frank. "What kinda creep are you?"

"He'll keep denying it for a while," Frank went blandly on, "they always do. But you keep after him on this, Jake, because before very long his own guilt feelings are gonna make him confess. As for that rap sheet of his you pulled off MINCIS," Frank told Bo, "I wouldn't worry a whole lot about the lack of any child-abuse record there. What you need to do is go in the sex offender file and find all the unsolved cases for the last six years or so, find the officers involved, and call them, go over the details with them. Chances are you're gonna find some descriptions that line up just fine. We're probably gonna have grateful cops from all over the area calling us before long, just lined up waiting to get a piece of this guy." He got up, set his chair neatly against the wall, said, "Very nice work, guys," and walked out. From the hall, holding the door ajar, he met my eyes and nodded toward his office.

I leaned toward Bo and said, "Tell you what, you two stay with the prisoner a few minutes while I get one of the support staff to start going through that sex offender file. Maybe you can ask him some questions about his childhood till I get back."

Bo and Darrell nodded solemnly. They didn't understand exactly what Frank and I were doing, but they knew very well we didn't go fishing for cases to hang around the necks of the prisoners we happened to have sitting around the station. I went out and found Frank, who said, "I believed his denial, didn't you?"

"Yes."

"What the hell, then? The ransom theory's bullshit, too, isn't it?"

"Yes."

"Well . . . he did it and we've got him, though, right? The ID is gonna hold up?"

"Yes. I'll get Schultzy and Jessica in here Monday and do a live lineup and confirm it, but yeah, he's our man all right."

"Okay. What did Bo find in the files?"

"Theft and drugs. Couple years in St. Cloud for robbery. Since then he's been picked up for dealing several times, but no convictions."

"Uh-huh. He went to St. Cloud and got connected," Frank said gloomily. "Ain't it swell how that works?"

"Still, though. He may not know how to spell 'pedophile,' but he's gotta know how child abusers get treated in prison. I say we put him back in his cell, give him no more phone calls and no visitors except his lawyer, and let him spend the weekend thinking about it. If he thinks we're really building a sex-offender case against him, he might decide to deal."

"I agree," Frank said. "It's the best we can do."

Back in my office, Bo was firing taut hostile questions at a mostly silent Alvin.

"All that time inside, and you're still not a crack smoker?" Bo asked him. "Come on."

"Never had no use for it," Bad Boy said.

"Whaddya use, then? H?"

"You looked at my arms?" He turned over two smooth forearms as big as fence posts. "No tracks." He looked at Bo's slender build condescendingly and flexed. "This body's a temple, man."

"Okay, guys, let's get down to business," I said, sitting down. "How long you had this weird thing for little kids, huh? You get off on boys, too, or just little girls?"

"I don't have no weird thing for nobody! Why you keep saying that?"

"Because you snatched a little girl off the street and tied her up, put a gag in her mouth, and took her to a filthy house where she didn't want to go. What am I supposed to think about that?"

He rocked his head, shrugged, raised his arms, and let them fall—thunk!—onto the chair arms again. "S'posed to think you made a mistake and got the wrong man."

"Bullshit again," I said. "You just keep bullshitting me, Alvin, and in the meantime the afternoon is passing, and by Monday we have to decide what to charge you with.

And it's gonna have to be kidnapping and attempted rape of a child, unless you start to make sense."

"No, it don't! What makes you so sure it was me? You got my record there, you see anything on there about me snatchin' up children?"

"No, I don't. But see, the two people who saw you and talked to you that day, the little girl and her mother, have both identified you positively." I looked at my watch. "I've got twenty minutes left, Alvin, before I have to put you back in your cell and get on with the day's work. Now, do you really think in the next twenty minutes you can explain to me why anybody who wasn't totally bananas, anybody but a nutcase with an out-of-control urge to abuse a child, would take her out of a yard and carry her off to a crack house and tie her up? Be reasonable, Alvin. What sane person is gonna look on that as anything but the work of a berserk pervert?"

He stared out my window at the power plant and finally said, almost kindly, "When my lawyer gets here, he'll fix everything."

We sent him back to his cell. Bo and Darrell went off to run checks on his gun and beeper. I took my tape recorder out to the support staff desk and left it for transcription over the weekend. Then I dialed Schultzy's number, waited through three rings, asked a giggling teenybopper to put her mother on the line, and then yelled over the background din, "Will you tell Miss Jessica Schultz that her many admirers on the Rutherford Police Force just locked that Bad Boy up in a cage where he belongs?" Schultzy was so tearfully, fervently grateful that for a couple of minutes I loved my job so much I'd have done it for nothing. Then my tired crew began filing into the small meeting room, and I came back to earth and concentrated on winding down the week.

"Just say what you learned today," I said, "but skip

how you found it, or we'll be here all night. I'll go first: We got a positive ID on the kidnapper from three people. Bo and Darrell and Clint Maddox went up to the North End and found him, and he's here in a cell right now. Damn good day's work. Now, let's hear what else we got. Bo?"

"If you get into the sewer through the hole in the crack house cellar, you can be at an escape hole at the river in just over a block. Plenty of bushes growing all around the escape hole, too."

"Darrell?"

"Randy Thorson had the keys to his mother's bar copied at the Package Depot on Twelfth Avenue Northwest. It's not the first time. He's had several other sets of keys made there before. Whatever he was up to has been going on for a while." He turned to me and said, "Aren't you gonna tell 'em how we picked up the kidnapper?"

"Sure. After Farah Tur gave us a name and a probable address, Bo and Darrell went up to the North End with Clint Maddox and nailed our suspect coming out of a store with his arms full of groceries." Everybody applauded, including the two who were in on the arrest. "I still have no idea why he did it, but maybe after a weekend in jail he'll decide to tell me that. The toughest part of the kidnapping case is closed now, and early Monday we should get most of the test results from BCA and begin to move ahead on the homicide. Very good news. Let's finish up here. Ray?"

"Well, as I told you earlier, my dad showed me where the river widens and gets shallow, just north of the Adelaide bridge. So I guess we're in for a search of those seven blocks of shallow water between the Adelaide bridge and the Second Avenue bridge. And I suggest we take a good look at the patch of woods that comes almost down to the water by the Adelaide bridge."

"Good. We'll hope to get started Monday. Rosie, how'd your afternoon go?"

"The lawyer says it's news to him if Babe Krueger was having trouble, she never asked him for any advice at all. The accountant says she was in a serious cash bind till early last year. Then she got a lot of group business—that's what he called it, 'all these groups on the weekends'—and paid all her bills, and she's been fine ever since. Jack Pfluege says business has been poor for the last three years, and getting a little worse all the time." Rosie smiled and raised her hands above her shoulders with the fingers splayed like fans. "Which story do you like?"

"Which one do you like?"

"Jack Pfluege was there six days a week, and he has no reason to lie. Otherwise, judging from the deposit books, I'd be inclined to believe the accountant. I'll tell you more when I get the bank records Monday."

"Good. Lou, you had a good day, tell 'em what you got."

"Huh. What I found out is pretty damned odd. Which is that most of the low-rent housing in town, including Rowdy's Bar and the crack house and Babe Krueger's house, as well as Jake's apartment, is rented by the same little girl who works in a two-bit office in the basement of the Kiowa Towers."

The other five crew members stared at him. Finally Rosie said, "So?"

"She works for four different real estate companies, has four phones and four sets of keys and four ledgers to keep up. But all these properties get their taxes paid by the Cigna Corporation, which also owns that tan hatchback we impounded at the crack house the other day. The kidnapper's car."

"I'm starting to get a weird hunch," Kevin said.

"What's the name of that girl in the office at Kiowa Towers?"

"Um . . ." Lou consulted his notes. "Tammi Fae Boe."

"See, there you go," Kevin said, "isn't that just the goddamnedest thing?" His Boy Scout face grew radiant; his eyes blazed with excitement, and he bounced around on his chair. "I just can't get over it!" he yelled, "It beats anything I've ever seen!"

"We're all glad you're enjoying yourself," I said. "Any chance you might share?"

"I told you I didn't get much fresh stuff from Babe's neighbors this morning," Kevin said, "so I spent the afternoon talking to Scott Rouse and his father. The father's not a whole lot of help right now, he's so pissed at his kid he can't think straight. He feels really screwed. He says he took a lot of time doing guy things with his son, ball games and fishing and hunting. And he felt sorry for Randy for not having a father, so he often included him, said he thought it was good for Scott to have a best friend. He says he has no idea why Scott would feel he needed to rob a bar, and you know what? I believe him.

"But Scott Rouse tells a completely different story, about how his father always wants to run everything, and Randy's mother was stingy, and Scott and Randy never had enough spending money, so they were practically forced to rob the bar. Listen, though, don't laugh, there's more to all this, something much bigger going on. I can feel it. Scott got right up to the edge of telling me about it this afternoon, he was dying to, but at the last minute he sucked up and backed off. Whatever it is, it involves Randy Thorson's steady girlfriend, a red-hot number by the name of Tammi Fae Boe."

"Ain't it beautiful when a case comes together?" Lou said. They all sat gabbing excitedly about the way these two cases kept merging, but nobody knew where to go with it yet, and before long we began to repeat ourselves.

"Go home," I said. "Enjoy the weekend. We'll figure it out on Monday." They filed out, and I heard them in their cubicles for a few minutes, putting paperwork away and resetting their voice mail, and then the elevator sighed a few times and the section went quiet. I sat making notes for Monday while the shadows lengthened in the parking lot.

At seven o'clock my body started a bitching fit about working all day with no lunch, so I drove to a specialty deli that's recently been added to a grocery store near my building and went mildly berserk. I selected a round loaf of bread full of raisins and nuts, found several pieces of wildly expensive cheese and a big slice of prosciutto, and at the last minute added a bunch of red grapes so elegant they could have been the centerpiece in a still life. I stood in front of a shelf of Italian wines for some time, finally choosing a Chianti with a description on the back of the bottle that made me hear peasants chanting. I carried my pricey treasures straight home and munched and crunched and quaffed while I watched a wrap-up of the week's news. Our local station used the kidnapper's arrest as the lead story. Frank had done a good job with them; the department got rave notices.

The weather prediction was good and then bad: Most of the weekend would be fair, it said, but by Sunday night we would see rain, hail, lightning, and high winds. "Summer's going out with a bang," said a kindly man in a sweater, "better get your outdoor chores done tomorrow."

The outdoor chore I had planned was no pleasure: I had a date to meet an insurance adjuster named Sven Torgerson, in the vehicle storage yard of Joe's Auto Repair. We were supposed to reach a settlement so that Joe could commence repairing my pickup. All week I had nagged the League of Minnesota Cities, which insures department vehicles, complaining that a pickup with a skewed axle, a crumpled truck bed, and two accordion fenders should be declared a total loss and replaced. "It's never gonna track straight again," I insisted. But Sven and Joe were adamant: My red sled could be returned to "like-new" condition. I didn't want like-new. I wanted what I had waited twelve years for and finally got, the loaded Super-Cab 4 × 4 cherry red creampuff Ford XLT I had driven to the golf course last Sunday. Spotless. Flawless. New. Sven was sympathetic but going by the book.

I had made up my mind to fight to the bloody, bitter end for what I wanted, but when I came out of my house Saturday morning, I looked at the late August sun pouring gold across asters and dahlias in the dewy yard across the street and suddenly thought, Screw it. It's a beautiful day. Get this behind you and have some fun. I was too tired from the week's work to make much headway against a professional haggler anyway.

So as soon as Sven had explained the deductible to me again, and I had groused about it and then persuaded him to include the cost of a new putter to replace the one I threw at Eugene Soames, I signed the forms he thrust at me and shook hands. As soon as he was gone I pried open the driver's-side door of the truck and hauled my golf bag out of the backseat. I tossed it in the trunk of the department's old Dodge Caravan, rolled down the windows, and cruised the sleepy Saturday morning streets across town to the municipal course.

Ted Bunting was in the pro shop, so I stopped in to order a new putter. I chose a Taylor-Made with a midsize grip. "Lemme see your old one," Ted said.

I dragged my bag up to the counter and handed him the bent putter. "Does the pitch on this head match your

stance pretty well? You want about the same offset?" He
waited a couple of seconds, and said, "Jake?"

I pulled my head out of my golf bag, stared at him a
couple of seconds, and said, "Yes. Fine. You got a phone I
can use?" He passed a phone from under the counter. I
found Bo's number on my wallet card and dialed. He
answered after four rings, "Dooley."

"I need you," I said, "just for a few minutes. Could you
meet me somewhere?"

"I have to bring my kid," he said.

"Not a problem."

"Where are you?"

"Municipal golf course. Where the chase ended up."

"I'll be there in fifteen minutes."

I dragged my golf bag to the bench in front of the pro
shop and waited there, sitting on the shady end of the
bench with the bag touching my left foot. Bo pulled his
Harley into the parking lot fourteen minutes later, set the
kickstand, and lifted a small girl in a sunsuit out of a
basket on the back of the bike. He helped her take off her
adorable tiny helmet, picked her up, and walked toward
me, carrying her. She had curly auburn hair growing close
around her head, like his, and the beginnings of his over-
bite.

"This is Nell," he said, and the toddler and I nodded.
She seemed poised, like Bo.

"Look in my golf bag," I said. He put the child down,
said, "Stay by me," bent over my golf bag, and looked
inside.

"Why, Jake," he said, "shame on you. What a place to
keep your crack."

"I've only ever seen it retail," I said, "a little nugget in
a twist of Saran Wrap. But this is what the big pieces look
like, is it?"

"Sure enough," he said, "we'll have to test it, of course,

but yes, this is by-God, sure-enough two wholesale portions of crack cocaine." He beamed at me. "In your golf bag!" He laughed happily.

Round and about the size of billiard balls, pale beige and slick-looking with a pebbly surface, they were in small plastic food bags caught under the handle of one of my clubs. I went and got some gloves out of my car, pulled the clubs out of the bag, reached in, and pulled the bags of crack out into the light. Holding them up, I saw the two balls were not really solid spheres, but tightly packed wads of hundreds of irregularly shaped nodules, melded together like popcorn balls but ready to break apart again at the tap of a mallet. As I watched, a fingertip-sized chunk fell off one of the balls and dropped to the bottom of the bag.

"I knew I saw that guy throw something away!" Bo crowed. "I kept saying it! You saw it too, didn't you?"

"Yes," I said, "but I didn't know what I was seeing. What would you say the odds are of his hitting the opening of my golf bag with a blind toss like that?"

"About a zillion to one."

"More to the point, I guess," I said, "what are the odds we can connect it to Eugene Soames now?"

"Well." He stood and pondered. "We can try fingerprinting the plastic bags, of course. Might get lucky. And there's the fact that he ran away; this gives him motive for that. Otherwise . . . a week after the chase? And we find it in your golf bag? Don't bet the farm."

"So Eugene's home free?"

"Oh, no. We know what we saw. The guys on the chase know. Soon's I get his mug shots and descriptions up to the Cities, all the cops in Minneapolis and St. Paul are gonna be watching Eugene. Sooner or later they'll catch him dealing."

"Right. Well! You go on back to whatever you were doing, Bo, and I'm sorry I had to call you."

"No problem," he said. "Nelly and I kinda wanted a ride this morning anyway." She was standing patiently by his side; at the mention of her name, she looked up and took his hand. "See you Monday," Bo said, and walked his self-possessed daughter to the parking lot.

I decided I wouldn't feel comfortable enough to play golf until the crack was put away, so I put my golf clubs back in the car and drove downtown. Standing at the counter in the evidence room, filling out forms, on an impulse I picked up the paper evidence bag that now contained the crack and walked down the hall to Frank's office. He wasn't supposed to be working on Saturday, but this summer he had been even more snowed than I was and often came in on weekends.

I found him hunched over his keyboard, typing at high speed. I stood in his doorway till he peeled his eyes reluctantly away from his monitor screen and said, "What?"

"You wanna see some crack?"

"I'm kind of busy, Jake," he said, as patiently as he could manage, and then, when I still stood there grinning, he said, "What? What is it?" I carried the bag over to his desk and set it in front of him. He looked in and said, "Oh, Jesus, that's a *lot* of crack, isn't it? Where'd you get this?"

I put gloves on, picked up the vanilla-colored balls, and laid them on top of the sack. "How much d'you think it's worth?"

"Retail? On the street? Twenty thousand at least. Maybe thirty. Wholesale like this, what the dealers charge each other is highly flexible, I guess. Where'd you find this, Jake?"

"In my golf bag."

"Whaaat?"

"Honest to God. See, when Bo and them chased Eugene Soames over the top of me last Sunday, Bo said Eugene threw something away, and I thought I saw it too, but nobody else did, and they never could find anything out there on the golf course but his dark glasses. Today I went out to play a round and found this at the bottom of my bag."

"Well, I'll be damned." He sat admiring the balls of crack a minute and began to chuckle. "Probably better keep this to yourself till we get it pretty well corroborated."

"Don't worry."

Then he began to thrash around in his chair, looking more and more discontented, and finally asked me, "This the biggest stash of crack you've ever come across? Here in town?"

"Yes. And in all my training they only ever showed us retail hits, one small rock in a wrapper."

"A find this size, you know what it means, don't you? The crack trade's moving into town in a big way. I've heard they do regular merchandising now, they—what's that expression they learned from big business?—'build a client base.' In plain English, that means getting kids hooked." He kicked his desk a few times. "If you hadn't ever seen a big chunk before, how'd you know what you had?"

"I called Bo. He came and looked and said yup, that's crack. I have to get it up to BCA for testing, of course."

"Uh-huh. Bo would know. He working out all right for you?"

"Fine. Gets his work done fast and doesn't complain. Only thing that seems to bother him is extra hours, but I guess that's because of his kid. What's he got, a shared custody or something?"

"No. His wife's in detox." Frank squinted out the window for a minute and said, "I guess maybe you ought to know. They moved up here from St. Louis because she was trying to kick a crack habit, and they thought getting out of the city might help. Evidently things went well for a while. She got clean, and they had a baby. But this summer she started using again." He squirmed, and his chair springs complained. "He came in and told me all this when she committed herself. He didn't want me to hear it from somebody else."

"Christ, that's rough," I said, thinking about the quiet redhaired child.

"I asked him, 'Is this job going to get too personal?' He said no, he thought he could remain highly motivated—that's how he said it, highly motivated—without going apeshit."

"As far as I can tell, that's exactly the line he's walking. I did wonder why he was wrapped so tight. I had him pegged for a little overly ambitious. Thanks for telling me, this explains a lot."

His keyboard was rattling again before I was out of the room. I went back to the evidence desk, checked in my stash, came out, and saw Rosie Doyle's ponytail swinging down the hall ahead of me. She was doing Saturday morning duty in exchange for one half-day off in midweek. I made this deal with her because I was sick of coming in Saturday every time we had a major arrest on Friday. We can only hold prisoners forty-eight hours without charging them; when we have to keep them over a weekend, we keep it legal by getting a probable-cause-to-arrest form signed by a judge on Saturday. Completing the paperwork, finding a judge at home, and running it out to his house for a signature can eat up half a morning.

"Hey, Rosie." She turned and waited for me to catch up.

"Hey yourself," she said, "thought you were going to play golf."

"I still am," I said. "That a Form Forty-four you're carrying?"

"Yeah. Just got it signed by Judge Meredith. Alvin Jackson is all yours till four P.M. on Monday."

"Good. Can you stand another task?"

"Sure. Gotta pass the time till noon somehow."

I showed her the request forms I needed filled out in order to test the big balls of crack in the state crime lab. I probably could have filled them out myself in the time it took me to explain, but it was more fun telling Rosie the story of finding crack in the bottom of my golf bag. By the time I finished and got back out to the golf course, it was lunchtime, so I ate a huge salami-and-Swiss hoagie and drank two beers. By the time I got to the ninth hole, I was bilious and sleepy and desperately needed to pee, so I hardly needed my crooked putter excuse to account for my double bogey six.

· E L E V E N ·

WEATHER GURUS KEPT BREAKING INTO MY MUSIC PROGRAMS to warn that a severe storm had moved inland off the Pacific Friday, crossed the Rockies yesterday, and was rolling across the Dakota border as they spoke. I kept switching stations to tune them out of my Sunday. Rolling merrily northward toward my date with Trudy, I didn't need any naysayers cautioning me to stay safe at home. The view from the highway was benign; red-winged blackbirds fluttered brilliantly in the ditches, the horizon shimmered with heat waves, and the sky was a cloudless bright blue bowl above motionless fields of ripening soybeans.

On the stairs to Trudy's apartment, bacon smells reached down to the newel post and pulled me up. She answered the door wearing an enormous white denim apron over her shorts, and the contrast between the chaste hausfrau of her front view and the perky homecoming queen in the rear turned me on so powerfully that I wanted to keep saying hello for hours.

"Come on, now, sit down," she said, "everything's ready but the eggs."

"Including me," I said, "let's have another hug." Nature intended Trudy for a soft, round woman, but her many athletic pursuits keep her muscles taut, so that holding her yields a delightful mix of tactile impressions: the pillowy softness of her breasts, the surprising strength of her arms. She pushed away suddenly and cried, "The muffins!" Pulling a pan out of the oven, she said, "Pour yourself a cup of coffee."

"Hey, this is beautiful," I said. The table in her tiny dinette was set with bright pottery, and daisies in a pot played off a daisy-print cloth. We ate her good breakfast slowly, talking about the series prospects for the Twins, the fishing reports from Canada. Anything but work: We had agreed early on to leave the work behind during private times. When she loaned me one of her enormous aprons for the washing-up after, I stuck a bowl on my head and did my Minnie Pearl impression, improvising banjos with a cutting board. Trudy seemed to enjoy the first couple of verses but interrupted my third "Howdee," looking at her watch and saying, "I guess we better get going."

In her bedroom, neatly sorted clothing was heaped on the bed and the floor. She was getting rid of many wool skirts, a couple of ski suits, a dozen sweaters. "I bet you looked cute in these," I said, holding up a pair of bell-bottoms.

"Isn't it ridiculous what you save sometimes?" She giggled, but she ran her hand so fondly over the fabric in the old gray pants that I could see she still found it hard to let them go. "How about taking that box of boots and shoes first?"

Distant thunder rumbled in the west as we loaded the trunk and backseat of my car. The wool clothing stuck to us in the punishing heat of early afternoon. The temperature hung relentlessly around ninety, and the air felt dead. Sticky heat stifled us as we parked in front of the Salvation Army, pulled all the heavy armloads out of the car again, and staggered into the dusty back room of the store. Drenched with sweat and sneezing after several trips, we stumbled at last back to my empty car, where I turned the air conditioner on the old Dodge as high as it would go. "This is fun," I shouted above the roar of the fan, "do we get to break up some rocks next?" She muttered something, and I yelled, "What did you say?"

Trudy said, "I said, one more load and I'm done."

"Done what? What is this, some kind of super house-cleaning job or something? Why are you giving so much stuff away?"

"Getting ready to move," she said.

"Move? You found a new apartment?"

"I kept trying to tell you the other day, but there was never any time. I've got a new job in San Francisco."

"You what?" I stared at her so long I started to drift into the oncoming lane. An air-horn blast from an oncoming eighteen-wheeler jerked me back to real time. I swung the wheel right and missed a colossal front bumper by a couple of inches, retaining an imprint of bright chrome and red lettering on my terrified retinas as the behemoth streaked angrily past me. Trembling, I found a strip mall driveway and turned into it, parked the car, and turned off the motor. Into the rapidly reheating silence, I said, "Tell me about it."

"I didn't mean to spring this on you, Jake. It all came up very suddenly, and I . . . we've both been so busy . . ."

"*What* came up very suddenly?"

"This neat job at a magazine in San Francisco. It's . . . uh . . . kind of a shopper's aid and tourist guide. Lots of pictures, so I'll really get to show what I can do with color shots. And they share customers and continuity with one of the TV stations, so I'll still get to use video as well as still camera, you don't get that combination many places—"

"You've got it here," I said. "Why would you move?"

"Oh, well, you know, I've never worked anywhere outside Minnesota, I thought it would be good for me to try another location. And San Francisco is such an exciting place. I've only been there for one vacation, but I know I'm going to love living by the ocean—" She went rattling on about the wonderful opportunity and the beautiful scenery and the marvelous food, while sorrow welled up in me to match the enormous black cloud that was overtaking the sky overhead. The Trudy of my hopes and dreams seemed ready to walk out of my life as casually as she would leave any of her peers at work, with cheery best wishes and a promise to send postcards.

My sense of impending tragedy grew and grew, until I began to dread that I would not be able to contain my distress and would burst into tears. I saw myself being led away by concerned strangers, wailing uncontrollably, leaving Trudy to cope with the balky starter on the Dodge and the gathering cloudburst. Luckily, a shaft of lightning split the sky in front of us at that moment, interrupting Trudy's soliloquy about sourdough bread and bike paths through the Presidio.

I said roughly, "Look, it's gonna storm, we better get back."

Trudy stared around her, surprised, as a gust of wind shook the car and the first big drops of rain splattered on the windshield. She said, "Oh, I'm sorry, Jake, I just wasn't paying attention, I guess—" as if the storm were her fault, and she had personally chosen to strand us on this cracked asphalt parking strip while a tornado bore down on us. She was abjectly contrite, then, helping me get back on the street, peering through the cloudburst into oncoming traffic, asked, "Are you all right?"

"Sure," I said, "it's a right at the next light, isn't it?" By the time we reached her street, the air was so full of water it was hard to breathe, and wind was blowing it against the car like wet bullets. I left the motor running when I stopped in front of her building, looking straight ahead while I said, "Guess we can't haul any more stuff today, huh?"

"No. I wish you didn't have to go home in this. Won't you come in awhile, and wait for the storm to let up a little?" She knew I wouldn't. I watched her run toward her front door, putting her feet down in the solid, capable style I had already begun to take pride in, adding it to my carefully tended list of things to feel good about, imagining myself telling someone, sometime soon, "You should see my girl run—"

Driving home would have been a nightmare if I'd cared one way or another how it turned out. As it was, I was just vaguely grateful for something to keep me occupied. Ten miles south of Fort Snelling the visibility went from poor to nonexistent, and as I crept forward I got a momentary impression I'd turned in to a used car lot by mistake. It turned out to be a double row of parked cars, southbound on the right, northbound on the left, full of people with sense enough to stop when they couldn't see where they were going. I threaded the single lane they'd left in the middle, and crept through the lashing downpour to Cannon Falls. I intended to stop for coffee there, but there were no lights on in the truck stop café, so I drove on. A few miles south, the road was blocked by a stream flowing across the road above a blocked culvert. A couple of farmers were out with shovels and pitchforks trying to clear the debris, and I jumped in the dirty fast-flowing flood to help. I'd been digging for ten minutes when a metal fence post reared up out of a tangle of barbed wire and tore a gash out of my left arm. I felt almost grateful for the gush of blood and the pain that gave me an excuse to double up and hold myself a minute. When the hay bales that were blocking the culvert broke apart and the backed-up water ran under the road with a voracious sucking sound, I slogged back to my car and drove the rest of the way home in sullen misery.

I stood under the shower for a long time. When I was finally warm and dry, I went into the kitchen and stared vaguely into the refrigerator for several minutes, finally selecting one of the three cans of Budweiser that stood alone on the second shelf. Looking for something to ease the throbbing in my left arm, I found four aspirin, washing them down with beer, which the label expressly forbade. As soon as I finished drinking, I curled up in bed so I could keep warm while I waited to die of disappointment. Unfortunately for my career as a tragic hero, I fell asleep almost at once.

So whatever else ailed me, and plenty did, I could not complain of sleep deprivation when the telephone woke me at 4:10 in the morning. It was the night sergeant at the adult detention center. "I'm sure sorry to call so early," he said.

" 'S okay. What's up, Norm?"

"Well, I can handle this if you want me to, but I thought you'd want to know. That Scott Rouse you brought in here a few days ago? He's been havin' a very rough night."

"Rough how?"

"He woke up about two-thirty havin' a nightmare, and we just can't seem to get him calmed down since then. He keeps crying and saying he's sorry. Can't seem to stop. I gave him a couple of aspirin, that's all I'm authorized to do. Didn't seem to help at all. He just sits in there *crying*. Now he's saying he wants to talk to you."

"He asked for me personally, or just a cop?"

"No, you, he knows your name. I was just over there talking to him again, and he came right up to the bars and whispered to me that he wants to talk to you right away before it's too late. He may be just flippin' out, but I'd say he's scared, too."

"I'll be right down."

"Helluva way to start the week, but—"

"No problem. Thanks, Norm."

Scott Rouse was sitting on the hard bench against the wall in his cell, curled up with his head on his knees. He had cried so long he was dehydrated, and now a little moaning sound came out of him, with an occasional sniffle. I took him into the visitors' room and brought in a blanket, a box of tissues, my tape recorder, and two cups of coffee. After I persuaded him to wrap up and blow his nose, he admitted he'd like something sweet, so I went out to the vending machine and found a pack of chocolate cookies. The sudden rich smell of them made my stomach growl, so I bought another pack for myself.

"I have to record this conversation, you understand?" He nodded indifferently. I pushed record, said, "Jake Hines talking to Scott Rouse," put in the date and time and location, and said, "You had a bad dream?" He started crying again, his face crumpled into the self-pitying outlines of a hungry baby.

"Wait, now," I urged him. "Have a cookie." We sat together munching sweets like buddies on a camping trip.

He whimpered and nibbled and blew. Presently he said, "Seein' Bad Boy's what did it."

"You know Bad Boy?"

"Well . . . sure. I mean, yes."

"Are you saying you saw him in here? Since he got booked?"

"Yeah." He ate another cookie.

"Where did you see him in here?"

"They let us out in the exercise yard together."

"So you talked?"

"Little bit." He pulled his blanket tighter. "He talked, anyways."

"And said what?"

"Said keep my mouth shut, or they were gonna squash me like a bug." He drew the blanket over most of his face. "It was just talk, probably." He shivered inside the blanket.

"You think seeing Bad Boy caused your nightmare?"

"Guess so"—he poked his head out of his self-made tent and sipped some coffee—"because in the dream he . . ." He whimpered and then was still.

"Who else was in the dream?"

He seemed not to breathe at all for half a minute, and then he whispered, "Randy."

"Did he drown?" He nodded. "Were you there? Not in the dream, I mean, but when he really did drown?" He nodded, emphatically, yes. I waited for him to go on. When he didn't, I asked him, "When did Randy die?"

"Well—" Somewhere his body found more water to lubricate his sorrow; he wept hopelessly for a full minute. "I guess—" he barely breathed it; I had to lean close—"probably a few minutes after we threw him in the water."

I waited while the big second hand on the wall clock swept past five, past six, and up to seven. Watching the tears run down through cookie crumbs on his sad face, I asked him, "You and who else, Scott?"

He whispered, "Me and Farah Tur." The air-conditioning cycled off with a muffled shudder of closing vents, and the console out at the desk began to signal monotonously, buzz buzz buzz buzz buzz. Norm bustled out of the bathroom and answered it, and the room went silent.

Finally I asked him, "Why'd you do it?"

"They made us."

"Made you?" He made a choking sound. "Who made you?" He blew his nose. "Come on, Scott, talk sense. How could anybody *make* you throw your buddy in the water?"

He lowered the blanket suddenly, blubbering, protesting, "They had a gun!" He reminded me, suddenly, of Jessica Schultz shouting, "I was scared!"

"Scott," I said reasonably, "you've got to explain this to me so I can understand. Who were these people with the gun?"

"Eugene Soames is the one I know. I never saw the other one before."

"All right. And why did Eugene and his friend want you to throw Randy in the water?"

"For a lesson, they said. So from now on we'd realize they were serious."

"About what?"

"About telling us what to do. About having us follow orders and not get cute. That's what they said: 'After today maybe you'll all think twice before you pull something cute.' See, they were pissed off about Rowdy's."

"About you and Farah robbing it, you mean?"

"Not me. Bad Boy and Farah. It was always Bad Boy and Farah doing the stealing."

"Then why did you and Farah come in and confess?"

"They said we had to."

"Who said?" I was getting a headache.

"Eugene and . . . that other guy that came down from the Cities with him. They wanted the cops to quit investigating Rowdy's Bar, so they said we had to confess."

"But why didn't they send Farah and Bad Boy, if they're the ones that did it?"

"They needed Bad Boy to do the kidnapping."

"Wait a minute," I said. "Back up a little. You said it was always Bad Boy and Farah doing the stealing? There were other thefts besides Rowdy's?"

"Sure. That's how we were getting the money to set up in the crack trade. Eugene figured out how to work it. See, me and Randy were white, and everybody in our part of town knew us, so we could walk through just about any building and nobody'd pay any attention to us. So we picked the marks. That's what they call it. Then Randy got the keys from Tammi and had copies made. We described the layout to Bad Boy and Farah, told 'em where to go and when to go, and then they did the job. Because they had more experience at that part. They'd go in at night with masks on, so if they did run into somebody, nobody could see they were black. And Bad Boy made a rule with Farah that they could never talk. He's touchy about his voice.

"But see"—he sniffled self-pityingly—"we got too ambitious, I guess. We were ready to make a buy from Eugene last Sunday, with the money we got from a couple of apartments and the liquor store, but when Eugene got there he had twice as much crack as we planned and he said we could have it all if we had the money. Just then the cops came along and he took off. But later we got to talking about how much we could make off that much crack if we could get it, and that's when Randy said, why not rob his mom's bar that night?

"But we never would have set it up if we'd known that Babe was laundering money for the same guys we were trying to buy from. We had no idea! She'd never told

Randy. So of course we couldn't know she'd be down there counting money in the middle of the night."

"Wait," I said. "You saying they really did rob the bar in the middle of the night?"

"Well, yeah, sure. We had to get the money Sunday night. Randy said his mom always went down Monday afternoon and made up her deposits, and took the money to the bank."

"She told me she was robbed in the daytime, early afternoon on Monday."

"Well—I guess she didn't want to explain why she was there at three in the morning."

"So she was taped in that chair for over thirty hours." I remembered her gulping water from the glass in my hand. "You and Randy, were you somewhere nearby while the robbery went on?"

"No. He stayed at my house that night. We were getting ready for a fishing trip with my dad. We left before daylight. Randy thought, if we were out of town, nobody would ever think we had anything to do with it. But somehow Soames found out anyway, and then they were mad because they said we were trying to buy crack from them with their own money. But shit, we didn't know it was their money! But Eugene said tough shit, you dickheads got the cops nosing around that place, it's no good for a money drop anymore, Rutherford's just gonna be a pile of shit for us for months to come. Eugene said, 'We gotta think about the cash flow.' They said we were all gonna hafta pay big time. So they made us—" He threw himself across the table in front of him, suddenly, moaning, "Oh, God, ohgodohgodohgod—" He sobbed so loudly that the sergeant heard him through the closed door and looked up from his desk.

It took some time to calm him enough to talk again.

When he finally sat up, I asked him, "Scott, do you know for a fact that Randy killed his mother?"

"Oh, sure. He called me as soon as the fight was over and said she didn't seem to be breathing anymore, and he had blood all over himself, and he couldn't think what to do. I said he better clean up and come downtown and meet me, and we'd find Bad Boy and ask him what to do. Bad Boy called Eugene in the Cities. Eugene said everybody stay cool, don't do anything, he'd be down in the morning and take care of it. So we went to the bar—"

"To Rowdy's?"

"Sure. Randy said the help would expect one of the family to be there for closing. So we played a few games of pool till closing time, and locked up and went home."

"You went to your house? Together?"

"No. Eugene said do everything normal. So I went to my house, and Randy went to his."

Randy had slept his last night in his own bed, with his mother lying below in the kitchen in a pool of her own blood. I remembered Babe proudly asking me, "Have you seen Randy since he grew up?" She had doted on her boy.

"Where did you meet in the morning?"

"At Bad Boy's room over the bookstore. Farah was there, and Eugene and this other guy that never even said his name, and right away Eugene and the new guy got in our faces, talking real mean about how we screwed up, and now we better do exactly what they said if we wanted to get out of this mess. So we said, 'Whaddya want?' They gave us the keys to an old car they had, told us to take it to Randy's house. Said wrap his mother's body up good and put her in the trunk, come up to Nineteenth Avenue and park by the trees south of the Adelaide bridge."

"How'd they know the place, I wonder?"

"Bad Boy picked it, I think. He was acting like he was Eugene's big buddy, all along, lording it over us other three. Then Eugene told him he had to go out and grab a kid in one of the neighborhoods and call the police and tell them he had the kid downtown and then go to the crack house till they told him to turn the kid loose. That way, he said, all the cops in town would be busy looking downtown while we were up at the Adelaide bridge getting rid of the body. Bad Boy didn't want to do it. He went, 'Wait a minute, I didn't kill nobody, what I gotta get in trouble for?' But Eugene said, 'Shut up, asshole, next time you decide to pull a heist that ain't authorized you'll remember how much trouble this was.'" Scott looked pained. "I never saw anybody so shitass *mean*."

"So you and Randy took his mother's body to the bridge—"

"They were waiting in the trees," he said. "We took her out of the trunk and carried her in there, to where they were standing. Randy says, 'What now?' and Eugene points at the ground and says 'Right here,' and we put her down, and then they jumped on Randy."

"All of them?"

He shook his head. "Farah and Eugene. Bad Boy was gone to grab the kid, and the mean quiet guy had a gun in his hand by then, and he just stood there holding it. He says to me, 'Don't even think about trying anything,' and I didn't." Tears sprang out of his eyes and watered the table. "I was too scared to even breathe hardly." He twisted in his chair, remembering. "They unrolled Babe out of that bedspread we had her wrapped in, and laid Randy down on top of her and tied the two of 'em up together like a package of meat. Randy was crying—" Scott broke down completely. His loud, heartbroken sobs were very hard to listen to; I concentrated on deciding if a water stain on the ceiling looked more like a swan or a dinosaur. When he could speak again, he whispered hoarsely from the depths of the blanket, "Even that wasn't the worst."

"What was the worst?" I asked him, very softly.

"When they got done tying all those knots, they made Farah and me carry Randy and his mother to the trunk of the car. Randy kept begging me to help him—" His voice broke. He shook his head, watering the area around his chair. "We all got in. Eugene drove. The mean guy held his gun. When we got to the middle of the bridge, he made Farah and me get out, and take Randy and his mom out of the trunk and—" He stared around wildly. "And . . . you know"—he flapped his hands forlornly—"hoist them right up over the railing and throw them in the river."

I waited. The next words were hard to catch, choked out in hoarse gulps from his heaving sobs. "Even then, Randy didn't give up. He tried to save himself. He couldn't swim all tied up like that, but every time they went down, he pushed off the bottom with his hands and feet. Whenever his face came out, he'd try to get a big gulp of air, but he kept getting water in, too, and choking. . . . Eugene saw him bob back up a couple of times and said, 'Aw, shit, the water ain't deep enough, you better shoot him,' but the guy with the gun said, 'Wait,' and after a while Randy . . . just . . . quit struggling."

I let him sob for several minutes. When he quieted a little, I asked, "What was the fight about?"

"Huh?"

"Between Randy and his mother. What were they fighting about, do you know?"

"Oh . . . he said she found out he was in on the robbery, and she was really mad."

"Who told her, do you know?"

"No idea."

"But why did he have to kill her?"

"Oh . . . he didn't *have* to. He said she slapped him, and he was pretty high on crack right then, so when he hit her back it felt good. So he hit her again, harder, and just kept on hitting her, and after a while he picked up the knife." Scott shrugged. "Goddamn shame. I mean, if he just hadn't of done that one thing . . . we probably coulda explained to Eugene and them if it had just been the robbery."

I got Norm to assign Scott to the only solitary confinement cell in Rutherford and put him under a close suicide watch. Actually, I didn't see him as self-destructive, but his sobbing had been plainly audible throughout the adult detention cells, and there was no way of knowing how much else Farah and Bad Boy might have heard. If they suspected him of confessing, they might try an assassination in the exercise yard. It seemed sensible to put Scott out of harm's way for a while.

Walking out into the fragrant morning glowing in the courtyard, I gulped fresh air gratefully. Two and a half hours in Scott Rouse's company had been a stiff sentence. Matricide is sufficiently discouraging to begin with, and filtered through Scott Rouse's bland greed and puerile indifference, Babe's death seemed more pathetic than ever. She had been a generous, warmhearted woman and a devoted mother. Her son had killed her without a moment's remorse, and his best friend saw her death as an inconvenience.

I had a confession to transcribe and a crew coming to work in less than an hour, so I hurried across the courtyard, walked up the broad staircase of the government building, and turned left into the morning hustle of the department. I took my tape recorder to the support staff area, left a note on Mary's desk asking her for a transcription ASAP, hung a note that said, "Good news," on Frank's door, and stopped to brew a fresh pot of coffee in the break room. Snarfing a jelly doughnut dug out of the morning supply some petty cash fund affords us, I opened my office and began mapping the day's work.

Scott's confession changed everything. We weren't looking for Randy's killer anymore; the motive for the kidnapping was clear; I knew who robbed Rowdy's Bar. Now we needed to prove it.

"Man oh *man*," Kevin Evjan said, jingling his coins in my doorway at seven-thirty. "You're gonna wear out the floors in this place, Jake."

"I've been here awhile," I said, "but it was worth it. Come in. I got news." I gave him a rundown of Scott's story.

"Wow," Kevin said, "talk about shortcuts! I feel like I fastforwarded into the middle of next week."

"If we can prove it. There's still a lot of work to do on that. Tell you what, instead of waiting for the meeting, how about going to work on this lineup we gotta do for Bad Boy?"

"Bad Boy? That's Alvin Jackson's street name?"

"Yes. And the catch is, somehow on a Monday morning in ninety-eight percent white Rutherford, you have to hunt up five public-spirited citizens with dark skins." I showed him the pictures I'd used, suggesting he might get Art McGee and my friend at the library again.

"I know a couple exchange students at the Junior College," he said. "Indian or Pakistani be okay?"

"If they're dark enough. Get 'em all back here by nine o'clock. Stick around, then, and help me run the lineup, and after that I want you to go to court with Bad Boy and the county attorney."

A few minutes later I had my crew in the small meeting room, telling Scott's story all over again. Lou said, "Hell, Jake, you keep closing a case a day like this, pretty soon we can all take a week off and go fishing."

"Oh, for sure. But not today. Today we gotta stay on a high lope. It's gonna take a mountain of evidence to make these charges stick."

"I'm wondering," Bo said. "These are wannabe drug dealers we got here. Any chance we can use 'em for bait to catch somebody farther up the food chain?"

"Good thinking," I said, "to begin with, right now you can get a warrant out for Eugene Soames, can't you? With this story I've got from Scott, and the balls of crack we found Saturday?"

"Wait a minute," Lou said, "what balls of crack? What in hell are you guys talking about?" We had to back up to Saturday morning then, and Bo and I got sort of silly, interrupting and finishing each other's sentences to describe how we found the crack in my golf bag. We were all laughing by the end of the story, enjoying a break from the string of tough days we'd been having, and we'd have stretched it out a little further if Frank hadn't appeared in the doorway, saying, "This good news of yours must be something terrific."

"It is. And we need your help with the media. We've had a big break, and we're hoping some front-page stories might flush out a drug dealer or two. That's what you had in mind, isn't it?" I asked Bo.

"Sure is."

"I'll help if it's feasible," Frank said. "Whatcha got?"

"Can I come see you in five minutes, soon as we finish here?"

"You bet," he said. "Can't wait to hear about it."

"He looks *pleased*," Darrell said in a hushed voice when he was gone.

"Can you stand the shock?" Lou said.

"Okay, now," I said, "Bo, you're going after Eugene, agreed? Rosie, collect your subpoena and hit the bank. Besides written records, talk to everybody over there that had dealings with Babe. They're going to be very antsy about any taint of money laundering, now, so assure them we're not out to do the bank any harm. Get them to open up if you can. See if they can help you figure out how the cutout worked: What was her percentage, where did she send the rest of the money? It occurs to me that Babe was probably not the only one in town laundering money. If you find out how she did it, we'll be closer to nailing the others."

"Am I free to threaten if I have to?"

"Sure. But probably you can get all you want with just a subpoena and your girlish charm." She crossed her eyes and stuck out her tongue, and we all laughed. Frank's little hint of praise had revved up my crew. They were all in overdrive now.

"Lou, get a squad car and a backup and go pick up Tammi Fae Boe. Scott says positively she helped set up the burglaries at Tom's Liquors and Kiowa Towers, and probably two or three others. They were all in buildings she was renting, and she gave the keys to Randy to copy."

"Ain't she a pip?" Lou said. He was breathing pretty hard through his mouth and his cheeks were flushed, but he was delighted to be in on the action.

"Ray, your hunch about that little stand of trees by the Adelaide bridge was right on. Scott says they tied Randy to his mother there, before they threw them over the bridge railing. Why don't you take a camera and some crime scene tape up there this morning, scout around, and see what you can find?"

"After the storm we had yesterday? Not gonna find much," he said mournfully. "I shoulda searched that grove when I first thought of it."

"Well, I know there won't be useful tracks or prints left. But we can't go back to Friday, and I think we ought to take a good look at it now before it gets any older.

Maybe they left something. Do the best you can. Now. Who's left?"

"Me," Darrell Butts said.

"Yes. You're gonna like this. I want you to hook up with Clint Maddox again and spend the day in the North End. I'm going to come up and join you after a while if I can, so be sure you keep your beeper turned on."

"Any particular targets?"

"Just the usual suspects, the pawnshop and the adult bookstore. Before you go, apply for a search warrant for Bad Boy's apartment above the bookstore. You don't need to wait for it, I'll bring it with me when I come."

"Can I check out the old van?"

"Sure." He left, smirking like a lottery winner, and the rest of the team scattered too. I went back to the chief's office.

"It sounds kind of incredible," Frank said when I'd summarized Scott's story. "He's claiming that Randy robbed his own mother's bar?"

"Scott and Randy set up the jobs. Farah and Bad Boy would go in at night and do the heavy lifting."

"And then Scott helped kill his buddy in cold blood? That sounds like part of his nightmare."

"His story matches the physical evidence, Frank."

"I still don't see how it all ties in to the kidnapping."

"You will, soon as you read the transcription. And if you listen to the tape, you'll believe it. Scott was really distressed. I'm sorry I can't stop to explain more, Frank, but I've got a lineup in five minutes."

"Oh, that's right, that's this morning, isn't it? Schultzy had to trade shifts so she could bring Jessica in. You gonna charge this Alvin Jackson after that?"

"Right away. The county attorney's meeting me at the jail to check his paperwork and take him before the judge."

"Ed's doing all this himself?"

"Hey, kidnapping's got profile. Before I forget, Frank, we need to take Scott and Farah back to court, get the charge raised to . . . well, what? Manslaughter, Murder Two?"

"Let's let the lawyers decide that. You got enough to do."

"Sure. Well. Will you call the paper?"

"Soon as I get all the details crammed in my noodle. It's weird how the kidnapping and the murder turned into one case."

"And the robbery at Rowdy's, and two or three burglaries before that. It's like a black hole sucking in case files."

Jessica looked pale and solemn in the harsh light of the overhead fluorescents in the jail. Schultzy was a little shaky herself at the prospect of confronting the shrill-voiced man.

"Remember," I said, "you'll see him, but he won't see you. This is one-way glass."

Mother and daughter held hands and walked where we showed them. We found a stool and hoisted Jessica onto it. Kevin had worked the phones hard and assembled a group of men similar enough to satisfy any judge. At the last minute, though, I noticed that he had put Bad Boy in the third position in the lineup, and since Greg had put his picture third on the strip I showed Jessica at home, I moved him to second place in the lineup. No use risking a future appeal based on the fact that he was always in the same spot in the row. When the curtain went up, Jessica stared at the row of dark-skinned men for three heartbeats, pointed, and said firmly, "That one."

"The first one or the second one?" her mother asked.

"The second one."

I had the men sit still while I took the Schultzes out

and brought in Scott Rouse. He was distraught and exhausted, his eyes red slits in his blotchy, swollen face, but he did not hesitate to identify Number Two as the Bad Boy of his story.

To speed things along, Ed Pearce had come over to adult detention and now huddled with me by the admissions desk, completing Bad Boy's paperwork while the deputy fitted the prisoner with leg irons and belly chains for transportation to court.

"Doris asked me to tell you she was sorry about the other day at the river," Ed said. "She felt pretty foolish for taking up everybody's time when you had so much to do."

"No problem," I said. "She okay? That was kind of a hard fall."

"Oh, perfectly," he said. "She's very strong. I've never known her to faint before. It was just the sudden shock, I guess. I blame myself for letting her see the bodies. We forget, don't we, that civilians aren't accustomed to the terrible sights we see all the time?"

"That's true," I said, with a straight face.

"Well," he slid the probable-cause application into his briefcase, "I guess this'll do it." He shook his head. "This case seems pretty nutty, doesn't it? Have you figured out yet what he had in mind, grabbing the kid like that?"

"Yes," I said. "We'll have all the motivation you need before it's time to try him. Right now Schultzy will just be very grateful if you'll keep him off the street."

Ed and Kevin took the prisoner to court. Back in the department, I found Bo in his cubicle, working his computer and phone simultaneously, on the trail of Eugene Soames. When I stuck my head in, he circled his thumb and forefinger in an okay sign, and I left him to it.

Lou followed me into my office. "She's gone," he said.

"Who?"

"Was I looking for the queen of Rumania?" he said. "Tammi Fae Boe, that's who." Having emerged from the cautious quiet his illness usually imposed on him, Lou was reclaiming some of the hard-edged glibness he used to have when I first met him. "The office in Kiowa Towers is locked up with the lights off. I asked around the building till I found a friend of hers in the pet grooming shop. She gave me Tammi's home address and phone number. When I got no answer, I went over there and got the landlord to let me in. The apartment's been cleaned out."

"So somebody tipped her off," I said. "Now, who would want to do that?"

"Whoever else was helping her clean out apartments, I guess. I'll put out an APB."

"And get it in the BOLOs," I said, "and MINCIS. Hell, go ahead and get it into NCIC, if you can."

"Will they take her? A little beginner thief in Rutherford, Minnesota?"

"Who says she's a beginner? She got ahead of you, didn't she?" He looked hurt. "If she's connected to the drug side of Randy's ventures, you can expect her to flee the state."

"Frigging databases," he grumbled. "I think they're run by elves." Ray was a dashing sleuth from the prewired era, when surfing was done on a board off Malibu.

"Get Mary to do it for you," I said. "Better check Tammi for priors while you're at it."

My phone rang. Ray's voice, oddly muffled, said, "Can you hear me, Jake?"

"Yes. Where are you?"

"In the grove by the bridge. I was poking around in here, and then I heard something, so I squatted in the bushes, and . . . a little kid just walked in with a spade. Looks like he's getting ready to dig. Can you come up?"

"Yes. How will I find you?"

"Park on the turnout east of the bridge and watch for my signal."

"Ten minutes." I ran down the hall, took the stairs two at a time, and burned rubber coming out of the parking garage. I didn't dare use the siren, but for once I hit every light just right. Ray popped out of the trees just as I parked, and I trotted down the slope from the bridge.

Crouching and squatting, we worked back to Ray's hiding spot. Ali Tur was a few yards away, between two big oak trees, digging steadily. He had made a neat mound of earth about three feet high. While we watched, his spade scraped against something, and he dropped to his knees, pawing dirt up out of the hole with his hands. He stood up with a bundle wrapped in a plastic garbage bag, unwrapped it, and I heard Ray stir beside me and stifle a chuckle.

"Coffee can," he breathed, and I grinned. An American child assisting his older brother in crime would surely have shopped the hardware stores for a heavy-duty plastic box with good chrome hinges and a hasp he could padlock. Ali, dutiful son of frugal immigrants, had eased one of his mother's used coffee cans out of the garbage and swiped a trash bag to wrap it in. He must have done a good job; the money looked dry.

Ali counted out a portion of his loot and stuck it in his pants pocket, replaced the rest in the can, and began to put it back in the sack. I nodded to Ray, and we stepped out of the trees. Ali dropped the can and bolted.

He was fast. I yelled after him, "It's no use, Ali, it's me, Jake Hines!" He was out of sight in the trees by then, but he stopped running and came back.

We met by the hole. I put on my latex gloves. When Ali got back to me, I held out my hand, and he gave me the money from his pocket. It totaled ten thousand three hundred and fifty dollars. I did a quick count of what was left in the can. Close to twenty-three thousand. If Scott's story was accurate, Ali must have their whole stash.

"Why didn't you take it all out?" I asked him.

"I only needed Farah's bail."

"Farah's bail is a hundred thousand."

"I found a person called a bail bondsman—" Ali Tur was learning fast.

"You can't pay him with stolen money, Ali." He gave a tiny, pragmatic shrug and said, "Now that you know it—"

"It wouldn't have worked anyway. This morning, Scott Rouse told me how they killed Randy."

"Scott is just a stupid liar."

"Stupid, maybe. But I think he's telling the truth about how Randy died."

Ali suddenly folded, literally, folding his small skinny body to hunker down on his heels in the wet underbrush. He put his face in his hands and wept. Stifled choking sounds came out of him, as painful and embarrassing as anything I've ever heard from a grown man. His breakdown made me realize how poised he was usually. He seemed at the same time much too small to be fourteen, and much too old.

His devastating loss of self-control only lasted a couple of minutes. Then he stood up, wiped tears off his face matter-of-factly, and got back to business.

"What will happen to Farah?"

"He's going to go before the judge again," I said. "This time we'll be asking for a finding of probable cause to hold him for maybe manslaughter, possibly second-degree murder. The lawyers will decide. The judge will set a much higher bail. I don't think you're going to be able to get him out, Ali."

"Am I under arrest?"

"That's up to you. If I could get your help—" He was already shaking his head.

"I'm not going to help you put my brother in prison."

"I'm not asking you to," I said, "but if you'd help us communicate with your parents and you'd all, the three of you, persuade Farah to give me some names—he could do himself some good, maybe. We're really after the dealers in the Twin Cities that were setting these boys up in business."

He gave me a piercing look, looking like a desert nomad wondering how much speed I could get out of my camel. "If I help you, can you get Farah a break? Help him plea-bargain?" Everybody watches *NYPD Blue*.

"His lawyer will do that," I said. "But if you all cooperate I'll push for all the help he can get, yes. He's going to do some time, Ali. He did some serious stuff."

"Uh-huh." He stared into the trees a minute and looked back at me. "If I go to jail, my parents have nobody to help them talk."

"I thought about that too."

"Okay." He shook his pragmatic little body and joined my team. "What's next?"

"Are your parents home yet?"

He shook his head. "Couple hours from now."

"Okay. Meantime come downtown with us and answer some questions, help us sort out where this money belongs. You know, don't you?" He nodded matter-of-factly. "Good. Come on up to Ray's car here. Your new career is about to begin." I put him in the front seat, closed the door, and told Ray, "This kid is your project for the rest of the day. Find out where they fenced the electronics from Kiowa Towers, where the booze from Tom's Liquors went. Dig out recent burglary files and see how many you can get him to admit to. One thing—" I opened the door again. "Tell me something. How come you were the one holding all the money?"

"I was the only one they all trusted," he said.

"Figures." I closed the door again. "Do the best you can to hold him harmless, will you, Ray? I like this kid, and his parents need him."

"Agreed," Ray said. "You know, I never had a chance to tell you what else I found in that grove of trees."

"What?"

"An old bedspread. Wanna see it?" He opened the trunk of his car. It was a cheap dark green chenille, dirty and rain-soaked.

"Could be the one they carried Babe in," I said. "Check it into the evidence room as soon as you get back, will you? Make sure they hang it up someplace and let it air dry. First guy goes to the Cities can take it along to get tested for blood and hair."

"Okay. You coming down?"

"In a bit. I want to check on my North End team first."

Instead of driving straight to the pawnshop, I poked along, exploring Nineteenth Street east to Tenth Avenue, turning south a couple of blocks on Tenth, and coming west again on Seventeenth Street, really just giving myself a little breather. The jumble of puzzles and evidence that I was beginning to lump together as "The Krueger Case" had rolled over me so fast, I was in a constant subliminal panic about losing sight of something important. When, by the way, was I going to get some test results back from St. Paul? I fished my cell phone out of my briefcase, punched the auto-dial button for BCA, and asked for Jimmy Chang. He came on the line sounding frazzled, and said, "Oh, Jake, I hope you're not just mad as hell at me. I'm sorry we're so late with your stuff."

"Have I got problems I don't know about?"

"Not you. Us. We're a mess up here. Let's see, I haven't got your stuff in front of me right now, but . . . Oh, wait, here it is. DNA won't be ready for weeks, of course,

but blood tests, let's see . . . a rather high level of cocaine in Randy Thorson, is that a surprise?"

"No. You find any evidence of a third party in the
kitchen fight?"

"None. All the blood we found in the house was from
Babe or Randy. We're saying Babe died of multiple stab
wounds and Randy drowned. Time of death is pretty uncertain for both of them."

"No problem, I'm getting that information now from
other sources."

"Oh, you are? Moving right along, huh?"

"A little too fast for comfort, yeah."

"Well, I'm pleased to hear you're solving your own
cases, Jake, because I'll tell you, the help you get from us is
likely to be pretty sparse for a while."

"What's going on, Jimmy?"

"Oh, Jesus, Jake, in the very same week my boss re-
signed, got this dream job doing research in Africa someplace—"

"That's a dream job?"

"Well you might ask. I think he's got his heart set on a
Nobel, why else would anybody take a pay cut to go risk
his health chasing new strains of Ebola virus? Just crazy.
And then Trudy quit, which is even crazier."

"You think so? I thought she seemed pretty happy
about moving to San Francisco."

"Yeah, well, I hope she really loves the view out there,
because the job she took is just shit compared to what
she's got here."

"You don't say."

"Why, hell, Jake, Minnesota pays as well as any state
crime lab in the country, and we've got all the bells and
whistles—we're cutting edge. And Trudy's a stone expert
on the still camera and coming right along with her
video; she belongs in a forensic lab, she's got good in-

stincts for the work. We've got a ton of applications already, of course, but still, Trudy will be hard to replace. I just can't figure out what's come over her."

I can, I thought. She's fleeing Jake Hines. I remembered watching her neatly balanced run through the rain yesterday, how much I loved watching her body and the way she moved it, and my chest filled up with pain so sharp that I gasped. I pulled over to the curb while Jimmy finished lamenting his upsets and said good-bye. Hunched over the steering wheel, rocking my aching chest and groaning softly to myself, I began to hope I was having a heart attack. I had a momentary vision of being wheeled along a squeaky clean corridor on a gurney while soothing voices told me to hang on till my angioplasty team arrived.

But no cure could fix the fact that I cared so much about Trudy Hanson, treasured my times with her, and constantly looked forward to seeing her again, and now it seemed that all she wanted was to get away from me. How could that be? It made me feel grotesque. I thought I had come to terms long ago with my strange face and unknown origins, the fact that just the sight of me, standing in the doorway, made some people nervous. Now I wondered, am I turning into Jabba the Hut? Will dogs bark at my approach from now on, am I destined to make small children cry?

Slumped in the car, groaning and clutching myself, it was a while before I realized I was looking at my ex-wife, Nancy, who had come out of the grocery store down the street and was wheeling a cart full of food across the parking lot to her car. On an impulse I could not have named, but following some desperately important trail, I got out of my car and walked toward her.

She looked up when I stopped by her basket. I reached

ut toward her bags of food and said, "Let me help you, uh?"

She pushed the basket a foot out of my reach and said, "What do you want?"

I held my hands up like the stagecoach driver facing bandits in an old Ward Bond movie. "Nothing! I'm not—I just came to say hello." She glared up at me suspiciously, and I blurted out, "I was hoping you'd talk to me. Will you?"

"About what?"

I took a deep breath and said, "About when we were married. Why did we—what went wrong for us? Mostly? We started out having a lot of fun together and ended up not speaking. Do you know why?"

She held the fingers of her left hand aloft and began to count them off with her right. "One, you were never home. Two, even when you were home, you were never really there. I could see your eyes glaze over when I started to talk. Three—" She stared at me a minute and sighed. "Actually, one and two pretty well cover it." She picked a grocery sack out of her basket. I moved to help her, and she held it out of my reach. "I don't need help!" She was suddenly fiercely angry. "I don't need any help from you ever again, Jake Hines! You got that? None! And that makes me feel very lucky, because what I did need from you all those years I never got!" She slammed her groceries into her car and unlocked the driver's-side door without looking at me again. I stood helplessly watching her while she backed out past me, spinning her tires, and drove away without a backward glance.

Back in my car, feeling hollow and whipped, I reviewed the charges: I was an insensitive clod, too seldom home, insufficiently responsive when I was home. This was not new information. In the long, noisy months we spent together on the scorched earth of our failing marriage,

Nancy had hurled these accusations at me many times. They were as true now as they ever had been, and just as hopeless. Because she was right: I didn't want to hear what she had to say.

It's not true I never listened. I listened closely during the happy first years of my sexual enslavement, usually without the foggiest idea what she was talking about. It's girl stuff, I thought; I'll get the hang of it. When lust eased its hold on me a little, I began to appraise the odd mishmash of airhead self-help manuals, New Age spirituality, health-food hype, astrology charts, and the worst gleanings of daytime talk shows that guided her life. I was appalled, but I figured she'd eventually outgrow most of this flimflam. Her convictions got stronger every year, though, and before long I couldn't stand to hear another word about the healing power of crystals or which house Jupiter was in. She would start stirring up some confection of Shirley MacLaine and Deepak Chopra with Oprah and Sally and Jerry, and I would find myself on the front step, headed out.

I wasn't aware of the extent of my disenchantment till she threw me out. After a few months alone it dawned on me that the regret I was feeling was mostly for my lost yard and workshop. I missed the tumultuous sex of the early years, and I hated the feeling of failure that divorce had loaded on me, but I was glad as hell to have escaped the unfettered flow of intellectual hokum that flowed out of my wife.

Her anger had been perfectly real today, however, and now I confronted a hateful conundrum: Having been lucky enough to start over, in an exciting relationship with a woman as different from Nancy as possible, how had I so mishandled it as to bring Trudy to the same feelings of rejection my wife had? Nancy was so fed up with me she wouldn't even let me touch her groceries;

Trudy was ready to move across half a continent to ensure that she would see me no more. Good old Jake Hines, what a way with women.

It was probably just as well my beeper went off. I found a public phone in the front of the supermarket. "Clint Maddox is looking for you," Neva said. "He wants you to find him in the brown van, parked on the corner of Eleventh Street and Seventh Avenue."

I drove west to Seventh Avenue and turned left. The brown van was tucked in behind an overgrown hedge on the north corner of the Eleventh Street intersection, where only a sliver of its left front bumper was visible from the front door of the pawnshop. Clint was in the driver's seat, pressed against the window to watch the store.

"Something new is going on up here today," he said. "At the bookstore and this place both. They been hauling stuff out all morning. And today the loads aren't all going to the warehouse on the highway. These guys have got another stash."

"They have? Where?"

"Damnedest thing," he said. "It's a nice big house in a good neighborhood. Almost a mansion really. On Clover Avenue, you know where that is?"

"Sure. Branches off Southwest Twenty-second Street, runs kind of up and around a hill and into a cul-de-sac."

"Exactly. Lot of big old trees out there, and all the houses have hedges. The house they're going to, Twenty-two-ninety-five, is on the circle at the end of the street, with a gate at the corner of the property and a long drive. Lotta bushes along the front of the house. Real secluded."

"And the pawnshop operator is taking stuff from his shop to that house?"

"Once, he did. Once to the warehouse this morning and once to the house. And after he delivered a load to the house, he went on out to the warehouse, left off some more stuff, put something from the warehouse into the van, and brought it back to the house on Clover Avenue."

"So—lots of shuffling going on. You see what any of it was?"

"No. I was afraid to get close, and he's using wraps, and those quilted pads that movers have. Really organized for his work, I'll give him that. Everything he's handling is small enough for one person to carry, he never had a helper."

"The bookstore operator went to the house too?"

"No. Just one trip to the warehouse."

"Anybody in the house, could you see?"

"The garage was empty when he raised the door. No lights on in the house."

"How are you covering all these places?" I said.

"Well, that's why I called you. We've been watching their two stores here and then following wherever they lead us, keeping in touch with each other by phone. But it's getting kind of dicey with all this activity, we're afraid they'll spot one of us. Any chance you can get us some help, and a couple of different cars?"

"You bet. Also, what about a break, you had any lunch?"

"Oh, we just talked to Putratz, he's driving the squad in section three this morning, he said he'd keep an eye on the bookstore while Darrell got us a pizza. You wanta join us?"

"Absolutely," I said. I called the department, got Bo, and asked him to check out a Crown Vic and come up. Darrell walked up to the passenger door just then with a flat box and said, "Anybody in here speak Italian?" He was in high spirits. We snarfed down hot cheese and mushrooms while we waited for Bo. He climbed in the van fifteen minutes later and sat nodding silently while we explained the operation.

"Be best if we park one car near the house and somebody just stay there," Clint said. "Then we could trail from here till we see which location they're going to, and pass 'em off and go on if it's the house. It's not so tough to follow somebody to the warehouse where there's plenty of traffic. But in that cul-de-sac it's hard to keep from being obvious."

"Then I think it's best if Bo takes the Crown Vic to Clover Avenue, that's the vehicle that'll look natural there. Clint, you can follow him in the Dodge I brought up here. Help him find an inconspicuous parking spot with a view of the house, and then come on back here. I'll take the van back downtown, and with what we have now I should be able to get a search warrant for the house on Clover Avenue. What's the number?" I wrote it down. "I'll come back in a different car and trade with you, Darrell, so where you gonna be?"

That's how we started the big shuffle that went on all afternoon. I widened the network to include Ray, hanging out in the parking lot near the warehouse in his father's pickup, and Kevin, shuttling between vehicles in Frank's old fishing car. When I had my search warrant I went back to Eleventh Street, found Clint Maddox, and sat beside him in the Dodge, which he had parked half a block south of Kwik Kash. We were watching the front of the pawnshop in the rearview mirrors.

"Anything more gone to the house?"

"No. Two more loads to the warehouse, from here, and one more from the bookstore. You got me some help just in time, these fellas are really goin' after it this afternoon. Tell you the truth, Jake, it's beginning to look like they're clearing out."

"I agree. I don't think I'll wait much longer to see the

inside of that house. I think I'll get Kevin to run me out there—"

I was reaching for my phone when he grabbed my arm. "You ever see Mr. Sewage?"

"No."

"Feast your eyes."

A sixtyish man in felt bedroom slippers walked out the front door of the pawnshop, turned, and went back along the alley at the side of the building. He wore a food-spotted blue chambray shirt with the collar open, and ancient pin-striped pants with the fly half unzipped. His mouth looked as if several front teeth were missing. The left lens of his eyeglasses was cracked, and the earpieces must have been bent, because they hung crooked on his face.

"Do you love him so far?" Maddox asked, starting the car. We watched the corner of the pawnshop building until a faded blue 1973 Ford passenger van nosed cautiously out of the alley and turned right. Maddox drove to the end of the block, turned left, and waited by the curb on Thirteenth Street.

"If he's going to the house on Clover Avenue, he'll come this way," he said. "If we don't see him in a couple of minutes we'll—no, there he is."

Maddox followed him while I called Bo. When Sewell turned into the cul-de-sac, we drove past it and parked in the next circle. Maddox parked and waited while I walked slowly back along the sidewalk. The old Ford van was out of sight. "You won't see it," Maddox had warned me. "They drive into the garage and close it every time." I inspected the leaves on the cotoneaster hedge of the house just outside the cul-de-sac, till I heard the garage door roll up and a motor start. When I heard the Ford coming out of the circle, I turned away from it and walked briskly along the sidewalk till it passed me. When Maddox had

trailed after him, I crossed the street and found Bo
Dooley in the easement between the two houses directly
opposite the cul-de-sac.

I slid in beside him and said, "Anybody in the house?"

"Don't think so. The driver of that van opened the
garage door himself, electronically. Which is kind of interesting, because he doesn't look as if he belongs here."

"Nobody inside the garage when he opened it?"

"No. No lights in there, no movement. Looks empty to
me."

"Lessee, what time is it? Four-twenty. I've got my
search warrant, I'm ready to go in anytime. I should have
backup, though, and you need to check out pretty soon,
don't you? I better call—"

Bo shook his head. "My sister came to help me for a
while," he said. "I can stay, I'd like to."

"Shall we do it, then?" I own a first-rate set of burglary
tools that I took off a petty thief a couple of years ago and
purchased from the evidence room during the next an-
nual spring cleaning and auction. The city owns a cheapo
set that sucks, and there are times when you need to get
through a door quickly without smashing it to bits. Bo
drew his weapon and held it flat against his leg while I
worked the door.

The lock slid open almost silently and closed again
behind us with a tiny well-oiled snap. We stood in the
dusky foyer, listening. As my eyes adjusted, I caught a
glint of polished floors, and of silver massed behind glass
doors. A deeply carpeted stairway led up to stained glass
on a landing. We eased together through the roomful of
gleaming silver, past a heavy mahogany table and a side-
board loaded with more silver: trays, a tea service, a tu-
reen. Bo pursed his lips and rolled his eyes. We eased
down a short hall and stood together with weapons in the
air, pressed against the wall at the door to the kitchen.

The refrigerator turned on, and we both jumped. "Shit," Bo whispered, and kicked the door open.

The kitchen stood empty and gleaming. It was fully, if somewhat sparsely, appointed, but showed no signs of use. I opened the refrigerator. Two bottles of Dom Perignon lay side by side on the bottom shelf, along with a jar of caviar and an unopened package of Brie.

Bo eased open the door to the garage. Across his shoulder I could see the empty garage, with half a dozen boxes stacked against the back wall. Bo shimmied sideways down three linoleum steps from the kitchen, looked in all the corners of the double garage, and lifted the cardboard top of a box with the butt of his gun. He rustled through a layer of crumpled newspaper, replaced it, and came back to the door. "Looks like more silver and glassware."

We crossed the ornate dining room again, tiptoed past the stairs, and peered into the living room, where velvet wing chairs faced each other in front of a marble fireplace flanked by two breakfronts loaded with fine china. More silver gleamed from picture frames and lamps, and the far end of the room was a luxurious grouping of velvet sofas and chairs heaped with satin and taffeta pillows. Everything seemed to have ruffles and beads and tassels.

We eased silently up the stairs. There were four bedrooms, all lavishly decorated like the rooms below and loaded to the doors with state-of-the-art music systems, a massive TV set with a thousand videocassettes, a walk-in closet full of velvet negligees, satin teddies, froufrou mules.

"What the hell is this," Bo whispered, "La-La Land?"

Then we both heard the heavy whir as the garage door opener was activated.

"Shit, how could he get back here so fast?" Bo hissed.

"Why didn't Darrell or Clint call us?" I said, and then, "Wait. They don't know we're in here. Maybe they won't come in." We were in the first bedroom at the right of the stairs; I pointed toward the hall, and we moved out there together so we could hear better. There was a period of silence in which nothing at all seemed to be happening, and then I heard steps come up the short flight of stairs from the garage.

The kitchen door opened and closed, and steps moved quietly across the hard kitchen floor and onto the muffled softness of the dining room carpet. I heard a sound I couldn't identify, turned toward Bo with my eyebrows raised, and then heard it clearer. Someone was in the dining room, moving things from place to place and absentmindedly humming scraps of a tune.

The song stopped; the steps came off the dining room carpet and crossed the hardwood floor of the foyer. Carpet muffled the step onto the bottom of the stairs, but I heard the creak when the railing was grasped. Bo was watching me; he knew as well as I did that the advantage of surprise would be gone in a few seconds. I flipped the light switch at my elbow, and the two of us stepped forward into the light with our Glocks trained down the stairs.

There was a terrified yelp and then a bump. For the second time in five days, Doris Pearce had collapsed at my feet.

·TWELVE·

I DON'T GET IT," MCCAFFERTY SAID, LATE TUESDAY AFTER-
noon. "Why would Doris Pearce need to mess around
with drug dealers?"

"She didn't *need* to," I said. "She *decided* to. Opportunity beckoned, she says, and she grabbed it."

"Getting bossed around by people like Bad Boy? What
kind of opportunity is that?"

"Doris wasn't getting bossed. She was doing the boss-
ing. Essentially, for the last couple of years she's been
running the whole Rutherford operation. Clout was a big
part of what she liked about it. That and the, uh, fantasizing."

"What fantasizing?" It's hard to tell Frank about sexual
peccadilloes; his nose wrinkles up, and he starts looking at
you like you're pissing on his leg. So I moved briskly
through a description of Doris's library of porn videos
and the array of implements in her bedside table at Clover
Avenue.

"Jesus," he said, "right under Ed's nose?"

"Ed's nose had a tendency to be elsewhere one or two nights a week. That left Doris with free evenings that Ed didn't want to discuss any more than she did. She used them for work as well as play; most of the illicit cash has been distributed on what she called her 'bridge nights.' And being the wife of the county attorney gave her the best cover you could ever have."

I yawned. Doris and I had talked most of the night, and as a result of the information she gave me, my crew and I had been very busy all day. "Ed didn't just give her cover. Unbeknownst to himself, he gave her names. Ed is lazy, so Doris helped him get through his files sometimes."

"So you're saying she hired some of the people he was prosecuting?"

"Sure. If they pleaded down and got time served, something like that, Doris would get in touch afterward and offer a little gainful employment. She got the people at the adult bookstore and the pawnshop that way, and most of her maintenance crew for the houses. I understand now why my apartment's going to hell; drug runners and petty thieves aren't selected for mechanical aptitude. Tammi Fae Boe got picked up for DUI while she was carrying a few bags of crack; Ed got her paroled on condition she enter a treatment program, and Doris took her from there."

"Wait now. You're not saying Ed Pearce was part of this business, are you?"

"Never. I'm sure not. He showed up in adult detention about midnight last night, after I'd left messages for him all over town, and when he found out what was going on, he was devastated. Someday when you're not busy, will you explain marriage to me?"

"Sure," Frank said, "right after black holes and cloning." He cocked an eyebrow. "Does this fit into the discussion somewhere, or are you starting to drift?"

"Ed and Doris," I said. "It's hard to see how that marriage works, but in some ways it's clear that it does. The other day when she fainted at the river, he was really concerned, he wasn't faking it, and she turned to him as trusting as a child. Then, last night, she was telling him this appalling story about accumulating a secret fortune from drug money and slum housing, and he never flinched, he just kept saying, 'We can beat this, Doris, trust me, I'll get you out of this mess.' But when he asked her, 'Honey, why did you want this other house?' she told him how she went there on his so-called poker nights to put on fancy negligees and get her rocks off watching porno movies. 'It made me feel like I was getting my fair share,' she said. And he broke down and cried."

"But you said he was playing around—"

"Well, in his mind that was no big deal, just a hobby like chess or model trains. He said to her very sincerely, 'I've always thought of us as the perfect couple.'"

"Aw, shit," Frank said. He sat shaking his head, looking dismayed. Then he asked, "Why did Doris faint that day by the river? Do you know?"

"She didn't know Babe was dead till then. When the news about the Rowdy's robbery hit the street, Doris called Bad Boy and told him to find out who had done it. He already knew all about it, so he told her. Doris was furious. She called Babe and told her she had to do something about her son, that he was going to ruin their deal for all of them. When Doris saw Babe and Randy tied together and drowned like that, she thought maybe the dealers had started a purge and she was gonna be next."

"Wow. She might have been right, too, who knows?" He thought a minute. "How much trouble are we facing with this house on Clover Avenue? Lotta stuff there?"

"Aw, shit, Frank, truckloads! It's her stash of all the best things that have been stolen in Rutherford and the surrounding towns for the last two or three years. We found Millicent Porter's spoons, can you beat that? And her punch bowl and cups, all that stuff she's been calling me about every week since last May. I had Kevin take the stuff back to her, I figured we had plenty without it. Do you know what she said to him? She said, 'I knew if somebody who really cared would take my case, he could find my things.'"

Frank loved it. He leaned back in his big chair and enjoyed his first good belly laugh in weeks. "Isn't it just perfect?" he said, wiping his eyes. Eventually he quieted down and asked, "I still don't quite see what Doris was saving all that stuff for."

"Doris is like the poster girl for the maxim that there's no free lunch. She's so proud of herself for never getting hooked on crack, she keeps saying, 'That's for losers,' and 'They're just weaklings.' But she started looking at the beautiful things that users brought in to fence, and she couldn't let them go. That's what she got hooked on, the treasure, the loot. She set up this cutout system with Mr. Sewage—"

"Now, that can't be his real name, is it?"

"Sorry. Sewell. His nickname is Mr. Sewage, and he looks the part. Doris had him call her whenever he took in something good. If she was interested, he delivered it to Clover Avenue. If she wanted it, she kept it and paid whatever he'd paid for it. If she decided against it, he came the next day and took it back. She has a mansion so full of treasures you can hardly move around. Sewell's been laundering money for her, too."

"Come on, there can't be that much crack trade going on in Rutherford."

"Well, there's more than we thought, but Doris was

funneling much more cash through here than just what was generated in town. She's really been a good soldier for those guys. Besides Babe and Mr. Sewell, she had the adult bookstore taking some of it, the massage and hydrotherapy shop on Second Street Southeast, one of the quick-stop gas stations. We might find one or two more places before we're done."

"And she got a percentage of all of it?"

"She got some, and they got some. Plenty for all. But bigger than that was the profit on all the substandard housing she eventually owned. One of her corporations owns the crack house, did I tell you that? Apartment houses and stores all over the North End. Doris could well afford to have Ed run for governor."

"Huh. Guess he can forget that now."

"And maybe his present job too. Though he hasn't committed any crime—but I don't think he cares about his job right now. He looks—broken."

Frank sighed profoundly and said, "Shit." He brooded a minute, then roused himself and smiled at me. "I must say I'm impressed," he said, "by how fast you got all this information out of her. How'd you get her to open up?"

I laughed out loud. It felt as good to my cheeks as a cool breeze. "I couldn't get her to *stop* talking," I said.

"But I mean, all you really had on her in the beginning was her presence in that house. Didn't she even try to make up an excuse?"

"On the contrary. From the minute Doris looked up and saw us there, it was like she'd found the audience of her dreams."

"Huh. What, she felt so guilty?"

"Guilty? Hell, no, Frank, Doris was proud! She'd been waiting for years to explain to somebody how clever she was. She set up this fabulous system for making money, and arranged to buy that elegant house and furnish it with shit so cheap it was almost free, but the catch to this sweet deal was, she didn't have anybody to share it with. There weren't any bragging rights! So she was dying to tell."

"But I thought you said she collapsed when she first saw you."

"Oh, she was still jumpy about the drug lords in the Cities, so when Bo and I stepped out to the top of the stairs, she thought they'd found her secret hideaway and were gonna kill her in it. Soon as she saw it was me, she put on her boasting cap and began telling me how much money she made off this bunch of dorks. She said to me at one point, 'We're just recycling misfits, Jake, that's all it is. You pick them up, and Ed puts them away for a while, and when the system spits them out again I find a way to use them over.' "

"Mercy," Frank said. Lulu opened his door and gave him one of her stern looks. He looked up and said, "In a minute," and she closed the door hard. "How are you doing with the mop-up from all of this? You need some extra help?"

"I will. Extra clerical help, anyway, by tomorrow. Mary can't handle all these transcriptions and probable-cause applications. My whole crew's spending today in the jailhouse, downloading tales of nefarious deeds from Mr. Sewell and the bookstore boys. And Bad Boy's dictating a regular book over there. Now that it's clear his big-city lawyers aren't coming to his rescue, he realizes he got stuck with this kidnapping, and he's telling us everything he can remember. One little nugget I can't wait any longer to tell you: It was Bad Boy made the nine-one-one call that got Pinky Predmore nailed for selling marijuana in the school parking lot."

"Bad Boy did that? Why?"

"Just clearing some of the miscellaneous competition

out of the way before he set up himself. He said, 'Little two-bit operators like that, they're just trouble for everybody. Better to get 'em off the street.' Isn't that cute?"

"Adorable. How about the two lads that started all this round of confessing, you getting them wrapped up tight?"

"Yes. Scott and Farah are cooperating totally. Scott's dad got him a lawyer, and Farah's being represented by the public defender's office. It's Scott's first offense—"

"Some offense, though, huh? Heaving his best buddy into the river to drown?"

"With a gun on him, though, don't forget. I've told his father I'll testify that he helped me make the case."

"To save his own neck, though, wasn't it?"

"Sure. He's basically a dumb greedy kid who's unluckily over eighteen. I think we ought to recommend St. Cloud. Still no picnic, but at least they're all young."

"Yeah. I'll put in with that. What about the African kid?"

"Not so easy for Farah. He's not a citizen yet. Lotta people at the church are doing all they can to help him, but he's nineteen. He's likely to get deported. Be tough on his little brother."

"That wormy-looking little runt that was following Ray around all day? What's with that kid? Everybody in the support staff seems to want to adopt him. Greg LaMotte claims he's never seen anything like him on the computers, a born gearhead, he said."

"I have no doubt. He's a tricky kid with great potential, fourteen going on fifty. He's helping us get most of the money and loot back where it belongs. He even knows where most of the liquor from Tom's store went. Some of it's in Rowdy's Bar, by the way. Randy robbed his mother in small ways as well as large. After they heisted the liquor store, he volunteered to fetch the liquor order for his mom, took her money, and filled the order from the free stock they had stashed in Bad Boy's room."

"Shee. This Ali's had himself a great set of role models, huh? Is he totally ruined, you think?"

"I'd say it's anybody's guess. I asked him today, 'Ali, what does your family want?' He said, 'My mother wants to keep us all safe. My father wants to go back to Africa and herd camels. My brother wants to be a drug lord.' I said, 'Well, what about you?' and he said, 'I want to go to MIT. You think I can do that?' and I said, 'Sure, if you really want it you can get it.' He laughed, not very pleasantly, and said, 'Well, I suppose I've got as good a chance as anybody else in the family.' "

"Huh. What school's he in? Hafta talk to his principal, see if he might get into some accelerated classes."

"You can try. Remember, I said he was tricky."

"I think I can accept that," he said. "I've got a son who wrote the book."

"What, it's not going so well with Kevin these days?"

Frank shook his head dolefully. "My ambitions as a parent get a little more modest all the time. Lately I'm just hoping to raise my son to college age without breaking his face." He tortured his chair a few seconds and asked me, "What about all those ideas you and Bo had for bigger fish?"

"Not netting any so far. Bo's working his networks, talking all the time to agents up and down the river, but he hasn't found Eugene Soames or his bosses. The drug business in the Twin Cities is suddenly very quiet, we're told. That won't last long; they're just reshuffling personnel. But we might enjoy a little vacation here in Rutherford."

"Well, Bo should be pleased we accomplished that much."

"Bo won't be pleased till crack is off the planet. He's a

helluva cop, Frank. Can I get him some family leave time when his wife gets home?"

"Absolutely. And you better knock off early today and get some sleep."

"Thank you. I believe I will."

And I really meant to do it. I was going to get my loaner car out of the parking garage, buy some Chinese takeout at Wong's, get a six-pack, watch the early evening news, and try for twelve hours in the sack. But I had been working so long that just being out on the street with a little free time made me giddy. I decided to drive around awhile and chill out. Hard to do since the bank thermometer said eighty-seven degrees, and the air conditioner in the old Dodge made more noise than cold air. But the radio worked. I rolled down the windows, dialed KQRS, got Pearl Jam playing "In My Tree," turned the volume to just below "self-destruct," and drove toward the highway with the reverb tickling the soles of my feet.

When I got halfway to St. Paul, I allowed myself to suspect that perhaps I was headed for Trudy's apartment. I could only think about it obliquely, since I had never appeared at her door without a firm date and had less standing to do so now than ever. I tried asking, "What's the worst that could happen?" but most of the answers to that were unbearable, so I counted backward from five thousand by ones, clinging to the wheel like a fruit bat, till I parked at the curb in front of her door.

She opened the door and stared at me openmouthed. "Jake," she said, and then, "Oh, my God, I'm so glad to see you," and she flew into my arms.

The next couple of minutes were very confusing. We both talked at once, very fast and loud, but interrupted each other with a lot of kissing and hugging.

"I've been so worried about you," she said.

"Please don't move to California," I said.

"I should never have let you leave in that storm," she said.

"I'll stay away from you," I said, "you won't have to see me at all." That may not have sounded entirely sincere, since by then we were wrapped tightly around each other and our bodies showed no disposition to disengage. In fact the more we explained ourselves the less we seemed to be wearing, until we had eased down the hall in a trail of cast-off garments and reached her bedroom. There, heedless of the welfare of her great-aunt Carrie's hundred-year-old handmade quilt, we sank together onto her sweet-smelling bed.

Love was kind to us that day. United in the country of our heart's desire, we whispered the language only lovers know, said, "Oh," and, "Yes," and, "Sweet, sweet," and understood each other perfectly. We touched and kissed each other in all the secret places of our bodies, until we tingled with delight. When the great wave of our pleasure lifted us, we rode it bravely to the crest, and cried out together from the heights. In the blissful silence that followed, we held each other in wordless trust and awe, until we slept.

We woke around nine o'clock, starving. "I've got some more bacon and eggs," Trudy said, "will that do?"

"Perfect," I said. "Can I make a lot of toast?"

"With cinnamon bread," she said, "and I've got some white Zin, you want a glass?" We cooked together in ravenous haste, bumping into each other and giggling, and ate double portions of everything. Sitting over the warm, soothing food in postcoital companionship, we drifted into a conversation about the week just past. I told her about finding crack in my golf bag, and getting called in the middle of the night to hear Scott Rouse's teary confession, and trailing Mr. Sewage to the astonishing finds on Clover Avenue.

I stopped once and said, "Oh, hey, I'm sorry to talk about work, I'm just so full of it right now—" and she shrugged and said, "Why did we ever make that rule? Actually, I love to hear more about the cases we work on." So we sat late over the messy table, got up and washed the dishes, poured more wine, and sat down to talk again. Somehow, around midnight, I found myself telling her about getting my start in life in a Dumpster. I described the pot-smoking janitor who found me, and the motel clerk who wiped the coffee grounds out of my eyes and called Health and Human Services.

"Who told you all this?" Trudy asked.

"A social worker I hated."

"Why did you hate her? What did she do to you?"

"Took me away from the best foster mother I ever had."

"Why?"

"My foster father got sent up for bad checks, and my case worker felt the environment in their house was unsuitable. I didn't care about him, but Maxine was good to me and I didn't want to leave her, so I swore at my caseworker. She decided it was time I knew how much Minnesota had done for me."

"What a pig," Trudy said. I looked at her, startled, and she said, "Not you. Her."

"Yes. Well, actually, I came to realize she wasn't entirely wrong about everything, and I am grateful to Minnesota now. It's better than a lot of places, for orphans. But I was nine at the time, and the merits of state supervision didn't grab me." Something stirred in my memory. I sat staring into my wineglass, letting it come back.

"You want some more?" she asked.

"No. I just remembered. That's when I first saw the wolf." I told her about the fierce animal that had stalked my dreams again this week. I had never described him to anyone before, figuring he made me seem crazy. But to my surprise, Trudy was impressed.

"Wow," she said, "a harbinger. Is he pretty reliable?"

"Very." I shivered. "I don't want to sound like a mystic. The wolf is probably the sum of a lot of peripheral messages that I try to ignore at the time. When the threat gets real enough he shows up and says, 'Heads up, asshole.' "

"Even so," she said, "what a convenience."

So, magically, in Trudy's hands, the ghoulish ghost I had kept hidden as a shameful secret was transformed into a handy hazard alert, like a smoke alarm. I stretched, luxuriating in my newfound respectability.

"Wanna stay over?" Trudy said. "It's pretty late to drive home."

"Could I, please? I'll have to leave early, but I'll try not to wake you." I broke that promise, at five in the morning, with a sudden desire for her so urgent that my response to it woke the neighbor's dog. A few minutes later I turned in the doorway and said, "Can I come back tonight?"

She put her head on one side and looked as if she might be going to ask where we were going with this, but then she just smiled and said, "Sure. What would you like for dinner?" The tiny anxious moment made me realize, though, that the time had come for plain dealing. All day long, while I helped a traumatized Milo Nilssen prepare the probable-cause papers with which to accompany his boss's wife before the judge, I got ready to plead my other case, with Trudy Hanson.

In the end she made it easy for me by dropping the spaghetti. She was tasting it for doneness every few seconds, while I dished up the salad, and when she said, "There, it's done!" she put on padded mitts, picked up the hot pan, and poured the cooked pasta into a big colander in the sink. She set the pan on the drain board, gave the colander a shake, and turned to pour the pasta back in the pan. Somehow one handle slipped out of her grasp, and the whole slippery steaming mess came pouring out onto the floor and her feet.

She screamed in pain and shock. I ran to the edge of the steaming lake of spaghetti, reached across it, and lifted her out. Wiggling strands of hot pasta slithered off her feet as I carried her down the hall by her armpits and thrust her into the tub. When I turned on the cold water, she yelled louder for a minute and then stopped and sat down on the side of the tub. I unlaced her sneakers and slid them gently off.

"I better do my own socks," she said. She got out of them without another squeak and sat surveying the damage. "Actually, not too bad," she said, watching the angry red streaks fade.

"If you can walk to the car, I'll take you to the emergency room."

"I've got some burn cream," she said. "Let's try that first." She spread some gooey aloe stuff on herself and declared that the pain was almost gone.

"I'm fine now," she said, "and I want to clean up that spaghetti before it gets really stuck to everything."

"You're going to supervise," I said. "I'm going to mop up. Sit here. Put your feet up on this stool. Drink this glass of water. Point and tell and I'll do as you say."

Cooked spaghetti is not easy. There are many small pieces. Each is undecided whether to turn into thick glue or a floppy rock. Every one is determined to stick to brooms, dustpans, sponges, mops, hands, knees, hair, and the underside of a cleaning bucket. By the time I had retrieved and discarded all the stray pieces of cooked spaghetti we had spread around Trudy's apartment, I had lower-back pain and a muscle spasm in my left thigh.

None of that mattered at all, because I saw that Trudy was pleased.

"Come and sit by me," she said. Smiling, she put her arms around me. "You're very handy to have around in a crisis, aren't you?"

"Keep me," I said. "I'll get better with time. My ambition is to be the perfect mate for you, do you know that? If you keep me and train me I can make you very happy, you'll see, I'll keep working at it till I do. I have a strange face and I don't know who I really am, but you can get used to that, can't you? Please don't go to California, stay here and let me love you."

"Stop a minute," she said. She looked at me thoughtfully a few seconds and asked me, "Do you really feel that way? Just what you said right now?"

"Absolutely," I said. "How can you doubt it?"

"How can I—" She stared at me and shook her head in wonder. "You don't have any idea what I've been going through, do you?"

"What?" I said. "Tell me. Say exactly what you've been going through. In plain English. Short words."

She laughed, thought a minute, and started. "When we were first . . . going out . . ." She shook her head and laughed again. "Now, there's a dumb expression! Mostly what we do is stay in, right?"

"Hallelujah," I said, and we both laughed.

"Okay," she said, "I'm gonna try to get this right, now." She got serious and determined looking, gripping her own elbows and looking straight into my eyes. "When we first started *making love* . . . I thought . . . we seemed so right for each other."

"We were," I said. "We are. Don't change your mind about it. We're exactly right for each other."

"Well . . . but then, why did it seem as if it was never going to . . . *go* anyplace? I was pleasant, you were pleasant, we had fun. But then nothing. Every time you left I wondered, Will I ever see this man again?"

"I was trying to give you space," I said. "You seemed so independent. My ex-wife said I asked too much, that I took everything and didn't give her anything back. I wanted to be sure I didn't repeat the same mistakes."

"Oh, the hell with that!" she said. "This is me! Aren't we entitled to our own mistakes?"

"Sure we are. I just mean I didn't want to get possessive right away and scare you off."

She flung herself into my arms. "I *want* possessive," she cried, with tears suddenly streaming down her cheeks, "I'm crazy about possessive! Why shouldn't we possess each other? Aren't we grown-ups, don't we know what we want?"

"Absolutely," I said. "Beyond question." I would have said I was spontaneous or dysfunctional or a member of the lost tribes of Israel, if it would make her stop crying.

"Well, then," she said, sitting up and smearing tears around on her face, "why don't you ever bring a toothbrush up here, or anything? Is that such a big scary step? Do you have to make me feel as if I have to seduce you all over again every time I want you to stay over?"

"No. I never meant to. Please forgive me if I did that. You don't have to seduce me ever," I promised, kissing her wet cheeks, "although I think I ought to tell that if you do, I'll probably love it."

Trudy got her old job back at BCA the next day. It didn't take a lot of doing, since she had never actually left the place, and since Jimmy Chang had stepped into his erstwhile superior's position and had plenty to think about without training a new photographer.

"How's he going to handle a big job like that and still get his Ph.D.?" I asked her.

"He's putting the rest of his degree work on hold for now," she said. "He just realized he loves the lab and hates teaching. I think that's what all his bad temper's been about. He was trying to satisfy everybody at once. Apparently all the men of his family are teachers. But when this job opened up, he saw what he really wanted and went after it like gangbusters."

"Well, so now we can all be happy."

"Wouldn't that be something?" she said, and kissed me. "What shall we do this weekend?" I loved having her take for granted that we'd be together. In fact I loved everything about our new arrangements, so much that I was behaving like a sap half the time, grinning inanely at everybody until Frank asked me sourly, "Whatsa matter, you got gas or something?"

Trudy came down to Rutherford that weekend and was polite about staying in my dingy apartment while she helped me look for a new one. On Saturday morning we saw three that seemed to have roughly equal merits, so in the afternoon we went back and walked through all three again, slower, looking for something that would set one above the other two. We quit at five o'clock, footsore and a little frustrated, because every time we picked one place, we saw something in one of the others that was just as good or better.

"I know why we can't decide," I said Sunday morning over breakfast. "It's because what we really want is a place between St. Paul and Rutherford where we could live together."

Trudy gave me a look I will always remember, which started as total disbelief and shaded gradually through questions and panic and hope, to end in utter delight.

"Wow," she said, hugging me, "you really don't mess around, do you? A few days ago I timidly suggested maybe you should bring up your toothbrush, and now you want us to buy a farm together?"

"Not a farm. But you know. Some place that's a short commute for both of us. A way to be together every day, instead of just weekends." I kissed the soft place where her neck met her collarbone, and started south toward further delights.

"Let me think a minute," she said.

I backed off and watched her respectfully. She does thinking the way she does everything else, with total commitment to the task at hand.

"I will say this," she said after a minute, very seriously. "I like your attitude, Jake."

I beamed at her. "I like yours too," I said. "I like your attitude and your outstanding bosom and your gorgeous tushie and the way you smell. So let's live together."

She laughed at last. "Jeez, what a list. I do get too sobersided sometimes, don't I?" She gazed at me, smiling fondly, and added thoughtfully, "I always wanted to live in the country."

I started toward her, but she held up her right hand, restraining me. "We'd have to agree on a few things."

"Of course. Pick your side of the bed first. I'm flexible." I reached out, but the hand came up again.

"I'm pretty careful about money. And I like a neat place."

"I'll put my socks in the hamper, I promise."

"Do you think we can . . . try it . . . ," she said, coming at last to the part that was really bothering her, "without getting too committed? So that if one of us wants to . . . just walk away . . . we can still be friends?"

"I doubt it. We're talking about sharing everything. If it works and we get inside each other's walls, we're going to learn all the things that let us hurt each other, and if it starts to come apart we'll use them. That's the way it works. But it's worth the risk, Trudy, because . . . you want me to be the first to say it? I love you."

She put her hand down then and crossed the space between us and pasted herself to my chest. "Oh, Jake," she caroled. "You beautiful man, I love you too."

"Now you've gone blind," I said, "isn't it lucky?"

Since we weren't looking for apartments anymore, we decided to take advantage of the glorious weather and went out in the country to ride the bike trail from Lanesboro to Preston. Some enlightened agency created it a few years ago from the roadbed of a defunct railroad, which winds through small towns by the Root River.

It was an idyllic afternoon, drifting through the dappled shade of the last hot weekend of summer. Loafing along, we stopped often to admire the view and talk to other bikers. At the tiny village of Whelan, we found an outdoor stand and bought triple-dip ice cream cones in three flavors, taking a ridiculous amount of time deciding on the combinations.

Trudy took her treat and hopped back on her bike, grinning. "I like to lick it while I ride along, don't you?" she said. She began arranging the paper napkin around the cone with meticulous care, as she rolled away down the trail no-handed, relaxed and skillful as an acrobat. I stood and admired her style while I slurped ice cream in the shade of the snack bar.

The skinny boy running the stand said, "Boy, she sure can ride that bike."

"You should see her run," I said.